To Tamara,
Thanks for the Support!

Oct 1/2011
Horror Con

Also Available by JW Schnarr

Collections

Things Falling Apart

Novellas

The Children of the Golden Day
Medal of Honour

eSingles

Birth Cycles
Green Hills

Edited Anthologies

Shadows of the Emerald City
War of the Worlds: Frontlines
Timelines: Stories Inspired by HG Wells' *The Time Machine*

Forthcoming

Big Pig (novel)
Atlantis: Ground Zero (eSingle)

A Fairytale of Sex, Drugs, and Murder

by

JW SCHNARR

Northern Frights Publishing

In the Great White North, Blood Runs Colder...

www.northernfrightspublishing.webs.com

Alice & Dorothy by JW Schnarr

Cover Art by Damian Pannell
Cover Design by Damian Pannell and JW Schnarr
Interior Layout and Design by JW Schnarr

FIRST PRINTING
ISBN: 978-0-9734837-8-9

"I wanted to clear all the lies and let the truth come out. I have hate crawling through my system."

—Aileen Wournos

A dream you dream alone is only a dream. A dream you dream together is reality.

—John Lennon

Acknowledgements

I'd like to thank everyone who has ever had a kind word, a criticism, or an interest in anything I've ever written. I'd also like to thank friends and family who have always stood by me and pushed me when I needed a shove; especially for all the impromptu book signings that have sprung up over the years. I'd like to thank my sister Janice for being an unending source of support and good ideas, and thanks to my parents Dave and Eleanor for putting up with me. As always lots of love and thanks for my daughter Aurora, my light.

Mostly I want to thank you, the reader, for taking a little time out of your day to make a dream come true.

—JWS.

For Jessica and Aurora,
For love.

'Begin at the beginning,' the King said gravely, 'and go on till you come to the end: then stop.'

—Lewis Carroll, *Alice's Adventures in Wonderland*

The Beginning.

Chapter 1

Rabbit dropped heroin into a soupspoon and smiled at Alice.

"Don't worry," he said. "Whatever happened, it's all gonna be fine in a couple minutes. You'll see." He let his eyes drop down over the swell of her tits, under the pink shirt she was wearing.

Alice sniffed. Her eyes were red from crying. She nodded. Black makeup and cheap glitter ran in streams down the sides of her face, like a birthday present in a mud puddle. She watched as Rabbit added a thumbnail of water to the spoon with a syringe, and then heated the mixture with a lighter. Part of her wanted to run screaming from the room; part of her knew this was the last thing she needed right at this moment with her life crashing down around her head and the *holy shit* meter going from 0-60 in under ten seconds.

The other part, *a much larger part of her*, saw the drugs dissolving on the spoon, smelled vinegar and baby powder as it cooked down, and smothered the first part of her with a pillow. Get high and forget it. Put it all behind her. *Life in the big city, baby.* That shit happened.

Right now Rabbit was looking at her, his smug mouth half turned in a smile. His two front teeth capped gold. His *namesake.* They made him look like Bugs Bunny kinda. His blue eyes were shining like a fat kid in a candy store. She knew the look. Rabbit was going to fuck her as soon as he finished fixing for her, and Alice was going to let him.

She rubbed her nose; her hand came away wet. Rabbit turned off the lighter and dropped the head of a Qtip into the mixture on the spoon. Then with his other hand he moved the cotton head around to soak everything up.

"You know, you're lucky you came by today," Rabbit said. "I already sold most of my stuff off for the week. This is from my stash." The message was clear. *Be grateful.*

Alice watched him and said nothing. She'd come to see Rabbit because there was nobody else. She'd been living rough too long; all her friends were gone. Her family was ashamed of her because she was hooking for party money. Or to buy groceries, though that was less often. She stayed where she could. She slept outside sometimes, and used motel rooms to get out of the weather when it turned bad.

Rabbit didn't care how much cock she sucked though. He still kissed her on the mouth. He let her crash whenever she wanted to get high and had nowhere to go. She paid him back with lots of freebies. Alice thought maybe Rabbit loved her, in his own way.

"Ok, Alice." Rabbit flicked the end of the filled syringe. "Roll your sleeve and let's find a pretty blue line."

Alice lifted her shirtsleeve and grabbed onto her bicep. Tight, so the veins below bulged under the pressure. She squeezed her hand open and shut to get the blood moving.

"*Good.*" He slapped her arm a couple times to bring them up even more. "You have perfect veins for this, you know that? I mean, mine are shit now, and I've seen girls who are already shooting in their asses. Big ugly sores everywhere, vein collapses, stuff like that. Sometimes it's like sticking your rig in a pound of steak. Don't know *what* you're hittin'. Yours are perfect though. Your skin is like fuckin *porcelain.*"

"Oh fuck," Alice snorted and rolled her eyes. "Rabbit, I look like shit. I *feel* worse. Quit talkin' so much shit."

Rabbit nodded. "Let's take care of those bad feelings, baby girl." He pushed the needle into a hungry vein. Alice took a sharp breath between her teeth. He pulled blood back into the syringe. It was the right colour. He slowly pushed the brown fluid into Alice's arm. It looked like Rabbit was shooting up with beer or vanilla flavoured cream soda. It always looked like something different to Alice. It helped her cope with her budding drug addiction, maybe.

Alice bit her lip. Spiking hurt like hell. Like hot syrup being pushing into her flesh and up her arm. The numbness was spreading. Here there were clouds. Here there was euphoria as the heroin started to be changed in to morphine by the chemicals in her brain. She didn't care how it worked though. Rabbit was right. She killed someone today. Who cared? Sunshine erupted from her chest, making her warm and sleepy all over. Reality faded under halos and sunbeams and the warmth of her soul.

"Good," Rabbit said again. He tossed the syringe on the table.

"*Ahhh*, much better." Alice giggled and licked her lips. She could feel her blood slowing. She tipped her head back. The man's face when she pulled the trigger. A little black dot under his left eye. It stopped him cold. His fuckin brains went *everywhere*. It wasn't like the movies. There was more blood than Alice had ever seen. Meat, hair, bone, just erupting from him. They were in his car. The windows were open. There was a starling somewhere close by. She could hear it barking out orders to other birds. *That bird sounds like metal*, she'd thought, before he'd stopped being a grateful John and turned into a vengeful one.

Alice had walked around the driver side of the car when she left, and it looked like someone had puked blood and raw meat all over the door of the car. Who the fuck was going to believe that someone had tried to rape a hooker? They'd gone out there for sex. He'd *paid* for sex.

Thing is, he'd *gotten* sex. And he wasn't ready to take her back to town. He wasn't ready to pay again either. He'd slapped her in the mouth and then tried to force himself into her ass. When she bore down, fighting back, he dropped a fist like a hammer just above Alice's hairline. And then he was inside her, pushing deep inside her bowels, his searing cock tearing and stretching her like a knife. As Carl Panzram said, Alice *wasn't broke to ride*. You had to be careful with that stuff. She'd heard it could cause infections or need stitches.

She screamed for him to stop. She scratched his face. He hit her again, and Alice swooned. Half in and out of consciousness, she reached into her purse under the chair and felt the cold shape of her gun. She pulled it out.

She stuck it in his fat piggy face.

There was a moment between the bullet and his realization of how fucked he was, a moment Alice saw slowly dawn on his face. Lust was replaced with fear.

"*Get the fuck off me!*" she screamed. She drew the hammer on her rage, and scraped his face with the barrel sight.

"Oh God," he whispered. And then it happened.

He started to come, inside her. As though a gun in his face had heightened the experience for him, as if raping a whore in his '79 Buick wasn't enough, ramming his dick into her ass dry wasn't enough, the cold circle of the gun barrel scraping a hot, angry line across his cheek *was* enough. The thought she might blow his pig head off made his orgasm come fast and hard.

"*I'm suh-horry*," he said. And then he closed his eyes. Breathed deep.

He's enjoying the ride.

His look of bliss sent Alice over the edge. Later, she'd give it some thought, and she could have seen herself emptying his wallet and letting him go. If it hadn't been for that fucking look on his face, like he'd just switched off the situation and tapped out, like nothing Alice ever did mattered, because *she* didn't matter. It was the same look she'd been seeing on men's faces since she was twelve years old, giving handjobs to the neighbour kids in the doghouse while her parents were at work. It was as though a light went on in her mind, a tiny singular ball of heat so terrible it had nowhere to go but out. And a moment later that light crashed through the car in an explosion of heat and thunder. The gun bucked in her hand. Then blood. So much blood…

On some level, she was aware that Rabbit had her shirt open and was fondling her tits. He could have them. They were attracting the wrong kind of attention from boys. That's what her mother said, when she'd finally been busted, her hand still hot and stinking like vinegar from those boys early teenage dicks, too young to come but old enough to get sticky. *You don't want to do that Alice, that's the wrong kind of attention.* Too bad she hadn't told Alice's dad and his friends the same thing. At the time, Alice had thought maybe they just didn't know any better.

Alice pushed on Rabbit's chest, but it wasn't enough for him to notice. Her fingers slid along the side of his head, down across his face.

She was covered in blood.

She had pulled his slack head up by his hair so she could crawl out from under him. Screaming and crying, like birth. His cock was still half full of jizz when she unplugged from him. Her asshole was on fire. She dropped the gun.

Rabbit was licking her nipples. The spring air was cold on her skin. It was hot in Rabbit's living room and she was sweating.

Alice tried to focus. It was like the heroin was splitting her in half, and she was living two lives at once. Everything was jumbling together. It made no sense. Rabbit with his hand down her shorts, fingering her clit. Alice washing blood off in a mud puddle, the water slick and rainbowed and smelling like motor oil. She found out the hard way that bone would float, if the pieces were small enough. Rabbit, with his groping fingers inside her. Alice had her hands on his shoulders. It was for balance, because she didn't want to fall into the puddle. Rabbit mistook it as permission to continue. The stink of gunpowder and humanity. The guy shit himself when the bullet turned his lights out. He probably pissed inside her. Rabbit splitting her legs. Spitting on her. His mouth rhimed with milkweed, like the big sacs full of plant jizz her daddy showed her when she was little. *Sometimes there's bugs in the spit, Alice,* he'd said . *Here, lemme show you.*

Her hands were tingling. They were covered in milkweed spit. It smelled awful and made her feel guilty to look at it. *Tell your momma and I'll kill her. Just like these bugs.* She never had to worry about that. Momma didn't need to be killed; she didn't care.

Motes of light appeared in both worlds. Alice was standing in the grass by the train yard, nobody around for a mile or two, surrounded by electric motes of light gently dazzling her skin. The motes danced around Rabbit as he fucked her. Her eyes fluttered back in her head.

The sparkling, tingling sensation moved up her arms and legs. Across her hips. Along her shoulders. She bit down, hard, until milkweed and rust welled around her teeth. Both worlds were washing out. Or maybe there were three worlds. She tried to focus her eyes but *Rabbit sparkled and fluttered too much. Halos, White light, the drum of her heart sparkling in her ears.*

Sparkle.

"*Shit!*" Rabbit yelled. He pulled out her, leaning back and putting his hands on her knees. His hard cock bounced as if tied to a string, slick and ridiculous looking. "*Shiiit!*"

Alice was thrashing. Sometimes when heroin users overdosed they just went to sleep and slipped into a coma. Sometimes they thrashed and spit like they were possessed. This was Alice now. She arched her back and bucked her legs and she fell on the floor even as Rabbit was trying to get out of the way. Alice was spitting all over the floor. She was moaning softly. It looked like electrocution. It was, in a way; her synapses were firing all over the place. Her body contorted and jerked in time.

Rabbit grabbed Alice by the shoulder and turned her on her side. He pulled his sweat pants over his dick and pushed the bulge to one side. He rubbed his face in his hands. His hands smelled like cigarette smoke and pussy. One more than the other, and the smells lingered in the sweat on his face.

"*FAWK!*" he shouted. That was how the word sounded, like in a comic book. Fawk. Not quite profanity, but close enough. He looked down at her fluttering body. He took deep breaths. If he didn't do something soon she would probably die in short order.

He had to get her the fuck out of here. *Now.*

Rabbit stepped out into the cold air. He zipped his plastic windbreaker all the way to the top and then pulled the sleeves down to his wrists. It wasn't much, but it would keep the chill off. Besides, the rate his body was running he could barely feel the cold finger bones of spring. He lit a smoke. He looked up and down the street. It was the middle of the night and the street was empty. It was still too early in the year for kids to be out wandering around, even for this shithole neighbourhood in which his parents had eventually settled. This is where he'd grown up, and eventually left for bigger and better. And this is where he'd come home and taken over after the old man had died and his mother had gone off to rot in a government assisted living facility. To Rabbit, it was home. He puffed his smoke, looking up and down again just to be sure. There wasn't a single asshole he could trust in the entire neighbourhood, but at least they were smart enough to mind their own business. Smart neighbours knew enough to look away when shit started to get loud.

He went in and thrust his hands under Alice's body. He'd moved her from the floor to the couch after carefully redressing her. Under the scent of her perfume and shampoo, under the talcum and strawberry deodorant, there was another smell of mingled sex and sweat, puke and blood. It was the real smell of a junkie. Sometimes they smelled like piss too. When you were high, it might be too much effort to use a toilet. When you were high, you were usually beyond caring. Rabbit smelled like that himself sometimes.

She was a small girl, but still a lot of dead weight to lift in her present condition. He wondered how much weight unconsciousness added to a body; the way television cameras seemed to add weight to actors and newscasters. He pulled her up and slung her over one shoulder in a single move. Then he stood, pulled his keys from his pocket, and crossed the threshold of his living room out the front door into the dark of the evening. He resisted the urge to press his face against her side as he locked and shut the door. There was something in her scent that he couldn't place. Something he loved, though. She reminded him of a better class of life than what he was used to. She was a whore, and homeless a lot of the time, but there was something in her that was like a rod of hot iron. Never bend. Never break.

But she *was* broken. She was unconscious and maybe about to die. If it was anyone else, Rabbit might have dumped her in a trash bin and started working on his alibi. He had too much shit going on to have the cops sniffing around his house. He threw her in the passenger seat of his car and ran around to the other side. He threw his cigarette away with a flourish. He jumped in behind the steering wheel, tossed the engine, then threw it in gear and drove away from his house.

The car was cold and he could see his breath. Looking over at Alice, he was relieved to see her breathing as well. It was a good sign. *At least she's breathing.* He turned onto a larger road, made another turn a few minutes later from an off ramp and jumped onto the freeway. Hitting the gas, his old car rumbled and groaned in protest. He lit another smoke. Then he flicked on the radio. He had a top end stereo in this yellow piece of shit. Pioneer deck, JBL speakers. All top of the line for their brand, and all stolen.

They were gifts from junkies that he'd traded for drugs. Drug addicts were like farm cats that brought their masters birds and chewed rats in hopes of garnering favour. He'd pat their heads and say *good boy, who's a good boy? Here's a little treat for you.* Pat, pat. The stereo was worth more than the car. *Alexisonfire* was screaming about the end of the world. *Preach on, fuckers. The end happened a long time ago.*

He got off the freeway and turned down a well-manicured side road. The trees along one side were all exactly the same size and shape. On the other side, gas powered lanterns cast yellow halos every thirty feet. When yuppies bought up inner city property and redecorated, the results usually looked something like this. Row after row of skinny infill houses with sports cars and sedans parked in front. Rich women were out in droves walking tiny dogs. Not a heroin crowd. They did coke over the holidays and smoked weed on the weekends and thought they were badass.

Alice moaned something about a clock. Or maybe she said *cock.* Rabbit wasn't sure. He made another turn, and saw the first lights of the hospital ahead. He flicked off his lights and slowed down. He saw a pair of lights splash across the road, leaving the lot. He pulled over and turned down the radio.

A big fat ambulance bounced light across the hood of his car as it turned toward him, then settled into the road. It drove slow as it passed. Rabbit looked up at them and saw the driver staring back. They locked eyes for a moment, and then they were gone, the ambulance picking up speed as it drove off. Rabbit realized he'd been holding his breath.

He flicked the lights back on and spun the steering wheel, and the vehicle lurched back out onto the road. At the entryway Rabbit turned, drove past two parking lots, and the followed a wide path up to the emergency exit. Two men were standing outside smoking.

"*Fuck,*" Rabbit whispered. He tapped the steering wheel and came to a stop 20 feet from where the men were standing. They both looked at the car, waiting for it to do something. *Dammit.* He looked at Alice, then back at the men. They were talking as they watched him. *They're talking about me.*

He couldn't drive up there. His plan had been simply to ditch Alice in front of the door and take off. They'd see what was happening. Maybe they'd try to stop him, maybe not. Most likely they'd yell for an orderly to call the cops or something. Either way, being caught with an overdosing junkie was grounds for Search and Seizure warrant. An S&S, as the cops called them, better known as a *Shit Sandwich.* On the inside, they'd say *the cops fed me a Shit Sandwich, and found my stash...* and he had enough shit in his house to make a very big sandwich. Might take him ten years in Fed to eat the damn thing. *Unless…*

He tapped the gas, pulling his car up toward the emergency entryway. One of the men flicked a butt out onto the road. Rabbit pulled his hat down low to cover his eyes. He stopped in front of the two men. Opened his door and stepped out.

"Hey," Rabbit said. "Can you boys help me out?"

"What's wrong son?" the man on the left said. He was in his late fifties and he looked exhausted. The man beside him could have been his son. Both were dressed for the country life, plaid shirts and ball caps. The younger man's over shirt was hanging open and he was wearing a *Lost Souls* t-shirt underneath. A couple days' growth and thirty years separated their faces, but the relation was easy to see.

"My girl is really sick," Rabbit said, avoiding eye contact with the younger man and looking squarely at the father. "Can you guys grab a wheelchair and help me get her inside?"

"Yeah," The father said, moving immediately. "Jason, grab a chair, boy." The father moved over to the passenger door and caught a glimpse of Alice.

"Jesus, is she alright? She looks unconscious."

"Yeah." Rabbit scratched his nose and adjusted his hat. "I *think* she is. She hasn't spoken much the last few minutes. Flu or something, I think."

"Flu doesn't make you go out like that," Jason said, wheeling a chair up to the door. The tone of his voice said he smelled bullshit on Rabbit's breath. The old man's eyes flashed on Rabbit for an instant, like he had been thinking the exact same thing.

"I'll get the door," the old man said. "Jason, go ahead and grab her under the arms when I get out of the way."

"Sure pop," Jason said. To Rabbit he said, "Can you grab the chair?"

"Yeah. Thanks a lot guys, I really appreciate this."

"Let's just get her squared away," the old man said. He popped the door and stepped aside for his son to get in and grab Alice.

"*Aww Jesus, she's got puke all over the place*," Jason said. He breathed though his mouth. "Come on *darling*, let's get you out of here."

"Grab that chair," The old man said to Rabbit. It was more like *at* Rabbit though, it had the sound of a man who was used to barking orders and having them followed.

"Right. I just gotta grab my wallet out of the car." He slipped in behind the wheel. Jason was watching him like a hawk through the open passenger side door. "Here it is," Rabbit said, looking down. He reached up and popped the car into drive. The car jumped forward.

"*What the fuck!*" Jason yelled as the car door slammed shut beside him. Rabbit heard the old man groan as the car bumped him and he went down. Rabbit punched the gas.

In the rearview mirror, Jason helping his dad get to his feet. Both of them watched as Rabbit drove off. Behind them, slumped in her wheelchair, Alice dropped one hand toward the cold pavement.

"Get better, baby," Rabbit whispered through his teeth. At that moment, he felt every bit the low life piece of shit his mother had always sworn he was. *Life in the big city.* This was his part in the big book of life. Asshole. Scumbag.

When the on ramp to the freeway approached, he skipped it. He lit a smoke and rolled the window down, allowing strong cold air into the car. It was a clear night, he could see the stars.

Chapter 2.

"*We need some help here!*" The old man yelled. He was standing in the yawning doorway on the hospital emergency room, faded John Deere hat in hand. He was using it to wave at the front desk nurses. In the sanitized emergency room waiting area, rheumatic, sad eyes looked up at the noise. Nobody moved. A few of those waiting for treatment looked over at the admissions desk.

"Sir?" one of the nurses said.

A fat Cuban in a white security shirt approached the man. He did his best to look like an authority figure, though he refused to make eye contact for more than a moment or two at a time. "Sir?" he said in a heavy accent, more street than island. "What's the problem?"

"Sick girl," the old man waved the guard through. "Some guy just dumped her and took off. She's totally out of it, man."

The mechanical entrance doors hummed to life and swung open with a puff of air. Jason appeared, He pushing Alice in her wheelchair. Her blond hair hung limp and sticky in her face, clothes mired with grey vomit. She was unconscious. The security guard pushed her head back so he could see her face. Her eyes fluttered. Mouth agape, her sewage stench breath exhaling shallow puffs of air. A duty nurse had come around the counter, through the sealed emergency room doors and past the twenty or so onlookers.

"*Overdose*," the guard said, earning a dirty look from the nurse.

She was a small, birdlike woman, a wisp of brown hair hanging down one side of her face. She had a light in one hand and a stethoscope around her neck. "Thank you Carlos." There was an edge of sarcasm in her voice, someone used to talking down to the men in her life. She pushed Alice's head back and then thumbed one eye open, shining the light in it. No response from Alice.

"Hey," Carlos said, turning to the old man and his son. "You don't know her at all?"

"Some asshole ditched her with us," Jason said. "Little wiry guy in one of those plastic coats. Said his girlfriend was really sick, and needed help getting her into a wheelchair."

"A plastic coat?" Carlos said. "Like, *uhh*, a rain jacket?"

"Wind breaker," the old man said. "One of those ones that fold down into a little square. You know, with a belt? Black. My boys had em when they were kids."

"Ahh yeah," Carlos said. "Anything else?"

"Ok sweetie I'm going to take you to the back," the duty nurse said, speaking loud enough for Alice and the rest of the people watching to hear. Being a big shot. "Katie can you open the door for me?"

There was movement behind the check in desk, and the twin frosted glass doors on the other end of the room opened to a maze of hallways and multi coloured strips of paint.

The older man watched the nurse disappear with Alice. He turned back to Carlos.

"Yeah," he said. "Uhh, he had metal in his mouth. Like gold teeth or something, I can't be sure."

"I never saw that." Jason scowled at his father.

"Big surprise," the older man said. He turned back to Carlos. "Hey, when can we get in and see my daughter?"

"Oh," Carlos said, biting the tip of his pen. He pulled a small notepad from his shirt pocket and was scratching a few notes down. "Uhh, I'm sure they will call you."

Jason shook his head. "All fuckin night."

"Whose fault is that?" his father said, glaring at him.

"Come on, Dad," Jason said, shaking his head. He put his hat back over his hair then pulled it down hard.

"*Yeah*. That's what I thought." There was a disgusted finality to his voice that marked the end of their conversation.

Jason looked up at the clock. It was just after 2am.

Alice was rushed down a long hallway following a single green strip. At a T-intersection, the single strip turned into a double strip, and the nurse continued to walk as quickly as her legs and comfortable shoes would allow. Eventually they came to an open area lined with beds separated by curtains. There were a few people back here, doctors quietly puttering around files and light tables, nurses walking back and forth, talking quietly among themselves. Some of the curtained beds were occupied. A woman was crying in one; in another a young man was whispering earnestly about getting out of his fucking bed and catching a score for the morning.

The nurse jotted down a few notes on her clip board. Looked up and smiled when the attending doctor came over to see. Dr Bale, tall and lanky, designer black framed glasses. Name brand expensive, for a name brand lifestyle.

"Know what it is?" the Dr Bale said, inspecting Alice's face but not touching her.

"I don't even know *who* she is," the nurse said. "I don't know if she has insurance or anything."

"Just wandered in off the street? Or was she brought in?"

"Dropped at the front door," the nurse said. "Apparently some guy got her into a wheelchair and then took off. She was brought in by the family of Deborah Angles, the abuse case in six." She corrected herself. "*Presumed* abuse. Looks like she got punched in the face. Orbital fracture, nose cracked open."

"Not on my list," he said. He waved a hand to change the subject.

"Sorry doctor, I just see these fuckers come in spouting some shit about hitting her head on the staircase or walking into a wall, I mean, *come on*." She raised her hands in mock surrender. "Like we don't see that twenty times a day, always the same stories. Same shit."

"*Still* not on my list," Dr Bale said. He made eye contact with the nurse and held it for a moment, making sure she got the point. *Not Interested.*

"So what's her deal?" He said.

"I checked pupil response, blood pressure's low, respiration laboured. She's almost in a coma. Looks like opiates. Heroin, probably. She has pinpoint pupils."

Dr Bale reached down and grabbed Alice's arms; thumbed this inside of her forearms. Made a clucking sound with his tongue.

"She's got some tracks, but not a lot of them. Recreational heroin."

"If you want to sign off on this," the nurse said, "I can start trying to figure out who she is."

"Negative," Dr Bale said. "I want you to start an IV drip immediately. I want you to dig me up a narcotic antagonizer. Naloxone, if we have it. Let me know when you're done."

"But doctor," the nurse said. Her eyes shifted back and forth. "We don't know what kind of insurance she has. We don't know anything about her."

"Interesting that you are more interested in her money than her health," Dr Bale said. He scowled. "Just do it. If anyone says anything, *which they won't*, ask them to come see me."

"Yes doctor," the nurse said.

"Cheer up," Dr Bale said. "You're probably going to give a girl her life back tonight." He snapped pen onto his clipboard and turned on a heel, not bothering to wait for a response.

"Yeah, If I don't get fired for it, *Dr Fuckhead*." She pointed the wheelchair toward an empty bed. "Come on sweetie," she said into Alice's ear. "Let's get you tucked away. You're about to have a hell of a trip."

The nurse called an orderly to help get Alice into bed. Then she secured the girl down with arm and leg straps and added another across her hips. She winched a strap across her chest. There were arm bars located on the sides of the bed, the nurse pushed Alice's right arm straight out from her body. She ran a thick I.V. drip into Alice's hand, the flesh puckering around the needle and immediately soaking up the bag of saline. Finally she ran a hose from the respirator in the wall to her mouth and nostrils. She secured them with medical tape; little X's on both sides of her mouth and one across her nose. A little piece over each eye would keep them shut.

She measured Alice's heart rate and temperature, then double checked by feeling the thrum of her heart on the inside of the girl's wrist. More scribbles on the girl's chart. At the top of it, she wrote "Jane Doe: Pending". More paperwork for the stack. Medicine these days was eighty per cent paper and twenty per cent drugs. Ahh, the miracles of modern living. She checked her watch.

At the bottom of the sheet she wrote *Naloxone 20cc requested by Dr Bale 2:30am.*

She'd have to make sure the good doctor signed off on the request. That way, when they asked who was going to do the paperwork she could step out of the way. With any luck, nobody would even talk to her about it.

Nalaxone was a drug designed specifically for junkies addicted to opiates – usually heroin, but just as often morphine or codeine addictions caused when people had to take pain medication for an extended time. When the Nalaxone entered the bloodstream it reacted with opiates in the blood and in the brain. It was a sticky cell; it collected the opiates in clumps and then flushed them from a patient's blood through their kidneys and out through the uterine system. The whole process took about four hours, was very expensive, and included follow up treatment for three weeks of taking Nalaxone tablets. It was a sort of miracle among heroin users; it allowed rapid detoxification without the weeks of agony associated with opiate abuse. This girl would have flu-like symptoms for about a week, and, as long as she kept taking the pills, opiates would have no effect on her. Hopefully in that time, she could get her shit together.

Myra headed to the pharmacy, found a small row of Nalaxone bottles among the dozens of other bottles, grabbed a 50cc syringe, and signed for it. Then she went back to where Alice was laying on the table, attached a heart monitor from the wall to Alice's finger, and filled the syringe from the bottle. She pushed the plunger forward to get the bubbles out of the needle.

"Good luck sweetie," she said, pushing the syringe into an entry point on the I.V. needle in Alice's arm. "We'll see you on the other side."

Chapter 3.

Alice stood outside of a large vanilla coloured house. The sun was warm on her skin, the grass a vivid emerald green. Cotton candy clouds sped across an aquamarine sky at an unnatural pace, sending shadows speeding across the landscape.

She had some sense of movement about her, a growing feeling. She had mushrooms in her mouth; the taste coated her teeth. The house was the general shape of a large rabbit; it had twin chimneys sprouting from a thatch roof in the shape of rabbit ears, while thatch rested between them like a tuft of brown hair. *The House of the March Hare*, she thought. She knew the place, but she had no idea from where.

There was a table set under a tree in front of the house. Sitting at the table, The March Hare himself was having tea with The Mad Hater. Between them was a large Dormouse, slouched over on the table asleep. The other two paid little attention to the sleeping rodent; indeed they used him as a pillow to rest their elbows and were busy talking over top of the creature.

The table was large, with many seats, but the three creatures were huddled down in the corner farthest away from Alice.

The Hater elbowed the March Hare; nodded toward Alice. Said something quietly.

The March Hare put a paw up.

"No room!" he cried. The Hater chimed in. "No room here! No room for your kind!"

"There's plenty of room here," said Alice. She waved at the table. "You guys are using three seats out of, *like*, twenty."

"No room, *whore,*" The Dormouse said, yawning and snapping his teeth. They were jagged shards of bloody bone. He tucked a hand under his chin and resumed his light snoring.

"Plenty of room," Alice said again. She yanked a chair out and sat at the far end of the table. The Hater and March Hare watched her intently. Finally the Hare stopped scowling and smiled.

"Have some wine," he said amicably.

Alice looked across the spread. High class silver, fine china cups and saucers, teapots with little ceramic paintings of flowers and grapevines. There were at least a dozen. Little painted bowls filled with milk and sugar. Clotted cream and jam. Vanilla.

"I don't see any wine," said Alice. "Just a lot of teapots."

"There isn't any wine," The March Hare said. He looked at Alice as though she was the dumbest bitch he'd ever seen. "It's all teapots, stupid girl."

"Why did you offer me some then?" said Alice. She crossed her arms. "Pretty shitty to offer me something that isn't even here."

"It was pretty shitty of you to sit at our table without being invited," The March Hare said.

"I didn't *know* it was your table," Alice said defensively. "There could be fifty people sitting here, and you three fags are bunched up in the corner. I figured there was room."

"*Your hair wants cutting,*" The Mad Hater said. He held a scalpel in his hand, pressed his thumb against the blade until blood stained his white glove. "Cut it? Close to the shoulders. *All the way around, girly. Clean and jerk.*" He smiled, and his teeth were aligned in perfect ceramic symmetry. A million dollar smile on anyone else. In the Hater's mouth, they looked like terrible weapons.

"Hey," Alice said. She tried to cover her shock at the creature's tone with a look of her own. "You just keep that sick shit to yourself."

"*Caw-Caww!*" The Hater said. "Bitch! You're dirty! Nobody loves you like I do!"

"Murderer," The Dormouse mumbled. He snuggled into the rook of his arm.

The March Hare broke into hysterical laughter.

"Why is a Raven like a writing desk?" he asked.

"I can probably guess that," Alice said. Anything to steer them away from their current topic.

"You mean you think you can find the answer?" said the March Hare.

"Yeah that's what I said."

"What are you, a *fuckin' retard?*" The Mad Hater's voice was like hot gravel. "Say what you mean."

"I *did*," said Alice. "I mean what I say."

"No," said the Hater. "Say what you mean."

"*It's the same fuckin' thing*," said Alice, exasperated. She hated they way they babbled. None of it made any sense.

"*Not the same!*" The Hater shouted. He slammed his hand down on a porcelain teacup. It shattered into tiny white shards, hot black tea spilling out across the fine lace tablecloth. "It's not the fuckin' same thing and you know it! *STOP LYING, WHORE!*"

"Whore," Dormouse agreed. He opened one lazy black eye for a moment, rolled it around, and then closed it again.

The Hater sat back down. He seemed to be disappointed that he had made such a mess in front of his seat. There were shards of teacup sticking into his hand, he paid them little mind. He pulled the gloves off one finger at a time.

His hands were black, scabrous claws. From his dinner jacket he withdrew another, identical set of white silk gloves. He put them on and pulled them tight. He made hard fists with them. Then he straightened his coat and flashed his hideous perfect teeth toward Alice. When he spoke again, his voice was calm.

"You may as well say that *I see what I eat* is the same as *I eat what I see*."

"He's right you know," said the March Hare. "You might as well say *I like what I get* is the same as *I get what I like*."

"Might as well say *I sleep when I breathe* is the same as *I breathe when I sleep*," Dormouse said between snores.

"It is the same thing with you," The March Hare said, elbowing Dormouse in the ribs.

"Shut it," Dormouse said. "I'll eat half of you and leave half on your mother's front step as a gift."

"You guys are fucked," Alice said. "It's a loony bin around here."

The March Hare smiled. "Have some wine," he said amicably.

Alice rolled her eyes and shook her head.

The four of them sat in silence for a time. Alice fingered the porcelain dishes in front of her. They were beautiful, like the ones she'd seen at her grandmother's house when she was a kid. Her grandmother had been a hoarder; she collected music boxes and McDonald's Happy Meal boxes and commemorative coins. She collected posters and books and old radios from the 1920s recorded on vinyl. She's also collected a lot of garbage; chicken buckets and plastic bags and old clothes. By the time they got around to having her committed, her house was so full you couldn't even get the front door open all the way.

"Lovely girl," The Mad Hater said. Do you happen to know what day it is?"

He'd pulled a large gold watch out of his front pocket. A filigreed chain anchored it to his lapel. He shook it several times, unnaturally fast, and then looked at it with a touch of fear on his face like he wasn't sure what he was seeing. Or perhaps he simply couldn't believe it.

Alice tried to remember what day it was. It took a moment, but then a number came to her from the foggy banks of her memory.

"The fourth," she said.

The Mad Hater shot The March Hare a murderous look. "Two days?" He asked angrily.

"*What*," said the March Hare. He was busy stirring sugar into a new cup of tea.

"My watch is two fucking days behind, you imbecile," The Hater said. "*I told you butter wouldn't be good for the works, didn't I?*"

The March Hare shrugged. "It was the best butter."

"It was *lung* butter," the Dormouse said. He yawned again.

"Quiet you," The Hater said. "Don't make me drown you in a bucket of water." He looked back at the March Hare. "I bet you got crumbs in the fucking thing. I *told* you not to use the butter knife, you *cock smoking faggot*."

The March Hare took the watch from him and shook it himself. He put it up against his ear and listened.

"Let me see it," Alice said.

Nobody looked at her. Nobody acknowledged that she had spoken. She was forgotten for now.

The March Hare dipped the watch in his tea and shook it out. He looked at the watch again and sighed. "It *was* the best butter, you know," he said again.

"Let me see it," Alice said again. This time the March Hare shrugged and tossed the watch to her. Alice caught it in both hands and flipped it over. It was as big as a large glazed doughnut, perfectly etched in gold and silver. On the back was a design made out of hundreds of tiny gems. There were diamonds and sapphires and rubies. It looked like a blue car sitting in a parking lot. At the bottom of the picture two stones were missing, and their empty sockets stared back up at her. "What is it? It's beautiful."

The Mad Hater shrugged. He was cleaning his teeth with a silk glove. The sound reminded Alice of the sounds bedsprings made when you fucked on an old bed. He gave the air of someone very bored with the conversation. The Dormouse was sound asleep but The March Hare was watching her intently.

Alice flipped the watch over. Instead of hands and a face, the watch face was barren of any features. It was polished, mirror-smooth gold. In the middle of the empty face, it looked as though someone had taken a sharp knife and gouged the number "2" in a childlike scrawl. She looked up at the Mad Hater, confused.

"This is your watch?" she said. "It doesn't even tell the time. Pretty useless, don't you think?"

"Why should it?" The Mad Hater said. He cupped his hands, motioning for Alice to toss it back. When she did, he fondled it like a lost child. "Does your watch tell you what year it is?"

"No, what would be the point of that?" Alice said.

"Exactly," The Mad Hater said. "That's just the case with *my* watch."

"Uhh, what?" Alice said. "That doesn't make any sense."

The Mad Hater sighed. "The Dormouse is asleep again," he said. He took his cup of steaming hot tea and splashed the entire cup onto the top of the sleeping creature's head.

"*Fuck!*" Dormouse screeched. It was an inhuman sound, like three or four voices screaming in pain at once. His head snapped up, and he snarled at the Mad Hater. His jagged teeth slashed into his gums and his snarl widened into a roar. Blood and saliva dripped freely from the wounds onto the tablecloth. Where the creature's fluids touched the silk lace, it turned black and thick bug hair sprouted forth like mold.

The Mad Hater looked back at him, unimpressed. The two held each other's gaze for a few moments. Something silent passing between them. Alice smelled violence in the air. It was thick, like summer gnats. Finally the Dormouse turned his head away from The Mad Hater and turned his eyes on Alice.

"I was just going to say that," he said to her. His voice had been restored to civility.

"Did you guess the Riddle yet?" The Hater said, smiling. All hints of violence were gone from his face.

Alice shook her head. "Why is a Raven like a writing desk? No clue. What's the answer?"

"Haven't the foggiest," replied The March Hare.

"Me either," said the Hater. The Dormouse mumbled in agreement. Alice noticed that in spite of the horrible red patch on the top of his head from the burning tea, he was on his way back to sleep already.

"Neither of you know? What a waste of fuckin' time," Alice said. "Why would you sit here telling riddles that have no answers? Actually, never mind. It's not that surprising, really."

"If you knew *Time* the way I did," said the Hater, "You wouldn't talk about wasting *it.* It's *Him.*"

"What?" asked Alice. "I don't know what you mean."

"What I mean, *little strumpet,*" The Hater said, leaning over the table toward her. His face had suddenly taken a vile, predatory slant to it. Alice's stomach rolled just looking at him. "I daresay you have no concept of time either as a *thing or a person.* You have never even spoken to him. I know this for a fact. He and I were grand friends,"

"You were lovers," said the Dormouse. "He ripped your sweet ass open like a hot knife through clotted cream."

The Mad Hater looked down at his companion, his face dark. "More tea?" he said quietly.

"Do it," the Dormouse said, "And I'll serve this whore your balls and your eyes with *her* next cup." He rolled his lazy eye back toward Alice. "She'll eat them, too. Every last bite."

"Jesus Christ," Alice said.

"*You've never even spoken to Jesus Christ…*" The March Hare began. He caught a look from the Hater and the Dormouse and immediately shut his mouth. Looked down at his teacup and fingered the handle.

"If you knew Time the way I did," The Hater said, resuming his discussion, "that is to say, as I once did, *on friendly terms*, why, the man would do anything you liked with but a whisper and a nod. For example, let's say you are being frigged in the exit by some fat guy, why you could ask Time to change the hours to days and stop time at a motel, skin hot from the shower, her lips…"

"There you go," said the Dormouse. "Off with your fantasies again."

"I wish you hadn't interrupted," The March Hare said, in a whisper, shifting in his chair.

"I was merely stating that Time would happily stop it for you at any point you wished. Stop it even; hold it there forever if you wanted."

"Is that how you guys get on?" said Alice. "Stuck on a moment? I guess my watch *would* be useless if I could pull that off."

"Not me," said the Dormouse. "These two are assholes are cuh-*razy*."

"Look," said the Hater, swatting away the Dormouse's comments. "I'll tell you. Last March was a bad year for us. We were sentenced to death by the Queen. It was my *big day*, I was singing for her High and *Mightiness*, tra la lah, singsong voice, very lovely, very, very pretty, I have a singing voice like my mother, when I wish it, you know?"

"Very lovely," said the March Hare.

"Like her big fat tits," mumbled the Dormouse.

The Mad Hater broke into braying, hysterical laughter. The March Hare pulled his hands off the table, watching his companion closely. There was a worried look on his face. The Dormouse snuggled his nose into the crook of his own arm.

Alice pulled back from the table. She'd been around unpredictable men before; her father had been prone to bouts of random fury much like this. The Hater actually seemed a lot like her father, when she thought about it. They even kind of looked the same, with their severe British faces and large teeth.

"Excuse me," said the Hater pleasantly. "As I was saying, I had merely gotten past a single verse when the Bitch Whore Queen began screaming—'He's murdering time! Off with his head! Chop off their cocks!' –and the like. Terrible things come from her mouth when she sets her mind to it."

"Much like this one, I imagine," the Dormouse said.

Alice said nothing. She was watching The Hater intently. He palmed a silver bread and butter knife, slid it up the cuff of his shirt. Looked up at Alice and smiled. Teapots reflected off their sheen.

"Ever since that day," he said quietly. "Time has forgotten us. It's been 6 o'clock since that day in March. Tea time."

The March Hare sighed, picked up his teacup and swished the contents sourly.

"I could use a beer, frankly," he said. "Always tea though. Always tea *time*."

"So," Alice said, looking at the teapots around the table. Sets of three, every one. The teapots were arranged in essentially the same setup that the three were sitting in now. "You guys just sit here and drink tea all day? Is *that* why this table is full of teapots?"

The Hater rolled his eyes.

"No, not all day," he said. "Tea is at 6 o'clock. Since it is six o'clock, we must have tea."

"We're supposed to wash up after tea," said the Mareh Hare, "but that time hasn't arrived yet."

"I don't get it," said Alice. "Why don't you just go do something else?"

"Because," the Hater said, lightning flashing across his face. "*It's 6 o'clock!* Why can't your deranged little girl-brain get a handle on this? We don't drink tea *because* it's 6 o'clock, we do it because at 6 o'clock we *must have tea*."

"Good God," said the Dormouse. "This again? How terribly boring. Thought you had it figured out by now."

"Enough," said the March Hare. "I think this fair-haired child of Eve should tell us a tale."

"What?" asked Alice. "I don't know anything."

"Then the Dormouse shall!" the Mad Hater screamed, bringing his hand down in an arc. The silver butter knife he'd palmed up his sleeve earlier reappeared in his hand, flashing in the yellow sunshine.

The knife went into the Dormouse's forearm, causing the creature to shriek demonically. Black tar spurted from the wound, splashing The Hater's face. The Hater laughed until his eyes bulged, face going from ivory to red to purple.

"I told you about that," the Dormouse hissed, cradling his wounded arm. "Now I'm going to pull your spine out and crack each bone with my teeth."

"I should love to see it," the Hater shrieked, his harsh, coughing laugh setting lose strands of drool from his mouth. "I should *loooooove* it."

The Dormouse wrenched the knife from his arm and held up to the Hater's face, pushed the blade against the skin at the corner of his eye. Ebon blood marred the Hater's perfect ceramic skin, which puckered around the spot where the Dormouse was holding the knife to his face.

"*Ahh yes*," The Hater said, his mouth open in an unnatural grin. He ran his tongue across the bottom of his teeth. His breath escaped like the hissing of a punctured tire.

The Dormouse moved as though he was going to punch the Hater in the face with his other hand, then, at the last moment turned and flicked his wrist. There was a flash of blood and something flew from the Hater's face into an empty teacup.

The Hater burst into his hysterical, shrieking donkey laugh again. He clutched at his face and sucked big gutfuls of air as tar ran down his cheek. The Dormouse smiled, winked at Alice, and threw a ceramic shard from the Hater's broken teacup onto the table. The jagged edge had a bright smear of blood, across the bottom half of it. He reached into his teacup with the same hand, and came up with one of the Hater's perfect teeth. There was blood and meat clinging to the bottom of it, between the roots. He flicked it back into his teacup, where it plunked and rattled around before coming to rest at the bottom.

"Oh, *haha!* You're going to pay…*haha!* For that one," said the Mad Hater, choking on spit. "Oh my little rodent companion, I'll not soon forget this."

"Please," said The March Hare. He held up his teacup and sighed. There was blood like spilled ink on the side of it. "Can we shift down a seat please? I should like a clean cup."

"Yes, let's," said The Hater. He grabbed a napkin, stuffed it in his mouth, then pulled a silk handkerchief and dabbed the blood from his face.

The three of them stood up and moved down one seat, closer to Alice. Now The March Hare was sitting at a fresh spread, while the Dormouse was sitting at The March Hare's old spot, and The Hater had taken the spot previously occupied by the Dormouse. The March Hare helped himself to tea and bread and jam. The Dormouse folded his arms, pushed the dishes aside, and laid his head down on them. The Hater picked up his teacup and smiled.

"Ah ha!" he said. He pulled the bloodied napkin from his mouth, revealing a black hole in his perfect white wall of teeth. "I was wondering where you got off to."

He held his missing tooth up in the light. A spot of tea ran down the white silk of his gloves, staining them brown and red.

"It was there the whole time," mumbled the Dormouse.

"So it was," said The Hater. He noisily jammed the tooth back in place. Then bit at the air a few times as though testing it out. Smiling, he turned to the Dormouse. "You were about to tell us a story, friend."

"Very well," the Dormouse muttered. "Once upon a time there were three sisters. Elsie, Lacie, and Tillie. They ate treacle and lived at the bottom of a well—"

"What?" Alice balked. The confusion and chaos of her hosts was starting to wear on her. She was having problems keeping everything straight in her own head, as though their madness was rubbing off on her.

"Confused?" said The March Hair. "Don't be. It's just the garbage floating around us."

"What's a treacle?" Alice said.

"Molasses," said The March Hair. "You know; *black tar.*"

"Yes, but this was *Treacle of Andromachus,*" said the Dormouse. "Very tasty."

"You can't live off molasses," Alice said. "It'll make you sick."

"And so they were," replied the Dormouse sweetly. "They were *very* sick."

"So, it made them sick but they kept eating it anyway," said Alice. "Doesn't make sense. None of this makes any sense at all."

"You're right," said the Hater. "Doing something that makes you sick is a silly thing. *Regardless of how good you feel when you do it.*"

"Some people never learn," the Dormouse said. "Some people are trash."

"There, there," said The March Hare. "Have some more tea, Alice."

She looked down at her empty cup.

"I haven't had any," she said. "I can't take *more.*"

"You mean you can't take *less,*" said The Hater. "It's easy to have *more* than nothing."

"What?" Alice said. She felt like she was drugged. The whole situation was overwhelming. "Nobody asked you."

"Ha!" cried The Hater. His smile was a crooked gash across the bottom of his face, but beneath that gash laid pearls. "Who is making personal comments now?"

Alice shook her head.

"The story—," she said. "Why did they live at the bottom of the well?"

"Yes," the Dormouse said. "They lived there because it was a treacle well. And because someone had tossed them to the bottom. Nobody loves bad girls, you see. They have to take care of themselves."

"Oh, she knows," said the March Hare. "All too well, don't you, blond girl?"

Alice answered with a confused look.

"Simply put," said The Hater, "They live at the bottom of the well because they *must* live at the bottom of the well, because if they didn't, then the story ceases to exist and all of this, *every bit of it*, has been for naught. Now please, shut your mouth so my friend can continue his story."

"They were learning to draw," said the Dormouse. "They drew all sorts of things. Anything beginning with the letter M. Mouse traps. Bleeding *Muffs*. Moustache rides. *Muchness*. Ever seen a drawing of a muchness, pretty plaything?"

Alice shook her head, no.

"I don't think—," she said.

"*THEN DON'T FUCKIN' SPEAK!*" The Hater screamed, jumping to his feet and slamming his fist on the table. "*IF YOU CAN'T FORM A SINGLE FUCKING THOUGHT IN THAT BOUNCY RETARD HEAD OF YOURS YOU KEEP YOUR CUNTING MOUTH FUCKING SHUT!*"

"You know *what*?" Alice said, standing quickly. She knocked the chair back behind her. Grabbed a rather nasty looking lobster fork in one hand. "I've had it with you crazy assholes."

"*Murderess*." The Dormouse said through his teeth.

"*FUCK YOU!*" she screamed, smashing the fork into the table. The wood was soft, like flesh, and she buried it up to her hand. The March Hare pulled his teacup away from the table, as though shocked by her sudden outburst. The Hater simply watched her, not moving or saying anything. The Dormouse rolled his nose on the table, yawned, and tucked his face back into the crook of his arm.

"Fuck this shit," Alice said. She swept her dishes off the table with a crash, and then grabbed a butter knife. "Anyone who follows me gets their balls cut off."

She walked backward away from the table, eyes on the three lunatics. Then she turned and stalked off toward the side of the large rabbit house. When she got to the corner she turned and spared one last look back at the table.

The Mad Hater was busy stabbing the Dormouse in the top of his head. Behind him, The Mad Hater had pushed the Dormouse's coat halfway up his back, and was mounting him from the rear. She could have sworn the Dormouse was sleeping.

Further into the woods there was a tree with a door on it. Having no direction in mind, no place to go, Alice opened the door. It was warm inside, brightly lit, and Alice stepped into a hallway. She slammed the door behind her, but at the last moment it stopped and drifted open again. Alice turned and looked.

It was the Hater, his clothes stained with blood and jam, one tooth knocked crooked in his perfect smile, fingering his watch and staring her down with bright, cheery eyes.

"Hello Honey," he said. "I'm home."

He dropped his watch. In that instant he was moving at Alice, moving impossibly fast, so fast he seemed to stretch out and elongate, as though she were seeing him in two places at once, still standing in the doorway and intolerably close to her face at the same time, his black claws tearing through his satin gloves and raking at her flesh, cupping her head in his hands like a Faberge egg.

"Shhhh..." he whispered, his face so close to hers she could see the writhing bands of muscle and jagged scar tissue under a layer of facepaint and stage makeup. The serene calm his face projected was only a facade. It was a parlour trick. The Mad Hater wasn't a creature prone to occasional bouts of fury, like her father was. The Hater was chaos incarnate wrapped in a pretty picture; like opening the most beautiful present under the Christmas tree and triggering the bomb that had been hiding inside it.

"It will all be over so quickly," he whispered, and a line of drool dropped from his mouth to Alice's teeth. It burned where it touched. The Hater rolled her like a doll in his arms, grabbing the side of her face and putting his mouth close to her ear. "It might sting a little, Pretty Plaything."

And then he was stretching again. Alice felt like she was falling into a swimming pool of The Mad Hater; he poured over her body like molasses (*treacle, she corrected*) and seeped into her pores. He flooded her nose and ears, forced his way past her lips and around her teeth. She felt him wiggle past the tears in her asshole, in to her cunt and under her fingernails. She couldn't breathe, couldn't scream, and when he poured into her eyes and flooded her tear ducts with his madness she couldn't see either. Her lungs were for screaming for air, but they were full of The Mad Hater and she could feel him swirling into her blood like a flushing toilet, sucking and snorting like a pig rooting in shit. And then it was over and she was lying on the ground sobbing and scratching at her ears and face.

I am always with you, The Hater's voice said from deep inside her mind. *I am always with you.*

Alice stood up.

Oh, you're going to be just perfect for what I have in mind. Let's walk a bit shall we?

Alice started walking. She had no idea where The Mad Hater was taking her, but something told her it was going to be terrible, no matter where it was.

Chapter 4.

Coming up out of the Rabbit hole was a lot like being deep underwater and quickly running out of oxygen; Alice had the feeling that no matter how fast she moved, she wasn't going to make it. The world was a black void behind her, ahead of her lay reality, murky and emerald. It was quiet. Pink, ambient light through her eyelids. She could hear the rise and fall of a respirator somewhere. Smells of alcohol and industrial cleaner; her own cigarette breath caught in her nostrils. Someone was crying nearby. *Something about rabbits…*

Alice focused on her breathing. Her lungs were sluggish, slow to react to her demands. She could feel a stitch deep in her chest, as though she had been sleeping with a weight on her chest. Her muscles ached. Her head ached. Her eyes were glued shut. Pain, everywhere, nerves stretched and singing. There was something in her mouth. Alice moaned, unable to speak.

Playing cards.

She'd been wrong. They weren't simply a pack of playing cards. That bitch queen and her idiot husband had somehow managed to knock her out. Maybe she'd tripped over something when the cards flew up into her face, struck her head…

Alice moaned again. She flexed her arms, and succeeded in sending shooting pains up into her shoulders. Whatever the Queen of Hearts had done, Alice was in a bad spot. She imagined herself tied to a medieval torture device, and any moment the ropes holding her down would tighten, pulling her limb from limb.

"Well hello," a woman's tired voice said. "Back from the dead, are we?"

Alice tipped her head toward the sound of the woman's voice but didn't say anything. She was like a goldfish flopping on linoleum; exposed, injured, and unable to defend herself. Whatever this woman was going to do to her, she was free to do as she wished and there wasn't a thing Alice could do about it.

"I'm going to take the tape off your eyes first," the woman said. "But I need you to keep your eyes shut until I'm finished, alright?"

Alice nodded.

"Let's turn this *overhead*—," a soft click, and the ambient light dimmed under Alice's eyelids.

"Just don't want you looking up into a fluorescent strip," The woman said. "It's a terrible thing to have to wake up to."

There was a moment of silence. Then a cool, dry hand was placed on Alice's forehead.

"This will just take a moment," the woman said.

Alice felt the skin around her eye tighten as the tape was removed, and the woman placed a hand over her eye at the same instant. Alice moved her head slightly.

"One more, just like that," The woman said. The skin tightened around Alice's other eye. "*Perfect*. That should be a lot better."

Alice opened her eyes. They were thick and gummy. There were spots in them. She blinked rapidly a few times, and the world came back into focus. There was a middle aged woman standing over her smiling pleasantly. Dark hair. Nurses smock. Flowers and pink blotches. A stethoscope. When she was a kid, her kindergarten teacher looked a little like this woman standing over her. Same soft face and dark eyes. Waking up from nap time was like this. Not as good as when your mom woke you up, but these kind looking women were a close second.

"I'm going to remove your respirator now," the woman said. "And then maybe you can tell me who you are and how your feeling."

Alice nodded. She was still half expecting the Queen of Hearts to appear, shrieking about her execution. Her mind flooded with blood and Alice shuddered at the thought...

"Easy now," the nurse was saying. "I had to tape this on. You were unconscious, and I didn't want you to pull it out when you started to detox."

Alice looked into the woman's eyes for a moment. Then looked away.

Then looked back.

The woman busied herself removing the tape from around Alice's mouth, and then pulled the tube away from her face. Alice responded by gagging hard and fought the urge to clench her teeth shut. And then the hose was gone, and the urge to vomit passed. Alice licked her parched lips.

"I imagine your mouth is going to be a little dry," the woman said. "We'll get that taken care of in just a moment or two."

"Where," Alice croaked.

"Mercyview General Hospital," the nurse said, finishing Alice's sentence. "You're in emergency right now. Do you remember anything about last night?"

Alice shook her head. No.

But it was a lie. She remembered it all. The tea party. Shrinking and growing. Being stuck inside the rabbit house and swimming in a lake of her own tears. Croquet in the Royal gardens…the Red Queen, face spattered with gore, chest heaving, the feral look of a wild animal on her face, screaming

Off with her head!

Animal heads on posts. The Mad Hater clawing his way into her skull, behind her eyes. She remembered it all.

"Do you remember overdosing on heroin last night?" The nurse said, intercepting Alice's train of thought.

What?

"Uhh," Alice said.

"Somebody thought enough to bring you to the hospital but didn't stick around long enough to give us any information on you," the nurse said. She busied herself with monitors and plugs and swabs, anything to avoid looking Alice in the face. "You are lucky to be alive."

Alice tried to think back. There was a fog wall in her memory right before the long hallway with the glass table and all the doors. Something about Rabbit. *Wait…*

"Can you tell me your name?"

"Alice Pleasance," she said automatically, without thinking. *Shit.*

"Ok, Alice," the nurse said. "My name is Dana Howard, I've been looking after you for the last ten hours or so. Can you tell me anything about the heroin you took?"

"What?" Alice said.

"Like, were you smoking or spiking? You don't have a lot of tracks on your arms, so we weren't sure if you were a long-term user or not."

"Long—uhh, no, not really," Alice said. "I do it once in a while, that's all."

"Uhh *huh*," Nurse Howard said, making a note on her chart. "And did you smoke the stuff last night?"

"I'm not sure, exactly," Alice said. "I think I might have used a needle."

"Pretty dangerous behavior," the nurse said. There was a hint of condescension in her tone. Alice didn't like it, but it wasn't anything new. Everyone was better than a heroin user. Some of them were just better at hiding their disgust than others.

"Hey, can you get me off this thing?" Alice said. She flexed the muscles in her arms. Made fists.

"Oh of course," Nurse Howard said. "I imagine that's not very comfortable for you after ten hours."

Alice nodded at her. She even managed to fake a smile.

Condescending bitch, she thought.

Nurse Howard put down her clipboard and undid the straps on Alice's arms first. Then she did her legs. Alice moved her hands, shook them out. The blood began to return to her fingers and toes.

"I have to ask, Alice," Nurse Howard said, picking up her clipboard again. "Do you have health insurance?"

"I do," Alice lied.

"Oh *good*! And what is it, state funded? Blue Cross maybe?"

"Yeah," said Alice. "*Uhh*, Blue Cross."

"You didn't come in with any identification," Nurse Howard said. "Is there any way you could round up your number for us?"

"Yeah," Alice said. "I can, *uhh*, call my folks."

Another lie. Alice's father had been dead since Alice was little. It had driven her mother insane with grief, and she'd concentrated her feelings into a little green heat ray and pointed it straight towards Alice. Now they didn't speak at all. The last thing Alice had heard her mother say was *go on, you little bitch! You killed him! You just couldn't get your shit together and you killed him! I hope* you *die too!*

"Oh. Good," Nurse Howard said again. "Well maybe we can sneak the phone call in before the doctor sees you this morning. That way we can get you all squared away in a proper room. Get you out of this area."

"Sounds good," Alice said. She'd already made up her mind. Getting out of the hospital would be first on her list of things to do.

She was deeply disturbed that there seemed to be two sets of memories in her mind regarding the last little while. She remembered vividly all the time she had spent down the rabbit hole, but underneath that was another, less soluble version of her life; one where she had been getting high and having sex with Rabbit. She'd been really upset about something in the foggiest part of her memories. She'd gone to Rabbit. They'd gotten high, and then…*had she followed him down into a cave or something?*

One set of memories filled with smoking cats and bizarre tea parties. Technicolor and fragmented, like an acid trip. The second memories made more sense, but they were dull and mottled copper-gray and seemed to just begin and end with no real beginning or ending. But worse, there was something black in that set of memories, like a dead patch of night between street lamps. A place where monsters might lurk; where she could step in and be dragged away screaming in eternal darkness if she wasn't very careful. But that was just the thing; her mind was being dramatic about it because it was simply a black hole with sepia and silver memories in orbit around it.

"Where are my clothes?" Alice said.

"Oh, they're in a bag at the foot of the bed here," Nurse Howard said. "No need to get back into those dirty things. We thought you had some kind of injury, there is quite a bit of blood on them."

She stopped for a moment, looking over charts and monitors again. Alice looked at the woman. Nurse Howard shook her head.

"No trace of injury though," she said. A quick glance into Alice's eyes, then darting away again. Trying to be flippant about the whole thing. Trying to act like it didn't matter where the blood came from, even though the nurses face had *WHAT THE FUCK HAVE YOU BEEN UP TO* pasted across it like a billboard sign.

"Your guess is as good as mine," Alice said.

"Well, we'll get it all squared away," Nurse Howard said. She double-checked the heart monitor. "Everything looks good here, why don't you relax and I'll get you some water."

"Oh good," Alice said. Beside her, the heart monitor blipped as her heart rate started to speed up.

Nurse Howard gave it a look, and then glanced at Alice. Looked away. She seemed on the verge of saying something, but then turned on her heel and walked out. The dividing curtain swished shut behind her.

Alice watched her shoes under the curtain. Nurse Howard was standing just outside, like a curious parent on the wrong side of a child's door, listening for any sign of wrongdoing. What was Nurse Howard up to out there? Writing on her clip board? Waiting for Alice to get off the bed and try to escape? Signaling security to be ready for anything? Whatever it was, the moment passed and Nurse Howard's feet disappeared from under the curtain. They turned and walked briskly down the hall.

Alice sat up in bed. If she was going to do this, she had to get up and moving. Her legs groaned in protest when she swung them off the side of the bed. Vertigo came, swished around behind her eyes, and drained away. Alice slid off the bed. Standing was an act of will.

She flicked off the finger sensor. The heart machine whined at her for a moment, and Alice hit the on/off button. She looked down at the IV needle in her hand. She was still being fed saline from a half filled bag on a post at the head of her bead. There was a touch of pink in the hose where the needle met her hand. The needle itself was deep inside her, in a vein. In spite of her recreational heroin use, Alice cringed at the thought of it. She didn't like needles at all; that's why she always made Rabbit fix her arms for her.

The needle was going to have to go.

There was a box of paper towels by her bed, and Alice grabbed a handful of them. Then she undid the tape around the IV needle and pinched the hose in her fingers.

Pulled it.

There was blood.

A line of dull purple-red shot from the hole in Alice's hand across the bed. She clamped her hand over the wound. Then she grabbed the bag at the end of her bed, pulling out her jeans. The nurse was right; there *was* a lot of blood on her clothes. Alice slid her pants on, the blood making them waxy. They smelled like iron; like when her period came early and got into her pants; like an unseasoned chunk of meat that had been sitting on the counter all day. She quickly did them up and grabbed her shirt. Yanked off her hospital gown. Pulled the shirt over her head. Blood was running down her fingers by the time she finished dressing, and she grabbed a folded washcloth from a pile of linens on a little shelf under her bed. She folded it in half and wrapped it around her hand, making a padded fist.

She stepped into her shoes. Then she walked to the curtain and took a quick peek into the hallway. It was filled with more of the same soft, yellow light that permeated her room. There were people milling about their workstations, but no sign of Nurse Howard. No sign of security.

Alice steadied her nerves. Took a deep breath, adjusted the bloodstained cloth on her hand. Then she stepped out into the yellow light of the hallway. It was familiar somehow, a yellow lit hallway filled with doors and curtains.

Familiar, yet different.

Chapter 5.

Dorothy sat in Dr. Weller's chair, avoiding eye contact and pretending to be interested in the silk plants hanging in the window just to her left. She was still in her pajamas, officially against hospital protocol but Dr Weller never cared enough to enforce it. Under her arm was a small black dog, one of those stuffed animal toys won at the carnival for popping balloons with darts or being able to get golf balls into the red goblets without them bouncing out.

"Good morning, Dorothy," Dr Weller said. He pretended to look busy; made a point of showing the girl that the long stretches of silence between them didn't bother *him* either.

"*Good morning to you*," Dorothy continued. "How is your mom?"

"Better, thanks," Dr Weller sighed. "She thinks it might be the flu." More paper shuffling.

Dorothy countered with a shirt adjustment, and then feigned a look of forgetfulness. She bit her lip, shook her head and then looked back at the silk plants.

"Something wrong?" Dr Weller said.

"*Umm*, no." There was a pause while Dorothy chose her words. "I was just wondering, *umm*, when I can watch television again."

"Well," Dr Weller said, leaning back in his chair. It was a power position for him, giving him the air of importance. "I just don't think that kind of stimulus would be good for you right now. I mean, you remember what happened last time, right?"

"Yes," Dorothy sighed, defeated. "But it wasn't *all* my fault. I mean, Tina was there first, yeah, but like, she was *sleeping* on the couch. I just switched the channel; she wouldn't have even noticed if Roth hadn't dumped his water on the floor and started crying."

"Well, either way, you were pretty upset weren't you?"

"Uhh, yeah. But still, not my fault—,"

"Alright," Dr Weller said. "Well, for you, watching the weather network for tornado warnings shows me that you are still spending a lot of time thinking about your incident. And if that's true, then you shouldn't be exposed to the television because you will crave watching the weather channel some more, and feed an unhealthy cycle of thought and behavior that ultimately may lead to you attempting suicide again. Does that make sense to you at all?"

Dorothy's shoulders sank. "I keep telling you guys I didn't try to kill myself."

"My apologies," Dr Weller said. It was time to push her, just a little. He folded his hands behind his head.

'So you ran away from your uncle's house. And you stole a car. Sorry, *allegedly* stole a car. Then you drove the car seventy miles to the Kansas state line, where you turned it into a field and drove straight into an oncoming tornado."

"He's not my real uncle," Dorothy said. "He's my dad's friend from the war. They only sent me there 'cuz of that, plus he takes in foster kids for the money. He calls us *strays*."

"You're right," Dr Weller said. "Sorry. But you can see how this looks, don't you Dorothy?"

"Yeah," she said. She bit her lower lip again. "I mean…*yeah.* It does sound a little *weird.* But that doesn't mean it's not true. I couldn't make something like that up, I swear, doctor."

"I know," Dr Weller said. He took a sip of cold coffee from a silver mug. "Sometimes, especially with people who have suffered greatly, it is easier for them to sort of wipe out the existing bad memories and replace them with extremely vivid fantasy memories. I think we can both agree that you have suffered a great deal, Dorothy."

"*But they're not fantasies!*" Dorothy said. She waved her arms, exasperated. She caught herself immediately. Dr Weller saw the lights switch off, and Dorothy's calm exterior shell once more took over. "I mean, I don't see how I could be dreaming all of it up. The Witch? *Scarecrow?*"

"I know," Dr Weller said. "That's why we have our meetings though, right? So we can discuss this whole Oz business, try to make sense of it."

"Em thought I meant Australia," Dorothy said, and smiled. She looked down and hugged her stuffed dog. The ratty old thing glared at Dr Weller with one scratched plastic eye. "She kept thinking I had some dream about going down there to live or something."

"Was she upset that you didn't want to stay with them?"

"A little I think," Dorothy said. "She was always talking about the boys around the area like I'd suddenly stop being into girls and run off to get married. Come home, do the family thing."

"But that's not for you," Dr Weller said.

"Nope," Dorothy said. "No thanks."

"How did Henry react to you being openly gay?"

"He didn't say anything at all." Dorothy cocked her head, looked out of the corner of her eye at the silk plants, and chewed her bottom lip. It was an incredibly cute gesture.

She does it to attract my sympathy, Dr Weller thought.. He made a point of keeping his gaze neutral.

"Mostly it was Aunt Em and her sermons about how I was this lost little sheep, and how God knew I was confused but wouldn't put up with me messin' around with girls. Like once I got back on track it would all disappear."

"Some people are like that," Dr Weller said. "Especially ones from the old way of thinking. How do you feel about that?"

"I don't really feel anything. It is what it is, right?"

"Sounds like avoidance," Dr Weller said.

"Well, they're *old*," Dorothy said. "They're not going to change on my account. Just like I'm not going to change for theirs." She turned her head down and then lilted her eyes up toward Dr Weller. she dangled a smile at him, and then shot a brief pouty face when he didn't respond.

"Would you like to talk about your parents today, Dorothy?" Dr Weller said. It had the effect of a punch in the stomach on the girl. Her shoulders sagged, and she dropped into a thoughtful, wounded look.

"There, *umm*," Dorothy said, fighting to regain control of her emotions. She shook her head and dismissed the question with a wave of her hand. "There's nothing really to talk about. They're dead, right? People die all the time."

"That's true. But these are your parents. They only die once."

"I know that," Dorothy said, looking down into her hands. "It's just that it can't be helped, can it? It was an accident. I don't know what to do about that."

"Well, for starters, you can allow yourself to be angry, and sad. Those are perfectly normal emotions to feel."

"Oh I do," Dorothy said, nodding quickly. She had begun to pick at the skin on the sides of her fingernails. "I'm just kind of beyond it right now. But I feel all those things you said."

"How?"

"*What?*"

"How have you been dealing with your grief?" Dr Weller said. He crossed his arms and looked down his nose at the girl. "How we deal with our grief is at least as important as the grief itself. Would you agree with that?"

"*Umm*, yes," Dorothy said. "I mean no. *I mean—*."

She sighed, and her shoulders sagged again. She looked up at Dr Weller and arched an eyebrow, flashing her playful, impish smile. "Can we maybe talk about this another time?"

"Absolutely," Dr Weller said. "We'll talk about it whenever you are ready. In the meantime I want you to try and think about the connections between their death and your life, if you can."

"I will." Dorothy said. "Promise."

"Anything else? Still having issues with the medication?"

"*Umm, no*," Dorothy said. "How much longer do I have to take it?"

"Tough to say. You have a small chemical issue that is causing you some problems, and we need to correct them before you see any real improvement." Dr Weller shuffled some papers as he spoke, piled a small stack together and tapped them out on the desk. He glanced at the clock.

"They make me feel like crap," Dorothy said. "Like I'm walking around in a mist kinda, I don't know. Not myself."

"It's called disassociation," Dr Weller said. "It's a result of the anti depressants you're taking. They're like a chemical wall we build in your brain to keep out the bad thoughts."

"Like driving into a tornado?" Dorothy said.

"Among other things, yes."

Dorothy stared into her hands.

Dr Weller smiled. "You know you don't have to be in here for the full half hour, right? I'm here to help you understand some of your feelings, kinda put things in perspective. If you feel like you've talked enough today, that's fine."

"I think I'm done for today, doctor," Dorothy said quickly. "I can go?"

"Sure," said Dr Weller. "Like I said, try to think about your connection to your parents, and how it's affected you. Maybe next time we can talk about it a little, if you feel ready."

"*Sure,*" Dorothy said, smiling. She got up off the couch and headed to the door. She paused at the threshold of Dr Weller's office. "You know, Dr Weller, I never intended to kill myself."

"I believe that *you* believe that," Dr Weller said.

Dorothy's face darkened for a moment. Then the look was gone, like the cloud passing by the sun on a summer day.

A moment later Dorothy herself was gone from the doorway, leaving Dr Weller to himself. "At least, that's what you *want* me to believe," he said, to nobody in particular.

Chapter 6.

Alice kept her head down. She felt sick and light headed, and several times she had to put her hand against the wall to steady herself. She'd never been this deep in a hospital before, and the soft emerald light made the distances deceiving. She tried to follow the stripes on the floor, but in her state she couldn't understand how they worked. She passed a hallway where 2 green strips and two yellow strips intersected, came to a "T" intersection and opted to follow a thick red stripe. She had the sense of someone standing right behind her, and she looked back often to see only empty hallway. She felt as though she were shrinking inside her body one moment and growing the next. The sense of movement within herself was making her dizzy, and she stumbled more than once.

There were people in the hall, but they were phantoms to Alice; she barely made note of their passing. She kept her head down and her shoulder to the wall. As she walked, her mind began to separate the two sets of memories mixed up in her head.

At some point she had killed a man, she was fairly certain. The electric ball of static at the center of that black and white world had slowly receded until bits and pieces of another memory began showing through; one where she was stabbed in her ass again and again and blew some guys brains out. She was also sure, at some point, she had seen her friend Rabbit dressed in a checkered vest and running for his life. He'd stopped and shot her up. She'd washed blood off in a mud puddle and fallen through her reflection in the water at the same time...

...into an emerald-lit hall with many doors and wisps of people floating like phantoms about her. Just like now. *But that was impossible.*

And there lay the paradox that was threatening to rip her skull apart. Things like that didn't just *happen.* You didn't just fall into a mud puddle and end up somewhere else. That wasn't how life worked.

Had she fallen into the hospital?

Alice stopped and looked around. Had she been in the hospital looking for Rabbit before the tea party? The hallway she was in now *did* seem like it was the same hallway from memory, except this hallway had doors...and that other hallway had only one tiny door. Her only memory of arriving to this point had been falling into the water while she was washing blood from her face and hands. And that just didn't make sense.

The nurse had been asking her about heroin. Was the answer so simple?

She couldn't remember looking for Rabbit in the hospital because she'd been *high* the first time she tried to find him. So she'd stumbled around not realizing where she was, and somehow ended up having tea with The March Hare, the Dormouse, and The Mad Hater. And she let Rabbit fuck her. *Before or after…*

The Royal Court. The Queen of Hearts. Alice had never seen so much blood in all her life. She'd never imagined the level of brutality the woman was capable of. And utterly, completely, insane. It was as though the Red Queen flipped a coin every time she opened her mouth.

Heads. Lucidity.

Tails. Chaos.

But more than the wet stink of the butchered bodies, shit and vomit on pressed silk smells and stark contrasting colours, ripped flesh and blood puddling around their feet and the sweaty grunting of the queen's servants as they cleared a path for their Bitch Goddess to her throne—more than all of that was the voice of the queen, when she opened her mouth and insanity poured from behind her teeth. Her parched, whisper dry voice screeching and chanting:

Meat is murder!
Meat is Murder!
Meat is Murder!
Meat is Murder!

The lines overlapped when Alice thought back to the Courtyard. She'd looked up at the Queen of Hearts, and the woman had looked back down, eyes wide and electric with her insanity. Her red hair splashed out away from her face like a crooked halo. Her mouth ripped across her face in a snarl, revealing crooked, yellow teeth. Hundreds of them, maybe. Jammed into her mouth haphazardly, angling this way and that way, and behind them her forked black tongue. And as she screamed in Alice's upturned face, her hot meat breath washed over Alice like an infernal baptism:

MEAT IS MURDER! MEAT IS MURDER! MEAT IS MURDER!

Alice had thrown herself at this woman's mercy.

It was hard to tell who was crazier.

Alice turned a corner and two darkened forms caught her eye. She looked up, tried to focus. Two pigs with white shirts. They wore black pants and shuffled along the floor, as though they were unsure of themselves on two legs. They had flashlights. Some sort of security? Did they work for the queen? A thought occurred to Alice, that any door she opened in this place may lead back to the Courtyard, and since she was totally lost she could have been walking in circles for hours and been walking back toward the Queen of Hearts without knowing it. Were these two of her soldiers?

"Easy *Miss*," one of them said, putting a hand up. They were walking slowly toward her, eyes sharp and alert behind piggy faces. "You're Alice, aren't you?"

"How did you know that?" Alice said.

"Relax," the other one said. "We're here to take you back."

Alice's heart plunged in her chest. She shook her head. "No," she said. Her jaw shook, and she began to cry. "*NO!*"

"Now, now," the first one snorted. "That's no way to behave, is it? You're just a little confused. Let's get you back to your room. The Doctor would like to see you still."

"You want to get better, don't you?" the other one said.

"You get the fuck away from me," Alice said. She matched their steps toward her with one of her own, back and away from them.

"It's going to be okay," The second pig said.

"*GET THE FUCK AWAY FROM ME!*" Alice screamed. Her voice strained and cut out on her, forcing her next breath to come out like a walrus barking at its mate.

"Calm down," The first pig said. "You need to go back, you can't stumble around in the halls all night leaving blood smears everywhere."

"Not going back," Alice said. "Not ever."

"Well, we have to take you back Missy," The first pig said. "We're *going* to take you back."

"*I'll rip your fuckin' balls off if you come near me, pig*," Alice said. They wavered for a moment. The first pig took on the shape of a man in his 20's with a crop of curly red hair. The other pig looked shorter. Darker. She shook her head, trying to clear the cobwebs. She could focus on the creatures in front of her. It was enough, for now.

"Real fuckin' nice," the second pig said. "Boy, I bet your mom is real proud of that mouth you have."

"I'm gonna drag you back to that room by *your hair* if I have to," the first one said. He had his hands up in front of him, and had stepped in front of his partner. In a lower voice, he said, "*But I bet you'd like that, wouldn't you?*"

Alice put her hands up, Balled into fists. The second pig snorted at her.

"*Aww come on*," he said. "Can we just do this without any bullshit please?"

"Too late," the first pig said. He made a grab for Alice's hand; and for a moment was surprised when it wasn't there. Alice slapped his hand down and away from them. Too late the pig noticed Alice's other fist pulled back like a spring on a hair trigger.

Alice hit the pig in the face with a perfect left cross, catching him just to the left of his nose and hitting his cheek. It was enough to cause his nose to angle off to the right; a subtle shift that only he and Alice were aware of. A moment later his face was gouting blood, and he fell back away from her holding his broken nose in his hooves.

"*Fuckin bitch!*" he screamed. "*Ahh Jesus Jackson she broke it!*"

Alice turned to the other pig. He had his flashlight out like a club. His head swiveled between his partner and back to Alice, as though he was unsure which one needed his attention more.

"I told you," Alice said. "I'm not going back to the courtyard. I'm not going back so she can cut off my goddamn head."

"What?" said the second pig. "What are you, high?"

"*I'm not going back!*"

"I have no idea what you're talking about lady," he said. "There's no fuckin' courtyard here. That's at *Barker* General Hospital. They have that big garden where you used to be able to smoke."

"Just let me leave," Alice said. "Please."

"*You're nod goin' anywhere, you fuckin bitch!*" the first pig squealed from behind his hands. Blood and snot was all over his face. It dripped from between his fingers like warm paint.

"Look, try to stay calm," the second pig said. "Doc just wants to take a look at you. That's it. Then I'm sure they'll let you do whatever you want."

Alice looked into his face. A moment too late she realized he was looking over her shoulder. It made her a moment too late to look behind her.

A third pig had come in behind her while the second one was talking. Now he hit Alice like a tackle dummy, ramming his shoulder into the small of her back and taking her to the ground. The air rushed out of her as she fell. She tried to twist her way around to face this new enemy, but then she was on her back and her skull bounced on the floor.

There was a wave of alternating blue and black behind her eyes, and sparks as the world bounced in her vision. Then things got very slow.

"Nice job, Mike," the second pig said somewhere above Alice. "You coulda played for the *Giants*."

"Heh, yeah," the pig named Mike said. "They could use me this year."

"You alright?"

"My fuckin nose, man," the first pig said. "She caught me good."

"Yeah, keep your hands up next time *Chuckles*," second pig said.

"Okay, hold her arms. Let's get her to observation. Go get that thing looked after, Charlie, your bleeding like a stuck pig."

"*He is a pig*," Alice said. "You're all pigs."

"What's that honey?" the Mike-Pig said. "Hey you're a real sweetheart, you know that? You think my friend here could get your number?"

"Yeah, thanks," Jackson-Pig laughed. "I bet my mother would love you. You kind of remind me of her."

The two men picked Alice up. She could feel movement, but she couldn't get a handle on where she was. The world was fracturing into shards of memory, as though she was observing her life a moment after it had taken place. Polaroids in a pile, shuffled like cards. The two pigs talking about football. The chimes of the Red Queen's Court somewhere in the distance. Her head black and foggy. She shot a man in the face because he was sodomizing her.

"*Fuckin killed him*," Alice said. "*His face asploded.*"

"You busted his nose," Mike-Pig said. "Take a lot more than that to kill Charlie though."

"She's on crack or something," Jackson-Pig said. "Said she wasn't going to the garden. You know that one in Mercy? She doesn't even know where she is."

"Hell," said M ike-Pig. "Come the weekend, I don't know where I am half the time either."

Jackson-Pig laughed. "Amen to that," he said.

The two men arrived at a small interview room a few minutes later. Dr Weller was waiting for them. Alice had slipped into unconsciousness. The two security guards laid Alice down on the couch and stepped away from her. Dr Weller checked her vitals, then shone a light in her eyes and felt the lump on the back of her head.

"So," He said, standing up and turning to the other two men in the room. "What did she say to you?"

Mike-Pig and Jackson-Pig looked at each other and shrugged.

"You may as well go first," Mike-Pig said.

Chapter 7.

Dorothy was sitting on the couch watching two men play pool When Alice was brought onto the ward. It was cloudy outside. Mid-April weather being what it was, that could have meant either rain or snow. She toyed with the idea of going downstairs and breathing in some fresh air, and then she'd know for sure. A single breath would give her all the information she needed to know. If there was rain in the air, she'd be able to taste it. She decided it was too far to go. It looked like rain, and that was fine for now.

Toto sat haphazardly on the couch beside her, his scratched plastic eyes watching her with sympathy? Boredom? Sometimes it was hard to tell with that little dog. Maybe she'd go down in a little while and check the weather.

The two men at the pool table were discussing a shot. In another room there were rows of reclining chairs, and the only television available on the hospital floor. Ward 9 was essentially two large box rooms with many small double-occupant rooms lining them. In the rec room, where Dorothy sat, there were couches and a pool table, and a punching bag hanging from the ceiling. There was also an air hockey table, but the nurses hated the noise it made and left it unplugged. The rec room also contained the nurses' station, and the only way off the floor via elevator. There was an emergency stairwell exit beside the elevator, but that door was alarm sealed. Behind the nurses' station was a small hallway with offices and storage space, and where Dr Weller had his sessions with patients. The other room was off limits to Dorothy; it contained the television and rows of comfortable chairs. If she'd been allowed near the T.V., she'd be able to flick on the weather channel and see what the forecast was for the rest of the week. Instead, she had to do it the old fashioned way; look out the window and take a guess.

And there were so many windows to choose from! As though the sight of the city surrounding them from the ninth floor of the City General Hospital would somehow calm their inner demons and make them feel sane again. Like it wouldn't make them aware of every single moment of their life ticking away. Dying, moment to moment. Like beach sand in the crack of their asses washing away in the shower. Like other things, too, but Dorothy was bored and didn't feel like coming up with them. It was cold; maybe it was snow after all.

When the elevator dinged, Dorothy looked up. The doors swung open and two security guards stepped out. Between them, a disheveled blond girl about the same age as Dorothy, her face a mix of anger and embarrassment. She looked like she'd been at it with someone. There were bruises on her face and a big lump over her eye. One of the security guards whispered something to the girl, and she shook her head.

She looked around the room. Her eyes fell on Dorothy. The pair looked at each other until the blond girl scowled and Dorothy looked away. She looked back out of the corner of her eyes, but the blond girl was speaking with security again.

"Alice Pleasance, unconfirmed," one of the security guards said to the attending nurse. "Transfer from Emergency."

"Ahh yes," the nurse said. "She's the one who made the big mess in the hall by the cafeteria."

"One and the same," the security guard said.

"Look Toto," Dorothy said. She lifted the stuffed animal so that its head was peeking up over the back end of the couch. Toward Alice. "We have a new neighbour." She moved the dog's head back and forth, and with her other hand wagged its little black tail. Then she picked him up and hugged him. "Yes," she whispered. She is very pretty."

She looked back at the Alice. Caught her staring; giving Dorothy a look that was equal parts confusion and amusement. Dorothy tipped her head. Caught her eye and smiled. Alice shook her head and turned to the security guard.

"You can't put me in here with these fucking psychos," she said.

Dorothy's face flushed. She spun around on her chair, face pulled down by a heavy pout. There were times when Ward 9 was almost like summer camp. Other times, like now, it was all she could do to keep from screaming and pulling all her hair out. People kept saying it, but it wasn't true. She *wasn't* crazy. She had her own mind. *What would the tin man or the scarecrow say if they could see me now?*

What was it the wizard had said to her? *Home is where you make it.* She tried to keep that in mind as she went about her day to day rituals in the nuthouse; mainly this consisted of watching out the windows for shifting weather patterns and taking her pills three times a day as ordered. Since she was not considered a flight risk, she was allowed to leave the floor and walk around if she wanted to get out for a bit; the nurses had to unlock the elevator in order to use it though, and after five o'clock the elevator shut down for public use and she was supposed to stay upstairs. Sometimes she went downstairs to be around other people, but there was so much misery on the other wards that this floor could be the calmest place in the building.

Of course, there was *one* thing she had to fight off the most terrible days, when the gloom of the hospital was too much or she was so bored she needed a pick-me-up; Aunt Em had sent along fifty dollars for ice cream. *In case you get a case of the nimbly bimbly's*, she'd whispered, stuffing the folded bill into her hand. Dorothy had accepted it gladly. Her life was nothing but *nimbly's* and *bimbly's*, often more of each than she could count.

Not knowing how long she might be in this place, Dorothy was very careful with how and when she spent that money. She saved it for those days when she was ready to claw out her eyes at the sight of another personality test, or slash open her wrists so the nurses taking blood could just take it all at once and get it over with. Some days, it seemed both were an imminent possibility. Then she'd grab two dollars, tell the nurse she was going to the cafeteria, and make her way down to the ice cream machine just outside the lunchroom.

There was a bench with a water fountain nearby, and some silk plants meant to relieve stress. Dorothy found it the perfect place to sit and be still and push all her bad thoughts away. Sometimes she would think about her life in Oz, sometimes not.

Sometimes she sat and thought about just walking out the door. Like her Aunt Em used to say, *Dorothy weren't no caged bird.* She was meant to fly. She was meant to sing. But like most songbirds that spent a long time in their cages, she wasn't so sure she could survive out there on her own anymore. She had a feeling her wings had atrophied beyond usefulness and were now just there to hold up her clothes. Anything resembling a killer instinct had been cowed by the drugs she was taking and the security blanket hospitality of the hospital. That, and well...she'd never been a killer had she? They were accidents.

So she'd fold her ice cream wrapper carefully so as not to get ice cream on her fingers, place it in the garbage, scoop up Toto and have a drink of water to get the ice cream milk off her teeth. By the time she got back upstairs she'd be smiling again. Just in time for more tests. Or more blood work.

"You take care, kiddo," one of the security guards said to Alice. Dorothy turned back to the nurses' station. They were getting ready to leave. The one standing to the left of Alice looked over at Dorothy and flashed her a predatory smile.

Dorothy could feel his eyes licking her skin. She pulled back from the edge of the couch. He smirked at her. His eyes moved down from Dorothy's face. To where her chest would be, if he could see through the back of the couch. Back up to her face. *Into her eyes…*

Alice saw the look and followed it down to Dorothy.

Dorothy's face burned. For a moment there were two sets of eyes on her, burning holes through her clothes and dancing on naked flesh. Then the blond girl looked over at the security guard and snickered.

"See something you like, pig? You got the *rape eyes* all over her."

"What?" the security guard said. He looked away from both of them, his face guilty. "Just shut up and go sit down."

"Aww Piggy can't get his eats." Alice's eyes flashed dangerously. "You're so fuckin disgusting, you know that? You probably look at little boys that way too, don't you, faggot?"

The guard clenched his hands into hammy fists. He was turning scarlet, and for a moment Dorothy thought he was going to hit the girl.

It was amazing to watch this woman handle men. She was the prisoner here, make no mistake, but she was the one in control.

"Mike," the other guard said. "Let's go man, we're done here." He stepped by Alice and patted Mike on the shoulder.

Mike shook his head. Crisis averted. In the end, the wiser course of action was just to move on and diffuse the situation. He'd met a lot of girls like this; girls used to men doing what they wanted or intimidated by their beauty; getting drunk off the power of their own cooze. Sometimes they turned mean, like the ability to make a guy have an orgasm turned them into some kind of sexual messiah.

"Take care of that pretty head of yours," he said, pointing to the swollen spot on the side of her head. "If I wrecked anything in there, they're liable to keep you on this floor for the rest of your life."

"Prick," she said.

The guards turned after they got onto the elevator, both smiling. Mike waved at her as the doors closed. There was silence as Alice watched after the elevator a moment then turned and stalked over to the couch beside the one Dorothy was sitting on. She flopped down, crossing her arms over her chest. She stared at the floor.

Dorothy watched her, a coy smile played on her lips. Sitting closer to the woman now, Dorothy could see Alice was a few years older than she herself was. Harder, as though she was made of wood and covered in flesh. Dorothy could *sense* the hardness in her. There was lot of stress on her face. She looked like she hadn't slept in days. Dark makeup under her eyes made her sympathetic.

But she was more than angry and stressed and exhausted, and Dorothy could see it plain as day. She was all those things *and beautiful.* Dorothy wondered what her lips tasted like.

"Well?" Alice said. "What the fuck are you looking at?" She'd turned to Dorothy and was staring hard at the girl.

"Umm, nothing," Dorothy said. "*I mean hi.* I'm Dorothy."

"*I give a fuck*," said Alice. "Quit staring at me or I'll bust your fuckin' face open."

Dorothy looked down at her knees and played with the hem of her shirt. "I just wanted to say thanks," she mumbled, her face in her chest.

"What?'

"I *uhm*," Dorothy said. She cleared her throat. Ventured a look at Alice. "I wanted to say thank you, *like*, for what you did with that guy and stuff."

"Shit," Alice said. "That goes back to before I walked in here. He fuckin' knocked me out downstairs, almost busted my head open."

"Really?" Dorothy said. "They actually hit you? I thought they weren't allowed to do that."

Alice smirked. "Yeah, well, the did. This was down in emergency somewhere, and there wasn't anyone around to say different. Fucker speared me in the side when I turned around to clock him. I went down hard, smashed my head on the floor."

"Holy crap," Dorothy said. "Are you alright?"

"Yeah, I'll live." Alice smiled; it was the most glorious thing Dorothy had ever seen. It was like sunrise on her face. "*Shoulda* seen what I did to his buddy."

"You *hit* him?" Dorothy said. She scooped Toto under one arm and held him tight. The move made Alice look at her funny.

"Busted him in the face," Alice said, mimicking the cross she'd used to down the security guard. "Broke his nose wide open."

"No *way*," Dorothy said. "Was he bleeding?"

"*Heh.* Yeah, like a pig. That's all they are." Alice fixed her sleeve. Straightened her shirt. When she spoke again her voice was soft, as though she'd suddenly thought of something important. "Just a bunch of pigs."

"That's so awesome," Dorothy said. "I've never been in a fight before. And I don't think I ever met a girl who was in a fight with three guys."

"Yeah well," Alice said. "Shit happens when you live rough. Girl's gotta know how to defend herself."

"I guess." Dorothy looked down at her dog, as though milling the words over. When the silence started to weigh on her, she looked up again. "So, *uhm*, how long you staying?"

"Not very. I gotta get out of here."

"Yeah, me too."

Alice nodded.

"So what's up with that dog?" she said, changing the subject. "Aren't you a little old for stuffed animals?"

"This is Toto!" Dorothy said, giggling. "He's just—well, I guess he's an easy friend. I've had him since I was a baby, you know? He's a Scottish terrier, and we had one when I lived with my folks before they died, and I guess Aunt Em thought it would make me feel better if I had a little stuffed puppy to pal around with." She shrugged, as though there were nothing else left to say on the subject. She bounced Toto on her knee, made him tilt his head with a flick of her wrist.

"Toto, say hello to the nice girl," she said.

"Alice. Nice to meet you Toto." She reached out to pet the stuffed pooch and Dorothy growled playfully. Alice withdrew her hand. "You going to bite me?"

"Maybe," Dorothy said. She smiled at Alice. "Never know what's down the road, right?"

Chapter 8.

Alice fingered a crack in the black leather of the couch she was sitting on. Across from her, Dr Weller folded his fingers and looked over his glasses at her. It was sunny outside, but the light that filtered into the room was green and sickly. Just like everything else in the hospital, it had a terminal feel that made Alice's skin crawl.

"So is this where I tell you how my dad fingered me when I was a baby and now I'm all fucked up from it?" Alice said. She laughed, uncomfortable by her own joke. She was uneasy though, and she sometimes said stupid shit when she was upset or nervous. She felt off keel here; she'd barely settled into her room when a nurse had dropped bye and told her about the meeting with the doctor. Now it was early afternoon, she'd been on the ward for two days, and she was ready to call it a day. But first she'd have to deal with Dr Phil and his psycho babble bullshit.

"Well," Dr Weller said. "We can talk about that if you like. I thought we could spend a couple minutes getting to know each other before I started coming up with excuses for your behavior."

Alice clapped her hands on her knees, took a big deep breath and flashed a smile at the doctor. "Great!" she said. "So where do you want to begin?"

"How about we start with an easy one?" Dr Weller said. "How are you feeling today, Alice?"

"Fine," Alice said.

"Just fine?"

"*Perfect!*" Alice said. "Never better."

"Any withdrawal pains or discomfort from your treatment?"

"Oh that," Alice said. "What the hell did you guys do to me? I feel like shit."

"They didn't tell you?" Dr Weller said. "They administered Naloxone because you were in the middle of an opiate overdose. It's like a vacuum cleaner for opiate molecules in your body. It's supposed to ease withdrawal pains as long as you keep taking it."

"I *know* what Naloxone is," Alice said. "And it doesn't ease the pain. I feel like I'm gonna barf. I have the sweats, too. Hot, right? Sexy." She laughed, but it sounded angry.

"Could be worse," I guess," Dr Weller said.

Alice grunted. There was silence for a minute as Alice distanced herself from the conversation. She sounded whiny and she knew it. Dr Weller probably knew it, too. She wondered if he thought her natural state was as one of those prissy, weak-willed bitches who needed someone to take care of them. If it was, he was sorely mistaken. She was her own woman. Not somebody's puppy.

"You're all settled in?" Dr Weller said, finally breaking the gulf of silence between them.

"Settled?" Alice said. She smiled again, sat forward on the couch. She spread her hands out in front of her. The gesture said *Let me lay it all out for you.* "In all honesty doc, this really isn't the place for me. I need to get out of here."

"Well," Dr Weller said. "That's a pretty normal sentiment. Nobody really likes it here. The walls, the paint. It's depressing. Even the drapes. I don't like being here sometimes."

"Like now?" Alice said.

"Not like now," Dr Weller said. "I love having someone to talk to. But a lot of my job is paperwork and going over charts and stuff, and sometimes I'd just rather be off somewhere else."

"Yeah," Alice said. "That must really suck for you." She settled back in the couch a bit. Let her hands drift to her sides.

"How about you?" Dr Weller said. "Do you like having people to talk to?"

"I guess," Alice said. "Dunno, I never really think about it too much. I'm happy to be on my own. I can live rough with the best of em, I don't care."

"It's good to be self sufficient," He said. "Really shows a person where they stand."

"You think half the suits in this town could live off the streets for more than three days?" Alice said. The idea seemed funny to her, like some sick universal joke. Truth was, she *knew* what half the suits in this town would be like after three days on the streets. They'd be sniveling, filthy, wounded little birds. That wasn't a knock on them maybe; it was just what the streets did to you if you weren't tough enough to stand on your own feet and face them.

"Oh I know they couldn't," Dr Weller said. "How long have *you* been on the streets?"

"Ahh, I dunno," Alice said. "Like four years I guess. You stop counting after a while. It doesn't matter so much."

"Sounds like hard times," Dr Weller said. "You ever talk to family? Your parents? A sister or brother maybe?"

Alice shook her head. "Naww, nothing," she said. Her face turned sour, like she smelled something foul in the air. "My dad's dead. He was a drunk driver. My mom and me...we don't really want nuthin' to do with each other, I think. I left when I was fourteen. I never looked back." Well, she *had* looked back…once. Just long enough to give the finger. Her mom was so shocked that spit came out of her mouth. *Don't you never come back here, blond bitch. Don't you never come back.*

"Something happen?" Dr Weller asked.

"Like getting fingered?" Alice said. She laughed again. "Yeah man, it fucked me up bad. Daddy couldn't keep his hands off his little girl, and now she's a junkie hooker living on the streets. *Christ.*"

"It was an honest question," Dr Weller said. "I was just wondering what would make a fourteen year old girl run away from home. Must have been pretty bad there."

"I need a cigarette," Alice said. "You got smokes on you, doc?"

"I don't, I'm sorry," he said. "Hospital doesn't let us smoke in here anyway. Makes sense I suppose. They'll kill you, it's hypocritical of them to let us smoke on the property."

"I need one bad," Alice said, ignoring the public service announcement. "*Fuck.*"

"Listen Alice," Dr Weller said. "If this line of discussion is distressing you, or you're getting upset, we can talk about something else. You can talk about whatever you want."

"*I'm not upset,*" Alice said. "I just need a smoke. I haven't had any in days. These fuckers won't let me off the floor to go out and bum one."

It was more than just the smokes though. *She'd killed someone.* It was possible they hadn't found the car yet, but how long after that before they found her DNA all over the guy? Wasn't that what they did on all those crime shows about Las Vegas and Miami? Find the DNA, arrest the bad girl. She was like a forensic Christmas present in here, just waiting for someone to put the pieces in the right order and come collect her. They'd already taken her blood, and they had her real name. Alice didn't think it took much more than that.

Worse, when she closed her eyes she was back in Wonderland. It made sleep a joke. She was beginning to wonder which was worse. Dealing with the nightmare of her waking life, or dealing with the nightmare that pulled her back in every time she closed her eyes. Maybe she *was* crazy, after all. Maybe not. Maybe this whole thing was the penny that would put her over.

She clenched her hands into fists. She scratched at her legs. She chewed her inside lip, looked about the room, and finally turned her gaze at the doctor.

"So how long are you guys going to keep me here?"

"Oh, I dunno." Dr Weller looked thoughtful. "We need to get a handle on your current frame of mind, make sure you're not too stressed out or anything. This is going to sound silly, but please bear with me. Do you ever feel like your shrinking or growing Alice? Like Rapidly?"

"*What?*" Alice said. *What does he mean? Does he mean the little glass bottle? The mushrooms and the birthday cake? The hand written placard with the words EAT ME scratched on with red crayon?* She'd gotten stuck in the rabbit house, she'd grown so fast. It wasn't just scary that she was suddenly ten times her height, she'd been fucking *terrified* because the walls were pressing in on her from every side, and the ceiling was pushing down on her, and the way she was hunched over like that, unable to breath…

"Just a silly question," Dr Weller said. "Sometimes people can feel like they're suddenly growing inside their skin, or shrinking away from it. Has that ever happened to you?

"No," Alice balked, and her face flushed. "That's crazy." The words tumbled out of her mouth. It felt like burnt ash was sticking to her tongue, and she clamped her hands over the bottom half of her face.

I am always with you, The Mad Hater said.

The words were in her ear but also inside her head, like the sound was emanating from somewhere in the middle of her brain. She'd once had one of those Japanese lollipops with the radios built into the stem; they let you hear their broadcast when you put your mouth on the candy and completed a short wave broadcast that you could actually *hear* inside your head. Alice was eight years old and she thought it was magic; the power of God incarnate. They'd been at Sunday school and the Friends of Jesus had been there for a little chat on obeying God's word.

At the end of the lesson they'd handed these suckers with a "special message" out to all the kids. Alice was one of the last kids in line and was stuck with Cherry, which she hated, but the magic of putting the treat in her mouth and hearing the lord's work made the flavour irrelevant. The suckers were wired to pick up the local Gospel station (WGOD, *Good for your ears, good for your soul!*) and long after the sucker was gone she kept the stick in her mouth, singing along with prayer tunes she knew from church or listening to Jack Van Impe preach about the end of the world until late into the evening. Eventually her mother threw it out on her, like she threw everything Alice loved away; like she threw her own life away by liquefying it and injecting the bad parts into her daughter.

But this wasn't religious radio coming through her thoughts, and it wasn't magical. The sudden appearance of The Mad Hater made her feel infected and dirty. It felt like being possessed by the devil. Any moment now she'd start jabbing her cunt with a crucifix, begging to let Jesus fuck her. Just like in *The Exorcist*. *WWJD* didn't refer to sexual positions. Alice had no interest in it *ever* referring to sex.

LIAR!

She could hear the Mad Hater inside her head, banging on a plate with a spoon and frothing at the mouth. *Goddamn liar! We saw you growing AND shrinking in the house of the Rabbit!*

How was this even possible? It seemed too crazy to be real. Maybe Alice—

"It's not crazy at all," Dr Weller said. "Like I was saying, it's sometimes common for people to feel that way. Doesn't make them crazy. Makes them sound like dirty cunts, right Fuckface?"

YOU'RE A CRAZY BITCH AREN'T YOU! The Hater shrieked. *YOU DON'T KNOW TIME! YOU'RE RUNNING OUT OF HIM BUT YOU DON'T KNOW WHAT YOU'RE LOSING! BUT I DO!*

"What?" Alice said, confused. It was hard to hear what the Doctor was saying with that lunatic shouting in her ears. "I haven't lost anything."

"What was that, Alice?" Dr Weller said. He was watching her closely. There was something Alice didn't like in his eyes. He looked like he was waiting for her to do something. Explode maybe.

Blow your top! The Hater said. *I have another for you! We'll take it to the Queen of Harts and she can stick it on a pig pole like the rest.*

"Shut up," Alice said. "I think I'm done."

"What are you done with, Alice?" Dr Weller said. "Are you alright? You're very pale. Maybe you should kill yourself. Then you'd be done, right?"

"I don't feel well," Alice said. She was beginning to get misty, like things were overlapping again. She could hear the Hater's voice, plain as day, overtop of the words Dr Weller was saying. But Dr Weller wasn't making any sense either. It was like they were all in the same room together, and the Hater had his face pressed against her head, shouting into her ear. Then a moment later he would be far away, sprinting toward her, his voice growing louder with each passing second.

PIG POLES ALICE! PIG POLES! YOU LOVE THE HOG DON'T YOU LITTLE BLOND GIRL? Come back to the table won't you? Things will be just as before. We'll have tea and you can scratch a new number in my watch and we'll piss on time. You won't miss him at all! If he does arrive, you won't even recognize him! YOU WONT RUN OUT OF TIME BECAUSE YOU HAVE NO IDEA WHO HE IS!

"Alice, what are you talking about?" Dr Weller said.

Alice looked at the Doctor, her mouth open. What was *he* talking about? Had she been speaking that insane bullshit *out loud?*

"I uhh," she began. She *what?* She was having trouble hearing him because some lunatic in a big green hat was screaming in her ears? But she couldn't see him because maybe he was sitting *inside her ear*, just next to her eardrum? What was the least crazy sounding thing she could say right now? "I feel sick." The words came out, but they sounded like how she might speak with her mouth stuffed with cotton. A classic Marlon Brando *Godfather* era impression. *I'm gonna do you this favour. Maybe someday you can do me a favour, Dr Weller. Maybe someday you can let me out of this place before the cops find me and put me away forever.*

Alice started sucking in deep, whooping breaths. It was just too much to think about all at once. There was too much going on inside her head. She needed to lie down, she needed to fix, she needed *something*. She needed out.

Dr Weller was beside her. When had that happened?

"It's alright, Alice," he was saying in a friendly, nonthreatening tone. The same voice male adults had been using on her since she was eleven years old and started growing breasts. He had a warm hand on her shoulder. Another on her back. *Too* low on her back, maybe. *Creepy low*. "We're going to get you something to calm you down. It's alright. And if you don't like it, fucking kill yourself. Slit your wrists. Pull your arteries out and hang yourself with them. Put on a show."

TEA AND BREAD! TEA AND BREAD! ALICE TOOK A THIRTY-EIGHT AND SHOT HIM IN THE HEAD!

"Try not to speak," Dr Weller said. "Or I'll kill you myself."

The Hater was trying to get her caught, and Alice knew it. He was screaming and making Alice say it at the same time. Dr Weller was hearing every word the Hater spoke to her, coming out of her mouth like a confession. And the worst part was Alice had no control over the Hater at all. She doubted if even the Hater could control himself. She had to do something to make it stop. Dr Weller's next phone call would likely be to the Homicide division.

"*Shut up!*" Alice screamed into the doctor's face. She sloughed off his groping hands and shoved him hard enough for him to fall off the couch. He felt like warm wax against her hands, and she pulled them back to save herself from sinking into his chest cavity. Then she was on her feet, stepping away and shaking the feeling of his flesh from her hands. "*Just shut the fuck up!*"

Dr Weller was standing beside the door to his office, and he popped it open. There were a couple women huddled around the nurses' station down the hall, and he motioned to them.

"Nurse? Little help, please." He said. He made a motion with his hand simulating the plunging of a syringe, and mouthed the word *Sedative.* Then he turned to Alice and made a blowjob motion at her, jacking an invisible dick and popping his tongue against the inside of his cheek.

"No!" Alice said. "*Tittle hee, tittle haw, broken girl, broken maw.*"

She stepped toward the doctor and planted a foot squarely on the office door. She pushed, hard, and the door flew out of Dr Weller's hands. It slammed shut with a rush of air and a bang.

"I just need a minute to calm down," Alice said. "I just need a moment."

"That's fine, Alice," Dr Weller said. "I don't want you to hurt anyone though, alright? Why don't you sit down? We can talk about the first thing that pops up. There's plenty of time for that, though you wouldn't know time if you met him, right?"

The walls were beginning to melt around her. The clock on the wall thudded in her ears, and when she looked up at it she saw someone had scrawled the word FUCK across the face of it in place of numbers.

"You think I'm a *fuckin idiot?*" Alice shouted at them. She had her hands in fists over her ears, her face contorted in rage. "*A clock that doesn't show time is fuckin' bullshit! Stop crawling around inside there!*"

THE ELECTRIC CHAIR! THE ELECTRIC CHAIR! THAT'S WHAT THEY DO TO LITTLE GIRLS WITH PRETTY YELLOW HAIR! The Hater's lip quivered as he shouted, above Alice, above the Doctor's soothing cradle voice.

"Alice!" Dr Weller said. He kept his voice firm, to keep her attention, but his eyes were elsewhere. He was looking at the glass on the sides of his door. There were two orderlies just outside in the hall, dressed head to toe in white uniforms, and when he nodded they pushed the door open. One of them handed Dr Weller a syringe.

The other one opened his wolf mouth and licked his yellow fangs with an overly long cartoon tongue. He was staring at her tits and he wanted to eat them.

"We need to sedate you, before you hurt yourself, alright?" Dr Weller said. "It's just a shot, and you can have a nap while we take turns digging around in your guts with a plastic fork."

"You don't understand," Alice said, almost pleading. "He's *inside* me. I don't know how he did it but he's in here with me and he's making me say lies." She pounded a fist against the side of her head to drive the point home. Dr Weller put out his hand and she swatted it away. "*He's making you say lies too!*"

The two orderlies moved on her, spreading out, talking softly, like they were trying to catch a chicken. Alice backed away from them, kicked over a silk plant by the couch, and slid into the corner.

"It's alright Alice," Dr Weller said, stepping in behind him. He popped the cap off his syringe, double checked the dosage. Then he pulled it into his body protectively. "This will all be over very soon. You are having an episode, maybe something left over from your drug use, and we're going to kill you for it."

"Ruined the tea party," Alice said. "Spilled tea and brains all over the dashboard."

One of the orderlies made a grab for her, and she lashed out with a savage kick. He pulled back, a little too late, and cried out when Alice's foot connected with his wrist. The other orderly grabbed Alice's arm then, while she was off balance, and yanked her forward. Alice fell face first, her captured arm jerking behind her back as she fell. Unable to catch herself, she fell hard on her chest, banging her face on the carpeted floor and losing her breath.

"*Oh Fuck*," she whimpered.

The orderly still holding her arm snapped it cleanly behind her back by the wrist, and then put a knee on the small of her back. The other orderly, still holding his hand, knelt down and put a knee across the back of Alice's legs.

"This is just going to pinch," Dr Weller said. "You know how it is." He knelt down in front of Alice, syringe out.

"Hold her steady," he said to the orderlies, "so I can jam my cock into her veins." Alice wasn't moving though. She could barely breathe with the weight of two men on her back, and she was still reeling from smashing her face off the floor.

Dr Weller stuck the syringe into Alice's shoulder. There was a pinch of for a moment, and then a soft spreading heat as the drugs took hold. Dr Weller rubbed the spot with a cotton ball.

Look at Time, The Hater whispered. *He's getting older by the second.*

Alice tried to talk. Her mouth was full of sand. *He's in here with me still*, she thought. Smashing an hourglass over her face. Pouring dust and broken glass into her eyes. Making them heavy. Her head filled with weighted balloons. Pushed her face in warm water. The Hater walked away from the front of her mind. Took his hat off. Ruffled his sweaty hair with a free hand, his too-big ears poking out under sand and sweat.

Try not to think of the Dormouse, he said. *Try not to think like that at all.*

Alice tried to shake the cobwebs and mist from her brain. They quickly turned to snow. She couldn't see the Hater anymore. Couldn't think of him.

Alice, The Hater said, snuggling up against her brain stem. *Don't worry dear, I have a plan. I'm going to help you.*

Alice's eyes rolled back in her head, but right before they did she caught sight of Dorothy standing in the doorway, holding her stuffed dog close to her chest, a worried look on her face.

Snow.

Static.

Exit.

Chapter 9.

As soon as Alice was unconscious, Dr Weller had the orderlies put her on a neck board and move her back to her room. On his way through the common he passed Dorothy, sitting on her knees looking over the back of the couch at the procession.

"Dr Weller," she said, putting her hand to her mouth. The other hand was wrapped tightly around Toto, her stuffed dog. "What did you do to her?"

"It's nothing, Dorothy. We had to sedate her because she was getting really upset. We don't want her to hurt herself, right?"

"I guess not." Dorothy balled her hand into a fist and rubbed it against her eye.

Is she crying? Dr Weller smiled at the girl, and resisted the urge to ruffle her hair. Then he was moving again, past the butter-coloured walls into Alice's room, where the orderlies had already unstrapped her from the neck board and were sliding her into bed. There were restraints in the small nightstand beside the bed, and Dr Weller moved around the orderlies to retrieve them. He began securing Alice into her bed.

"I need you to double check these," he told the orderlies. The restraints were nylon straps with buckles and velcro. One for each arm, two for each of her legs, and then two more for the torso. Dr Weller ran one under Alice's breasts to keep it from sliding down to her throat, another across her hips, and then one across each thigh and shin. When he was done, Alice would be able to breath and move her head, but very little else. Of course, she was going to be out for a couple hours so she wouldn't be moving at all. In that time, Dr Weller hoped he could get the ball rolling on some kind of diagnosis.

When he finished double checking the straps, he nodded to the orderlies, and then followed them out into the common room. "Just check on her every half hour or so," he told the nurse in attendance. He leaned in close and spoke softly because he didn't like the other patients overhearing him. "She should be out for a couple hours. If she wakes up and is lucid, have the orderlies remove the straps. If she starts having an episode, make sure you let me know at once."

The nurse behind the desk nodded, and then shot him a tired, resigned look. *You must think I'm the biggest idiot*, it seemed to say. Dr Weller ignored it. He nodded back to her, uttered a quick thanks, and returned to his office. Once there he closed the door, straightened the plant Alice had kicked over, and then sat down behind his desk. He pulled the file marked *Pleasance, Alice* and settled back in his chair.

He was going to have to do a little research, but a tiny worm of suspicion had been digging around in the meat in the back of Dr Weller's brain. She had been agitated when she came in, nervous about being in therapy. Probably upset about being stuck in the hospital in the first place. It was obvious she didn't trust any authority figures. Probably had a history of abuse from people caring for her. That was a pretty common diagnosis.

What bothered him was how rapid her episode had occurred. It had actually occurred *mid sentence*, while he was watching her. It was like a light switch flicked on in her head and she began spouting nonsense. Then the light flicked off. Alice had seemed unaware that it had even occurred at first. This was what most concerned Dr Weller. If she had been faking, he would have been able to tell. Most often people's perception of mental illness compared to the realities of it were like night and day. People in the field of mental health chalked it up to what they deemed "The Hollywood Effect".

Hollywood lunatics were most often hyper-realistic sociopaths, stark raving mad. They were twisted minds bent on death or sex, and often a combination of both. Anthony Hopkins in *Silence of the Lambs* may have been an interesting and riveting character, but in reality he was far from the sociopathic genius *Hannibal Lector*.

True sociopaths were rarely monsters you knew. They were more akin to playground bullies, tyrants manipulating their little worlds for their own gain and amusement. They were the button pushers of the world; they were con men; they did what they wanted with little regard for other people's feelings. This was because they didn't feel things the way people normally did, and as a coping mechanism turned to mimicking the emotional responses in others. They didn't *act* like they were mentally ill; they acted like other people *because* they were mentally ill.

The episode Alice suffered from had similar hallmarks. There was no halting at the cliff of sanity, she'd simply been walking along and slipped off the edge without noticing. Her confusion was the key to her sincerity. Alice had lashed out angrily because she had been trying to sort out whatever was happening in her mind when the orderlies came in and threatened her physically. It was unfortunate but necessary. Dr Weller couldn't allow Alice to go through a complete breakdown in his office for the sake of letting her try and work out her problems alone. It was better she was sedated now, and the episode allowed to pass, so that later they could begin working on it rationally. They would be able to discern whether this was an isolated incident or something that had been ongoing in Alice's life.

If it was isolated, and not the result of an emerging psychosis, it could have been brought on by a specific factor. Her overdose was an obvious one. Perhaps she was suffering from a trauma related stress disorder.

Dr Weller sighed, rubbed his face with his hands. It was a habit he'd picked up from his mother, something she did when the world was big and ugly and messy and stressful. The subconscious act of wiping her face off with her hands symbolized her need to separate herself from her stresses. Dr Weller smiled inwardly thinking about his own inherited behavior. Human beings really were amazing machines. The clockwork that made them run was more complex than any computer could ever be.

It was a wonder everyone wasn't crazy. Of course, there were those in the field of psychology who firmly believed everyone *was* crazy to some extent; and that the ideal of well being was long due for an overhaul. No matter what the ideal was though, there was something terribly wrong with Alice.

If she had been repeating something she thought she was hearing in her head, it could be an indicator that she was suffering from a schizoid disorder. Longtime drug addicts often suffered from what was known as *narcotic induced mental illness*, usually schizophrenia, brought on by their heavy dependency and abuse of street drugs. Schizophrenia covered a wide blanket of symptoms, however, and a diagnosis like that might mean long-term care, even institutionalization. Provided there was somebody around to foot the bill. If not she'd be back on the street with a prescription for an anti-psychotic. *Anti-insanitories*, his mind joked, something funny from his university days. Of course, back then the word mostly pertained to beer and shots of tequila.

It was also possible that Alice had some form of MPD. Multiple Personality Disorder. MPD had once been the "in" diagnosis back in the 80s, before a lot of work had been done in the field to really figure out what it was and what caused it. It was generally accepted now that MPD occurred in individuals suffering from heavy physical and emotional abuse as children, and found a way to disassociate themselves from the terrible things happening to them by separating themselves from the act mentally.

Doctors speculated that, the splitting of these actions could, under the right circumstances, actually cause smaller, mini-personalities to appear. Since they were created to deal with only one aspect of a person's life, they usually only exhibited traits of one or two emotions, and were often tied to cliché personality types. For example, a scared child or an angry old woman. It was these universal cliché's that made some scientists wonder if MPD was a real disorder at all, and not some offshoot iatrogenic condition.

And although an MPD diagnosis might be difficult because Alice was a drug user, she could have been using drugs in an effort to self medicate an undiagnosed illness. Then, *again*, perhaps the whole thing was brought on by stress. Or perhaps it *was* a heroin-related episode. A leftover opiate particle getting loose in her brain and causing a glitch in the system.

One thing was for certain, and it took him in a circle back to his original thought. *Something is definitely wrong with Alice.* He just hoped he'd get a chance to dig into her a bit before her insurance ran out or she was moved. He'd like to give the smug assholes who worked out at the Pine Woods *Centre for Well Being* a ready and working case file if they came to collect her. Something to show them he wasn't just some transition doctor working patchwork psychology on emergency room rejects and junkies. *Thank you doctor, we'll take it from here*, they'd say, as though administering institutionalized medicine made them the Alpha and Omega of mental health.

It was petty, and he scolded himself for thinking that way. Of course the only thing that mattered was for Alice to get the help she needed to cope with her life. Still, he'd been at this job a long time. It was important, to be on the front lines, working in a hospital for a major city, but it didn't always let him sink his fingers into his work the way he'd like to. The dismissive attitudes of his peers didn't really help things any.

Dr Weller sighed. He closed the folder marked *Pleasance, Alice* and tossed it to the side. He swished his cold coffee, staring down at the reflection in the bottom of the cup. A tired face looked back. Rippled in the coffee. He'd been here too long maybe. He'd bled for this job, and his life had suffered because of it. He'd been held back while his peers had simply climbed around him up the ladder of success.

He'd never married, either. He supposed that had something to do with his present attitude. His *funk*, as his mom would have said. *Boy look at the way your face is dragging on the ground*, she'd say. *That must be some funk you got there.*

It was futile to spend too much time dwelling on this stuff. He knew that. Good Mental Health 101 – don't dwell too much on the Negative Aspects of Positive Being. Was that a *Bad Religion* song? Something like that. If he didn't have the heart for his work anymore, he would have to find *new* work or else find his heart. He was fast approaching the crested hill marked *50* though, and the sign read *Caution: this road is closer to the end of the line than it looks*. He was over qualified for anything other than what he was doing right now, and too close to retirement to start thinking of a new career. He supposed he could look at a change of scenery, apply at the Pine Woods Centre himself and take on long term patients. That might be just about as bad, since he'd be the low man on the totem pole and likely would remain that way until he retired.

He drank the swish out of his mug. Rubbed the coffee smell from his moustache and flipped through the *Pleasance, Alice* folder again. There was something to this girl. Something about the way her switch had gone off. His intuition was telling him there was a story here somewhere.

If only Alice trusted him enough to talk about her life…

Oh but she has, his mother's voice said. *She was ranting about killing someone.*

He wasn't so sure. It may have been all part of the psychotic episode.

What does your heart tell you?

His heart told him nothing. He hadn't heard from it in a long time. If it wasn't for the pulse pounding headaches he got from stress, he'd honestly doubt if it was even there anymore.

Chapter 10.

When Alice finally opened her eyes again she was greeted with a miserable stiffness running the entire length of her body. She was also greeted with the sweet, smiling face of Dorothy, sitting in a chair beside her bed with a magazine and Toto in her lap.

There was a black gap in her memory. Had she been sleeping? Or had she just closed her eyes for a moment? She rolled her eyes around the room; h er plain brown and yellow bedroom. Brown curtains. Sunlight leaking in around its edges, dripping down the wall and pooling on the floor. There was a moment of calm as her brain started up again, no noise or feedback or Mad Haters screaming unholy confessions. No guilt. No remorse.

She looked back at Dorothy, sitting beside her bed beaming at her, beautiful face cocked slightly to the side like a puppy. She wondered if anyone had ever looked at her that way before; the look of someone who was so into you that they would sit quietly by your bed for hours, careful not to disturb your sleep but barely able to wait until the moment you opened your eyes and came back to them.

And she barely knew the girl beside her now. But her face was welcome. Softly magnetic.

"Good morning!" Dorothy said. "Sleep well?"

"I feel like a truck load of ass," Alice said. She tried to sit up but found she was strapped to the bed. She rolled her eyes. Sighed heavily. "*Again?* What the *fuck*."

"Yeah, I hate them," Dorothy said. She reached up and rubbed her finger along the strap holding Alice's hips down. She bit her lip and looked into Alice's eyes. "I had them on me before. When I first came in. I kept trying to get off the ward. Every time the elevator opened."

A moment of silence passed between the girls. Alice tried not to think about the past few days a moment longer than she had to, focusing instead on keeping the mental dikes in place. Already, they were springing leaks all over her mind. On the other side of the wall was an ocean of guilt and remorse. An ocean filled with sea monsters that had tea parties and had their heads blown off in late model sedans.

"What are you doing?" Alice looked down at Dorothy's hand, still rubbing the strap on her hip. She looked back into Dorothy's eyes.

Dorothy smiled again, but pulled her hand back. "I can probably loosen them for you." Her eyes danced. "If they're hurting you, I mean."

"*Hell yes*," Alice said. "Get me the fuck out of here."

Dorothy stood up, eager to please. After a moment's consideration, she reached across the bed and began to undo the strap on Alice's chest. She tugged on the strap, but the buckle didn't move. Dorothy pressed her breasts against Alice's for a moment, seemingly needing to get leverage on the buckle. It was an obvious grope; in spite of herself

Alice laughed. "Oh God. Just get off me. You're worse than a guy."

"What do you mean?" Dorothy said. "That was an accident."

"Uh huh." Alice smiled, but the smile withered when she saw the look on Dorothy's face. "Look, I was just fucking around. Can you undo these straps please? My back is really starting to hurt."

"I guess," Dorothy sulked. She went back to work on the buckle, this time flicked it open with one hand and pulled the strap loose with the other. Wordlessly she did the same to the other straps, and Alice stretched out, a soft groan escaping her lips.

Dorothy sat again, deflated, and hugged her stuffed dog close to her chest.

"What's wrong?" Alice said.

"*Uhh*, nothing,"

"I didn't mean nuthin' by it. Just, *you know*, it was pretty obvious. Believe me. I know a lot about this stuff."

Dorothy looked at her with dark eyes.

"*I didn't say it was a bad thing*," Alice said after a moment. "Just obvious."

This time Dorothy smiled. She rolled her eyes, put a hand up on her face. Toto slipped down between her thighs.

"Oh God," she said. "I'm such an idiot."

"You're not an idiot. That doctor in there is an idiot. *You're* not an idiot."

"Doctor Weller?" Dorothy smiled. "Uhh, he's okay. Just a little tired maybe. He always shuffles his papers when I'm in there, like he has something else he'd rather be doing than listen to me rattle off about my life."

Alice could hear the Midwest dripping off her voice as she spoke. It was most obvious when she said things like *mah lahhf*, but it was always there. It gave the sound of her words a welcome, soothing lilt; something Alice could listen to and actually hang on to as they streamed out of her mouth. She found herself smiling again, almost to herself, watching Dorothy speak. The way her hands animated everything she said. The way her face changed to reflect every word she spoke. Alice had a feeling she could watch this girl without hearing a word she was saying and still be able to pick up on the gist of her stories. "So what are you in here for?"

"Uhh, *well*," Dorothy said. She smiled; it was the guiltiest and cutest thing Alice had ever seen. Dorothy shrugged. "Officially I'm in here because my aunt thinks I tried to kill myself."

"Did you?"

"Oh no," Dorothy said quickly, shaking her head emphatically. "It wasn't nuthin' like that. I stole a truck, and uhm, *drove it*. Somewhere."

She stopped then, watching Alice's face carefully.

"That's it?" Alice said. "That sounds like *Grand Theft Auto*, not suicide."

"Well," Dorothy replied, slowly. "Can I ask you something? And you won't think I'm crazy?"

Alice laughed.

"Shit, you're in here," she said. "I already think your fuckin' crazy."

Dorothy rolled her eyes and laughed with her.

"No, silly," she said. She stopped smiling. "I uhh, I shouldn't be here."

"No shit. Me either."

"You don't understand," Dorothy said. "I'm not *supposed* to be here. Like this place. This country, this world, any of it. I don't belong here. I'm supposed to be somewhere else."

She stopped, watching Alice's face carefully, waiting for any sign of ridicule, any sign of disbelief. Alice recognized the look instantly; it was the look of a deer who thought it might have smelled a wolf in the air. They stood really still, barely breathing, all five senses going on overdrive, and waiting for the snap of a twig, the sound of a mouth closing, or thick hair rubbing against the grass, anything, *anything* to tell them to get the fuck out of there as fast as they could.

Alice didn't want to be the wolf. "I know what you mean." She hoped it would be enough. A simple sentence. Five words. Hopefully Dorothy didn't take it as a joke and run for the door. She wasn't sure why it mattered so much that she stay, but it mattered all the same.

Dorothy reached down and grabbed Toto from between her thighs, and pulled him up close to her face. She looked away from Alice, down at her feet. "Do you believe the world is what other people say it is?" she said quietly.

"No," Alice answered quickly. That was the truth too; she knew from experience that the world was never what people thought it was. Her time with the Hater was proving it true.

"I *mean*," Dorothy said. "You watch the news, and countries are going to war, and there's people sick and dying all over the place, and people are getting raped and killed and in the meantime the world itself is causing earthquakes and mudslides and tornadoes. But what if all of that horrible stuff isn't what they say it is? What if it's like, something completely different?"

"You mean, like the news is lying to us?" Alice said. "Well, yeah, no shit they are. I heard that like CNN, Fox News, even big chunks of the internet, they're all controlled by the C.I.A. or something. Like mass media brain washing, telling us what to eat and what to buy, when to shit even. Hell, it's *all* a big lie. Rabbit used to talk about that shit all the time."

"Not lying," Dorothy said, stone faced. "Like they just don't know." She paused dramatically, like what she was saying had just that moment occurred to her. "What if there is something else going on that is part of the world, but it isn't at the same time? Like the real world outside of some crazy movie."

"Yeah," Alice said, slowly. She wasn't really sure where this girl was going with her current topic, but there was a feeling there, underlying all her words, and it reminded Alice of her time *Down The Hole*. It was like things were real and a dream at the same time; as though maybe they were unfolding in her reality but it had all been sanitized, maybe scripted somehow. There were big cogs grinding and moving behind the scenes of her life, and something was in control of the button that started and stopped every part of it. Junk made it worse, sometimes. Mostly being awake made it worse though. Knowing that the Queen of Hearts was out there in the world somewhere, and at the same time knowing that something like that couldn't possibly exist, well, that seemed to fit perfectly with what Dorothy was saying. "Duality. Yeah, I get what you're saying."

"What did you say?" Dorothy said.

"I said it's like duality," Alice said. "Like two worlds overlapping each other. Like when two TV channels are coming in on the same station and you can see them both."

"Yeah," Dorothy said. "That's exactly what it is."

"It's not fucked up," Alice said. "I know what that's like, believe me." She wanted to add to the conversation. She wanted to tell Dorothy about how she'd followed a rabbit down a hole and had ended up standing knee deep in blood and body parts with a shrill ginger queen screaming at her from atop a heart shaped throne. She also wanted to tell her that her trip back to this world hadn't been a single ticket trip. Someone had come back with her, someone who smelled like tanning chemicals and fresh leather and was picking through Alice's memories like a filing cabinet and shouting all her dirty secrets to the world. She wanted to tell Dorothy about that moment in the hallway, when the Hater had appeared and then crawled inside her, and where he was now roosting behind her eyes, inside her brain, not as a metaphor or some abstract bullshit but as a real person in their; like if they took an X-ray of Alice's skull they'd see him in there curled up around her optic nerves like some kind of grotesque parasitic twin.

Instead she said nothing. And then, thinking something might be better than nothing, she said: "So, are they going to let you out anytime soon?"

"I'm on medication right now," Dorothy said. "Antidepressants, and another one might be an antipsychotic, I'm not sure. The nurses won't really tell me what I'm taking. I'm going to be here for a little while, and then they might ship me up to the nuthouse if I need it. I hate the medication though, it makes me feel like shit all the time."

She smiled a little, tossed Alice a *What can you do* look. She played with her hair. Toto was back in her lap, staring up at the ceiling with scratched plastic eyes. His tongue was hanging half out of his mouth, far to the side, like a summertime mutt trying to beat the heat.

"So why do you take them if they make you feel like crap?" Alice said.

"I dunno," Dorothy shrugged. "I guess if I just do what they're telling me, they'll let me out sooner maybe? It kinda makes sense."

"Fuck," Alice snorted. "They won't be giving me nothin', unless they got those two fatass pig guards with them every time. I need a clear head if I'm gonna get out of here."

"Where you gonna go?" Dorothy said carefully. "Back to your boyfriend?"

"Oh yeah," Alice laughed. "Back to my hot big-cock boyfriend." She shook her head and her blond hair danced off her shoulders. It was flirty, and she was a little surprised to catch herself doing it. She saw Dorothy looking at her. She didn't look sad, exactly; maybe disappointed was a better word.

"I'm *kidding*," she said, smiling at her. "I'm ready to swear off men forever at this rate."

Dorothy was quiet, looking at her hands.

"I don't have a boyfriend," Alice said. A pang of emotion shot through her. Another crack in the wall she kept up around her. "I don't really have anyone."

"Yeah," Dorothy whispered. "Me either."

The door opened and a heavy nurse walked into the room. When she saw Alice and Dorothy together the crease on her face deepened into a full blown frown. She was carrying a chart and four little paper cups, and was dressed in one of those fruity nurses coats; one with bananas, oranges, and grapes scattered about in a repeating pattern. Harmless for adults, mildly entertaining for kids. Like getting needles, pills, and diaper changes from a clown. The *really* funny thing was how miserable these old nurses could be. That was a *big* joke, because they looked fun and happy until you talked to them, and they pissed bile in your face with every word they spoke.

Two of the cups had water in them. Two of the cups contained pills.

"You're not supposed to be in here, are you *Ms Gale*?" she said. She stretched out Dorothy's formal name longer than necessary, like she was proving a point by even speaking it. *Mizzzzzz Gaaale.*

She looked at Alice sitting up and shook her head. "And how did we get out of our bindings? That stuff should be left up to the professionals, don't you think *Ms Gale*?"

"I guess," Dorothy said. She scooped up her stuffed dog and held it to her throat.

Alice watched the girl wilt under the domineering presence of the woman in the room. Having her in there with them was like spilling a can of grey paint on the floor, and then watching it slowly reach for the corners. She brought a creeping malaise with her, and it was turning Dorothy into a miserable, pathetic little thing. Watching her stirred something in Alice. She wanted to put an arm around the girl and drag her away from the cloud of misery emanating into the room. She wanted the spritely, adorable, slightly crooked grin and the sparkling eyes that made her feel like smiling herself.

"Those fucking straps were killing *me*," Alice said. "I made her take them off."

"Well *you* should have waited until someone could come and check on you," the nurse said. Switching to Dorothy she handed a paper cup toward the girl. "While I have you here, you may as well take your evening medication. I was going to come and see you after I was done helping *Ms Pleasance* out of her harness."

Dorothy took the cup from her outstretched hand and cupped it with both of her own. She looked over to Alice for a moment, then back at the cup.

The nurse turned back to Alice. "And for you, *dearie*, Doctor Weller would like you to take these." She held up a small paper cup to Alice and shook it. The pills inside rattled like teeth.

"Like fuck. Don't give me any of your mind bending shit." Alice said rather loudly, hoping Dorothy might take a cue from her bravery. "I'm not taking anything that's gonna fuck me up."

"It's Naxolone. It's so we can kick all the heroin out of your body," the nurse said impatiently. "If you don't want to take them you're going to go through withdrawals and we'll probably have to sedate you again. This *floor* isn't prepared to deal with that kind of bullshit, if you get my meaning." She looked from Alice to Dorothy, then back to Alice again, just to drive the point home.

Alice caught it. If she made life too miserable on the attending staff she'd be moved away from her little friend. She might not even notice, however, as these needle crazy nurses were liable to put her in a coma.

Dorothy was staring at Alice. Her face was a mask, but was there a tiny bit of accusation there?

Alice caught her eyes. "It's nothing." She felt defensive suddenly. Like she had to explain to Dorothy how she wasn't really a junkie, just a girl who liked to play sometimes when the world became too fucked up. *Like last week*, when she'd blown a guy's face off and had to wash his brains off in a mud puddle.

"Pills, Ms Gale," the nurse said again. "Both of you."

Dorothy looked down into her pill cup. Then she dumped the pills in her mouth, gulped half the water in her other cup and got up. She finished her water and tossed both cups in the garbage.

"Very good," she marked the time on one of her charts. Then she flipped them around and nodded at Alice.

Alice took her own pills and drank all of her water. Whatever shred of good mood she had from being around Dorothy was gone now. She could feel the last of it draining away, like scented water in a bathtub, leaving behind grime and filth and soap scum to mark its passing.

The nurse marked the other chart and then turned to Dorothy.

"Come on, let's get you out of here," she said. "The doctor will be in tonight after dinner. If you girls don't fill out your dinner cards you're both going to end up with oatmeal and dry toast on your plates." She moved toward the door, and swept her arm toward it, trying to get Dorothy to walk in front of her.

"Oh, just a minute," Dorothy said. She sidestepped the woman and moved to the chair she'd been sitting in, scooped up Toto in her arm. "I guess I'll talk to you later, Alice."

When Dorothy smiled at her Alice laughed and nearly spit water in her face. Instead she snorted, swallowed the water and beamed at the girl.

"I'll be out on the couch later, if the doctor doesn't have me lobotomized," Alice said. She gave the girl a little wave, which Dorothy returned with a wink.

"Come on," the nurse said. "Back to your room."

When the girls had left, Alice lay back down on her bed and cupped her face in her hands, giggling into her fingers. Dorothy didn't hate her for being a junkie, as she'd first thought. In fact, Now that she and Dorothy were sharing secrets, she felt closer to the girl than ever. It had been a long time since she'd connected with anyone who didn't just talk to her because they wanted to fuck her. Although Alice was sure Dorothy wanted that too, she was happy to be her friend first. She knew all of this the moment Dorothy had grabbed her stuffed dog and smiled at her.

Capped under her gums, like rabbits teeth, were the pills Dorothy so dreaded taking. The ones she'd only taken when she was alone and outnumbered by the hospital staff. The ones she hated because they made her feel sick all the time. The ones Nurse *Fattie* had thought she watched Dorothy swallow already, because Dorothy was a good girl who did what she was told and was all alone in the hospital with nobody to have her back.

Except now she wasn't alone. Neither of them were.

Now they had each other.

Chapter 11.

Dr Weller entered Alice's room shortly after the nurse left. He had a folder in his hands attached to a clipboard and had a neat row of pens across the top. They exchanged greetings, and then he settled into the chair Dorothy had been sitting in by the side of the bed. Alice instinctively pulled up into a sitting position and crossed her arms.

"So," Dr Weller said. "How are we feeling?"

"Kind of spacey," Alice yawned. "Like I was up drinking all night."

"That's the shot we gave you," he said. "Thorazine, with a sedative. It was designed to bring you out of your little episode."

"It knocked me right out. What is that, like a reset switch for my sanity?" She smiled but it felt foreign on her face and she got rid of it in a hurry.

"Just long enough for the episode to pass." He jotted something down in his folder. "Can you tell me what you remember of your session earlier this morning?"

"Not a lot really," Alice said. "We were talking, and then it gets kind of spotty. I remember little gaps, and you were asking me stuff that was confusing me, and then I remember some big guys and the needle." She stopped for a moment, lost in thought. "No, I remember the *prick* of the needle, but I don't remember seeing it." She didn't mention that Dorothy had snuck down into the room to see what was going on, and that Alice herself had seen her moments before passing out. Somehow, it seemed like it would be a betrayal.

"Basically what happened was something in your mind was seeping past your conscious self," Dr Weller said. "What we need to find out in order to treat you properly is what exactly was causing it."

"Drug use?" Alice said immediately.

"Well, yes, that's certainly a strong possibility," Dr Weller said. "But it's not the only thing. Tell me, can you remember when these episodes began?"

"That was the first time," Alice said. "I've never had a reaction like that before."

"I see."

"No," Alice said. "That's not *totally* right. When I woke up after my overdose it was like I was coming up out of the ground. Like inside the ground was another world."

Dr Weller was writing furiously in his notebook, but he stopped when Alice said this. "What do you mean?"

"I dunno," Alice said. "Just a dream, I guess. A vivid one though. Lots of talking animals. Playing card people. Just the kind of shit you think of when you're high."

"How are your relationships with your family?"

"Same as a lot of people," Alice said. She shrugged. *Had he already asked her this question?* She thought so, but she wasn't sure. And then she wondered what she'd told him the first time. Maybe he was doubling back like the cops did sometimes when they were trying to make you trip over your words. There was no way of knowing what she'd said originally, so she decided she'd plow ahead with the truth. "I dunno, I don't really have contact with family. My mom lives in town here but she threw me out when I was fourteen. I've been living kinda rough since then."

"That's a long time to be on your own," Dr Weller said.

"Whatever," Alice said. "It's nothing really. I mean, you get on alright by yourself. Now I prefer it, you know?"

"Yeah. Okay, this is an important one," Dr Weller said. "Has anything happened recently? Anything terrible? Like a fight, or...or an attack?"

"No," Alice said too quickly. "Nothing."

"You're sure."

"What kind of question is that?" Alice said. She clenched her fists. "I'd fuckin' know if something like that had happened, right? What, am I totally crazy now? I don't even know when bad shit happens anymore?"

Dr Weller put his hands up. "I'm sorry," he said. "I had to ask. Try to take a deep breath and calm down."

"I *am* calm," Alice said. It's just a stupid question."

"Alright," Dr Weller said. "Forget I asked. It's not important." He closed the folder and clipped his pen to the clipboard. "I would like to see you in the morning. I'll schedule a time, and we can get you on a little Thorazine just to take the edge off. You shouldn't need a sedative with it though, thankfully. And let's keep up with the Naloxone to flush the last of those nasty opioids out of your system."

"Perfect," Alice said. "*More* drugs."

"Well, these ones will help you get back on track. In the meantime we can do some talk-through sessions, and maybe we can get a better picture of what's going on in that noggin of yours."

"Whatever," Alice said again.

Dr Weller said a quick goodbye and left the room. Alice got out of bed and stretched. The Thorazine shot made her feel gummy inside, like they'd cracked her head open and poured a litre of milk over her brain. And she didn't know why she'd bothered to tell the Doctor about her dream; if anything they'd be watching her more closely now that they thought she was a genuine wackjob.

Another time, another place, she might actually consider sticking around and seeing what they had to say about the mess she'd made of her life. But there was a body sitting in a car somewhere. Surely it was found by now. Which meant the cops had a murder on their hands. It was only a matter of time before they tracked her down. Maybe they'd talk to Rabbit, and maybe he'd give her up. Had she taken an ambulance to the hospital? She didn't even know. Knowing Rabbit, he probably ditched her at a bus stop or something to be found by strangers. She wondered if he'd cum before he bothered to wrap her up and dump her off.

Then there was Dorothy.

She'd felt the connection to the girl the moment she'd walked onto the ward—short brown hair, soft eyes and skin, a dusting of freckles across her nose. Alice wasn't a lesbian, but she had been around long enough to realize it was really a person's insides that you were attracted to. Like Rabbit, kind of, he was a scrawny white kid with a lot of drugs and guns hanging around the house. But he'd always been a nice guy. Even if it was because Alice had great tits and would fuck for dope.

Dorothy was different though. Alice was attracted to her cherubic face. But the girl seemed to need Alice, for whatever reason, and that feeling of connection was really doing good things for Alice. When she broke out of the hospital, she'd have to at least ask if Dorothy wanted to come. The girl probably had some problems, but she didn't like her treatment in here anymore than Alice herself did, and Alice couldn't imagine the girl saying no.

They were connected, after all.

Alice got up and went to her door. She scanned the common room and saw Dorothy with her knees up on the couch. Reading. Dorothy caught her eye, beamed a smile, and waved her over. Alice smiled back. The look was infectious. She opened the door and went over to where the girl was sitting.

"How did it go?" Dorothy said, sliding over to make room.

"Meh," Alice said, shrugging. "More bullshit. I told Dr Weller as much too. I said I wasn't going to put up with any crap from the staff, and he better not try to knock me out again." A lie, meant to impress. It accomplished its goal beautifully.

Dorothy's face lit up. "No way!" she said. "I wish I had the guts to talk to them like that. I probably would have been off my meds a while ago."

"How's that going?"

"Oh, fine," Dorothy said, whispering. "I guess we'll see tomorrow though."

"What are you reading?" Alice said, changing the subject.

"*Twilight*," Dorothy said. "It's pretty good. I found it on the book rack. A girl is in love with a vampire. How cool would that be?"

"I dunno, isn't that like necrophilia or something?" Alice said.

"What do you mean?"

"Vampires are dead things right?" Alice said.

"Oh, *gross!*" Dorothy said, laughing. She closed the book and swatted Alice playfully with it. "I don't think that's what the writer had in mind. Or maybe she did, I dunno."

"Can we go watch the news?" Alice said, changing the subject.

"I'm not supposed to watch television" Dorothy said. "It's one of my triggers. Especially the Weather Network."

Alice stood up. "Well, I'm going to go watch the news. I need to see about something. Come with me if you want."

Dorothy's face twisted in mock-panic. She eyed the nurses' station. Then she shook her head. "I maybe better stay here," she said. "I don't want to get in shit."

"Suit yourself," Alice said. She walked out of the rec room and into the television area. It was on but nobody was watching it, so she flicked the channel over to the local news station. They were going through football scores. Alice dropped down in one of the reclining chairs and leaned back in it. Out of the corner of her eye she saw Dorothy checking out the nurses' station. There were two on duty at the moment; one was off working in one of the back rooms and the other was sitting at the desk watching an ongoing game of pool.

Dorothy watched her carefully. A few minutes later fortune smiled on her, because the phone rang and the nurse behind the station turned away for some privacy. Seizing the moment, Dorothy got up and walked over to where Alice was sitting. She had a big grin on her face, like she'd never been bad before. It was a kind of high school rebellion look; Alice had known it a time or two when she was younger and the shine hadn't warn off of being your own master.

She flopped down in the seat beside Alice and impulsively reached out and squeezed her hand. "So what are we watching'? She said.

"News," Alice said. The sports ended and a woman with a business casual blouse and tight red hair smiled on the screen. Behind her, a map of the local area flashed on a green screen.

"*The weather for next week will be seasonal with a chance of thunderstorms toward the weekend*," The woman said. "*We're keeping an eye on the weather patterns as you know, this is tornado primetime.*"

Dorothy perked up at the mention. Then she chuckled, self conscious. "I'm not supposed to watch the weather channels or any weather news," she said again.

"No problem," Alice said. "We can change it if you want."

"Naw, I'll be okay. I'm a big girl."

"I won't tell on you," Alice said.

"Aww, thanks!" Dorothy said. She reached out and rubbed Alice's shoulder. She gave it a firm squeeze. Her fingers lingered a moment on the hem of her shirt before retreating. Alice smiled. The weather report ended and the anchor came on, sitting behind a nondescript blue desk with the station logo splashed across the front in lights.

"*In local news, police are asking for the public's help in finding this man's killer*," The Anchor said, and Alice felt her heart stop. The man from the blue car appeared in the screen, very much alive in the photo. He was smiling, and standing in front of a barbeque full of sausages. Maybe a kid's birthday party. *Oh my dear*, a voice in her head whispered. It was not her own. *Why so much fear?*

She fumbled with the remote, trying to hit all the buttons at once, but her fingers were rebellious and she knocked the device into Dorothy's lap.

"You alright?" Dorothy said.

"Change the *chah-hannel*, please," Alice said. She squeezed her eyes shut.

"...*Police say Greg Haines, fifty-two, a local resident was found brutally shot to death in his car in the Marlborough industrial park early Saturday morning. They are looking for a woman with blond hair in her twenties, of average height and slim build who was seen leaving the area. The woman may be injured...*"

"Please turn it off," Alice said.

Dorothy grabbed Alice's hand, and with the other hand she used the remote to flip the channel to *Dancing with the Stars*. "Hey," she said. "Easy. Take it easy. You're alright."

She's a pretty girl, the Hater whispered. *Would you hurt her? Commit another murder?*

Alice clenched her eyes shut, willing the voice out of her head. The Hater didn't speak again, but Alice could sense him in there somewhere, lingering like smoke on a warm breath. On the television, minor celebrities were dancing to what Alice could only describe as droning bees set to a human heartbeat. Their voices were warbly and faintly sinister. She couldn't make out any words though. She thought they might be talking about her.

"You okay now?" Dorothy said. "You look like you're kind of fading in and out. You want me to get a nurse?"

Alice looked up into Dorothy's face. She was bathed in soft yellow light. Warm light, like the feeling she always got from heroin. Warm amber blanket of light that wrapped around her soul. That face promised more than love; it promised pure bliss.

"No," Alice said. "I'll be fine. Listen. I need to get out of here. As soon as possible. There's shit I gotta deal with and I can't do it in here."

"Oh," Dorothy said, her eyes clouding for a moment. Disappointment broke out on her face, and Alice fought the urge to kiss it off.

"*Dorothy*," Alice said. "Do you want to come with me?"

"What? *Where?*"

"Well, I gotta make a stop when we get out," Alice said. "But after that the open road could be our plaything. I mean, we could go wherever we want to, right? It doesn't matter. I need a beer, and I need a cigarette. Where I get it, well, it doesn't matter much to me."

Dorothy bit her lip.

Alice put a hand on Dorothy's neck and stroked it gently. She'd been hooking long enough to know how to get a person's wheels going. It was old hand to her now.

"I would love some company," she said.

Dorothy looked up at her. She flashed a crazy grin."Yeah!" she said. "Let's do it. I'm *totally* in."

"I'm glad," Alice said. "Now we just need to figure out a way to get off this floor. I think we can pretty much walk out of the hospital then."

"Well," Dorothy said. "I can easily get off the floor. I'm not a flight risk at all. And I think I know how we can get you out of here. Won't even be a hard thing to pull off."

"Really?" Alice said.

"Well, yeah," Dorothy said. "It's not like this is a prison. I could just leave if I wanted to and none of them could really stop me. Probably wouldn't even notice me gone 'til pill time."

"Okay," Alice said. Impulsively she leaned in and planted a quick peck on Dorothy's lips. Dorothy closed her eyes for a moment, shocked, opened her mouth for a longer kiss, and Alice pulled back. The two women stared at each other.

Finally, Alice said: "Tell me." And Dorothy did.

Chapter 12.

Dorothy was standing at the water machine. She filled a cup of water and took a drink, and then jumped when the bottle garbled back at her. She tried to breathe deep and calm her nerves, but it didn't work. She closed her eyes. *A kiss. A sweet kiss, but what did it mean? Did Alice love her?* No, that was ridiculous. They'd only been friends for a short while. And yet the connection was there, she could feel it. Butterflies in her stomach, like she'd been eating grubs in the garden and they were hatching. The thought of Alice's face and the smell of her hair calmed Dorothy, and she took a deep breath.

You can do this, she could almost hear Alice say. *Easy as a pie.* Dorothy turned and walked up to the front desk. *Maybe it is easy for a girl like Alice,* she thought. *Someone brave and beautiful and sharp. But Alice isn't here. I am. And I'm boring and lame and clunky.* Alice was sitting on the couch pretending to watch television. And waiting.

"Yes?" The duty nurse said. Dorothy had never seen her before. She was young and cow eyed, perfect for what Dorothy was planning to do. Alice had said as much when they were going over the escape plan. If Dorothy stayed calm and acted like she belonged there, the nurse would assume it was true and they'd be home free.

The other part of their plan involved the two of them watching carefully and waiting for just the right moment to strike; a moment when the senior nurse was off busy with something and the new nurse was all alone at the station. Just a couple minutes was all they needed. A bathroom break or a coffee run. They needed to have only one nurse at the station, and they needed someone who might not think to watch the elevator *and* handle a minor crisis at the desk.

The window of opportunity finally opened two days later. The head nurse burped, and then blew her breath out and waved it away with her hand. Then she laughed.

"Oh god," she said. "Don't get me wrong. I love my husband, but that man needs to stay away from shellfish."

"Sounds like you do too," the other nurse said. She was much younger, and new to the ward.

"Garlic clams," the head nurse said. "I don't know what else he added, but I've got a double dose of the turkey trots today." She laughed, and the younger nurse curled her nose.

"Better make that a triple dose," the head nurse said. She pawed at her stomach. "I'll be right back." She got up and waddled into the nurses office, where their private bathroom was located. The younger nurse sat at the desk struggling through paperwork, a sour look etched across her face. The air was ripe with brine and garlic.

Dorothy approached the desk carefully, her cup of water tight in her hand. "I'm going to go get a little air. Something *stinks*." She felt like she was stepping outside herself with the very first lie. She was on her way now, no turning back. No chickening out. She'd told Alice she could deliver, and Dorothy wanted to be known as a girl who could be depended on. That kind of thing would probably impress a girl like Alice.

"Ugh," the nurse said, "Tell me about it. You need to sign out first. *Wait*, are you allowed to leave the floor?"

"Sure am," Dorothy said. She put her cup of water on the counter. Had she said that too defensively? *No.* The duty nurse wasn't even looking at her. She was shuffling papers. Maybe she was trying her best *not* to look at Dorothy. *Did she know? If I blow this Alice will hate me forever. Please God don't let me blow this.*

Dorothy pressed the pen hard onto paper. *Is the nurse watching?* She felt like a hundred pairs of eyes were on her. She didn't dare look up because she knew if she did she would lose it and chicken out. Sweat broke on her brow. She didn't dare wipe it away. *Would I be sweating if I wasn't doing something wrong?* She didn't want to seem out of the ordinary. *I'm just a normal girl signing out for some fresh air,* she thought. *I promise.* Stretching her legs. *Maybe I shouldn't have gone off my meds.* The pen was slippery in her hands, and she fumbled with it as she wrote. *Oh God, what if they look at my penmanship and see how nervous I am?* She felt like she was in a roller coaster with nobody at the control switch.

She finished writing her name and put the pen down. It clunked on the table.

The duty nurse smiled at Dorothy and hit a switch behind the counter, unlocking the elevator. It would be allowed to travel up to the psychiatric floor now. Ward Nine.

Dorothy smiled at Alice, pleased as punch that her plan was going off without a hitch. *I am dependable*, she thought. *You can love—*

The water!

Dorothy spun around, unsure of what to do next. Her original plan was to spill water on the desk when she was writing her name in the book. But she was done that now. She felt exposed and guilty. She considered throwing the cup of water on the desk anyway. That would be too suspicious. *How did I screw this up so bad?*

The elevator would be there any moment, she was sure of it.

"So," Dorothy said. "*Uhm*, what are you doing?"

The duty nurse looked up. "Me? Paper work. What else?" She had a light accent Dorothy couldn't place. She couldn't focus on the nurse's voice at the moment, however. *Spill the water!* She thought. *Spill it now!*

"Maybe I could help," Dorothy said. The words were falling out of her mouth before she could register them. Any moment she'd say something completely ridiculous and blow the entire thing.

"I don't think so," the nurse said.

"*No I'm good with paperwork!*" Dorothy exclaimed. She stepped forward. The cup of water hit the counter awkwardly, its paper shell crumpled, and Dorothy tipped it onto the corner. The water ran across the tabletop and spilled down onto the pile of papers below.

"*Oops,*" Dorothy put her hands over her mouth.

"Ahh shit!" the nurse exclaimed. She started grabbing sheets and pulling them off the counter. "I'm supposed to have these in before lunch!"

"*I'm so sorry*," Dorothy said, backing away from the desk. The elevator behind her beeped. It had reached the floor. Dorothy turned.

"I'll just get out of your hair," she said. She stepped toward the elevator. On the other side, of the room Alice stood up and went to the wall beside the elevator door. With the duty nurse distracted, she'd be able to get into the elevator unseen. The plan was as easy as it was simple.

A bell went off. Dorothy walked toward the elevator. Alice leaned back against the wall, her hand resting on the doorway. Dorothy stood halfway between the desk and the elevator, trying to block any prying eyes. Her heart was in her chest. The doors clunked open.

I'm doing it! I'm doing it! I'm do—Dorothy froze in her tracks. Her stomach lurched.

As the door opened fully, two uniformed police officers stepped out into the room. They looked like two bulldogs with guns on their hips.

"Alice Pleasance?" One of them said.

Dorothy simply stared at them, too terrified to react.

Chapter 13.

Alice shrank back against the wall the moment the door opened. She'd caught a glimpse of a badge and instinct took over. Dorothy, apparently, didn't have that particular instinct. As the two cops stepped off the elevator she froze, a look of guilty horror on her face.

"*Alice Pleasance?*" One of the cops said to Dorothy. His badge said *Sgt Pepper*. Any other time Dorothy would have laughed at that. Now all she wanted to do was piss herself and then crawl away to hide.

Dorothy said nothing. She stared at the cops like she'd just been caught red handed murdering a kitten. In a way, it worked perfectly, because their attention was now drawn away from their target: the blond woman slinking against the wall. Alice made her move, sliding along the wall and stepping into the elevator. She stood very still against the wall closest to the two policemen, jammed into the front corner and well out of sight if one of them should happen to look back.

"Are you Alice Pleasance?" The other cop spoke this time, a brick wall with a shaved head and a badge. His eyes were bloodshot, and they were mean.

"I *uhm...no*," Dorothy said.

Come on, Alice thought. *Come on, get in here.* Any second now the elevator would close. Not a disaster, but she really wanted Dorothy away from those cops before she said something stupid and set off their bullshit radar. Plus if she headed downstairs by herself she'd have to find somewhere to hide until Dorothy could get down, and she wanted to be out of the hospital as soon as possible.

"What's your name?" The Wall said.

Alice couldn't see which one was speaking. They seemed to be interchangeable though. Carbon clones pumped out of a factory in some hidden industrial complex to keep the machine in place.

That's right, The Hater whispered. *You got it girl, spot on.*

Alice clamped a hand over her mouth. Jesus Christ, had she said that out loud?

"Dorothy Gale," Dorothy said.

"You don't know a blond girl named Alice Pleasance?" the wide cop said. "Came in the other night? About your age."

"*Oh*," Dorothy said. Her voice was getting higher and higher in pitch, ambling toward all out panic. "*Maybe...I think. Actually, no, I don't.*"

"Tough question, hey?" Sgt Pepper said. He raised his hand to wipe his brow and revealed an armpit dark with sweat.

They can smell her lies, Alice thought. *Why can't she just shut up and get into the elevator?* She still had her hand clamped over her mouth.

That idiot is going to blow it. They're going to catch me and put me away forever. The elevator bell went off and the doors began to close. Alice would have to hide downstairs and pray Dorothy could make it on her own. Hopefully she was smart enough not to give them away.

"She's just a baby," the Hater whispered through Alice's fingers.

"My elevator," Dorothy said.

The doors were about to shut when a large hand appeared and knocked the safety tab, popping them open.

"Can I help you?" Alice heard the rookie nurse say.

"Alice Pleasance?" the cop said. The other one still had his hand on the elevator door.

Alice could see scrapes on the man's knuckles. She wondered if they had been caused by someone's face.

"One second, I'll go get Dr Weller."

"Thank you," Sgt Pepper said.

The other one tipped his hat to Dorothy. "You have a good day."

"Thanks," Dorothy rasped. She stepped into the elevator. She was shaky and pale.

She looks like she's about to pass out. Alice thought. *If she does, they'll be in here in a heartbeat. Maybe she should have stayed behind.*

Dorothy stared at the ground and gasped for air. She kept her head down as the elevator bell went off. She collapsed into Alice's arms as the doors were closing, but nobody seemed to notice. The elevator lurched, and the two girls began their trip down to the main floor.

"Hey," Alice said. "You alright?"

"I feel sick," Dorothy whispered. "I almost blew it." Her eyes were wet.

"You did real good," Alice said. She pulled the girl into an embrace, and Dorothy wrapped her arms around Alice. She ran her fingers through Dorothy's hair. "You're a real pro."

Dorothy looked up into her face.

"No I'm not," she said. "I suck at this. I'm not used to lying."

Alice kissed a large tear off Dorothy's face. Then she shared the tear with Dorothy on her lips.

Dorothy gasped. Her leg started to shake.

Alice opened her mouth and gently sucked on the girls bottom lip. Dorothy responded by turning her head and running her tongue along Alice's teeth. Alice put her hands in Dorothy's short hair, directing traffic, as she'd done a hundred times with a hundred different men. A few women as well.

Alice moaned and withdrew from the kiss. She rubbed her nose against Dorothy's cheek. "Better?"

"I'm sorry," Dorothy said. Her eyes were wide and dark, and she peered sadly into Alice's blue ones.

"Try not to sweat it," Alice whispered. She hugged her tight and then the girls kissed again.

The door popped open on the main floor, and someone clucked their tongue.

The girls turned and looked to see a fat old woman in expensive clothes eyeing them in disgust. Her son stood beside her, maybe sixteen or seventeen, sporting skinny pants and a *Rise Against* T-shirt. He was watching them with a smile on his face.

"Come on," Alice said, taking Dorothy's hand. "This is our stop."

Dorothy smiled at the woman as she stepped past She wiped the kiss from her mouth with the back of her hand. Alice winked at the boy beside her as he stepped aside to let them pass. His smile widened. He was part of their little secret now, three against one. His mother would not approve. At that age, it was a good thing.

The main floor of the hospital had a balcony that overlooked the cafeteria, straight across from a large waiting room for ingoing and outgoing patients. In the center, in front of two sets of automatic doors, the receptionist smiled at the girls as they passed. Alice was still wearing her hospital gown, but down here nobody seemed to care. Dorothy was fully dressed in her street clothes. They looked like everyone else at the hospital; just a good friend coming to check on someone who'd had a rough go of things. They acted natural, holding hands and walking quickly toward the front doors. Dorothy wouldn't stop smiling at everyone, and the look was infectious. Everyone they passed returned the smile in kind.

The girls stepped out of the hospital and into the morning sunshine. It felt good to be alive. Good to be free. Dorothy snuggled up to Alice as they passed ingoing patients, and elderly long term care patients standing around smoking and gossiping.

"Where are we going?" Dorothy said after a while.

"I need to go see a friend about something," Alice said. Rabbit, of course, would probably not be happy to see her. But if the fucker was going to dump her at the hospital like so much useless garbage, well, he was going to pay for it.

Alice found the bus stop she wanted, then sat and invited Dorothy to sit on her lap. Eventually the bus came, and the girls paid with part of Dorothy's ice cream fund. Then the bus pulled onto the road and was swept away in the traffic.

Chapter 14.

Dr Weller came out of his office wiping doughnut powder from his face. He followed the duty nurse out into the main room of the ward and met the two cops standing at the front desk. "Yes?" he said. "How can I help you?"

"Alice Pleasance," The Wall said.

"What is this about?" Dr Weller said. One of the officers was wearing an expensive smelling cologne but he couldn't be sure which one it was. *Probably the dark one,* he thought. *They usually smell better.*

"Is she here?" Sgt Pepper asked.

"Yeah. Listen, guys. I don't want to be a bother, but I'm Alice's acting doctor, and you really need to tell me what this is about."

"One of the security guards she assaulted has pressed charges," Sgt Pepper said. "So we need to discuss it with her."

"Are you planning on taking her out of here?" Dr Weller said.

"We are probably going to need to set up a time for her to take a statement and to get fingerprinted, if warranted. We saw the guy yesterday, he's got a busted nose. Looks like he got hit in the face with a baseball bat." He made a slicing motion across his face to show the doctor where the man had been hit.

"It happened while she was still flushing opiates out of her system," Dr Weller said. "I can hardly see how she could be responsible for her actions." He crossed his arms, an unconscious show of defiance. He was like most people dealing with police; he felt intimidated by their rough manner and the uniform. These men were exuding violence; it dripped from their pores and tainted the air. *Not here though. This is my territory and I will not be intimidated in my own yard.*

"Yeah, well, that's why we want a statement instead of taking her in."

"She really needs to stay here," Dr Weller said. "She's suffering a breakdown. She has diminished mental capabilities."

"She's crazy?" The Wall shook his head. "Terrific."

"I didn't say that. I can't tell you exactly what's wrong with her."

"Well," Sgt Pepper said. "We still need to talk to her. Can you point us to where she is?"

Dr Weller looked at the nurse, who was quietly but blatantly eavesdropping.

"She's in her room," the nurse said, suddenly self conscious.

"Ahh. It's right over here then," Dr Weller said. He came around from the back of the desk. Moving past the two policemen, he stopped and turned. "I will need to be present for this, of course. I'm Alice's legal guardian while she is under my care."

"Of course you are," The Wall sighed. He looked at his partner and shook his head before nodding at the doctor. "Hey, whatever you say, *legal guardian*."

That's right, Dr Weller thought. *We will do things my way here.* He'd been dealing with men like this his entire life. They responded to direct commands much better than Dr Weller could ever hope to appeal to their softer sides. He turned and walked to Alice's door, giving it a sharp knock. The two police officers walked up behind him. "Alice. You have visitors."

He opened the door.

"Alice?"

The room was empty. There was a bathroom to hide in, but it was dark and empty as well. The bathroom door was hanging half open.

The two cops looked at each other. Dr Weller caught the silent discussion they were having and didn't like it one bit. *They think they've won,* he thought. *Perhaps they have. Alice just made me look a fool.* "Hold on a sec."

Dr Weller walked back out to the front desk. There he stood very close to the duty nurse and spoke softly. "She's not in her room. Is she maybe somewhere else?"

"Well, she'd have to be, right?" the nurse said. She looked at Sgt Pepper's nametag and started to smile, but the look on the doctor's face killed the smile at birth. "I'm afraid I don't know where she is. She was out here a little while ago, and then she got up and left. I assumed it was to go back to her room, because the door was shut."

Weller looked around the room, frowning. "Where's Dorothy Gale?" His gut was suddenly telling him something he didn't want to hear. *They're both gone. Right out from under your nose, old boy.*

"She signed out just as these cops were showing up," the nurse said.

"Any luck?" Sgt Pepper said.

"And Alice was nowhere near the elevator when Dorothy left, right?" Dr Weller said, waving them off. The not now gesture wouldn't sit well with their alpha male egos

"Well, no," the nurse said. "I mean, wouldn't the cops have seen her? They were talking to Dorothy when I looked up—,"

"What do you mean?" Dr Weller said. "You weren't watching her?"

"*Of course I was.* It's just that Dorothy spilled water all over the counter so I was busy trying to save all this paperwork. Besides, those cops were talking to her."

Dr Weller walked around the outside of the table, around to where the sign out book was sitting. It was still in the same spot Dorothy had left it. He ran his finger down the entries until he came to the last one. Then he looked up at the duty nurse. His face was a mix of sour and anger.

"What is it?" she said, putting a hand over her heart.

Dr Weller shook his head. "I think you two should take a look at this." He motioned the two cops over.

"I think Alice Pleasance might have fled the hospital with another girl," he said.

"What?" Sgt Pepper said. "Wasn't anyone watching the elevator?"

"*I was,*" the rookie nurse said, with a touch of dread in her voice. She looked as though she might start crying at any minute.

"See this?" Dr Weller said, his finger on the last entry. "This is the girl she is with.

The Wall read it, and then looked at the doctor. "*Ozma of Oz?* What the hell kind of name is that?"

"Those women are both very disturbed," Dr Weller said. "But Dorothy Gale is more so. She lives in her delusions full time, but she has been able to integrate them seemlessly into her everyday life. She actually believes that somewhere out in the world there is a land of magic and fairies where she is a princess."

"So?" Sgt Pepper said. "Sounds like every other nutcase in here."

"Dorothy is suffering from severe post traumatic shock," Dr Weller said. "Last year there was a tornado near her town and her family was killed. Dorothy reacted by attempting to drive a stolen car into the tornado because she believed she could reach her fairyland if the tornado picked her up and carried her there. Natural disasters are the only way to travel to Oz, apparently."

The Wall stared at Dr Weller. His face was a stone. "Uhh, no offense doc, but that's seriously fucked up."

Dr Weller sighed. *Brutes.* "I know. The danger here is that Dorothy may try it again. And Alice is suffering from some kind of breakdown that I haven't been able to pin down yet. I believe she suffered a trauma before she came to the hospital, and that her overdose on heroin was her attempt to self medicate her pain. This could all be temporary, though, and in her state I believe she could absorb Dorothy's delusions and make them her own."

"Really? So what, *crazy by proxy?*"

"Well, that's a gross oversimplification," Dr Weller said. "But I guess in a way it could be seen like that. It's not guaranteed, mind you. Most of the time things like this don't happen. Anytime you have people with reality impairments, though, it *is* a possibility."

"So?" Sgt Pepper crossed his arms and scowled. "She trades in one crazy fantasy for another?"

"The thing is," Dr Weller said, "Dorothy Gale's fantasy is not harmless. Her attempts to reach the Land of Oz have caused her to attempt suicide at least three times. The first time she tried to burn the family barn down while she was in it. After her parents pulled her out she tried to fight them and get back into the fire. The second time she was caught trying to burn a schoolhouse down."

"Christ," said the dark cop. "What a nut job."

"After that she spent some time in juvenile custody. It was in there that her delusion evolved so that her trip to Oz could no longer be completed with a manmade disaster. It had to be natural. I believe this was an attempt by Dorothy to keep herself out of prison."

"What about Alice's fantasy?"

"I honestly can't tell you much," Dr Weller said. "We didn't have enough time to dig into it. And Alice had a breakdown during our first session." Dr Weller stopped. Something had suddenly occurred to him. "During her initial session, she began screaming about having killed someone."

"What?"

"Yeah," Dr Weller said. "I wouldn't trust that it actually happened, but *something* happened to her. If it is a temporary episode, it could well have been brought on by a rape or murder."

"Or both?" the dark cop said.

"Definitely, yes," Dr Weller said. "That would explain a lot of things. She blames her addiction to heroin and the forced detox we put her through. But that's not the case at all."

"Call it in?" the blond cop said, looking at his partner. "We can check and see if anything like that has happened. Recently."

"Yeah, let's get on it."

"Thank you doctor," the blond cop said. The two men turned to go. The dark cop spoke into the small walkie talkie attached to his shirt.

"Officers," Dr Weller said, following them toward the elevator. "Could you keep me up on what's happening please? I'm the doctor in charge of both of these girls. They are my responsibility."

"Yeah," Sgt Pepper said. "You got a card or something? I'll give you a call if we hear anything."

"They should be brought back here for continued treatment," Dr Weller said, handing the officer his business card.

"Well, let's focus on finding them first."

The elevator door opened, and the two cops stepped onto it. Dr Weller stayed on the floor.

"Good luck, officers," he said, as the doors started to close. "Please bring them back safely."

"We'll do what we can," The Wall said. "Thanks."

The door shut. Dr Weller looked at his warped reflection in the steel door for a moment, then turned and faced the duty nurse. She was standing there watching him. She had a pen in her hands but wasn't writing anything.

"That's it, I guess," Dr Weller said. He ran his hands through his hair.

The nurse didn't say anything. After a few moments, Dr Weller returned to his office and shut the door.

In the nurses' office, the bathroom door opened to the sound of a flushing toilet. The older nurse walked out to the desk and put a hand on the younger nurse's back. "I wouldn't go in there," she said, chuckling. Then she clapped her hands. "So what did I miss?"

Chapter 15.

The bus stank like piss and was full of odd looks for both Alice and Dorothy. Dorothy clung to her stuffed dog and kept her eyes on the floor. Alice met each stare with a sneer. She knew how fucked up they looked together: A young girl carrying a toy dog and a blond girl still dressed in her hospital gown and robe. At some point she'd have to get clothes if they were going to be out in public; she imagined herself as a beacon for emergency calls from good Samaritans.

Finally they drove to a neighbourhood that Alice recognized, and a short time later they were getting off the bus. The neighbourhood looked like a dozen other run down areas Alice knew of in the city; she could count them off on her fingers. Old houses with big yards, slowly torn down one at a time and replaced with cheap duplexes and townhouse developments. The air was muggy and carried a faint industrial smell. It was the kind of neighbourhood that held many different races of people, most living in close proximity to one another but keeping to themselves as much as possible. Between these groups were houses owned by the elderly poor. Everything felt run down. Even the tires on the cars parked on the side of the road seemed flat.

"Great place," Dorothy said. "Why are we here again?"

"I'm going to see my boy Rabbit," Alice said.

"You *do* have a boyfriend?" Dorothy said, exasperated.

Alice laughed, and then put a hand to her mouth when she realized Dorothy was being serious. "No, he's not a boyfriend," she said. "He's just a friend."

"Yeah right," Dorothy muttered.

"He's my *dealer*, actually," Alice said. "And he ditched me off when he knew there would be cops lookin' for me. So now he's going to make it better."

"How?"

"He's going to give us enough cash to grab a bus ticket or something. Hell I dunno, we can grab a motel and figure out where we're headed next."

"But you were overdosing, right?" Dorothy said. "I mean, that's what the nurse said..."

"Bullshit," Alice said. "I would have been fine. Rabbit did what Rabbit always does when shit gets real: He bolted. And anyway, he owes me. He owes me *bigtime*." That wasn't entirely true, and Alice knew it. In reality, Rabbit didn't put up with a lot of shit from anyone. She'd seen him beat the living hell out of junkies who brought drama and bullshit to his grandmother's house; she was going to have to be very careful how she handled him. Thankfully, she had an idea about how she could level the playing field in a hurry. She just hoped it was still there when she got into the house.

Dorothy smiled. She took Alice's hand and laced their fingers together. "Okay," she said sweetly, smiling up at her. Alice couldn't help but smile back. Dorothy was too cute to do anything else.

They walked along cracked sidewalks and past garbage strewn allies, and kids playing basketball and hockey in the streets. They would pass three houses of unkempt lawn for every one that was groomed and trimmed; most of these yards had whirly-gigs and garden gnomes. Alice noted that almost every one of them had some sort of announcement on the lawn claiming to be protected by various home security companies; the elderly were besieged in their homes in the last days of their lives. Too afraid to leave their yards, and yet afraid to stay in their houses as well. Alice hoped that she never reached the point in her life where fear overtook every aspect of it.

Eventually the manicured lawns became less frequent, and the dirty, rotting duplexes and cheap community living townhouses took over. The streets became more cracked and weed strewn. There were broken bottles in the gutter. Kids on bikes rode past, giving the girls a wary eye and a wide birth.

And then there was Rabbit's house, a little bungalow on its own property. The house was run down and ratty looking. It was badly in need of a paint job. The lawn was uneven and hadn't been cut in months, and there was garbage strewn from the front step all the way out to the street. It was a pile of shit, but it was paid for; Rabbit had inherited the property from his parents when they died. It had never been a prized mansion, but at least it had been clean at one point. It might have once been one of those manicured lawns they'd been passing on the way here. Maybe this was the true end result of life; destined to end up a run down old pile of garbage. An eyesore and a burden. A forgotten object of desire.

Rabbit's car was parked on the street. He didn't have a driveway. The girls walked up to the front door. It was hanging open. They could hear Rabbit talking on the phone somewhere inside. The television was on *The Price is Right.*

"Stay behind me," Alice said. "And be careful. He's quick."

Dorothy nodded.

Alice opened the door and stepped inside, Dorothy on her heel.

The room was dark. The shades were pulled all the way down. Rabbit was paranoid about junkies and cops looking into his house from the street; he'd nailed the blinds in place so they couldn't be opened for any reason. The place was as much a mess inside as it was outside. There was a large flat panel television in one corner where Drew Carey was about to grant a wish. The furniture was old, dirty, and unmatched. Rabbit was sitting on the couch in a pair of shorts and a *Hardship Post* concert shirt. It was blue and said *my only aim is to please you* in swirly yellow letters. He was wearing a John Deere hat off to the side. Gold rings. He was smoking a cigarette and talking into a black cell phone. He rubbed his face absently while he talked. His voice was slurred and he looked sleepy. Or high.

"Rabbit," Alice said. "*HEY!*" She snapped her fingers.

Rabbit looked up, had a moment of confusion and then shook his head. "Alice." He stuck one finger up to plead for another second. "*Uh, let me hitchoo back in a bit...alright. Alright.*" He hung up the phone.

"So?" Alice shrugged, her hands in the air.

"How the hell are you?" Rabbit said. "You look good."

"Forget about that. I need some clothes."

"You don't *need* them," Rabbit smiled. The look on her face made him think twice though, and he stood up quickly. He chewed his thumb. "It's just *ummuh*, you know I don't like people showin' up unannounced."

"Clothes," Alice said again. "And none of that hootchie bullshit you're always trying to get me into."

"Alright, alright," Rabbit said. "Calm down, I'll hook you up." He walked into the bedroom.

Alice and Dorothy looked at each other, and Dorothy mouthed the words *we should go.* Alice squeezed her hand. Then she walked over to fridge and popped open the freezer.

"*You want a hoodie or a shirt?*" Rabbit called from the bedroom.

"Shirt," Alice replied. She lost her grip on a frozen steak, which bounced off her arm and hit the floor loudly. Her breath hissed in her teeth. "*Shit!*"

"*Oh my God.*" Dorothy put both her hands over her mouth and shook her head. "*What are you doing?*"

"What was that?" Rabbit said. Alice didn't know if he meant the noise or her clothing choice.

"*Uhh, hoodie!*" she called back. "It's cold out."

"*Alice!*" Dorothy hissed.

Alice looked at her and smiled. "Got it." She pulled her hand out of the freezer. She had a sandwich bag in her hand. She reached into the bag and pulled out a snub nosed revolver with a taped handle.

"Alice!" Dorothy said again. Her eyes bulged at the site of the weapon.

Alice smiled at Dorothy, then gave her a little wink and blew a kiss her way.

Rabbit walked out of his bedroom, his hands full of clothes.

"Hoodie. And a shirt, because you can't seem to make up your damned mind. I—"

He stopped in the middle of the living room when he noticed Alice pointing a gun at him. She pushed the frozen barrel of the weapon against the side of his head, and the contact with his warm flesh caused a flash of white mist to form around the lip of the weapon.

"What the *fuck?*"

"Put the clothes down," Alice said. The smile was gone from her face. It was replaced by a look that said *don't fuck with me, I'm all business right now.*

"Alice, put the gun down." He dropped the clothes at his feet and put up his hands. "This is some *bullshit.*"

"I need cash, Rabbit. And you owe me."

"What? You're out of your fuckin' mind, aren't you? I *knew* you were." He was talking tough but his face was red and he was huffing like he'd just run up a flight of stairs.

"Shut the fuck up," Alice said. "And stop talking. All you have to worry about are the words coming out of *my* mouth. *Do what I say or I'll kill you.*"

Rabbit squinted at Alice. She responded by pulling the hammer back on the gun.

"Don't even think about it!" Alice growled.

"Take it easy! *I saved your fuckin life!* You were so far down the hole you prolly would have died. I had to take you to the hospital." Sweat danced on his brow.

"You shot me up in the first place!" Her voice had gone from inside to outside. She was on the verge of shouting. "You fuckin' left me in the parking lot like a bag of garbage."

"It ain't like that," Rabbit said. He grimaced, flashing his gold teeth.

"Oh it ain't?" Alice said. "Nobody wants to hear your lies. Dorothy and I need some cash. Give it to me."

"So that's it huh? You just gonna rob me now. After all the shit I gave you."

"*I got my ass kicked by security guards!*" Alice yelled.

"Aren't you forgetting something?" Rabbit asked.

"What?" The gun wavered for a moment.

"Uhh...*nothing*," Rabbit said. He looked like he'd just been hit in the balls with a brick. "Look, let's just stay calm, alright? I'll give you whatever you want. You say you're in shit, I believe you. I want to help."

"Money. *Now.*"

Rabbit reached into his shorts pocket. He pulled out several crumpled bills. "This is all I got."

"How much?"

"Uhm...I dunno," He looked at the wad of bills and did some quick math. "It's like thirty-eight bucks."

Alice shook her head. "Not good enough."

"*I told you it's all I got!*" Rabbit's voice squeaked.

"Maybe we should take that and leave," Dorothy said weakly.

"Hey, I'm not the bad guy, doll. You came to me, remember? You were talkin' all crazy shit 'cuz you said some guy raped you—"

Alice grabbed the gun with both hands and squeezed the trigger. It roared fire and bucked in her hand, and Rabbit ducked instinctively. Dorothy crumpled and screamed. A hole opened up in the wall behind where Rabbit was standing.

"*SHUT THE FUCK UP!*" Alice screamed. "And stand up, I missed on purpose. Next time maybe I'll shoot your balls off."

"*FUCK!*" Rabbit put his hands over his head and laced his fingers together. His head was on a swivel, rolling between Alice's gun and the whole in the wall. "*Alright!* Alright. Just...don't shoot that thing again. This is my grandmother's house."

"It's a shithole. Where's your stash?"

"What stash?"

Alice pulled the hammer back on the gun again.

Rabbit sighed. He rolled his eyes and shook his head petulantly. "The bathroom," he said. "In the back of the toilet."

"*You're kidding*," Alice said, and laughed. "That's the first place the cops would look, you idiot."

"Don't call me that," Rabbit said. "I'm not an idiot."

Alice waved the gun toward the back of the house. "Let's go, *idiot*," she said.

Rabbit shook his head. "I'm not gonna forget this Alice. I hope you realize, they call me Rabbit but I got a memory like an elephant."

"Spare me the one-liners." She motioned toward the hallway leading to the bathroom again. Come on, *do* it."

Rabbit stepped into the hall and made his way toward the bathroom.

"I take care of you," Rabbit said. "*Bitch*, I shoot you up all the time for nothing."

"You got paid for it," Alice growled. "*Every fucking time.*"

Alice looked back at Dorothy and smiled. Dorothy looked like she was going to throw up, or pass out. Or both.

"Why don't you put the gun down?" Rabbit said. "We can still be friends, right?"

"Why don't you shut up and give me what I want?" Alice said. She poked Rabbit in the back with the barrel of the pistol for effect.

"You won't shoot me." He reached the bathroom. He flicked on the light and looked at her over his shoulder. "You know you won't shoot me."

"You know that for a fact right?" Alice said.

I know you will, the Hater whispered. Alice tensed. Rabbit felt the change in how she was holding the gun where it contacted his skin.

"Whoa," he said. "Easy. Easy, girl. Don't be stupid."

Just do it, the Hater said. *Pull the trigger and we'll play in his blood. It'll be like when you were little and played in the garden sprinkler.*

"Fuck!" Alice said. "Shut up!" She put her free hand against her temple. She used the other hand to jab Rabbit in the back with the pistol barrel.

"Hey," Rabbit said. "We're still friends, right? Don't shoot me, babygirl. You'll regret it forever."

"*SHE ALREADY KILLED A FUCKER!*" the Hater screamed. The voice erupted through Alice. It was throaty and guttural.

Behind Alice, at the front door, Dorothy cried out. Alice flicked her head back for a moment, then back on Rabbit.

"Do you know Time?" she said. *Not me, I'm losing me, I'm losing—*

"Yeah." He checked his watch. "Two-thirty, baby. Now—"

"*WRONG!*" Alice barked. "*You have no idea what you're talking about. You're not even a real fucking Rabbit, are you? You have the shortest ears I've ever seen.*"

Rabbit pulled the lid off the back of the toilet, then fished into the cold water and pulled out a sealed black bag. At first Alice saw a dead cat pulled out of the water, rotted and wilting, but then it was a brick covered in a tightly wrapped garbage bag and she had no idea where the dead cat had gone.

"Hand it over," Alice said. The light in the bathroom flicked on and off as the power in the room surged and dropped off again. She could hear the electricity running through the filament, droning like an angry fly. The light flickered between pink and blue. The bathtub took on a waxy, rotten fruit sheen and the finish began to bubble and slide toward the drain. She glanced up at the bathroom light and confirmed her suspicion. The light bulb was filled with angry, buzzing flies. They were lit up like a filament, but she could plainly see them wiping their hands and rubbing their faces. *Little schemers. They're planning something.*

Rabbit turned around. The bag was now a big black roach, and he had it between his hands."It's a fucking water gun," Rabbit said. "Go on, pull the trigger and see. It squirts raspberry jelly."

You can't trust her anyway, the Hater mumbled. *She's killed a man. Scooped out his brain! His mind rotting and stained!*

"Shut *UP!*" Alice yelled. She pounded the sides of her head with her hands.

Rabbit held out the bag. Alice reached for it with her free hand. The gun was no longer on Rabbit, she was using it to try and keep the voice of the Hater from spilling out of her mouth.

It was just the opportunity Rabbit needed. He dropped the bag.

Instinctively Alice made a grab for it. The moment her eyes shifted to follow the cockroach, Rabbit made his move. He slammed a fist into Alice's mouth and grabbed for the gun. Alice flew back into the hall. Her mouth was a bloody mess. Her eyes danced under her eyelids. She stumbled against the wall and slid to the floor in a heap.

Rabbit spit on her. He had the gun in his hands now. "*Fuck you!*" he shouted. "You want to point a gun at me? I'll *fuckin' kill you!*"

"*ALICE!*" Dorothy screamed. She was crouched over by the door, crying. Rabbit looked at her.

Alice heard Rabbit say: "You're gettin' it good, bitch. Nobody rolls in here like that." He stepped past her, his hands clenched in fists. Alice reached out and grabbed his ankle with one feeble hand, and he looked down at her, smiling.

"*I told you,*" Rabbit said. He turned and planted a sharp kick squarely in the side of Alice's face. There was a wet meat sound and a sharp clack of her teeth coming together, then her head flopped stupidly on her neck and she let out a *HYUNNH*. For Alice, the world sputtered in hyper colour flashes. She floundered on the carpet, too dazed and stupid to move.

"*Stop it!*" Dorothy looked like a trapped, panicked deer. Glancing around, she looked at the front door of the house. Her head snapped between Alice on the floor and Rabbit, standing between them.

There was death in his eyes.

"Don't even think it, bitch. So help me God I'll take your head right off." Dorothy looked back at the door.

"*HEY!*" Rabbit shouted. He waved the gun at her.

"Okay," she whimpered. She put her hands up. "Please." The air was thick with the smell of gunpowder and electric with tension. She snuffled and sucked back tears and snot.

Rabbit approached her with the gun held out in front of him. He grabbed her by the back of the head and shoved her back into the living room, away from the doorway. Away from freedom. Dorothy howled at his touch.

She stumbled toward the coffee table, tripped over her feet and went down on one knee. Rabbit walked in behind her, gun at his side. Dorothy wiped the tears from her eyes with her sleeve. One hand on the floor, the other on the table, she saw the green glass ashtray just inches from her fingertips.

"Get up!" Rabbit nudged her with the edge of his foot.

Dorothy stood up. As she moved, her fingers curled around the lip of the ashtray. And then she was turning, ashtray in hand, swinging it in a wild arc. Rabbit ducked instinctively. The corner of the ashtray grazed the top of his head, leaving an angry red streak in his hairline that carried down his forehead and stopped over his eye. He fell back on the floor, overbalanced, then threw his hands back and caught himself at the last moment.

And then he was back up again, and fending off her blows. Dorothy was screaming and swinging, her face puffy and streaked, her eyes mixed with equal parts rage and terror. Rabbit stuck his hand into her next swing, knocked her arm wide, and then brought his gun-hand up and caught her on the chin. Dorothy's knees buckled. She dropped the ashtray, threw her hands to her face, and collapsed in a weeping heap in front of Rabbit.

"*FUCK!*" he screamed, grabbing his head. There was a line of fire where the ashtray had struck. He went around beside Dorothy and booted her in the ass. She wailed in pain and tried to crawl away. Rabbit grabbed her by the shirt and pulled her hard onto her side. He planted a knee into her side and she squawked in protest.

Rabbit pulled her hands away from her face. She looked up at him with rolling, terrified eyes and he slammed the side of his gun into them.

Dorothy gasped, choked on a cry, and gagged again. She buried her face in her arms and tried to turn away.

"*Don't fuckin' puke,*" Rabbit said quietly. He smacked her again in the side of the face with the pistol. He grabbed her hair with his free hand and pulled her head back, then slammed his gun hand into the fingers covering her eyes. Somewhere under the tangle of her hands her nose was bleeding. She was moaning softly, instinctively covering herself as best she could. Rabbit socked her in the jaw. The gun came away sticky with blood and saliva. He rolled her on her back and straddled her hips. She tried to curl into a ball on her side, but it was a weak attempt. She was barely conscious.

Rabbit grabbed the neck of her shirt and pulled hard. Dorothy's head rocked. Her shirt ripped open. She was wearing a green bra. Her pale skin was dusted with freckles and streaks of blood. Stress made her milky flesh red and blotchy.

"Oh yeah," Rabbit said. He grabbed her breast with a free hand. He squeezed it until Dorothy moaned. She tried to cover herself with a clumsy hand. Rabbit knocked it away and latched onto her again. "You want to party?" His voice was a dirty whisper. "*You do, don't you.*"

He grabbed her hands and pinned them over her head. Then he leaned down and licked the top of her breast. Dorothy gasped. A fine crimson mist danced off her lips. She shook her head slowly back and forth. The eye that had been repeatedly slammed with the gun was swollen shut. The area around it was turning into an ugly black and purple bruise.

Rabbit flicked the button on her jeans. He yanked on the denim. Her zipper popped, and her pants opened to reveal buttermilk flesh and sensible green panties that matched her bra. Rabbit grunted. His lips parted and he ran a finger along the waistband. Organic heat radiated out from her to his fingertips. He pulled the waistband down with his finger. He traced a circle in the light dusting of auburn hair beneath. She smelled like sweat and cunt down there. Rabbit's cock went stiff and he rubbed the head with the damp finger, pushing against his piss hole through the denim of his jeans.

Dorothy bucked hard at his touch, and Rabbit slid to one side. She kicked and flailed and screamed and suddenly Rabbit wasn't on her anymore; he was lying on his side and scrabbling for his gun. A flutter of movement from the corner of his eye caught his attention. He looked up to see Alice charging toward him. He looked at the black rage on her face and thought *THAT'S NOT ALICE.* Then it was too late for anything else.

"Fuck *YOUUUUU!*" Alice screeched. She had a weapon in her hand, a heavy porcelain square stained with years of water marks and chemical deposits. It was the lid off the back of the toilet. Blood was in her eyes, but her target was an easy one. Her fingers locked on the lid, she let go with one hand and swung like she was throwing a bowling ball.

Dorothy scrabbled out of the way, grabbing at her clothes and retreating to the far side of the coffee table.

Rabbit was staring up at Alice with a dumb, shocked look on his face. The lid caught him square in the mouth and continued past him. Alice lost her grip on it at shoulder height, and it sailed across the living room. It smashed Rabbit's plasma TV before hitting the floor and snapping neatly in three pieces.

The force of the blow knocked Rabbit backward and he slammed his head against the floor. He moaned softly, his legs folded underneath him in a painful yoga pose. He had blood and bits of broken teeth on his face. His bottom teeth had cut though his lower lip and now peeked out of their bloody holes like little yellow maggots.

Alice grabbed Dorothy. "Come on," she said. "Get up."

Dorothy was shaking her head. Her eyes were fluttering and dopey.

"*Come on!*" Alice yelled. She grabbed Dorothy under her arms and hauled her out from under Rabbit. She pulled the girl into a sitting position against the couch. Then she ran over and grabbed Rabbit's gun. It was warm and sticky with blood. She turned back to Dorothy and shook her arms. "*We gotta go!*"

Dorothy opened her eyes. She looked up into Alice's bloodied face. Then she reached for her and let out a sob.

"Dorothy," Alice said, wiping her hair out of her face. "We have to go. *Now*. I might have killed that fucker. I still might, I dunno."

Dorothy nodded. Then she looked down at her torn clothing. She gave Alice a hurt, confused look and tried to cover herself. Alice helped her to her feet. Rabbit's car keys were on the coffee table; she grabbed those in one hand. The gun was still in the other.

"What did he do?" Dorothy said, softly pulling her ripped shirt closed. she spoke like she was half asleep.

Alice pulled her toward the door.

"He didn't do nuthin'," she said. "He didn't get a chance. Now come on."

Dorothy took a few steps on her own. She buckled and grabbed Alice for support.

"I got you," Alice said. "It's okay, I got you." She walked them to the door. As Dorothy stepped outside onto the front step, Alice turned suddenly and looked down the hallway. Rabbit's black bag, the one from the back of the toilet, was still sitting on the floor near where he'd knocked Alice out.

"Wait here," she said. She ran past the living room, down the hall to the bathroom and scooped the bag up in her hands. There were syringes on the table in the bathroom in a little white box. On the way back she grabbed the clothes Rabbit had dug out for her. She handed the hoodie to Dorothy. "Put this on," she said. As Dorothy was pulling the sweater over her head Alice grabbed the syringes and stuffed them deep into her pocket.

Dorothy pulled the sweater down and then inspected the length. The sweater was at least two sizes too big, but it had a big poison symbol on the front, just above the pouch. Dorothy put the hood up and looked at Alice.

"Beautiful," Alice said. "Now let's get out of here. I got his keys."

"Off with your head," Rabbit muttered, and Alice stopped dead where she stood. Dorothy carried on like she hadn't heard him.

"What did you just say?" Alice said, standing over him.

"Alice come on," Dorothy said. "He didn't say anything. Let's go. I think I hear the cops."

Alice pointed the gun at Rabbit's head. "Do it," she said, but it wasn't her voice. It was the Hater's.

"You got a bad secret," Rabbit bubbled. "You're gonna have to kill me or I'm gonna kill you."

"Alice!" Dorothy cried. She reached out and grabbed Alice's arm and pulled the girl toward the door. They made their way out to the street and jumped into Rabbit's car. Alice sat behind the driver's seat.

"He was talkin," Alice said slowly. "He said he was gonna kill me."

"No he wasn't," Dorothy said. "*You* were."

"Do up your seat belt," Alice said. When the buckle snapped into place, Alice fired the engine, and they pulled away from the curb. Dorothy watched Rabbit's grandmother's house in the rearview mirror until Alice turned a corner. Then she buried her head in her hands and cried.

Chapter 16.

They drove for a while, not talking, Alice seething behind the wheel. Her head felt like a giant, pulsing bruise. The blood on her face felt like syrup on her skin, a distracting irritant. The Hater was mumbling somewhere in the corner of her mind, and that was also distracting.

Dorothy had her face buried in the sleeves of the sweater she was wearing. She hadn't looked up since they left Rabbit's house. She was turned away from Alice, curled up against the passenger door. Occasionally she let out a whimper or a little sob; Alice would have assumed her asleep otherwise. *Or dead.*

Alice turned on the radio to fill silence. The song was *Prison Sex* by Tool, and she flicked it off after the first chorus. There was a gas station on the right side of the road and Alice pulled into it. She skipped past the gas bar and went around to the side of the building. There was a rusted and broken air machine for pumping tires and two steel blue doors marked as bathrooms. In the space between the doors was a little white and blue sign politely requesting that those wishing to use the bathroom facilities would need to track down an attendant and get the keys.

"Wait here," Alice said. She looked at her bloodied, puffy face in the mirror and decided there was no use attempting to hide it. "I'll get the keys. Then we can wash up a bit."

Dorothy didn't respond, and after a moment of silence Alice shut the door and walked into the gas station.

Thankfully it was empty. She threw the glass door open and was hit with the smell of hot coffee and chemical cleaners. The store was a big blue and white rectangle lit by yellow striplights that flickered on unsteady power. There were cockroaches inside them; they fluttered and scrabbled on the plastic covers. Near the coffee machines and the slushie dispensers was a rack of fruit, blackened and rotting. Lazy flies droned in the updraft of two industrial sized fans hanging from the ceiling. The fan blades looked like they were coated in shit, and they were spattering the walls with filth. There was an attendant behind the counter, but his face was covered with smoke.

Alice looked around, confused. *What the fuck is going on here?*

"Can I help you?" the attendant said. Alice blinked, and the smoke was gone. The store was clean and bright.

It was a mistake, she thought. *I was confused.*

The attendant balked when their eyes met. "Jesus *Christ*. What happened?" He was tall and thin, and had the dark eyes of a stoner. Video games, pot and pizza.

Alice knew the type. *Men my age were all boys still.* "I fell off my bike and landed on my face," she lied. "It's worse than it looks. Hurts like a bitch." She'd screwed that up. Gotten it backwards. The clerk didn't seem to notice though, so she didn't bother correcting herself.

"I'll call an ambulance if you want," the clerk said. They'll be here in like five minutes probably. The hospital isn't that far away."

"No thanks," Alice said. "Four hundred bucks for them to tell me to be more careful next time and give me a band aid? I just need the keys to the washroom so I can clean up."

"You got it," the clerk said. "We have bandages in aisle two there, beside the motor oil and stationary."

Alice walked to the section containing pharmacy supplies. From the rows of cold medicine, lip balm and energy supplements she grabbed two tubes of *Polysporin*, a roll of gauze, and a small box of rubber bandages. She also grabbed two Cokes and a bag of chips. When she got to the counter she checked her pockets and realized she had no money. *These are Rabbit's clothes, that's why. Everything I own is in the hospital still.* "Ahh, shit. I think I have some cash in the car."

"It's alright," the clerk said. "Just take it. Go get cleaned up."

"Really?"

"Yeah," the clerk said. My boss is a fuckin' prick anyway. I don't give a shit about this job; I'm going to school. And you look like you might need your cash for more important shit."

"Thanks," Alice said. She even managed a smile.

"Don't mention it," he said. As Alice left the store, he added, "I hope whoever did that to you is lying in a ditch somewhere."

Alice went back out to the car. She knocked on Dorothy's window and got the girl moving. She dropped the Cokes and chips into the passenger seat and kicked the door shut, then went over and opened the bathroom door for Dorothy. The room was a small concrete cube illuminated by a flickering yellow light. It was clean, though, with a white sink and toilet along one wall and a sign on the other.

ANY DAMAGE TO PREMISES WILL RESULT IN CHARGES BEING LAID.

"Friendly," Alice said. Dorothy stepped into the bathroom and Alice slammed the door shut. It automatically locked the moment it closed. Alice stripped off her clothes, but Dorothy stood mute. Watching.

"Come on," Alice said. She had already taken her shirt off and was in the middle of undoing her pants. She stopped when she noticed Dorothy wasn't moving. "What's wrong? If you're shy, I can turn around."

Dorothy scowled at her. She crossed her arms. Her eyes wandered down to Alice's breasts and then she looked away.

"Okay," Alice said. She stepped very close to the girl. "It's alright." her voice was a whisper. "Here, lift your arms up."

Dorothy stared at Alice for a moment, as though she was trying to decide if she was walking into a trap or not. Then she relented and lifted her arms. Alice pulled the sweater up over her head. Dorothy immediately covered herself again. Alice smiled.

"Now I'm just going to get a little warm water," Alice said. "It's going to be okay, really. I've had my ass kicked before. Rabbit tried to do something to you, but you have to remember that he *didn't* do it. You're okay now." She opened the gauze with her teeth, ran a part of it under the steaming water in the sink, and then applied it to Dorothy's face.

She closed her eyes and sighed and the heat touched her skin. Alice moved slowly, allowing the hot water to do the work so she wouldn't have to scrub the girl's flesh. Dorothy's face was badly bruised, but not as bad as Alice's own face.

She's soft. She's not used to being hit by men. It was possible that Dorothy had *never* been hit by a man before. Judging by how the girl froze in terror in the doorway while Alice and Rabbit were fighting, Alice thought it was possible Dorothy had never even been in a fight before today. And now here she was, standing quietly and biting her bottom lip while Alice wiped blood off the freckle-kissed skin of her face.

Alice felt Dorothy's hands on her hips. She responded by wiping the blood from around Dorothy's lips. The girl sighed and leaned in to Alice's touch. Their breasts touched; Alice felt the heat of her body as she leaned close. Under the metal scent of blood Dorothy smelled like lavender and poppies.

Dorothy planted a kiss on Alice's lips.

"Stop," Alice said, smiling. "I'm covered in blood."

Dorothy looked into her eyes, her emerald irises blazing. "I don't care." She brushed her lips against Alice once, and then again, before opening her mouth and licking the girl's bottom lip.

They kissed like that, mouths open, tongues dancing, and Alice tried to wipe the blood from her mouth but eventually gave up. Dorothy's hands were everywhere. They grabbed at Alice's hips and breasts; she traced lines with her knuckles across Alice's belly. She ran her fingertips down Alice's spine, across her ribs, up under her chin and over her neck. They held each others' faces and Alice ran her tongue along Dorothy's chin, down across her neck and shoulders.

Finally Alice moaned and withdrew. She bit her lip and wiped the blood from around Dorothy's mouth.

"You look like a clown," Alice said.

"We both do," Dorothy said. "You have blood from your nose to your chin."

Alice checked herself in the mirror. She looked like she'd been washing her face in strawberries. She clucked her tongue, ran the water extra hot and soaked the guaze before using it to scrub her face clean. She sipped from the tap and spit bloody water back into the sink.

"It's disgusting," Alice said.

"Thanks," Dorothy said, miffed.

"Not you," she said, playfully elbowing Dorothy in the side. The girl responded by cupping her hands under the tap and bringing hot water to her face. She scrubbed herself clean with her fingers, and then wiped her face on the hoodie they'd taken from Rabbit's house.

Once they were both clean Alice applied *Polysporin* to both their wounds. Dorothy received a bandage across the top of her nose. Alice put one on a cut under her eye, but it wouldn't stay put and she ended up rolling the bandage into a ball and flicking it into a corner of the bathroom. Dorothy's eye was in bad shape, but when the swelling went down it would be fine again. The bruise followed the hollow of her eye to the line of her nose and halfway down her cheek.

"What do we do now?" Dorothy said as she got dressed. "I don't want to spend all night in here."

"Now," Alice said, smiling, "we go spend some of Rabbit's cash on a motel room. I figure he owes us, right?"

"Can we eat too?" Dorothy asked, rather sheepishly. "I'm starving."

"Of course," Alice said. She ruffled the girl's hair impulsively and Dorothy made a sour face.

"Can we have cheeseburgers?"

"We can have whatever you want," Alice said. "We can *do* whatever you want."

Dorothy leaned up and planted a kiss on Alice's lips.

"I like the sound of that," she said.

The girls walked arm in arm out of the bathroom a little while later, shivering in the cool air but happy. Their arrival caught the amused stares of several young guys getting gas. Dorothy caught their eyes and smiled flirtatiously and Alice laughed.

"Even all banged up your hot as hell," she said, and kissed Dorothy's cheek. They got in their car, Alice started it up and hit the gas, and the two of them were on their way.

The black bag from Rabbit's toilet was at Dorothy's feet. She flicked on the car radio then reached down and scooped it up in her hands. She looked over at Alice and motioned for her to open it.

"Go ahead," Alice said. "You be in charge of seeing how rich we are, I'll be in charge of the driving."

"Deal," Dorothy said. She ripped into the bag with her fingers and tore it open along the side. Her face lit up. She clucked her tongue, then reached into the bag and pulled out a wad of folded twenty dollar bills. "Holy shit!"

"Looks like we're in business," Alice said, and then she laughed. "How much?"

"I dunno," Dorothy said. "Like three hundred bucks maybe?"

"Check the bag again," Alice said.

"Umm..." Dorothy said, the smile on her face replaced with a puzzled, slightly cautious look. She pulled the black bag away so the contents were more visible. "Alice?"

Alice looked over and her smile suffered a stroke; it melted into a frown.

"Shit," she said through her teeth. Dorothy was holding what looked like a block of powdered cinnamon wrapped tightly in cellophane. It was a perfect rectangular brick, two pounds or so. The bag wasn't full of money. At least, not the kind of money Alice and Dorothy could easily spend on a motel room. It was filled with dangerous money. Blood money. The kind that could get them both killed if they weren't careful about it. The brick caused the back of Alice's brain to itch slightly, the soft whisper of a warm lover calling her back to bed.

"What is it?" Dorothy asked again.

"It's junk," Alice finally said, forcing her eyes back onto the road. "Heroin."

Chapter 17.

Rabbit came back to the world with a pounding headache and the taste of blood. He lay on his back, on the floor, not moving, as reality pushed itself out of the dark and slowly came to the forefront. The bottom half of his face was numb and sticky. He could feel the electric bite of exposed nerves in his mouth, cracked and chipped teeth whining and threatening to erupt in screams. He ran his tongue over the sharpest parts of his mouth, his heart sinking as he felt each splinter. The shattered bits in his mouth were like the candy shell of broken M&M's. He resisted the urge to bite down. He was afraid to bring his splintered teeth together; afraid of the ball of pain humming in there. He opened his eyes, wincing at the influx of unwelcome light. He brought his hand up and felt the numb, sticky parts of his face. There was a metallic smell in the room, like live wires and ozone. There was blood.

My jaw might be broken. The ceiling of his Momma's house came slowly into focus, and he lay there for a while staring at the cracks in the cheap paint. He frowned when the image of Alice coming at him with the lid off the back part of the toilet danced across his memory. He'd never seen that look on a woman before. Pure, chaotic rage.

She killed someone. Like an idiot he'd nearly blurted it out when she had that gun on him. The freezer gun. *I* am *an idiot. I should have never left them alone out here. I should have kicked her in the face the moment she walked through the door.* He was actually lucky to be alive, if he thought about it.

That thing with the brown haired girl had been a mistake. He shouldn't have tried to fuck her. Not when he didn't know if Alice was awake or not. His stupid rage had gotten the best of him. She'd just looked so fucking useless. *Just wanted to make sure she knew I'm the boss.* He ran his fingers through his hair but it hurt and he stopped. And then he remembered the black bag he'd grabbed out of the toilet.

He sat up. Nausea and dizziness met him halfway. He closed his eyes until the wave passed. Slowly. He mustn't rush it. He grabbed the table for support. He braced his other hand on his knee. He got up on one shaky leg. He was standing now. Good. *I can stand, at least.* He took a few steps on his rubber legs, found the hall, and braced himself against the wall. A picture of Dali's melting clocks leapt free of the hook as he passed; it crashed to the ground behind him. Glass splintered and spilled across the floor. *Old Grammy would have liked that. She always hated that picture.*

He couldn't see into the bathroom yet. He was blind with pain. It didn't matter though. That blond whore and her skittish friend had taken the bag, he was sure of it. He'd used it for bait, to buy some time, and now it was gone. The blood and slivered candy coated bits of teeth weren't enough to mask the sour tang of shit in his mouth. He owed a lot of money on that bag. *I am an idiot*, he thought again.

He reached the bathroom and a quick glance around confirmed what he knew was true. The lid off the back of the toilet was missing. There was water and blood on the floor from his fight with Alice. *I should have gone to the freezer first.* But he hadn't gone for the gun because he'd never seen Alice as a threat before she pulled his own frozen gun on him.

The strange thing was that he actually thought he was doing her a favour when he dropped her at the hospital. She had to know he couldn't stay there with her; he'd given her the drugs. But Alice hadn't seen it that way. She'd seen another betrayal from another man in her life. There was a long list of them now, Rabbit had no doubt. He wondered if the little brunette was Alice's lover now. If she'd given up on men forever.

Shit.

Alice had been his friend, hadn't she? He always thought so. As good of friends as they could be under the circumstances. Rabbit liked to think that he and Alice had crossed some kind of line that went past the usual dealer and user relationship. They'd been close. He'd showed her things. Like where he'd stashed his backup gun, just in case shit ever went down when she was in the house.

He walked back to the living room, being careful to avoid the glass from his poster. He grabbed his smokes off the table. He plunked down on the couch. He popped a smoke into his mouth, flicked his lighter and took a drag. In response, his teeth shrieked in pain, and Rabbit pulled the bloody stick from his lips.

"*FUCK!*" He mashed the smoke in the ashtray. He cupped the green glass in his hands and spit a bloody wad into the bed of ashes. When he breathed out the ashes caught the air and puffed out around him. His teeth glittered back at him like tiny bits of yellow pearl. He thought of the stripped meat look of a dog bone.

Twenty thousand dollars. Those bitches had taken it all. Rabbit was a business man; he had people who depended on him on both sides of the ladder. He answered to his connections. He answered to the junkies who came to bang and pretend to be his friend. But he'd convinced those Mexican fucks to trust him with more this time, and now he was out a whole lot of money. And if Alice started selling it before he had a chance to cut it again, he'd be out twice as much. Forty thousand. *Fuck*.

Alice wasn't a heavy user. She still had a brain. She wasn't particularly bright when it came to Mr Brown though, and she might just as easily kill herself as kill someone else. She had high octane shit. Not pure, by any stretch of the imagination, but not some bullshit baby powder mix that you'd have to shoot a full grain of to get high. A grain would kill her. And she wouldn't even know how much that was.

Rabbit touched his teeth with the tip of his tongue. The exposed nerves were like nine volt batteries in his mouth. They sent a charge up inside his face and made his nose twitch. He coughed and whimpered, rubbed his face with his hands and they came away bloody. He snorted blood and smoke. He looked over at the television and sighed. His head was killing him. It felt like his brain was about to burst out of his face. A wave of nausea passed. He had to get his fucking shit together. He had to find those cunts before the Mexicans came looking for their cash.

But first he had to get rid of the lightning show in his mouth.

Rabbit reached down under the couch and felt around until his fingers closed on a cool metal box. It was an old cigarette tin he'd picked up years ago during a promotion. Back when smoke companies were still allowed to advertise to Average Joes and before they'd lost all their ad money in class action lawsuits to dying smokers. It was bound in yellow and green rubber bands. The top of the box had a sticker of a skeleton smoking a long tipped cigarette and sporting an oversized top hat. Rabbit thought the skeleton might have been *Slash* from his Guns N' Roses days, but he wasn't sure.

He pulled the bands off the box and popped it open. There were bags of dope, a lighter, new unopened syringes, his baby spoon from when his momma fed him by hand (and wouldn't she be proud of her son for using *that* particular heirloom to cook junk), and a tightly wound bundle of Q-tips. Everything a growing boy needed to blast his brains out.

He didn't need the blast though. He just needed enough to turn the lightning spikes in his broken teeth into warm fuzzies. He needed to keep enough of his head so he could figure out how the fuck he was going to find Alice.

He scooped up a bag of dope and placed a chunk of heroin about half the size of his little fingernail in the baby spoon. The pale brown powder broke apart easily enough and he pushed it around on the spoon to even it out. There was a half a beer sitting on the coffee table, but he was afraid if he used it as mix he'd end up sleeping on the floor. Instead he pursed his lips, forming suction in his closed mouth and drawing blood out of the wounds left by his broken teeth. Then he pushed the blood to the front of his mouth with his tongue and very carefully spit into the spoon. He stirred it with his baby finger. The mixture of blood, spit, and drug turned black on the spoon. Sticking the finger in his mouth caused a small lightning bolt to hammer along his jaw and he winced accordingly. His finger tasted bitter and bloody.

Rabbit carefully put the spoon down on the table and gabbed a cotton swab out of his kit. Then he picked up his lighter and warmed the bloody rig. It bubbled for just a moment, and then he put the lighter down and dropped the cotton swab into it. The cotton soaked up the contents of the spoon and became a dull, reddish brown colour. *It looks like a partially deflated eyeball,* he thought. *I'm gonna have to remember that one.*

He stuck a clean syringe into the cotton ball and drew the rig. The cotton was more than just a gross-looking way for him to pull heroin into a syringe; it was a filter used to keep particles out of the bloodstream. From the look of the cotton swab, there were a lot of them. Rabbit counted flecks of broken enamel among the more usual impurities that came from heroin use. He slapped his arm to bring up a vein. He followed it with his finger to make sure it was strong enough to hold a syringe. He wasn't sure what saliva might do to his blood, but he was sure the blood in the syringe itself wouldn't do anything harmful. All the same, he needed a stable vein to take the shot. He found it, as always.

The needle slid in smooth, with practiced ease. Rabbit was a regular user himself, but he also fixed rigs for a lot of his customers; party girls like Alice and college kids who were sick of spending all their tuition on junk they smoked or snorted. New heroin users getting onto the needle could get blasted for less than it cost to buy a cup of coffee. Unfortunately that didn't last. Rabbit knew those kids would be back to spending their tuition cheques before long, unless they somehow managed to kick (unlikely) or overdosed and died (probably) with cash in the bank still (almost never).

Rabbit wasn't here to judge though. People did what they want. That was the great fucking thing about being alive. You got to choose what kind of directions your life went. If you wanted to be a slave to the buck, you were welcome to it. But Rabbit wasn't part of the rat race, he was in a different hole altogether. And something big was going to happen in his future, he could tell. All he had to do was look at his watch and he could see it, plain as the nose on his face. *A nose with little arms for a moustache, swinging wildly while his eyes rocked back and forth like one of those black cat clocks...*

...what was he thinking about? He'd lost his train of thought for a moment. It was all good though, because another train was going to come along sooner or later. He didn't have to worry about being late, he lived in the city. And though the city was full of demons and monsters, there was one thing you could always count on: You could never be *too* late for anything, could you? There was always another one coming along.

Rabbit shook his head. He was drifting. He looked down at the syringe in his arm and giggled. There was a small crust of blood forming around the entry point, and a long thin line of it had dried to his arm. How long had he been sitting here? It didn't matter, someone had pushed the plunger on the syringe all the way in. He felt warm and snuggly and safe, and the room smelled like blood and baby powder and burning electronics. The door was open. The sun had just about set, and it was a beautiful blue-gray outside. He had to find Alice and Dorothy, but there was time for that. That was the great thing about living in the city. There was always time for everything.

Chapter 18.

Dorothy stared at Alice as she drove. "Well?" she said finally.

It was clear Alice was doing her best to ignore the girl. "Well what?" She glanced at Dorothy for an instant and then back at the road. Her blue eyes looked black under the reflected glare of the streetlights.

"*Well what*?" Dorothy repeated. "Well what do we do now?"

"Now we get you some cheeseburgers, and we find a hotel room. *That's* what we do now."

"Alice." She pushed the bag toward Alice's face. "This looks like a lot of dope. Isn't it a little dangerous?"

"Naww," Alice said. "Rabbit will hardly notice it's gone. Put it down. People can see it."

"You're lying."

"Am I?" Alice said.

"How much is this worth?"

Alice looked at Dorothy, then at the opiate shield in her hands. She shook her head. Then she reached over and pushed the brick back into Rabbit's bag. "It's a lot, okay?"

"*How much*?" Dorothy repeated.

"I honestly don't know," Alice said.

Tell her, the Hater said.

She didn't want to. She really wasn't sure of the value, to be perfectly honest. She had a thought that it might be worth quite a lot. It was just a feeling though.

Tell her.

No.

You're so useless, darling.

No.

"*Alice!*" Dorothy shouted.

Alice blinked, saw the red light out of the corner of her eye just as she passed under it. She slammed on the breaks, but the car was moving too fast and slid into the intersection. Alice straightened the wheel and pumped the gas, then floored it. The cab of the car lit up for a moment to the sound of shrieking tires and angry horns from other cars.

"*OH FUCK YOU!*" Alice shouted. Her face collapsed in a snarl.

"*...the hell!*" Dorothy said. "Are you crazy? You could have killed us!"

"I would not," Alice said. "Don't be so fuckin' dramatic all the time."

Dorothy's eyes bulged like she was choking on a toffee. Her mouth flapped open, and then she shut it. After a moment her fish-look was replaced by black hurt, and she sank back into her seat. "Go to hell." The bag of heroin was still in her hands, and now she threw it to the floor like it was a lump of dogshit.

The girls rode in silence for a while. The car seemed to be in two distinct temperatures: Ice cold on Dorothy's side and seething hot on Alice's. She could feel the heat of her anger spewing up from her chest and spilling over her forehead. She smelled garlic and onions (*armpits*) and thought of something her father might have cooked when she was younger. Hot chicken soup, spilling up over her face and into her eyes. She could taste it. It tasted like body odour. *That's right, be a good girl. Drink it all up. Sooo goooood....*

Push the gas pedal down as far as it'll go, the Hater said. *Go! do it! Betcha can't jerk the wheel into oncoming traffic. We'll make a game of it. Undo your seatbelts and see which one of you flies further. Windshield Longjump. Keep your arms out in front of you and you'll win, I bet. You're a lot taller than she is.*

Lights danced in her eyes. Was it that easy? Windshield Longjump definitely sounded like something she could win. Dorothy would completely suck at it. She was wearing her seat belt, for Christ's sake. *Wait.*

What am I even thinking about? I'm not seriously going to jerk the wheel into oncoming traffic, am I? What the hell was wrong with me? She needed to stop for a moment. She needed to catch her bearings. There was a blank spot on the shoulder of the road up ahead, and Alice pulled the car over toward it. She needed to clear her head for a minute or two. She slowed down and pulled over, then put the car in park and let out a long sigh. "I can't drive anymore," she said finally. "Any chance you can take over?"

"Why," Dorothy said. "What's wrong with you?"

"You wouldn't believe it," Alice said.

Tell her, the Hater said. *Tell her, then bite her throat open like a fuckin' tiger. Look at her vanilla flesh. I bet it tastes as good as it looks.*

"Whatever," Dorothy said. She popped her door open and went around to the driver's side. She knocked impatiently on the window.

Alice opened the door and looked up at her. In the cool evening air she seemed backlit by Heaven's gaze. She had a rainbow halo around her head and her eyes sparkled like emerald jewels.

"What the hell," Dorothy said. "You want me to drive or not?"

"You're so beautiful right now," Alice said. She reached out to touch Dorothy's hand, but the girl pulled away.

"Whatever," Dorothy said, rolling her eyes. She looked away, shaking her head. She was fighting a smile and losing. She moved her hand back so Alice could touch it. "Just shut up and let me drive."

Alice got out of the car. She leaned into Dorothy's body as the girl moved past her.

"Get out of here," Dorothy said playfully. "I'm mad, and you're a huge icky jerk."

"I *am*," Alice said. The air was cool and damp, and a few deep breaths seemed exactly what she needed.

Dorothy sat behind the wheel and shut the door. Alice moved along the back of the car in a series of yellow Polaroid shots that left her dizzy and panting. She kept one hand on the car to keep her bearing, and when she got to the passenger side she dropped into the bucket seat. It was still warm. Dorothy's warmth, and it felt good.

"You alright?" Dorothy said.

"Perfect," Alice said. "Let's get some cheeseburgers. And beer. I know a good place to crash. It's cheap. *They rent by the hour.*"

Dorothy laughed. "Oh baby. Sounds classy."

"They know me by name," Alice said, smiling.

"Slut," Dorothy said. She slapped Alice's leg. She drummed the steering wheel with both hands. "*Okay!* I have no *effing* idea where I'm going, so we're probably gonna get way lost."

"Burger King!" Alice cried. "Take a left soon."

"Gee, thanks," Dorothy said. "Soon hey?"

Grab the wheel, the Hater said cheerfully. *It's not too late. You can still beat her at Windshield Longjump. Look at her face, it's oozing blood already, you won't even know the difference. If you love her, kill her. She's going to betray you one day.*

Alice put her hand to her head and gritted her teeth."We need music," she said suddenly, reaching over and cranking on Rabbit's stereo. A wall of angry, muddy guitars hit the girls mid-stroke as Korn lamented their fucked up lives. Dorothy banged her head and threw up her devil horns. Alice screamed and growled every word. If the Hater was saying anything now, Alice couldn't hear him

"*Turn here!*" Alice shouted over the music.

"*Okay!*" Dorothy shouted back.

Burger King gradually appeared on their left side slick and well lit and inviting among the dreary rows of commercial buildings, video stores, liquore shops, and gas stations. Alice pointed to the drive through. The girls screamed their orders over Metallica's punishing guitar riffs and paid for their meals out of the rolled up ball of cash.

They made a quick stop at the liquor store across the street, grabbed a case of beer and a forty-pounder of Vodka, and then Alice directed Dorothy toward the motel. A short time later they were pulling into a large empty parking lot. The sign over the office was a large crescent moon with the words BLUE MOON underneath, and Dorothy shook her head, smiling. Mudvayne screamed that they were everything and nothing, and Alice had to agree.

Dorothy reached over and turned down the music. "I think I saw this place in a horror movie. A really bad one."

"You might have seen it in a porno, actually," Alice said. "*For serious.*"

"Eww!" Dorothy cried. She threw her hands up in front of her face as if to try and keep them clean.

Alice laughed. "Yeah there's a couple college guys who make movies down here with *rentals*. They drive hummers, so I guess they're making money at it."

"Hummers," Dorothy chuckled. "How fitting."

"I know, right?"

The car squeaked as they pulled to a stop in front of the manager's office. "I'll just be a second," Alice said. She started getting out of the car.

"You want me to come with?" Dorothy said.

"Umm...naww, I'll get it. You keep the car warm."

"Okay, good luck!" Dorothy said.

"Thanks."

"*Don't get any porn rooms!*" Dorothy shouted after Alice slammed the door. She turned and gave Dorothy a double thumbs up.

The door chimed when Alice opened it. There was a skinny guy in a Charlie Brown shirt sitting behind a wall of yellow panel board and Plexiglas. The man had his feet up in front of a small television and was sucking the barbeque sauce off a chicken bone. A plate of greasy wings sat in front of him, and the smell made Alice's mouth water.

"Hey Steve," Alice said, smiling. "Busy as always I see."

"*Denise,*" the man said, licking his lips. He grabbed a paper towel and began the monumental task of getting the barbeque sauce off his fingers.

"The one and only," Alice said. She was different people to different men. To this guy, in this place where she sometimes brought men when the weather was bad, she was Denise. Just another hooker looking for someplace warm and out of the rain for a few minutes.

"*Whatchu* need, the usual?"

The usual, for Denise, was one of the front rooms for an hour or so. Twenty bucks, cash, which went right into Steve's pocket. A couple times he'd saved them up until he had sixty bucks and then handed them back to Denise. Then she'd fuck him, and pretend his weird, banana shaped penis was the hottest thing she'd ever seen.

"Not tonight," Alice said. "I actually need a room for the next couple days."

"Oh yeah?" Steve said. He eyed her from behind the Plexiglas and reached for a cigarette. His eyes darted across Alice's bruises like a mosquito. "Anything special?"

"No," Alice said. "Well, actually, I just got out of the hospital. Had a bad party a couple nights ago, and my friend and I need a place to crash for a bit."

"Yeah, you look like shit," Steve said. "I'm not just sayin' that because I'm your friend."

Is that what we are? Alice thought, but didn't say. A spider web had begun to creep along the edges of the glass, framing Steve in a delicate portrait frame. Black shadows skittered around the edges of her vision.

I wonder if you could pull his face through that little slot in the glass, the Hater said. *Think you could get at him if you offered to blow him?*

"So you need a room?" Steve said. "What, single?"

"Umm...Double, I think," Alice said.

"Double hey?" Steve said, as though he didn't believe his ears. "Alright then. It's fifty bucks a night. How many you want?"

"Better go three nights," Alice said. She pulled the roll of cash and started counting tens and twenties off it, against the counter and out of sight from Steve. Fuzzy black pipe cleaner spiders danced across the money and onto her hands, and she shook them off only to watch them fall to the ground in lazy somersaults. They hit the floor with the sound of fat raindrops hitting a car windshield.

"*Hunnert and fitty bucks*," Steve said, and smiled. "*Plus tip*."

Alice looked up at him and regarded his predatory look with her best hooker's smile. "Only the tip?"

"Oh, you're a bad bitch," Steve said, molesting his cigarette. He blew hot ugly smoke against the Plexiglas and his smile widened, revealing teeth the colour of old ivory.

"You have no idea," Alice said. She slid the cash through the open slot where the glass met the table.

Steve grabbed it up, gave it a quick count, and then grabbed a key from under the desk. "Room 108," he said, sliding the key toward her. "Don't wreck the place, and don't fall asleep with a lit cigarette."

"No worries," Alice said. "Thanks baby!"

"Anytime, sexy," Steve said as Alice turned and walked out the front door. It chimed as she passed. Steve's eyes never left her ass until the door closed and he was alone again.

Alice walked around to the passenger side of the car and hopped in. Immediately Dorothy reached over and turned the music down.

"Got it," Alice said. "Room One-oh-Eight."

"Was it a porn room?" Dorothy said, making a scared little girl face.

Alice laughed. "Yeah. Big orgy in there this afternoon. Probably still smells like cocks and rubbers."

"Eww!" Dorothy chirped. "You're so nasty!"

"You don't know the half of it," Alice said, and had a moment of Deja-vu.

Dorothy pulled out of her spot, drove over to a spot marked *108*, painted in yellow road paint on a short concrete divider and parked the car. Alice busied herself collecting their supplies. She grabbed the heroin off the floor last and stuffed it in her pocket. Dorothy laced their arms together and they walked to their room. Alice popped the key and flicked on the light, and held the door open for Dorothy so she could go first.

"Wow," Dorothy said, kicking off her shoes. "It's like the seventies never ended for this place."

"Yeah, pretty awesome, hey?" Alice said.

The room was a mix of cream and orange trim, with a heavy brown carpet. Two identical beds stood side by side in the middle of the room, their brown and orange top covers a perfect match. There were two small night tables beside each bed, sporting ashtrays, menus, and small bulbous lamps with orange covers. It had a vaguely sanitized feel to it, but Alice knew better. These rooms, especially the front rooms overlooking the parking lot, were anything but sanitized. She would be happy if the rooms had been cleaned in the past few weeks. From the stale smell of the air, though, she thought they might be out of luck with that.

"You got a double," Dorothy said, staring at the beds.

"Yeah," Alice said. "I didn't know…what the sleeping arrangements would be."

Dorothy smiled and bit her lip. Stepping up onto her tiptoes she did a little ballerina spin and finished facing Alice. "I guess we'll have to see, won't we?"

"Guess so," Alice said. She tossed the food down on the closest bed, and then kicked the door shut with her foot.

"Let's eat!" Dorothy said.

Chapter 19.

Rabbit didn't hear the door the first time it banged. He was sound asleep on his couch, drifting in a warm opiate bath and dreaming about sparklers running up and down his arms and legs. The second time it banged the spell broke like a golden bubble around him, and he felt himself coming up out of his stupor. It was like standing up after being in a hot tub all afternoon, he could feel cold consciousness stroking his skin and he suddenly wanted nothing more than to sink back into the confines of warm sleep.

"*Yo Rabbit!*"

"*Jesus—fuck is stinks in here—Holy shit!*"

Rabbit slowly opened one lazy eye and rested it on the two large dark figures standing in his living room.

"Rabbit, what the fuck, *niggah?* You get jacked?"

"*Yeah,*" Rabbit said slowly. "*Bitch hit me in the mouf wif the fuckin' thing...*" he waved a hand, dismissing them, and drifted away from the conversation.

"*Torlet lid?* Fuck man, a bitch did you like that?"

"*Yesh,*" Rabbit said. He opened his eyes again. He knew the two men, he realized. Two regulars, Devon and Eazy. Big, strong, healthy looking black men. They were his friends. They'd never hurt him. They were his boys. They worked for him, and he paid well for their services. More often than not, he paid them in drugs. Especially Eazy.

"Jesus man, look at his face," Eazy said. "Hey Rabbit! Are *all* your teeth busted?"

"I *fink* so," Rabbit said. he brought his fingers to his lips. there was dried blood and tooth shards all over the lower half of his face, like broken M&M shells filled with gore and nerve endings. Or eggshells. They kinda felt like a mouth full of eggshells too. "*Yesh, all da front onesh are gone.*" He reached down into the ashtray and pulled his mangled, bloody gold tooth grill out of the ashes, holding it up for them to see.

"That's messed up," Devon said. "Christ I think I'm gonna puke."

"*It was Alish,*" Rabbit said, tossing the dental appliance aside. It rattled on the coffee table and broken teeth came loose. They spilled out around ashes and gold wires, and when they stopped moving they were sitting in little pools of blood like white ants drowning in cherry syrup. "*Her and her little bitch friend did it.*"

"That skinny bitch?" asked Eazy. "You sleepin' or somet'in?"

"*I wash fighting with the other one. Didn't she it comin'.*"

Rabbit took a couple deep breaths. He had to clear his head a bit more if he was going to figure this out. Now that Devon and Eazy were here he could get them to look for the girls. They were basically paid thugs anyway, and he knew he could have them if he promised some free junk.

And he *did* have to get that brick back. Soon. If Alice started dipping into it she might overdose again, and with nobody to help her the best Rabbit could hope for was her death. At worst, she'd end up back in the hospital, and his dope ended up in some precinct lockup while they pushed on those girls about where the brick came from.

Which would lead them to Rabbit's grandma's house."*We need to find thoshe bitches,*" Rabbit said. He quickly rehashed the details of the past few hours, being careful not to mention exactly *how much* heroin the girls had stolen. No sense getting the dogs all worked up over something they couldn't have. When he finished explaining everything, he picked up a cigarette, winced, and then slowly put it down again. "So you in?"

Devon and Eazy looked at each other. "Yeah," Eazy said. "Sure as Christ. Got any idea where you wanna start lookin'?"

Rabbit thought about that. He didn't really know where Alice went when she wasn't at his house. He knew she fucked for money, so she must have had some regular hangouts, but Rabbit didn't normally concern himself with where she went to make a buck. And to be honest, he kind of hadn't *wanted* to know until today. He thought she might have mentioned a room somewhere before, but there was too much fog behind his eyes to recall the conversation exactly. Something about a moon? or the Fall? Full Moon? It made sense, for a flophouse to be named after being bare ass naked with your ass up. *Should have called it the bicycle stand,* he thought. *Bury your head in the sand and stick your ass in the air so you can park your bike between the ass cheeks.*

No, that was stupid. It wasn't the Full Moon. It was something like that though....

"*Hey!*" Devon snapped his fingers in front of Rabbit's face. "Yo, wake up man!"

"I'm awake," Rabbit said. *Am I though? Maybe this is all some stupid dream.* He rubbed his hands on his swollen face but stopped short of his mouth.

"*He's Jesus Juiced,*" Eazy said. "He needs to have a nappy nap."

"Naw," Devon said. "You was mumblin' something about bein' bare assed. What the fuck are you talkin about?"

And suddenly it came to Rabbit, like a lighthouse beam through the fog.

"*Shit!*" he cried. "*My shell phone!*"

He felt his pockets. It wasn't there. He looked around his couch, in the cushions. He started to get up but his legs failed him and he crumpled back into his seat. He cursed his useless state and tried again.

Alice had called him a couple times last week, and if they were lucky enough one of them might have been from her hotel. She went there when the weather was bad. Something Moon something.

"*Where the fuck is it?*" He yelled, and lightning flared in his mouth. He grabbed the side of his face.

"*FAWK*!"

Devon slapped Eazy's chest.

"Call it man," he said.

"*YESH!*" Rabbit barked. "*Call me and we'll lishen for it. Good idea.*"

"'Course it is," Devon said.

Eazy pulled an iPhone out of his pocket, scrolled down his list of numbers and hit a button. Devon and Rabbit stopped dead. Rabbit's ears were pounding in the silence, but a moment later MC Hammer started twittering about how you couldn't touch it. The sound was coming from the hallway.

"Damn," Eazy said.

"*Go get it!*" Rabbit said.

"Why you got this old shit on your phone?" Devon said. He walked into the hall. "Holy shit there's blood all over the place. What the fuck happened over here?"

"*I beat her fuckin ash,*" Rabbit called out. "*But she snuck up on me when I wash gettin wif her friend.*"

Devon reappeared with the phone in his hand.

"You *need* to get rid of this old shit on your phone," he said again.

"*Shut the fuck up,*" Rabbit said. He made a grab for the phone. "*Gimme that.*"

"I'm hangin' up now," Eazy said. "I don't want my gramma showin' up cuz she heard *Hammer* comin' out of your phone." Devon laughed, and the two men bumped fists.

Rabbit ignored them. He was flipping through his call history. Finally, near the end of his call list, the words BLUE MOON MOTEL appeared, and he pointed a finger at Eazy.

"*I got it,*" he said. "*You call, I can barely fuckin' talk. Use your good guy voice. No thug shit.*"

"I'll make them think it's the king of fuckin' England," Eazy said, switching to a mock British accent. "Or Christ on the cross."

"*Just sound like a normal human being.*"

"Now that's impossible," Devon said, and the two men laughed again.

"You got that right," Eazy said.

They're enjoying this too much, Rabbit thought. *If I didn't have a busted face they wouldn't be fucking around this much.*"Get fuckin' serious. You two are about to get bounced out on your ass."

"Alright, alright," Eazy said. He put his hands up in mock surrender.

"Yeah just chillax, boss," Devon said. "You know we good people."

Eazy turned, putting the phone to his ear. With his other hand he motioned the other two men for quiet. "Yes, Hello?" His voice bounced up an octave. All trace of his street accent disappeared. He sounded like he could be selling bibles or vacuum cleaners. "Is this the Blue Moon Hotel? It is. *Good.* Would you be able to tell me if a pretty little blond thing is down there?"

Eazy listened for a moment, then laughed. "Oh I'm sure. No we are supposed to meet up a little later and she said she was going to be there, but I forgot which room. I know I should really learn to write this stuff down. Name? Yeah, it's Alice."

Eazy grimaced in Rabbit's direction, and started snapping his fingers frantically.

"Last Name?" he said in his false voice, staring hard at Rabbit.

"*Pleashansh*," Rabbit mumbled, and a line of bloody drool ran down his chin. "Shit! *Pleashansh. PLEASANSH.*"

Eazy mouthed the word *WHAT*? He looked at Devon, but the other man just shook his head.

"What did you say?" he said to Rabbit.

"*PLEASHANSH.*" Rabbit said again, louder this time.

"Presents," Eazy said, smiling. "Yeah, Alice Presents."

"NO!" Rabbit started to yell then immediately put his hand to his mouth.

Eazy looked at him. "One second sir," he said, then mouthed *WHAT?*

Rabbit began spelling the letters out.

"*P...L...E...S...E...N...T...S. Pleashansh.*"

"Pleasance," Devon said.

"Sorry," Eazy said. I must have read that wrong. "Alice Pleasance." He cupped his hand over the phone. "He's just checking the roster."

"Good," Devon said. "He better not take all damn day."

Rabbit looked down at his rig for a lustful moment, then closed the tin and grabbed his smokes again. This time he had the smoke in his hands when he remembered how much it hurt to smoke.

"Yeah," Eazy said. "Yeah, I'm still here."

Chapter 20.

They ate cheeseburgers and licked the grease off their fingers. When they were finished eating, Dorothy set the empty food bag up on the dresser against the wall, at the foot of the beds. They took turns with their rolled up cheeseburger wrappers trying for baskets and discovered they were both terrible shots. So much so that finally Alice got up and slammed her wrappers into the bag and then tossed the entire mess into a small garbage can sitting on the floor by the television.

When she turned around Dorothy was watching her. The expectant stare unnerved her a little. Not because she didn't like seeing that jubilant smile on Dorothy's face, but because her mood had changed with a frightening suddenness that left Alice breathless. Was this the same girl who had been cowed into submissiveness by an attempted rape just a few hours before? It couldn't be. Yet here she was, smiling, joking, and acting like nothing had happened. Alice herself was reeling from her fight with Rabbit. Her face was on fire, and the throb of the muscles beneath her skin was an echo of her heart. But not Dorothy. Even though she was sporting a similar purple bruise on her face and her nose was badly swollen, Dorothy seemed a million miles away from it all.

Why shouldn't she be happy, Alice thought. *She got what she wanted in the Gas Station bathroom. I'm all hers now*. The thought was ugly. Even her inner voice was angry and traitorous. Then she heard cackling in her ears like glass breaking, and she knew it wasn't her voice at all.

"So," she said.

"*So*," Dorothy said, beaming at her.

"That was pretty crazy today," she said quietly. She sat on the bed beside Dorothy.

"Oh my god!" Dorothy said. She was vibrating with her newfound energy. "That was a little more than crazy. That was *way* off the hook. I thought we were going to fuckin' die."

"I wasn't worried," Alice said. "I've known Rabbit a long time. He's no killer." *Not like I am, anyway. I wonder what you'd think if you knew you were sitting beside a monster, sweet thing.*

"If it's one thing I've learned watching T.V., it's that anyone is capable of anything, under the right circumstances. Your old Grandma could kill someone if she had to."

"That's how it is, hey?" Alice said. "I guess television never lies." *What do you know? You know nothing.*

"Well, I'm just saying that people do what they have to so they can survive. I'm sure if someone was trying to kill me I could muster the balls to do something about it."

"Oh yeah?" Alice said coldly. She didn't like the way the conversation had turned. It was too close to reality. Too much like her life.

Scrape her pretty face into that burger bag so we get the fuck out of here.

"I'd blow their head off, or set 'em on fire or something, I don't know," Dorothy said. "Drop a fuckin house on them."

"You're a real bad ass," Alice said. "Stone cold killah."

Dorothy laughed, and her hand slid down Alice's arm and onto her thigh. "Yeah, I'm a tough chick," she said. "Okay, maybe I couldn't kill anybody. But I bet you could. I thought you *did* kill that guy when you hit him with the toilet lid. Holy shit, man. I ain't seen nothing like that."

Kill her. Then kill yourself. Do it, before the Queen finds us and puts our fucking heads on poles.

"Leave me alone," Alice said.

"Oh," Dorothy said. She pulled her hand away from Alice and shifted away from her. "Sorry."

Alice shook her head. "No, it's not—,"

She stopped, closed her eyes, and shook her head gain. "I get migraines sometimes," she said, tapping her temple with her finger. "I kind of feel one now. It feels like I have another person inside me. Banging around in my skull, behind my eyes. smashing pots and pans and blowing a coaches whistle. He's so loud sometimes I can barely stand it."

"*What?*" Dorothy said. "Who?"

"Oh," Alice said, catching herself. "Nothing. I was just making an example. I meant *it*, not he."

Dorothy touched her hand, and Alice immediately laced their fingers together. "Is that why you were in the hospital?" Dorothy said softly.

"No," Alice said. "I overdosed on heroin, I told you that."

"But there is someone in there with you," Dorothy whispered.

Alice smirked. Then the Hater began screaming *FUCKING TELL HER NOW AND THEN CUT HER HEAD OFF! YOU WORTHLESS CUNTY BITCH! CAN'T KEEP SECRETS! SHE'S READING YOUR FUCKING MIND AND ALL SHE HEARS IS ME! ALL SHE HEARS IS–*

"—I just get distracted easily," Alice said. She winced. *How can she not hear this?*

Maybe she can and she's pretending she can't.

The last thought disturbed her, and she immediately pulled away from it.

Dorothy squeezed her hand."Sounds awful. Poor thing." She leaned in and gently kissed Alice's shoulder. Alice turned to her. Their lips touched. Dorothy moaned and breathed cheeseburger breath on her cheek.

Alice's mind flashed on The Mad Hater. He was jumping on a pogo stick on her brain. At the bottom of the pogo stick were square razor blades. Every jump was accompanied by a great whooping shriek and a fountain of blood rising up from the wrinkles in her brain. He got off the pogo stick and began snorting the wrinkles in her brain with a rolled up trillion dollar bill. Rabbit's face was where the Queen should be. He was leering at her and making a cock-sucking motion with her gun.

Christ...where was that gun?

Oopsie, the Hater said.

She stood up suddenly, almost knocking Dorothy over in the process. Their heads kissed with a thunk and a shard of pain.

"*What the hell!*" Dorothy, sat up, rubbing the spot where their heads connected.

"Sorry. *I*...I need to have a shower. My head is killing me. Maybe some hot water will loosen it up."

"Oh," Dorothy said. "Okay. Need someone to wash your back?"

"Maybe next time," Alice said. She grabbed two beers and then showed them to Dorothy. "For the road."

"I'll see if I can track down some Tylenol," Dorothy offered.

"Don't bother. I'll be good. Just need some hot water and a couple cold beers." Alice pressed the beers against her cheek and sighed. "Right, warm beer it is then."

"Holler if you need anything," Dorothy said.

"Will do," Alice said. She retreated to the far side of the room, into a dirty beige bathroom. She shut the door behind her, and put the beers on the floor. She took a deep breath.

"Sure you don't want some aspirin or something?" Dorothy called from the other side of the door.

"I'm fine!" Alice called back. Her hand slid down and clicked the lock on the door. She coughed into her hand to cover the noise. At least, she hoped she covered it.

She picked up a beer and cracked it, then drank half of it in one long pull. Then she walked over to the small dirty sink. It was lined with the usual motel refinery; little packets of sharp smelling soap, a couple ketchup packs filled with shampoo and conditioner. Hand towels the colour of the walls folded and sitting there under the soap, waiting to be used. She turned on the water. There was a mirror over the sink, and she looked up into her own face. It was filthy and haggard and tired looking. She barely recognized herself.

In the other room the television snapped on.

"*She'll eat your mind*," The girl in the mirror said. "She'll find the blue car and the guy with his cock in your ass and his brains all over your clothes, she'll pick them out like maggots on a dog in the hot sun and that will be it. You'll get the fucking chair. You're worthless. She's going to fuck you up because you're nothing to her. Kill her now, or kill yourself."

"Shut the fuck up!" Alice hissed, staring hard at herself. Her mirror-self had taken on a cruel, alien slant, and its mouth twisted into a sideways smile. She watched as the Mirror Alice grew scrabbling, rubbery baby fingers out of her mouth in place of teeth. They scratched bright blood lines into her tongue.

"Yeah," Mirror-Alice said. Her baby finger teeth turned her words to mud and silt. "That's what I thought. You can't do nothing right, can you? That's why I'm taking over this joint. I'm gonna put up blue curtains 'cuz I know it'll remind you of that fucking car."

"You aren't in control of me," Alice said. "You're just a psycho that loves to fuck rabbits."

"*SO ARE YOU!*" Mirror Alice screeched. "Reminds me of when we were little. We *looked* like a rabbit back then, didn't we? All ears and fuckin' teeth. Maybe that's why Daddy and his friends used to come and tuck us in at night. Everyone loves to pet a bunny, right?"

"Shut up," Alice said. "You look like me, but you aren't me. That shit never happened. Those are just your lies."

"I'm *not* you?" Mirror-Alice slammed her hands against the inside of the mirror. It shuddered on its hooks and drywall powder dusted the sink. "I am wearing you like a fucking Halloween costume. *You* look like *me*."

"It's not true." Alice reached for her beer. Her hands were shaking so badly she almost dropped it.

"Oh it is," Mirror-Alice said. "Watch this!" She opened her mouth. At the back of her throat was a solid ball of white flesh. It was engorged and lined with veins. Alice thought of a hard cock sliding into an ass. A crack appeared on the mass near the top of Mirror-Alice's mouth.

Alice swallowed hard. She could feel that mass in her own throat, cutting off her air. It was like swallowing a long sausage. It was like (*COCK IT WAS LIKE COCK GOING DOWN YOUR THROAT OH YES*)

The crack in the flesh sprouted from the roof of Mirror-Alice's mouth and continued as the mass pushed further down her throat toward her lungs. The crack widened. Split. Alice's mouth filled with hot blood. Fly legs erupted from either side of the crack like broken sutures. They were barbed on the end; they reached around blindly before hooking into the soft flesh of Alice's mouth. Then, as one, they pulled.

There was more blood. It was like watching a vagina being born. The barbed legs sank into her cheek, into her teeth. There was pressure back there. Alice gagged. The barbed insect legs pulled her tongue back toward the wound.

And suddenly the wound pulled apart, and sparklers were going off in the bathroom behind Alice. *Or in front of her*. She could no longer tell for sure what side of the mirror she was on. The gash in the back of her throat was filled with a sickly vanilla orb, like a hard boiled egg, slick and shiny and veined with the red bloom of arterial networks. The fly legs curled away from the egg. And then it rolled.

It was no egg, after all.

It was a single, angry red eye. The Hater's eye.

The Hater's Eye.

It blinked.

Alice screamed. *GET IT OUT GET IT OUT GET OHHHHH GODDDDDD GET IT OUT…*

She slammed her mouth shut and clamped both hands over it. She clawed at her face. The open beer flew into the sink where it banged against the steel basin and foamed in the running water.

She had to get it out.

Without thinking she jammed two fingers into her mouth and pushed them as far into the back of her throat as they would go. Her teeth scraped the knuckles on her hand. Her fingernails pushed against something soft, like egg flesh. *It's not an egg. It's not an egg.*

She pushed harder and the resistance against her nails gave way, and then the tips of her fingers were swimming in slime.

There were a series of rapidfire explosions of light and colour and smells behind her eyes, like fireworks mixed with birthday cake and crotch sweat and dogshit. Her ears were ringing, but the magnetic whine was forming words. *My eye…My eye…*

The Mad Hater.

Alice leaned forward and vomited beer and cheeseburgers into the sink. The vomit was viscous and oily; it looked like there were raw eggs mixed in with her supper. *It's eyeball guts*, she thought, staring down at the black and clear globules floating in the burger slime and beer. The scalding tap water was cooking the puke in the sink. The slime turned white. *I was wrong. It is an egg. It's poaching.*

There was a fly leg on Alice's lip, and she spit it into the sink. There was blood in her mouth and her throat was raw where she'd scraped it with her fingernails. Her fingers were red and covered with puke, and her knuckles had been scraped raw from the force of her attack. Movement in the mirror caught her eye and she looked up.

The steam from the heat was fogging the glass, and Mirror-Alice smiled. Her teeth were shards of broken china. Alice recognized them from the tea party. Every tooth was a smiling image of Dorothy waving and holding that stupid fucking dog. Some of them had tornados in the background. Some of them had blue cars.

Alice waved and the steam from the sink suddenly filled the room. Then she staggered over to the toilet and puked bile, cheeseburger and foaming beer. The force of the act packed her nose with vomit, and for a moment she couldn't breathe. She panicked, snorted partially digested hamburger back out of her sinuses and into her throat, setting off her gag reflex again. She vomited a bright stream of rainbow coloured froth into the toilet. The beer and grease smell seemed to be dripping from her pores like hot sweat. Bubbles popped in her ears, and sparkles were dancing on the edge of her vision. She gasped a long, jagged breath, bringing tears to her eyes, coughed more hamburger meat out of her nose, and tried to wipe the tears from her eyes. There was slime all over her hands. She'd had her hands in the toilet.

Now she reached out and grabbed the throttle on the back of the toilet. There was a *woosh* of cold air as the toilet washed away her filth, and Alice was on her knees, hands curled around the toilet seat like a life preserver, her face inches from the streaming ice water. She could smell toilet cleaner, but there was also a lingering, forbidden taint of human waste. She gagged again but caught hold of herself. She ran her tongue along her teeth, collected a puke slime coating and spit it into the toilet. Her face was rippling in the water and she felt a splash of ice on her cheek. Her reflection in the water was alien. As the water calmed Alice saw that it wasn't her at all, it was the Hater. He looked like his face was turned inside out. He smiled up at her and maggots dripped from his teeth. His left eye was a bleeding mess. His eye was deflated, giving him a fiendish, squinting look.

I can have you any time I want, he said quietly, inside her ear. *Just remember that girlie. I'm not in here with you. You're in here with* me.

"You don't own me," Alice whispered. "I'm nobody's whore."

You are. You are everyone's whore. You belong to the world now.

"No. I'm free."

Really? the Hater said. *His voice was crushed glass on her eardrums. Riddle me this, girlie. Where's your gun? We'll see how free you are when the cops match it to the hole in that guy's head.*

"He was...*he raped me*," Alice said, and started to cry.

Shh, pretty plaything, the Hater said. Alice felt him rubbing her head. *We both know you deserved it, didn't you?*

Slowly, Alice nodded. "*Yes*. Yes I did."

It's alright, the Hater said. *I am always with you. Sleep now. Sleep.*

And Alice did.

Chapter 21.

After Dorothy watched Alice retreat to the safe haven of the bathroom, she could only think of one thing: *You've done it again.* All it took was four words and Dorothy's good mood, like a house of cards stacked on the back of a sleeping dog, came crashing down around her.

She hated the thought of Alice being mad at her. The girl was like a magnet; Dorothy could feel it whenever she was near. She was being dragged along with Alice because her heart and her body felt that pull, like a jar of ball bearings, rolling along toward Alice and unable to stop. Tumbleweeds, maybe, but that didn't do her feelings justice. Neither did ball bearings. Ball bearings were too cold. What she felt around Alice was white hot and screaming, and it wouldn't be denied.

She got up and walked over to the door. Waves of Alice's presence tickled Dorothy's senses. Her blond haired beauty was inches away, her perfect body pressed tight against the door in case Dorothy tried to open it. Probably looking at herself in the mirror and thinking *What the fuck have I gotten myself into?*

Dorothy pressed her hand against the door. "You sure you don't need any aspirin or anything?" She said quietly.

"*I'm Fine!*" Alice barked. There was a quick moment of fumbling in the bathroom and then the lock on the door clicked into place. Alice coughed, to cover it up, but the click was louder on *this* side of the door. Everyone knew that.

It was *loudest* in Dorothy's heart.

Dorothy ran her fingers along the painted faux-grain of the wood. The sound of the lock was like a slap in the face. Rejected, she withdrew and walked instead over to the television. Without thinking she flipped it over to the weather channel.

She wasn't allowed to watch it in the Hospital because Dr Weller thought it encouraged her to think about tornados. She still thought, sometimes, when the nurses were busy or when Dr Weller was with a patient. It was good to know which way the wind was blowing. Aunt Emily used to say *it pays to be on your toes*. Growing up in the American Midwest had given Old Aunt Emily a keen nose for the weather. She could tell days before a storm hit that one was on the way. Like most old people, she was equipped with built in barometers and weather detectors: her hips ached, her sinuses acted up, and she would get what she termed *The Terrible Arthritis* in her wrists and hands.

Dorothy had never been so blessed, and so had to rely on the science of the weatherman; Low and high pressure fronts, cyclical weather patterns, prevailing winds. And, as Aunt Emily had sometimes said: *When in doubt, open the window and stick your nose in the air.* The sweet, earthy smell of a tornado was mixed with the yellow stink of brimstone. Aunt Emily wouldn't hear about conflicting pressure systems that funneled topsoil and pollen into the air. A tornado was the work of the devil, through and through.

Auntie Em always laughed at Dorothy's insistence that tornados started on the ground and were flung into the sky by circumstance. *If that was the case,* the old woman said, *there'd be tornados springing up everywhere. I'd be able to grow 'em in my garden.*

But she was wrong. Dorothy had science behind her, and all Untie Em had was a million years of homespun country logic. That was fine if you wanted to find the best fishing holes or you needed to know when to plant your crops. Predicting tornados was a science. Hell, it was even more than that. It was a high *art.*

Dorothy heard Alice muttering something in the bathroom but she couldn't make out the words. She wondered if talking to herself was something Alice did a lot, or whether the stress of the last few days somehow made it worse. The word *crazy* danced across her thoughts, but it was a dirty word that tasted like burnt onions. She pushed it as far back in her brain as she could, until it was grabbed by flying monkeys and disappeared from sight.

The weather man said a warm wet front was coming. Expect rain. Dorothy decided she would go see if she could track down some Tylenol, just in case Alice changed her mind. The woman had saved her life today. She deserved to take it easy. *If that's not love, I don't know what is.*

Dorothy grabbed one of the door keys and stepped outside. The weatherman was right; it was definitely getting warmer, and the wind had picked up noticeably. It was crisp and left her skin tingly. She skipped past the other motel rooms and across the parking lot. The main office was just ahead. It was a bland looking stucco building with large windows and cancerous yellow light seeping out into the night air. She sidestepped a puddle and pulled the door open, and a chime rang in a back room somewhere. Behind two panes of glass was a skinny guy in a Charlie Brown shirt. He was watching television with his feet up. A tray of half-eaten chicken wings was sitting on the counter.

"Hey," he said, looking up. "You need a room?"

"I'm actually here already," Dorothy said. For a moment she misheard him. She could have sworn he'd said *Back so soon*, but of course that didn't make sense because she'd never been there before.

"Oh yeah?" the guy said, sitting up. "Funny, I don't remember seeing you come in." He cocked an eyebrow and was speaking with a fake accent, like he'd just become involved in a racy secret between the two of them.

"My friend got the room for us," Dorothy said. "I just came looking for some Tylenol or something for a headache."

"Which room?" the guy said.

"What?"

"I asked which room," he said. "I didn't see you come in, so I can't be sure if you're telling the truth or not." He smiled lewdly at her and winked at some joke Dorothy couldn't begin to guess at.

"Oh," Dorothy said. "Umm," —she pulled a door key out of her pocket."108."

"*Denise,*" the guy said, laughing. The phone started ringing. "Hold on a sec." He picked up the line.

Dorothy stood there a moment, unsure of what to do next. There was a coin machine in the corner full of condiments, however, so she headed toward that.

"Yeah, Blue Moon Motel," the guy said into the phone. Then: "I just said it was, didn't I?"

The machine contained shampoo, cigarettes, little bars of soap, and hand sanitizers. There were condoms and antacids. On the top row were Aspirin *and* Tylenol, for the discerning taste.

"I dunno buddy," the guy behind the counter said. "You gotta be a little more specific than that. They're all pretty blonds."

Dorothy half turned. Suddenly the painkillers weren't so important. Slowing her heart down and being able to breathe again were.

"Last Name?" the guy said. "What? *Presents?* Yeah, I'll hold on."

He looked up at Dorothy and shook his head. He brought up his hand like a gun to his temple and pretended to shoot himself with it. Dorothy didn't respond. She was still trying to stop the boat engine that had suddenly fired up in her chest. *Someone is looking for Alice. Oh god please, no more cops or drug dealers. I'm not sure I can take it.*

"That doesn't sound like anyone who's been here," the guy said. "Hold on a sec, I'll check the roster."

He pulled the phone down from his face and pushed the receiver against his chest. "You need change for that machine?" he said, smiling at Dorothy.

"*Yeah.*" She shook her head. "I mean *no*. I got some, thanks."

The guy nodded. He put the phone back to his ear. "Yeah," he said. "I got nobody here by that name...No. Oh, *Pleasance?*" The guy behind the counter suddenly snapped his fingers and motioned for Dorothy to come to the window. "Wait, he said. Do you mean *Denise?*"

Dorothy's heart double-flipped in her chest.

"Oh, okay. Well listen pal, if you don't know who that is then it's not the right person. No, I'm not gonna put you through to her room...Because it *obviously ain't* who you're looking for. *Oh*, Okay. I'm a big asshole then. Yeah, fuck you too."

He slammed the phone down. "*Christ,*" he said. "This town is full of fuckin' morons."

"Yeah," Dorothy said. She was suddenly too sticky and sweaty, too afraid. The walls and the lights in the room were too yellow. The guy behind the glass looked too much like a caged tiger.

"You get your Tylenol?" the guy said, grinning at her.

"No," Dorothy said. "I umm—I forgot my change."

"Ahh, yeah?" the guy said. "Hold on a sec." He ducked down behind the counter. It was all Dorothy could do to keep from turning on a heel and running out of the room. When he reappeared he had a handful of small packages in his hand. They were single serving Tylenols.

"Here," he said, tossing them under the slot in the glass.

"Oh," Dorothy said. "Really?"

"Yeah," he said. "Delivery guy is a fuckin' moron too. I've got a box of these things back here. Besides, you're my favourite customer."

"Thanks," Dorothy said. She scooped the pills into her hand.

"Hey," the guy said. "You wanna buy some weed?"

"Oh, no," Dorothy said. She shook the packets of pills in her hand. "This will do the trick."

"Sometimes it does, sometimes it doesn't," the guy said. "You change your mind you let me know, *huh?*"

"Yeah," she said. "Thanks."

"Anytime," the guy said. "Say hey to Denise for me. You guys get bored you come back and see me."

Dorothy didn't respond. She didn't trust her voice. Instead she turned and walked out of the room. She could feel the guys eyes on her ass, but she didn't care. All she wanted to do was get back to Alice. *Or Denise.*

Whoever she was. More importantly, who was on the phone? The hospital? She dismissed the thought immediately. How could they possibly know where they were. Unless they had spies around watching for the girls...

No. That wasn't possible. The hospital wouldn't waste their time on something like that for a couple runaways. Either Alice and Dorothy would come back to the ward or they wouldn't. They didn't hunt down strays. But the cops might be looking for them. Or worse. Maybe Alice's druggie boyfriend was looking for them. Either of those might be true. They'd stolen a car, ripped a dealer off for what she figured was a lot of money worth of drugs, and Alice had done something horrible in the hours leading up to her overdose and arrival at The General. There was a solid argument for both scenarios in the basic facts of their past few days together. It could be police or drug dealers. Hell, for all Dorothy knew, it could be both.

Dorothy let out a long breath and hurried across the lot back to their room. *It's too big for you to handle,* she thought. *Let Alice do it, she's good at this stuff.* Alice was strong and smart. She was the Lion and Scarecrow in one. She even had hair the colour of the Lion's fair mane. *Meeting her was more than life affirming. It's fate. We belong together. Forever.*

She reached the door and slipped the electronic key into the slot, and when the light over it turned from red to green she threw the door open.

Alice was sitting on the bed wrapped in a towel. Her hair hung like wet straw across her shoulder. In her lap was the brick of heroin, the corner peeled back and exposed. She looked up when the door opened but made no attempt to cover the drugs.

"Oh hey," she said, her eyes cloudy and dream-like. "You're just in time."

Chapter 22.

"What's...going on?" Dorothy shut the door behind her. "What are you doing?"

"Nuthin," Alice said. "I got sick. My stomach is really doing funny things. And my head is killing me." She wiped her hair away from her face.

"So...you're going to do *heroin* to get rid of it?"

"Well no," Alice said. "Well, a little. I'm just smoking it."

Dorothy shook her head. "Are you kidding me?"

"It's not as bad when you smoke it," Alice said. "It's like smoking pot."

Dorothy sat down on the bed beside her and tossed the little packets of Tylenol in front of her. "I got you these." She folded her arms and looked down at Alice's thigh. The room smelled like beer and vomit, but Alice smelled clean. Her thigh was a patch of milk white perfection.

Alice leaned over and kissed her cheek. "What a sweetie," she said."You want to take a pull of this?"

Dorothy made a sour face. No thanks. I don't wanna *overdose*."

Alice laughed. "You can't overdose when you're smoking it. You'd have to smoke this whole brick."

"Really?" Dorothy said. She scratched at an itchy spot in her hair."I didn't know that."

"Oh yeah," Alice said. She elbowed the girl playfully. "You can't believe those Saturday morning T.V. drug warnings for kids. They're all bullshit. Most people who do heroin are smokers. That's how I started."

"But you shoot needles now," Dorothy said.

"Well yeah, *now* I do," Alice said. "You know how much it costs to shoot heroin? I can get bombed off my head for like five bucks. I used to burn through a hundred bucks a night easy when I was a *Jolly Popper*. Smokin' is nuthin'. Smokin' is what you do to get rid of the blues."

"What's it feel like?" Dorothy said.

"Kind of like a warm bath, but inside you," Alice said. She smiled when she said it, like she was thinking of Christmas. "You should do some with me."

"I don't think so," Dorothy said. "That shit will kill you."

"It's safe. *Trust me.*"

And those were the words that stuck in Dorothy's head. *Trust me.* This was a girl she had escaped from the hospital with. She'd watched Alice beat a man half to death saving her from being raped and probably killed. Would Alice ever do anything to hurt her?

The answer, sadly, was *yes*. Dorothy wasn't an idiot. She could see the instability in Alice's eyes, the way she mumbled and talked to herself, or the way she'd suddenly fly into a rage and spout half sentences of random gibberish. There was something wrong with Alice. She might be totally crazy. Of course *the world* was totally crazy, and the world would also like to hurt Dorothy, but there wasn't anything to be done about that. She could escape the world, given half a chance. There was no way to escape Dorothy though. The blond goddess was inside her forever..

Alice pulled the foil from her cigarette pack and ran her lighter under it. When the paper lifted she peeled it off, tossed it aside, and flashed the foil with the lighter again to burn the rest of the glue.

Dorothy sat down beside her.

"You fold the foil in half so it makes a little valley," Alice said. "Then you cook it from the bottom. The junk turns into a liquid when it's heated, and then it'll burn off."

"That's how you smoke it?" Dorothy said.

"It's *one* way of smoking it," Alice said. "It's called chasing the dragon. You roll up a piece of paper or a dollar bill and catch the smoke as it burns off."

"Sounds simple," Dorothy said. She unfolded her hands and sat on them, and inched closer to Alice. She leaned down and smelled Alice's bare shoulder. She smelled faintly of wild flowers and baby powder.

"Oh, it is! Nothing to it. You can watch me, if you want. Then if you want to try it I'll set it up for you. Then we can lay in the dark and listen to some music or something."

"That sounds really nice," Dorothy said. *Am I really going through with this?* Looking at Alice, she realized her mind was already made up for her. Yes, she was. Because it's what Alice wanted.

"Ah-*ha!*" Alice said. She reached over and pulled the straw out of her drink, then clamped it in her teeth and smiled up at Dorothy. She broke a piece of the heroin off with her fingernail, looked at it for a moment, and then did it again. Then she flicked the lighter under the foil and the brown clumps turned to an amber liquid. After a moment of bubbling, a white smoke rose off the foil and the smell of vinegar and talcum powder wafted toward Dorothy. Alice sucked deeply on the straw and coughed into her hand, then looked over at Dorothy, eyes watering, and smiled. She reached out with one hand and pulled Dorothy's head until their noses were touching.

Alice kissed Dorothy's bottom lip. When Dorothy opened her mouth in response, Alice blew smoke into her. The taste of vinegar and Alice's spit flooded Dorothy's senses. She held her breath as long as she could, then blew out the last of Alice's toke into the air. The world began to slow down.

"See?" Alice said, kissing Dorothy again. "Not so bad."

"Umm," Dorothy said, and then giggled. "No."

"Let me set up another one for you," Alice said. She scraped a bit more off the brick and set it in the centre of the foil. Then she handed the straw to Dorothy.

"So I just suck on it?"

"Yeah. Slowly though, so you can get it all."

"Sounds kinda dirty."

"It's not dirty. It's beautiful. Just wait. And try not to cough." Alice flicked the lighter and heated the dope. When it began to smoke, she nodded. "Okay, *now*."

Dorothy drew in her breath slowly, like Alice told her, and her head filled with vinegar. The smoke was extremely rough, even though Dorothy was a smoker, she found herself fighting off the urge to gag on the bitter taste.

"Keep it in!" Alice cried happily.

Finally Dorothy pulled her head back and drew a deep breath to cool her smouldering throat. She lay back on the bed awash in the unfamiliar disconnect of an opiate high, as though her soul had come undone from her body and was now flapping around her like a loose tooth. Alice finished her hit for her and then leaned over Dorothy.

"So?"

"I think I'm in love," Dorothy said, looking up into Alice's ice water eyes.

Alice laughed, misunderstanding. "I felt the same way after my first hit," she said. "Let's do some more. That fuckin' shit they were giving me in the hospital is making it hard for me to get high."

"In a minute," Dorothy said slowly. There was piano music in her head, melancholy and beautiful and spreading out from her heart and filling her veins with sunshine. It was like smoking pure joy.

Alice set up another hit and smoked it herself, coughing lightly and blowing a plume of smoke out over Dorothy.

Dorothy imagined she could see the particles of smoke like tiny bits of blue-gray caterpillars. "Oh," she said, suddenly remembering. "I think someone might have called for you."

Alice laughed. "*What?*"

"When I was looking for the Tylenol, the guy in the booth got a call and I thought maybe it was for you, but he asked for someone else. Then he called you that other name, so it was confusing." She folded her hands behind her head. She wished she was outside so she could look at the stars, but the bed was comfortable and she didn't want to get up.

"Here," Alice said, handing the foil back to her. "You're not making any sense."

"Probably nothing," Dorothy said. She sat up and took the rig. This time when she breathed the smoke in, her throat was mostly numb and she didn't cough. Instead she leaned over and kissed the smoke into Alice's mouth. Then she handed everything back and lay down again.

"It's so peaceful," she said.

The lighter flicked and Alice smoked and smoked.

"How's your head?"

"Much better," Alice said. "I can't hear him at all anymore. It's like he went to sleep or something. Poof. Back down the hole."

"Him?" Dorothy rolled onto her side and looked up at Alice. She'd never gotten high with someone she loved before. She felt so connected. So warm.

"Yeah," Alice said. Then she shook her head. "Not important. I think I pulled something out of my dream and it won't go back."

"That doesn't make any sense," Dorothy said. "Dreams aren't real."

"What if you dream about real things?" Alice said. She rubbed her teeth with her fingers then lay down beside Dorothy. The girls' arms found each other, and they lay in a tangled heap staring up at the ceiling.

"I dunno, I guess so," Dorothy said. After a while, she said: "Do you think we're going to be alright?"

"Yeah," Alice said. "Once we sell some of this brick we'll have enough cash to go wherever we want."

"I want to go to Oz," Dorothy said.

"Point me in the right direction," Alice said.

"It's out in the desert somewhere," she said. "It's surrounded by sand."

"Arizona?"

"Maybe. You can only get there when something really bad happens. It's like, a door or something. An earthquake, tornado. something like that."

"I dunno," Alice said. "That sounds pretty fucked up."

"It is," Dorothy said. "I guess I don't really believe it. I just want it to be true so bad. After my parents died it was the only thing I had to hold on to. These stupid baby stories my dad used to tell me."

Alice propped herself up on one elbow so she could look down into Dorothy's face.

"Were you trying to kill yourself when you drove at that tornado?"

Dorothy looked down at her hands and then looked away. When she looked back, her eyes were bright with tears.

"Yeah," she said.

"You shouldn't have been up in that ward at all," Alice said.

"No. When I got in there they asked me all this shit about what I was feeling. I started making up stuff. I don't know why. Maybe the attention was nice, for once."

"I get it," Alice said. "It's hard to be a ghost sometimes."

"They gave this paperwork to fill out, and it was really easy to see what they were looking for. It had a sliding chart you know, like *agree*, *disagree*, *strongly agree*, and stuff like that. All the questions that asked about fantasy lands I checked *strongly agree*. Then I added in stuff about the world trying to get me and how I needed to get away. They signed me in the next day. Had a room full of brain doctors in there. Dr Weller was the first one."

"He's a fuckin' prick," Alice said. "I hate that guy."

"He's not so bad. He listened a lot to what I was saying. He said I was a flight risk but I was also a voluntary patient so they couldn't keep me. That's why I was allowed to go downstairs for ice creams and sneak out for smokes sometimes."

"Boy was he wrong," Alice said. She smiled, then leaned down and kissed Dorothy's nose.

"He didn't know what a bad influence you'd be on me," Dorothy said, wrinkling her nose and smiling. "Probably thought he could save my soul or something."

"*Probably* thought he could get down your pants," Alice said.

"Yeah well, that too."

Dorothy lay still, smelling Alice's hair and enjoying the places where their bodies were touching. The heroin made her feel drifty. Alice was right. It did feel like a warm bath inside her. Her heart was pumping sunlight as thick as amber maple syrup through her veins. She felt every beat. "I guess I just always feel out of place," she said. "I don't know what I'm doing most of the time. I wish I could just sit and watch the world go by without me in it sometimes."

"I hear it," Alice said.

"Yeah. I guess you do."

"That's why God invented heroin. So you could have a little time out now and again."

"He knew what he was doing," Dorothy said.

"He always does."

Outside the world skipped by, and the girls laid together in the warm dark and watched it go. After a while, they melded into a single, beautiful form.

Chapter 23.

Hours later the rain had stopped, and Alice lie in the dark staring up at the ceiling with Dorothy sleeping beside her. Her face was twisted in a cruel smile and she mouthed the words *Your hair wants to be cut* over and over again. Dorothy mumbled something in her sleep and pulled Toto close. Alice nuzzled the side of the girl's face with her nose. She pulled back her lips in a hideous grin and snapped her teeth like she was about to bite Dorothy's nose off. At the last moment she turned away. Teasing.

"Your hair wants to be cut," she whispered, careful not to wake the girl. She wondered how people could sleep with another person in the bed. How vulnerable they were, and how little people really knew of each other. And people were capable of anything. They were horrible to one another. The Queen of Hearts was an absolute butcher and yet, she still went to bed at night. Still slept with other people in the room.

Alice carefully unraveled herself from Dorothy and got dressed. Moments later she was standing outside the hotel room, Rabbit's freezer-gun in hand, breathing in the wet night air. She crossed the parking lot to the front office and tucked the gun into the back of her pants. Dorothy had something queer when they were smoking up, and now Alice and the Hater were going to go check up on it. *Somebody called for you* Dorothy had said. That simply wouldn't do.

She could see Steve through one of the side windows, smoking a cigarette and watching television. Thanks to the yellow light of the flourescent bulbs that lit the office, however, Steve couldn't see outside at all. The windows would look like blue-black sheets of plastic covering the glass from where he sat.

"*Tweedle - dee - dee*," Alice said. "All alone, in need of some company." She cocked her head as she watched him. The glass booth he was sitting in looked like a fishbowl, complete with lazy air bubbles and gulping, bug-eyed goldfish. Their heads were swollen with blood. Their eyes were bloodshot and glassy, and they looked like they might just fall out of their socket at any moment. They swam and gulped the water, and when their gills flashed they vented fans of bloody pus.

Steve seemed not to notice how sick the fish were. He was suddenly Steve the Diver, with an air hose rammed up his ass so he could swim up to the top of the bowl. Then he'd flop back down into his chair in front of the television. He had a pink *Fleshlight* in one hand and a spear in the other, only it wasn't really a spear at all. It was more like a leg bone that had been ground down to a point on the business end by rubbing it on the sidewalk. The Fleshlight wasn't pink latex; it had a real pussy on the end of it. Occasionally the pussy smiled, or lapped at its lips with a long slick tongue. It smiled and flashed more pottery teeth like the girl from the bathroom mirror. The sight of the lapping cunt filled Alice with a bile of rage.

I want to fuck your mouth, Steve the Diver said. *Then you can blow your wad in my ass*. When he spoke, the words came out as pink and blue soap bubbles. As each one popped the sound traveled to Alice's ears. One of the goldfish was shitting intestines out into the bowl, and as the free end of the fleshy tube drifted by Steve he suddenly reached out and clamped onto it with his teeth. The Fleshlight vanished from his hand and he began to suck the intestine like a cock, jerking it at the same time like a macabre porn star.

When the rotting goldfish above him started to cum, it bucked and shuddered. The way it was gulping made Alice think about biting Dorothy's face while she slept, but then Steve was sucking the pus and blood out of the fish and taking it all, really sucking dick like a champ, gulping fish fluids down and letting some of it spill onto his face so it would be more sexy.

The goldfish buckled like a stomped tin can, and Steve the Diver was showered in little gold scales. They came to rest with the sound of hammer strikes and gunshots, but Steve didn't seem to notice.

He was watching television again, his diving costume gone, sipping hot tea and belching loudly.

Tweedle - dee - dee, he belched. *Tweedle Dum. Make me cum.*

Alice walked to the front of the building and opened the door. The television was screeching static and jumbled nonsense she couldn't understand; the pounding of steel on steel from the fish scales settled into a semi regular drumbeat. It took a moment for Alice to pick out a vocal line in all the shrieking, grating noise; *your hair wants to be cut, your hair wants to be cut.* It wanted to be cut, oh yes, and she was just the one to do the cutting. She didn't have a knife, but she was sure Rabbit's gun would do the trick. A girl could accomplish anything if she just put her mind to it, wasn't that right? Anything at all. Of course, if her mind was someone else's, well, all bets were off. May as well give her the gold medal ribbon and tell the other contestants to go home, because Alice had handed something over to a man truly capable of anything, and was about to show her just how capable.

Like cutting hair with a gun. Or sticking it in his ass to make him cum. The screeching television had been reduced to a steady *hyugh, hyugh, hyugh*, like the sound of a washer with a blanket in the spin cycle.

Alice walked up to the desk and planted a pink lipstick kiss on the glass. She caught sight of her reflection as she did. It was warbled and defiled, but there was no doubt that it wasn't Alice. Alice was back in the room, sleeping off her dope high. Or she was tucked away safely in the back of her mind. The Hater was driving now. And he had some very specific ideas about how little girls were supposed to behave.

Steve looked up and smiled when he saw Alice.

Alice smiled back.

Chapter 24.

The next morning Dorothy woke before Alice and untangled herself from their ball of warmth in the middle of the bed. Her mouth was raw and fuzzy. She swished with some tap water in the bathroom then decided a shower might be in order. Her brain was coated with cobwebs and garden lattice from the drugs. Steaming hot water and packets of shampoo seemed like the perfect cure.

She turned the water on and the pipes groaned. She undressed and stepped into the tub. The fugue of the night before washed away from her skin under hot, soapy water, and soon was swirling around the rusting drain, gone forever. She tried to remember when exactly they had fallen asleep and found she couldn't. There were little Polaroid images of them laying in the dark and talking, and snippets of conversation between episodes of smoking and resting. The heroin made her feel asleep and awake at the same time. Maybe she had dreamt the evening. Maybe she'd been awake all night.

One of the Polaroid flashes was of Dorothy admitting to faking her hospital tests. Guilt bloomed in her stomach. She would have never told Alice if they'd both been sober. The drugs had stripped her inhibitions away, however, and it had seemed a natural topic to discuss. She loved Alice. Love meant no secrets. She wanted to take that back now though, standing in the light of sobriety. She wondered if Alice might hate her for it, or think she was pathetic.

If Alice woke up and hated her, Dorothy would have no one to blame but herself. And what would she do? Alice would get dressed, tell her to fuck off, and probably head out on the road alone. She could picture the girl, face pink and flushed, blue eyes blazing and flaxen yellow hair dancing around her as she left a sobbing and begging Dorothy alone in the motel room. Dorothy's makeup and nose would be running, and her simpering, blubbering noises of pity would make Alice hate her even more. Then she would get in Rabbit's car, flip Dorothy off, and be gone forever while Dorothy stood alone in the rain.

Maybe Alice would spit on her before she left. Dorothy wouldn't blame her. She was a weak and pitiful thing. An *ugly* thing. Nobody ever loved ugly. Dorothy started to cry, and lifted her face to the shower head. The movement was a familiar one. Letting the hot water pound her face while she wept would keep her tears from staining her face. It was a trick she'd learned early in her life and put to good use.

Thing was, she hadn't lied about *everything* on those tests. Some things she'd been truthful about. She really did think the world was out to get her sometimes. It just felt like she was going to spend the rest of her life digging herself out of a hole left behind by her childhood. Random chance had taken her parents from her, left her scared and confused and terribly lonely. Aunt Emily and Uncle Henry had been nice enough, but taking kids in was their job, and with all those other needy hearts begging for attention her own little voice could get lost. She was just a paycheck, and that was that. Sure her dad and Uncle Henry had been war buddies, but when her dad died she saw the change come over Henry's face, a change that said *you mean nothing more to me than how much the government will pay to keep you in food and clothes.*

So Dorothy started spending all her time in her room with her dolls, writing stories of distant lands and little girls who were unlikely heroes in their own little dramas. She started watching the Weather Channel and reading up on Tornados, and how they were a mix of different fronts crashing together. She saw the parallels to her life perfectly, and the more she watched those twisting balls of chaos on television the more sure she was about it.

By the time she stole the car and headed toward Kansas, she could almost tell herself Oz was out there waiting for her somewhere.

But of course, it was all a load of bullshit. Dr Weller had been right in his assessment of her; she'd been trying to kill herself. She'd just been able to rationalize it as a way to get to a magical land she'd made up on her own, and maybe that place existed because she thought about it enough and wished hard enough to make it so. Then again, maybe not.

If she'd been anyone else, a strong woman, like Alice, she would have never headed toward that tornado. She would have gone out on her own and made something of herself. But she had no direction and she didn't know what she was supposed to do to make her life unfold the way it should. She supposed that was what marriage was for, so she could stay at home and be blissfully dependant on a man to make all her decisions for her. Do all her thinkin', like a good woman was supposed to.

She couldn't though, because she was young enough to believe love was the most important reason to get married and old enough to realize that being attracted to women was more than just confusion brought on by her sadness, like Pastor Dave had told her at confession, that it was who she was and it was about the only thing she was completely certain of.

Dorothy reached down for the bar of soap perched on the soap dish and let it drop down to the drain by her feet. The bottom of the soap was covered in a slick, lumpy red mess that ran clean in the shower. The water that had collected in the soap dish was pink and flecked more red. It was blood, and she knew it right away, the way you instinctively knew when a dog was wagging its tail but wasn't being friendly, or how you could always tell when a spider was about to drop off the ceiling and land on you. Sometimes, you *just knew*. The soap had blood all over it.

She looked down at the little packs of shampoo and conditioner and saw they were torn open and used. The empty packs had been discarded. Had they not bothered to clean the suite before they rented it out? She hit the water and stepped out of the shower. She grabbed at the towels on the wall and found the top one damp. She picked it up and rubbed it between her fingers. There was more blood on the towel, washed pink with water.

The first thought that went through Dorothy's head was that Alice was bleeding again, and maybe Rabbit had messed her up worse than she was letting on. And maybe she was not only hurt but possibly trying to *hide* it from Dorothy. Why would she? And if she was hiding this could she be hiding other things?

There was something on the mirror. Dorothy moved closer so she could see it better. There were lines coming up where the steam had clouded the mirror over, revealing what Dorothy thought looked like tiny pussies, and then quickly saw that they were eyes. In the center of the mirror was a big one, unlidded, glaring into the bathroom with the words *I AM ALWAYS WITH YOU* scrawled under it.

There's no telling how long that has been there was how her mind processed the image. These motels didn't get cleaned too often from the looks of things, so that was certainly plausible. But how long would the oil from a fingertip last on a mirror so it would still affect the shower steam? Hours maybe. Not *days*.

Maybe it was just a cool art project Alice had done while waiting for her hair to dry. Maybe...but that didn't quite sit with Dorothy either. She suddenly had a flash of their time in the hospital, right after Alice had woken up from the shot Dr Weller had given her to put her down, and Dorothy had started telling her about Oz. What had she called it?

"*...it's like* duality. *Like two worlds overlapping each other. Like when two TV channels are coming in on the same station and you can see them both...*"

She hadn't paid attention when Alice had first said it, but what if Alice had been hinting at her own life and not relating to Dorothy's troubles as she'd first thought? It made sense when Dorothy thought about what Alice had told her last night, about how she had pulled something through her dreams and it wouldn't go back. She looked at the mirror again and a shiver of fear prickled her neck. *Is Alice truly crazy?*

Then another thought popped into Dorothy's mind.

Did it really matter?

A moment later: *No.* It didn't really matter. It was the two of them against the world. That's what mattered now. It wasn't even a choice really; Dorothy's heart had chosen for her already. She felt connected to Alice's soul. Like they were extensions of each other. She wasn't going to give that up for anything. And when people started looking for her, or the police came like Alice said, they'd just run away and find somewhere else to be happy. A home on the beach. Oz. It didn't matter.

Like Alice had said: *The open road could be our plaything*. She liked the sound of that. Besides, Alice had saved her life in Rabbit's house. Saved her from being raped. If Alice needed a little help now and then telling her fantasies from her realities, Dorothy could certainly help her with that. She was a bit of an expert, after all.

There was a knock at the bathroom door.

"Hey, you fall in or something?" Alice said from the other side.

"Just making myself pretty for you," Dorothy said sweetly.

"Hell, you don't even have to try to do that," Alice said.

"Aww," Dorothy said. "You're a sweet thing. I think I'm going to keep you."

"Deal. Now get your hot ass out here. I really need to pee."

"Be right out," Dorothy said. "Just one more thing to do." She looked back into the mirror, then grabbed her towel and scrubbed off all the glaring eyes and the words *I AM ALWAYS WITH YOU*. Then she wrapped herself in the towel and popped open the door. "Good morning, Sunshine," Dorothy said, smiling.

Alice smiled back. There was dried blood on her teeth. It looked like brown scabs stuck to the enamel.

"Ugh," Dorothy said. "Brush your teeth while you're in there. Your mouth looks like a train wreck."

"Thanks," Alice said, and Dorothy laughed.

"I'm going to check," Dorothy said, kissing Alice on the cheek. "So hurry up."

"Sounds good to me," Alice said. She disappeared behind the bathroom door.

When the water in the sink started running, Dorothy went and sat down on the bed. *I AM ALWAYS WITH YOU* flashed in her thoughts. It was almost comforting, if she could forget all those awful eyes Alice had drawn around it. Beautiful even. She could make it beautiful, if she put her mind to it. She could train herself to believe almost anything. She pictured Alice whispering it sweetly into her ear. *I am always with you. I love you.*

She felt better about it already. She was still feeling good about it a few minutes later when there was a series of sharp knocks at the door. Dorothy threw it open without thinking; the smile on her face melted into a look of horror.

The two police officers standing in the doorway weren't smiling at all.

Chapter 25.

They stared at each other from across the threshold. Dorothy had a hand on the door and the other on the wall; like she was using her own body as a last line of defense from intruders. *Gawd,* she thought. *This is just like the hospital all over again—*

"Excuse me," The first officer said, holding up a clipboard. "Sorry to bother you, but there's been an incident in the motel office, and we're going room to room checking names and looking for witnesses. Who are you?"

"Dorothy Gale," she said immediately, without thought. She instantly regretted her words.

"Are you alone in here?" One cop was jotting down her name in a small notebook. The other stared her down hard. *He's waiting for me to crack,* she thought. *One misstep and he'll be on me like a pitbull.*

Already, Dorothy felt like a cornered cat. Talking to police had a way of doing that. Especially when you had something to hide. Like stealing a drug dealer's car after nearly killing him and breaking out of the psychiatric floor of a General Hospital. And Alice had been confined there, so if they found her they might take her back. Or worse. It would be better to tell them she was alone.

On the other hand, if she walked out of the bathroom after Dorothy told them she was alone they'd want to know why she'd lied about her presence, and would almost certainly do some kind of background check. Maybe there was still a way out of this though...

"I'm alone, *officer.*" Dorothy said loudly. Hopefully loud enough for Alice to hear.

"Okay," The cop said. "No need to yell. We have a bit of a discrepancy here, between you and the logbook. Says there shouldn't be anyone in here right now, and yet here you are. Can we see some I.D. please?"

"Yeah," Dorothy said. She stepped back from the door and grabbed her wallet off the table. She slipped her license out of its holder and handed it to him. Then she bit her lip and looked up at the cop with her most helpless face. "I didn't have a credit card, so that guy behind the glass said he'd take cash and keep it off the books. *Umm...*"

"Something else?" the cop said. The officer standing behind him snickered, looked down for a moment, then looked away.

"I kinda had to...do...something. For him," Dorothy said. She made a little curtsy when she said it, as though the words were heavy on her shoulders and she was unused to carrying the weight.

"Oh yeah?" the cop said. "Like something, what? Something sexual?"

"I don't really want to say, because I know you're not supposed to do it. For favours, I mean," Dorothy squeaked.

"That's true. You're definitely not," the cop said.

"I didn't have a credit card," Dorothy said again. She tried to look as sweet as possible. *Please don't come out right now Alice*, she thought.

"Okay, *Dorothy Gale*," The cop said. "So when did you get here?"

"Last night," Dorothy said. "I stopped for Burger King and then came here about nine o'clock I guess, and it was dead here. Like, nobody in the parking lot, nuthin. That's why that guy said I could have a room even though I didn't have a credit card. Then he said, "*Oh, you're going to have to give me something in return, because if you trash the room while you're in here I'm gonna get shit canned.*" And I said *like what?* And he said *Well, why don't you come in here and we'll talk about it.* And I knew what he wanted because he had that look in his eyes men sometimes get, like they don't see a person standing in front of them but maybe a big juicy steak or something, but I went in there anyway because it was raining and cold and I didn't want to sleep in my car again and sometimes it isn't such a huge deal, if they're *clean* down there, I mean I've done it before for my boyfriends and it was okay. I just felt like such a piece of garbage after though. I finished up and he didn't even look at me...he just tossed the keys and told me not to trash the room again."

Dorothy was weepy and high-voiced by the time she stopped talking, and now she looked up at the officer with wet eyes and said, "I know it's bad and it makes me a bad person and I'm so sorry, but it was raining outside and I just wanted a hot shower and somewhere warm to sleep for a couple days."

"Okay," the officer said, his voice softening. "Just calm down. It's not the end of the world, people are just jerks sometimes and they take advantage of sweet little things. This is a bad neighbourhood for a girl like you. There are wolves around every corner."

Cute is the best weapon I have. "I'm sorry," Dorothy said. She wiped tears from her cheeks and bit her lip.

"So, did you hear anything last night at all?" The cop said. "Like shouting, or screaming or anything?"

"Umm," Dorothy said, pursing her lips in thought. "Nope," she said. I came in here, washed my mouth and brushed my teeth like four times, then had a shower and went to bed with the T.V. on. Why?"

"Did you see anyone strange? Anything that stuck out in your mind at all? Like someone sitting in their car for a long time, or any strange people hanging around?"

"I'm from the country," Dorothy said. "They're all strange to me. But no, nobody. There were some cars in the lot, but I didn't notice anybody in 'em. Why?"

"The motel manager was murdered last night," the cop said gravely. "Some kind of ritual killing, from the looks of it. Happened sometime before dawn, when the guy who delivers papers showed up and found him."

"Oh my God," Dorothy said, covering her mouth with her hands. "I just...I mean. *Oh God!* And *I*...Ohhh, I don't feel so good."

"Calm down," the cop said. He put a hand on Dorothy's shoulder.

Dorothy reached for it, giving him a quick squeeze and flashing a sad smile. "I just feel so awful. Do you know who did it?"

"That's what we're trying to find out," the officer standing in the back said. He was lanky and hiding behind his Aviator shades.

"We don't have anyone in custody just yet," the first cop said. "Right now we're just going from room to room making sure everyone is where they should be."

"And I'm not," Dorothy said. "Oh, I'm so sorry I came here now. I should have never left Kansas."

"Well, unfortunately, the motel is shut down while we do our investigation, so I'm afraid you're going to have to find another place to stay. Do you have any friends or family in town you can stay with?"

"No," Dorothy whimpered. I'm going to have to find another motel I guess. I'm up here looking for work and trying to get a place of my own. I want to go to school next year, if I can save up enough money."

"Smart decision," the cop said. "I wish my daughter made smart decisions like that."

"Is she the same age as me?" Dorothy asked. Her eyelids fluttered sweetly.

"Just a couple years older, from the looks of it," the cop said. "No school for her though. She seems to think Daddy's going to be around to pay the bills forever."

"*Aww,*" Dorothy said. "You sound like a good dad. She's very lucky to have you."

"Oh I know," the cop said. "I'm sure she'll realize it one day, too."

"She knows." Dorothy said. "Believe me. *She knows.*"

"Anyway," the cop said, withdrawing his hand from Dorothy's shoulder. "I'll leave you with my card, and if you remember anything could you call it in?"

"Absolutely, officer," Dorothy said, taking the card from his outstretched hand. "Anything I can do to help."

"It's usually something little that you don't think is important," the cop said. "That's the kind of stuff that makes the best leads. So if you remember anything at all, no matter how small a thing you think it is, just ring us up and let us know."

"I will," Dorothy said. "Promise."

"Good," the cop said, pleased. "Oh, which one of these cars is yours?"

"Umm," Dorothy said. She stood on her tiptoes and looked around the two cops, who parted to either side of the door so she could see better. "There it is. The ugly yellow thing."

"The *Rabbit?* Good Car. Very reliable. You pretty much have to shoot them to get them to stop running."

"That's what I hear," Dorothy said. She giggled. "Let's hope it doesn't come to that."

"Thank you for your time, Miz Gale," the officer said. "We're going to need you to vacate the premises as soon as possible." He quickly wrote down the vital information off Dorothy's license and handed it back to her.

"Thank you officer," Dorothy said. "I hope you catch whoever did it."

"Oh, we will." He replied. "Thank you for your time."

Dorothy closed the door. She felt dizzy, and she braced herself against the wall as she took deep breaths and tried to calm down. She turned when the bathroom door opened behind her.

"They gone?" Alice said. Her face was dark, and her voice was husky. Mannish.

"Yeah," Dorothy said. She smiled weakly. "I can't believe they didn't say anything. I thought I was gonna hurl all over them. I swear I've never been so scared in my—"

She stopped mid-sentence as Alice came out of the bathroom and placed rabbit's gun on the table by the television across from Dorothy's wallet.

"What the hell," Dorothy said. "Were you going to *shoot* them?"

"I was going to do what I had to do to keep us safe," Alice said coldly. "So, Steve is dead? That's fucked up."

"Uhh, yeah," Dorothy said. "Some kind of ritual killing, the cop said. What does that mean?"

Alice flicked on the television. "Let's find out," she said.

Dorothy sat down beside her. Alice was giving off a weird, scary vibe that made her nervous.

"Were you really going to shoot those cops?" Dorothy asked again.

Alice turned and looked at her, then put her finger to her lips asking for quiet. Then she slowly turned and pointed at the television. There was a live news feed from a reporter across the street, and the words *Motel Massacre* splashed across the bottom of the screen.

Chapter 26.

Rabbit and Eazy had managed to go about two hours without television, personal records for both of them. Then Rabbit had Eazy and Devon fish his old 32" tube screen out of the spare room and the three of them set it up where Rabbit's plasma T.V. had been. The plasma was going out to the side of the house. He'd never be able to get it fixed. He'd gotten it from a drug addict. Rabbit had learned that the kind of warranty the average junkie offered on their gear only lasted as long as their junk did. Then all bets were off. He'd gotten it in trade for a quarter ounce of heroin. It was hard to see it go. He'd felt like a real high roller with it sitting in his living room. But there would be more T.V.s; more junkie gifts when he got his drugs back from Alice and her whore.

Besides, the plasma screen had a fuckin toilet lid smashed through it. Try telling the faggots at Best Buy that *that* was a factory defect.

"It ain't really heavy at all, is it?" Eazy said as they moved the television carcass out onto the side of the house. "I mean it looks like it should be heavy, but that other T.V. is heavier I think. Half the size too."

"This thing is like two inches thick," Rabbit said. "The other one is two *feet* thick, and it's full of glass. Plus, there's a big-ass magnet at the back of it, like in a subwoofer. Thing weighs twenty pounds on its own."

"Listen to this guy," Eazy said, grinning. "Fuckin' Maytag Repairman over here."

"That's washers and dryers, you dumbshit," Rabbit said. "Everybody *knowsh* how these things work. Common knowledge."

"Whatever you say, *professor*," Eazy laughed. "Why don't you triangulate us a spot where to put this down?"

"I'll triangulate *you*," Rabbit said. Exposed roots in his mouth touched, like crossing live wires on a car battery, and he winced.

"You should see a dentist man," Eazy said. "Your shit is *all* fucked up."

"*Yeah yeah*," Rabbit said. "First we find that bitch and get my shit back. When I sell off that brick, I can get all new teeth. Gold ones, if I want. Say *PayaNiggah* on them."

Eazy laughed. Rabbit motioned to a spot beside the gas meter. The two men set the television down with the screen against the side of the house.

Devon popped his head around the side of the house. "Better come check this shit out," he said, and disappeared again.

"Probably titties," Eazy said. "You know how he gets."

Rabbit followed Eazy back into the house and Devon was sitting on the couch as far away from the bloodstains as he could get. He had Rabbit's old T.V. set on, and the channel was set to the local news.

"We just talked to this muthafuckah last night," Devon said. "Ain't it a trip?"

Rabbit looked at the screen. The words "Motel Massacre" were across the bottom of the screen.

"Holy shit," Eazy said. "Is that the Blue Moon Motel?"

"Yeah," Rabbit said.

"Somebody killed the guy behind the desk," Devon said. "Last night."

As if on cue, the screen flashed to an interior shot of the motel office. It looked like a scene from a horror film. There was blood on the walls and the glass booth, and there were officers milling about. Someone had drawn eyes all over the glass.

"*Authorities haven't begun to speculate who is responsible for the grisly, and apparently ritualistic murder*," the voiceover said. The screen flashed back to the parking lot of the Blue Moon Motel and an attractive young news reporter.

"Apparently this motel is a known flophouse for prostitutes, drug addicts, and occasional pornography film crew," she said.

"Police have started combing the neighbourhood, starting with the tenants of the Blue Moon Motel themselves. They have had limited success in getting any leads, as gunfire and violence can be pretty common up in this part of the city, and people are nervous about getting involved. Especially with the grisly way the victim, who police say is 32 year old *Steven Marsh*, a long-time employee of the motel, was murdered."

"Holy shit!" Eazy said again. He flicked his fingers at the screen. "Rabbit, is that your *car?*"

Rabbit knelt down and put his face close to the screen. The background of the parking lot was blurry as fuck, but there was no mistaking the shape of the Volkswagen Rabbit parked in front of one of the blue doors of the motel. About as far from the motel as you could get and still be on the main floor. Still, his car was far from unique. A lot of kids had those old Volkswagens; the damn things were nearly indestructible and cheap as hell on gas. It was like a Ford Taurus; the perfect high school car. The less you worked on them the better they seemed to run.

"Naww, that ain't my car," Rabbit said slowly. *But what if it is?* His mind kept telling him, over and over again like a skipping record. *What if it is? What if it is?*

"Looks like yer car," Devon said. "*Jes* like it."

"What are you, retarded?" Rabbit snapped. "I just said it wasn't. Now shut the fuck up about it."

"Dude," Eazy said. "We just called there last night. What are the chances? It ain't a coincidence. It can't be. That's too convenient."

Rabbit didn't respond. He turned his attention back to the T.V. screen, and to the thrumming in his head. *What if it is.*

"*Shore* look like it," Devon said again.

"Fuck me," Rabbit said. It really did look *jes* like it. *Could I be this lucky?* It hardly seemed possible. That bitch had smashed in the side of his face, robbed him of a *lot* of scratch, busted up his T.V., and stolen his car. Shit. Maybe he deserved a little luck. Alice had fucked him over bigtime. And if he didn't get the drugs back in a hurry, they were liable to sell it off or smoke it all and then he'd end up in the river with a shank in his belly. Because he wasn't even a real pro yet; this was his test, and if he failed at it the Mexicans who were supplying him wouldn't honour him with a double tap to the back of the head like real pros got.

They'd cut his balls off, gut him like small game and throw him in the fuckin river. They'd stick a blade in his lungs so he wouldn't float when they dumped him. Hopefully he'd drown before the cold water got into his chest cavity and started pressing on his heart. But like his dad always said, *hope in one hand and shit in the other, kid, see which is heavier.*

Let's just take a ride by, *dig*?" Eazy was saying. "Real calm. Just three mahfuckahs out for some Denny's.

It was worth it just to take a look. Sure. It beat sitting around here doing nothing. *Less chance of unwanted company if we're out on the road, too.* Sure, hope in one hand, shit in the other. This trip could either be the hope or the shit, like his daddy said. Didn't hurt to take a peak, at any rate."Yeah. Let's do it." He got up and grabbed his sweater.

"I'll drive," Eazy said.

"Like fuck you will," Rabbit had one knee on the couch, and was digging around in the back of the seat behind the cushions.

"My car, my ride. We get your car back, you can drive all you want."

"Yeah," Rabbit said. He pulled up the item he was looking for. A snub nosed revolver. A thick fucker, .44 calibre. There was blood on the barrel, but Rabbit either didn't notice or he didn't care. "Usually, that's how we do, but I got the gun. So I'm driving, *Eez*. You got a problem with that you take it up with my little friend here."

"Shit," Devon waved a hand toward Rabbit. "I ride in the back, I don' give a fuck."

"When we find that little bitch, I'm gonna give this thing back to her," Rabbit said softly. "She's got mine, anyhow."

"Great," Eazy said, shaking his head. "You never said shit about guns. You know I don't play that shit."

"Fine," Rabbit said. "You can wait in the car like a bitch. Devon and I will take care of it. Now give me the fuckin' *keysh* before I give you another hole to cry out of."

"Man, whatever." Eazy tossed the keys toward Rabbit, who caught them with his free hand. "You fuck up my car at all you're payin' for it. I mean scratches, dents, anything."

"Shut the fuck up," Rabbit said. "Get out my house, *niggahs*. Let's do this."

"Not cool!" Devon said, but he followed Eazy out the door just the same. "Shouldn't talk like that, son. 'Bout to gitcho ass chopped."

"*Shpare* me," Rabbit said. "We find Alice, I'll spring for cheeseburgers." Once outside he slammed the door to his house shut and was sure to lock it. The wind was gusting. It smelled faintly of motor oil and wet grass. Devon and Eazy were down by the car already.

"Fuck your cheeseburgers," Eazy said quietly. He flopped the door open for Devon, who climbed in the back of Eazy's silver Grand Prix, then shot Rabbit one more exasperated look before climbing into the passenger seat.

Rabbit went around to the driver's side. When Eazy didn't move to unlock the door immediately, he tapped the driver's side glass with his pistol.

"Lazy fucker," Eazy said, but he reached over and flipped the door handle, which popped the lock.

Rabbit climbed in and started it up. *Shit in one hand, hope in the oth*er, his daddy had told him. *See what weighs more*. Usually when he was hoping to get something cool for Christmas (shit), or he needed money for school supplies (shit). Poppa Rabbit was a clever fuck indeed. He laughed every time he said it. Rabbit popped the car into gear and flicked the lights on. The car rumbled out onto the street and into the evening.

Here's to hope, he thought. *Just this one time.*

Chapter 27.

Dorothy grabbed Toto up in her arms. There was a brief moment of panic when she thought she'd lost him somewhere, like left him in that gas station bathroom where they'd washed the blood and violence of Rabbit's house off, or oddly even at the Burger King where they'd gotten drive-through, somehow stuck on the counter waiting for some small child to claim him....

But no, he was down along the side of the bed in that little channel that made it seem like there was space underneath instead of some kind of fitted flooring mould that opened like a vase and held the mattresses in place.

She had a sick feeling in her stomach. It was twisting in knots like a wet snake around her spine, and there was nothing she could do but watch as the parking lot outside was taped off around the motel office, and where a brief glimpse of the inside of the room Steve Marsh, 32, long time employee of the Blue Moon Motel, was carved up like a Christmas turkey.

Dorothy recognized the garish yellow light and the lame 'seventies style decorating plan that permeated the whole of the motel. But it was on the protective window glass surrounding Steve's desk that Dorothy focused on. It looked like a fish bowl kinda, if Steve was a fish. Only now, it looked like a nightmare straight out of Dorothy's own head.

It looked like the mirror, in the shower, before Dorothy had scrubbed it all down. Those eyes. Those goddamn eyes. *I AM ALWAYS WITH YOU*, it said. Here, on the T.V., in true to life Technicolor, was proof. She looked over at Alice and found the girl staring at her already, her face painted with a thoughtful, yet slightly distasteful look. The way you might look if you had just taken a big slug of milk from the milk carton in the refrigerator, only to realize that the slightly cheesy aftertaste might mean the milk was starting to go south. *Might* be, because you were looking at the expiry date and trying to think about what day it was, and if you were safe or not because that little blue stamp with its blurry date was in the past or somewhere in your future still.

"That's fucked up," Alice said slowly, her eyes like snake eyes, waiting for Dorothy to make a move or say something dangerous. Something that would mark her as prey.

Dorothy didn't speak, but she nodded. "Who would do something like that?"

"Whoever did that is pretty fucked up," Alice said, after a moment's thought. "I'd say they were like a landmine. Those ones that bounce up to your belly and blow your balls off. Just waiting for someone to come along so they could blow their wad and rip someone to pieces."

What is she trying to say? Is she blaming me? "Or *s-someone* who just has a few issues," Dorothy said. "I mean, come on. Some bum or something passing through, all high or...maybe just...," she stopped and looked down at her hands, twisting poor Toto into knots. "I don't know. Shit. Someone far away from here by now." Dorothy felt like a dandelion wilting under a magnifying glass. She could almost feel the heat of Alice's gaze on her petals.

"Can I trust you?" Alice said suddenly.

Was this the moment of truth for them? Dorothy bit her lip. She rubbed her face. She looked at Alice again, but found she couldn't hold that molten stare. She looked down at Toto instead. It reminded her of a driving class she'd taken in high school. *Never keep your eyes on one thing too long,* her instructor had said. He'd put his hand on her thigh while she was attempting a parallel park. She'd looked at his hand for only a moment before looking away. She was always such a good student. *Look at the road. Look away. Look at the speedometer. Look away.* Look at Alice, look away.

If you stuck your fingers under hot water but pulled them away fast enough when you were doing the dishes, you wouldn't get burned. That's how Aunt Emily had been able to rinse them in scalding hot water so they dried faster. It wasn't some magic trick, as Dorothy had originally thought. She didn't have super tough hands or a really high pain threshold (she *definitely* did not have that), she just knew that when you were faced with something scalding like straight hot water from the tap, you could pull your hands out of it fast enough that your nerves wouldn't have time to register pain or danger.

That's what it was like now, looking at Alice. *Look away*. Could Alice trust her? *Look away*. Of course she could. Could she trust Alice? Well, that was the big question. If she miscued on it, she was liable to burn her hands bad. She was liable to end up like Steve Marsh, 32, long-time employee of The Blue Moon Motel. Because Alice was more than just a beautiful girl who had a drug problem, she was scalding hot water straight from the tap.

And maybe that's why Dorothy loved her so much, because hot water was something important. Something alive. It was something that you could curl up in with candles and a Stephen King book, and soak the pain of your life away until your fingertips were all wrinkled like the slipped skin on a dead girl, but your muscles were sore and relaxed and the heat radiated out of you like molten steel. So could she trust Alice?

Did she have a choice?

No. *You don't pick who you love*, she thought. *Love picks you*. Look away.

"Of course you can," Dorothy said, looking up and meeting Alice's gaze. "You can trust me to the end of the road."

Alice leaned over and kissed Dorothy's ruby lips, full on, their mouths partly open.

Dorothy didn't look away. She met Alice's ice blue eyes, head on, and let the molten heat fill her completely. *Love doesn't look away,* she thought. *Love goes head on, a hundred and eighty miles per hour with its seatbelt off and screaming to holy hell the entire way.* To the end of the road. Dorothy had no idea where that road was headed, but she was willing to go. *Fuck the world. We have each other.*

"Come on then," Alice whispered into Dorothy's mouth. "Let's get out of here."

Dorothy grabbed her bag, and they went.

Chapter 28.

Across the street, parked far away from the news anchor but still close enough to see the entire parking lot, Rabbit, Eazy and Devon sat in the silver Grand Am and waited. It had taken Rabbit about two seconds to discern that the yellow Volkswagen in the parking lot was indeed his missing car, and now he felt so close to his heroin he imagined he could smell it's tangy, pissy stink. His teeth were killing him, throbbing in time to his heart beat, so he lit a joint to smoke.

"You fuckin *crazy?*" Eazy waved at the parking lot. "There's like a homicide investigation goin' on across the street."

"Exactly," Rabbit said, taking a pull and passing it off. "Across the street." His nerves in his mouth screamed in protest as hot smoke bathed them in filth, but almost immediately the pain receded. He could taste blood and pot, but there was a pinch of Brown in the joint as well, because it was good to mellow you out.

The motel door in front of his car opened briefly, and two women made their way to where the VW Rabbit was parked. They didn't have much of anything with them. The shorter, brunette woman was carrying a bag and what Rabbit thought looked like a black pillow. The blond was driving. The brunette was watching the police cruisers on the far side of the lot. Then she disappeared into the yellow car as well.

"And here we go," Rabbit said. He started the car. A moment after the yellow Volkswagen pulled out of the parking lot, Eazy's silver Grand Am came out of the lot across the street and slid in smoothly behind it.

Chapter 29.

A few hours and several motels later, Alice and Dorothy weren't any closer to finding a place to stay. Alice had no I.D. whatsoever, and Dorothy didn't have a credit card. Now they were driving around in circles trying to come up with another plan, and Alice's head was starting to hurt. The Hater was murmuring obscenities in the back of her head, but even he seemed like he wasn't in the mood to cause trouble.

"This is hopeless," Dorothy said. "We're so screwed." It was coming on to suppertime, and rush hour traffic was in full swing. Dorothy's stomach was growling; they'd driven around all afternoon and not bothered to stop anywhere.

"Naww, we're alright," Alice said. "We just need to find another place that doesn't care whether you trash their shit or not."

"Which is, like, *everybody*," Dorothy said.

"Not everybody," Alice said. "There are a couple cash motels downtown, we'll check those out. I didn't really want to go down there but fuck it, right? All we need is a place to crash and maybe smoke a bit, then we can figure out where we're goin' from here."

The rode in silence for a minute, then Dorothy said, "*You said butt fuckin'*."

Alice looked over at her. Dorothy was stealing sidelong glances back, a small smile playing on her lips.

"Oh god," Alice said, laughing. "That's fuckin' awful."

"You said it," Dorothy said. She reached out and turned up the stereo. Rammstein was singing about *Amerika*. "I love this song."

"They sound like Nazis," Alice said.

"Yeah, a little," Dorothy said. She banged her head in time to the pounding guitars.

"None of this shit is in English, either."

"I like it."

"Yeah?" Alice said. "Well, you're fucked up I guess."

"Ouch!" Dorothy said. "Don't be mean."

Alice laughed. "I'll make it up to you when we get to our room, I promise."

"Oh yeah?" Dorothy said coyly. "How?"

"Oh wouldn't you like to know," Alice said. They were driving in the inner city now, rows of sad old Victorian style houses with boarded windows and dirty looking kids hanging out on the street. Sometimes the houses had tall chain fences around them; the inner city version of a white picket fence was chain link steel and seven feet tall.

"Wow," Dorothy said. "It really looks like hell around here, doesn't it?"

"I used to live down here," Alice said. When Dorothy looked at her, she nodded vigorously. "You bet. Actually just a few streets down. The neighbourhood wasn't quite this bad a few years ago, but it's always been shitty. "

"Sounds wild," Dorothy said, and let it sit there. She stared out the window listening to music and Alice didn't disturb her.

After a while the houses were replaced with warehouses and strip malls, and then there were a series of motels and fast food restaurants along one side of the road. Alice turned at a set of lights and followed a service road that linked all the motels and fast food places together.

"Any preference?" Alice said.

They drove past a place called Emerald City Motel and Dorothy pointed to the *WE TAKE CASH* half of the sign.

"This looks good," Dorothy said.

"Good as any other."

They pulled into the parking lot and Dorothy had a flashback to the last Motel office she had been in, looking for aspirin with creepy Steve who was nice enough to toss her a handful of pills (she still had them) from his own private stash. Steve, who had been butchered by something maybe living inside Alice, maybe Alice herself, for God knows why. Certainly wasn't drugs, they had plenty of those. Money maybe, but Alice hadn't said anything about a robbery. The news hadn't mentioned it either. She kind of thought that if Alice really felt like grinding someone up and spitting them out, she didn't need a reason for it.

Alice parked the car and then turned to Dorothy. "You want me to come in with you?" she said. "I don't have any I.D., so it's gonna have to be you."

"I can do it," Dorothy said. "Money?"

"Oh yeah," Alice said. She reached into her pocket and pulled out a handful of twenties. "Take it all, I have no idea how much a room costs. Get us something for a couple days. I'll run over and grab some lunch while you're in there."

"Okay," Dorothy said. She cupped the money in her hands. "Where did you get all this?"

"Santa Claus," Alice said.

Dorothy looked down at her feet. Then, wordlessly, she stuffed the wad of bills into her pocket. At the last moment Alice snaked a hand out and grabbed Dorothy's wrist. It was all Dorothy could do not to scream.

"What do you want for lunch?" Alice asked softly.

"Wh-whatever you're having," Dorothy said. That dangerous serenity had returned to Alice's face. Dorothy shrank away from the look; from her touch.

"I'll getcha somethin' good," Alice said. Then she slid her fingers into Dorothy's pocket and grabbed a stray bill. Her fingers pressed into Dorothy's thigh as she slid them out of the girl's pocket, but her other hand lingered on the girl's wrist.

"Sounds good to me," Dorothy said. *She did it. I have the proof in my hands, right here. We spent this money last night and now we have it back again because she robbed Steve after she butchered him.*

Alice withdrew her hand, and the Dorothy popped out of the vehicle. She made her way around the car, jamming her fists into her pockets as she moved toward the motel office door.

"Hey babe?" Alice said suddenly. Dorothy turned back to her.

"What?"

"Thanks," Alice said. "For everything. *I love you.*"

The words were like warm hands cupping Dorothy's face. She suddenly felt like such a heel for ever being afraid of Alice; for ever doubting anything more than her loyalty. Why did she have to keep telling herself Alice was a good person? She could see it now, on her face, plain as day. She wasn't dangerous, not to Dorothy anyway.

That look she was afraid of was insecurity, and Dorothy had seen it plenty of times on her own face. That look you got when you loved someone but you weren't sure if they loved you back or not; feeling balloons of warmth but also icy pins lining the walls of your heart. When it was even money they'd tell you they loved you or they'd tell you to fuck off, and all the while you were whispering *I love you* into a pillow because they might leave if they heard you say it.

She rushed to the car and grabbed Alice's face in her hands. "I love you," she said back, and kissed Alice deeply. "*I love you so much.*"

Alice smiled, her upturned face like a bowl of sunshine to Dorothy. "I'm gonna go get us something to eat," she said.

"I'll be here," Dorothy said. "I swear." She stepped away from the car, and Alice backed out of the stall, smiling broadly. She flashed a little finger wave from the car then hit the gas. Dorothy waved back. She'd cast her lot with love, for better or worse.

Dorothy turned then, and skipped into the Emerald City Motel. The office was a large, open area with seating and coffee tables piled high with old newspapers and Time magazines, and in one corner was a double desk with computers and a sign saying INTERNET ACCESS FREE WITH ROOM RENTAL. On the other side were a row of telephones and a magazine stand filled with tourist pamphlets. The walls were green and yellow; the ceiling was a different kind of green. There was a young woman behind the desk who smiled when Dorothy walked in, but otherwise the room was empty of people. She was pretty but tired looking, and at first glance Dorothy took her to be ten years older than she appeared on closer inspection.

"Hello," the woman said, smiling. "Welcome to the Emerald City."

"Thanks," Dorothy said. "Great name."

"Oh," the woman said. "Well, thank you. Do you need a room?"

"Yeah. You guys don't need a credit card, right? 'Cuz I lost mine."

"Not a problem," the woman said through her teeth. Her smile seemed painted on. "There is a deposit of a hundred dollars, then it's forty dollars per night. Can I sign you up?"

Dorothy pulled the wad of twenties.

"They get your wallet, too?" the girl asked.

"Yeah," Dorothy said.

"That sucks."

"Two nights," Dorothy said.

"Ohhh-kay," the woman said. "Do you have some I.D.? I just need to make a copy for our records, then that will be eighty dollars for two night's rental plus a hundred dollars deposit that you'll get back at the end of your stay." She didn't say what she really meant, which was *you'll get it back if you haven't destroyed the room or stolen all the towels out of the place.* She didn't have to.

Dorothy slipped the woman her driver's license and counted out nine of the twenty dollar bills. She still had five left. She wondered if any of the money they'd taken from Rabbit's house with his drugs had somehow found its way back into her possession, then reminded herself she didn't care, because love picked her and she would be better off if she just went for the ride.

The woman behind the desk had Dorothy sign a contract, and then made a copy of her license and the contract together. "That's yours," she said, handing the license and the document back. She scooped the cash off the table. "This is mine." She disappeared behind an office door for a moment then came back without the cash. She grabbed a serving tray with an electric teapot and some instant coffee and tea. There was also a plastic cup of sugar packets and artificial whitener. A handful of little wooden stir sticks had been dumped haphazardly along one side.

"This is also for you," the woman said. She held out a small brown envelope. "Your door keys."

"Perfect," Dorothy said. "Thanks a lot."

"No problem. Your room is 202, right around the corner. Just give me a holler if you can't find it, but it's like right beside us. Should be no problem."

"Thanks," Dorothy said again.

The girls said goodnight to each other and then Dorothy walked outside. Someone was sitting in a silver car on the far side of the parking lot, but she gave it no more than a cursory glance. She found room 202 easily enough, and then stood in the parking spot and waited for Alice. When Rabbit's car reappeared, she waved the girl in and motioned to the parking spot.

"Everything all good?" Alice said, sticking her head out the window.

"Yeah, *Easy-Peasy*," Dorothy said. "I had enough for two nights, so I got that. There's still, like, I dunno, a hundred bucks left."

"Sweet!" Alice said. She parked the car, got out, and pulled a bag of food from the front seat. In her other hand she scooped up a six pack of beer. "Later we can go for more, if you want, the liquor store is right around the corner."

"Oh yeah?" Dorothy said. "Plannin' on gettin' me drunk?"

"Maybe," Alice said. She was walking by Dorothy, but the girl had other plans.

Dorothy leaned in and kissed her on the mouth. "You don't have to," she said.

She took Alice's arm and walked her to their room. She fumbled with the tray in her hands while trying to get the lock to work, but finally managed to swipe the cardkey. A little red light turned green, and the door popped open.

The room inside had a green ceiling and pale yellow walls. There was a single bed against the wall, and a small flat screen television on an IKEA-style table beside the bathroom door. It smelled like pine needles, and when Alice hit the light switch beside the entrance the room was bathed in a soft yellow light from a pair of emerald lamps on either side of the bed.

"Fancy," Dorothy breathed.

"Your favourite colour, too," Alice said, and laughed when Dorothy elbowed her. She tossed the food on the bed and set the beer down on the table in front of the television.

"Seems familiar," Dorothy said, putting the coffee tray down. There was a single cushion recliner-style chair facing the television, and she sat there.

"These motel rooms pretty much all look the same," Alice said. "Same everything. Towels too small, lights too dim, bed too hard. Only thing that changes is the colour scheme."

"Sounds depressing," Dorothy said.

"Hey, that's why the almighty invented beer," Alice said. She pulled two cans off their plastic loop and tossed one to Dorothy.

"I thought he invented it so the Irish wouldn't take over the world," Dorothy said.

"Yeah," Alice said. "That, and so you wouldn't care so much that motels all look the same."

"Amen," Dorothy said, swigging her beer.

There was a knock at the door, and the girls stopped dead.

Cops? Dorothy mouthed.

Get rid of them, Alice mouthed back.

Dorothy shook her head, no.

"Get—," Alice said, her eyes blazing. Then *GO* as loud as she dared whisper.

Dorothy stood up, scowling. *What do I do?* she mouthed.

Alice got up and headed for the bathroom. She pointed at the front door.

Dorothy approached the door just as a second, louder knock banged around the room. She leaned up and took a peak in the spy hole but the view was completely black.

"Hello?" Dorothy said.

"Ice delivery," a man's voice said. "You forgot to grab the bucket when you signed in, ma'am."

She turned and looked back at Alice, with her head poking out behind the bathroom door. Alice shook her head once, *no*.

"Uhh, no thanks," Dorothy said."We don't need any ice."

"That's fine ma'am. May I leave the bucket with you then? It's supposed to be in the room anyway, I can't believe they didn't give it to you when you first signed in."

"That's fine," Dorothy said. "Just leave it outside, I'll get it in a bit."

"Alright. Just so you know though, if anything happens to it, you will be responsible for replacing it."

"Fine," Dorothy said.

"Have a good evening ma'am. The bucket is right outside your door."

"Thanks." She looked back at Alice again and shrugged her shoulders.

Alice motioned for quiet. The girls stood motionless for several minutes as they listened for any hint of noise outside. Dorothy took another look out the spy hole. It was still black. Finally Alice shrugged. Dorothy nodded, and then turned the latch on the door. It snapped open with a click—

Chapter 30.

—and the moment the latch clicked open the door seemed to explode out of Dorothy's hands, like she was holding on to a wall that *suddenly attacked her*, Or a big flapping rat trap that had snapped down on her. The door slammed inward, catching Dorothy square and sending her flying into the wall, and not just trapping her but biting into her with its brass tooth of a doorknob, and she screamed.

But all that was far away because all Alice saw was Rabbit with his foot out from where he'd booted the door, the instant that doorknob *clicked* he'd given it a good bash with his leg, and now he was standing there with two of the biggest black guys Alice had ever seen, and all she could think was *OHSHIT OHSHIT OHSHIT.*

Funny how when moments like this happen, your brain goes into overdrive and fragments everything into pieces; like your memory is trying to catch up to the moment as you are watching it happen, and you are in fact, remembering and experiencing things at the same time. In her mind, Alice saw that boot come down and Rabbit shout *BOOOOM.*

"*BOOOOM!*" Rabbit shouted, stepping into the room. The force of the door knocked Dorothy flat against the wall, and she blocked the door from smashing into the wall by taking it in the chest with a puff of wind from her lungs. He'd had his thumb on the spy hole, such a juvenile trick. But an effective one. Down by his feet there actually *was* a bucket of ice, and Alice almost laughed that he'd put so much preparation into his trap. Almost laughed, but this wasn't a *haha* kind of moment. This was an *ohshit ohshit ohshit* moment.

Rabbit had a gun in his hand. When Alice saw it, the Hater squealed in delight. It was her gun. And now Rabbit scooped up Dorothy under one arm, and she was semiconscious so she didn't really know what was going on. Rabbit knew, and he put the business end of Alice's iron against Dorothy's temple.

"Ah, ah, ah, baby girl," Rabbit said. His face was a mess; his jaw line was a solid, swollen bruise from his cheek to halfway down his throat. There were rich hues of reds and purples and a line of black where the toilet lid had taken him. When he spoke, he drooled blood and spit, and there were shards of teeth in his mouth that reminded Alice of the china smile the girl in the mirror had flashed. There was no sign of his gold grill. His smashed mouth made him slurr when he spoke, so he sounded high. "Don't you fuckin' move. You move a goddamn inch and I *shwear* I'll make soup out of her pretty little face."

"Okay," Alice said. She put her hands up in front of her. "Whatever you want man, don't do anything stupid."

"Where's my gun?" Rabbit said.

"In my pocket," Alice said. "I swear I won't touch it."

"Eazy," Rabbit said.

One of the black guys moved around Rabbit and stepped carefully over to where Alice was standing by the bathroom. When he got within arm's reach he put his hands on her shoulders.

"I'm just gonna reach in real slow and take it out, alright girl? No need to get jumpy, everything is cool, right?"

"Right," Alice said.

Eazy pulled the gun out and then turned it on Alice. "Good. Eazy does it. Just the way I like it. Now put your hands on your head like they do on *Cops*."

Alice complied. She laced her fingers together and rested them on the top of her head.

"Good." Eazy stepped behind Alice and draped an arm across her chest. He was still holding the gun on her, and now he put it to her head. "Good," he said again. "*Real good*."

Rabbit pushed Dorothy toward Devon.

"Hold this bitch," he said. He kept the gun, though. Devon grabbed Dorothy around the middle and put another arm around her neck. It looked like she was trying to carry a brown bear on her back.

Rabbit stalked over to where Eazy was holding Alice and slapped her in the mouth.

"Fuckin bitch," he seethed. "I should kill you right now."

"*Fuck you!* You're a piece of shit!"

"*You smashed in all my fuckin teeth!*" Rabbit shouted. He thrust the barrel of the gun into her forehead hard enough to push her head back against Eazy's chest.

"They were rotten anyway!" Alice shouted back.

Rabbit pulled the hammer. The gun clicked as the chamber rotated, and Alice stopped talking. "There we are. That's better. That's a girl. Keep your fuckin mouth shut. If you're lucky I won't kill your girlfriend first."

"I hate you," Alice said through her teeth.

Rabbit grabbed her face. "You're so cute when you're angry, you know that?"

"Fuck you."

Rabbit grinned, and his face split in a bloody tear filled with shark teeth. "So, baby girl. Where is it? Why don't you tell me so I don't have to hurt you."

Alice watched his eyes for a moment. Hate poured out of them, heating the room and making it hot and uncomfortable. Finally she sighed and rolled her eyes.

"In my purse," she said.

"How much did you skanks sell?"

"None," Alice said truthfully. "We partied with it though. Not bad."

Rabbit grabbed up Alice's purse off the bed and pulled out the brick of heroin. He sucked his teeth when he saw the corner of the bag torn open. He held the corner up for Eazy to see. "Why the fuck everybody gotta rip the bag," he said, disgusted. "Nobody can unwrap these things properly. They don't realize what a pain in the ass it is to wrap a brick of junk. It takes time. Hey Alice, where's the money?"

"Spent it," Alice said. "On cheeseburgers and motel rooms."

"You spent—," Rabbit stopped, getting his temper under control. He took a couple deep breaths and then smiled. "Well, there's one more thing you owe me for."

"I don't owe you shit," Alice said. "You owe me."

"Yeah right," Rabbit said. He reached over and slapped Alice again, splitting her lip. "I thought I told you to shut the fuck up."

"*Leave her alone!*" Dorothy shouted, struggling against the weight of the man on her back.

Rabbit chuckled. To Devon he said, "See this shit? Told you guys they were fucked up. They got guns in their faces and they still won't quit talkin'."

"You said it," Devon said. He tightened his anaconda grip on Dorothy and she squealed in pain.

"What'd I say?" Rabbit growled. He lifted the gun in his hand and brought it down, hard, across the bridge of Dorothy's nose. There was a wet *crack*, like a chef splitting chicken bones for stock, and Dorothy's face broke open. She screamed at the sight of it.

"*BOOOOM!*" Rabbit yelled, raising his fists like a champ. "Told you! *I told you!*"

The sight of Dorothy bleeding and crying and being smothered by that big black bastard was more than Alice could bear. It was just the opening the Hater needed.

Let go, darling, the Hater said, his voice like a snake and dripping venom.

"Just a second," Alice said. Her eyes had taken on a spacey, faraway look. "*Just a second.*"

There you go again. Time wastes, for no ham.

And then Alice was far away, sitting in a waiting room with melting plaster walls and burnt roses. There was blood in the room, and squeals, and when Dorothy looked down at the floor she saw rabbits fucking and cannibalizing one another. But she was far away from the Emerald City now. So very far away…

"You shouldn't have done that," Alice growled. "Dear, sweet thing, oh dear, oh dear."

She knelt slightly, just enough to bring Eazy forward over her. He still had the gun to her temple, so he wasn't being especially careful with how tight she was being held. When she knelt just a little bit, his first response was to lean forward.

Exactly what she was hoping for.

She flexed her thighs and sprang up like a bullfrog, and the back of her head caught Eazy square in the face. She felt the crunch of his teeth and his nose against her flax golden hair and against her skull. He let out a garbled squawk and stepped backward. The gun went off in his hands, but by this time Alice was already moving away from him, arms outstretched, claws reaching for Rabbit with a banshee's howl on her lips. The sound of the gun in the motel room bounced off the walls and stunned them with the level of noise, but not Alice. She was making an unholy *CHEE CHEE CHEE* sound and gnashing her teeth as she flew across the room toward Rabbit.

He was so shocked by her speed he tripped over his own feet trying to get out of the way.

And then she was on top of him, raking his face, biting the flesh on his arms and chest, beating his face with her fists and screaming the entire time.

"*Mahfucker!*" Eazy shouted, bending over at the waste and bracing himself on his thighs. Blood poured freely from his mouth and nose. "*Fuggin bitch broke it!*"

"*GET HER THE FUCK OFF ME!*" Rabbit screeched, his face raked and bleeding. Alice's gun disappeared from his hands. He closed his fist on her hair and punched her in the jaw, but that was all he had time for before Alice let out another banshee-like howl and unleashed a barrage of fists and raking fingers upon him.

Eazy had cupped his hand over his face to stem the blood, with little effect. It had splashed down his shirt and was running like hot red milk down his arms. He pointed the gun toward the violent ball of flesh on the floor that was Alice and Rabbit.

"*Git the fugg ub!*" he yelled. "*You lookin' ta git shot!*"

Alice definitely wasn't lookin' ta git shot. The problem was Alice was more like a bulldozer of hate and rage now, and she wasn't driving. She was sitting in the passenger seat watching while the Hater worked his magic. He'd kicked the machine into high gear and set cruise control somewhere past the redline. There weren't even any numbers to mark the speed.

At the moment he had Alice's hands tied into Rabbit's hair, and was smashing his head onto the floor. At some point in the chaos she glanced over and saw Rabbit's gun *(my gun, it's mine I own it, you asked me where it was in the bathroom and I can tell you now!)* lying on its side under the bed, and that's when the engine throttled back a bit. Maybe there was a way out of this, after all.

Her hand shot out and closed around the steel (*GET THE FUCK OFF ME! I'm suh-horry...*) and the nameless man she'd killed in the car came to her mind, that look of guilt and fear and ecstasy as she pushed the gun into his face and forced him into an orgasm. It was a million years ago now, another lifetime. Another Alice. She shook his face away and his head fractured with a gout of blood from his nose and eyes, like when she'd opened a hole in his face and a much bigger, sloppier one in the back of his head, and all those arteries had begun pouring blood into the burnt hole left by a little rounded piece of lead travelling at twice the speed of sound.

As though filling the space with blood would help fix the problem. The human body was a marvel of nature, for sure, but it was scary how quickly it could go from a living, breathing organism to a pulsing, bloody piece of meat.

Alice looked down into Rabbit's face. His mouth was a bloody mess. She'd scratched through fragments of broken enamel and ripped into nerve endings with her fingernails. The pain must have been unimaginable, because he'd shut down after that. His mouth was hanging open, and he was listing badly, like a ship taking on water. His eyes were rolling in their sockets, trying to find a reset button so he could get his shit back in order. But he was there, like Alice was there, kind of off to the side and no longer driving.

The Hater was there, too, and now he had the gun in Alice's hands and as she stood up she pushed the gun into the lengths of sweaty blond hair on the back of her head. Then she turned and faced Eazy, standing over Rabbit like a lion gloating over a fallen Gazelle.

"*Git the fug away from him!*" Eazy barked, his voice teetering on the edge of screams. He looked like a shaken bottle of beer barely able to contain the energy he was holding in.

Alice kept her eyes on Eazy. Her hands were buried in her hair. Her breath was heaving in her chest. Behind her, Dorothy was crying and blowing the blood from her nose off her lips. Devon was holding her tight to his chest, and when Alice's hand move his eyes bulged.

"*Look out!*" Was all he had time for.

Dorothy shrieked.

Alice brought her hands out from the back of her head. The guns flashed at each other, like they were speaking to one another, barking concussive blasts through the room. Alice tripped over Rabbit's body and sprawled out over top of him.

Eazy staggered back against the bathroom door and slid to the ground, leaving a long red snail's trail behind him. He coughed and a vomitous mass of blood dropped from his lips.

Alice looked down the length of her body and didn't see any blood. She spun around on top of Rabbit and came up with the gun pointed at Devon's face. Rabbit was moaning softly and trying to roll over on his side.

"Get off her," Alice growled. "Now. Or I'll kill you."

Devon let go of Dorothy and stepped back, his hands up over his head.

"*I got nuthin*," he said. "*I won't do nuthin' neither.*"

Dorothy stepped forward and fell into Alice's arms, sobbing and clutching at her like a lost child. Alice switched her over to one side so she had a clear line of sight on Devon with her gun.

"Now, get the fuck out of here," Alice said. To highlight her point, she pulled the hammer back on her weapon.

"Alright, alright," Devon said, backing away toward the door.

"Grab our shit," Alice said, pushing Dorothy toward the bed.

"Let's just go," Dorothy sobbed.

"*Grab our fucking shit!*" Alice's nostrils flared, her cheeks red. Her eyes were glossed, but there was no mistaking the intent of her words.

Dorothy stopped crying instantly. She looked at Alice as though she'd just been slapped, then wordlessly turned and started grabbing up their bags. Alice knelt down and placed her knee on Rabbits chest, then stuck the barrel of the gun under his eye.

"You try to follow us, you so much as raise your head until we're gone, I'll kill you. If I *see* you, you're dead. Got it?"

Rabbit stared up at her, his mouth shut. He was bleeding from both eyes and his nose. The lower half of his face was a giant bruise.

"Yeah, I got it," he garbled.

"Good," Alice said, standing up. She waved at Dorothy. "Let's get the fuck out of here."

Dorothy pressed her body against Alice's side and grabbed her around the waste. They stepped over Rabbit and walked out the door of the motel. Outside, on their right, Devon was standing about ten feet back from the entryway. Alice pointed her gun at him, and he put his hands up.

"No problems," he said. "*Jes* be cool."

Dorothy walked Alice to the yellow car, and Alice climbed behind the wheel. Moments later the girls were peeling out of the parking lot. There were people milling around watching the action.

Devon poked his head back into the room. Rabbit was sitting on the bed holding his face in his hands.

"You *aiight*, boss?" Devon said. "Best get goin'. Cops *goan* be here soon."

"*Fuck!*" Rabbit shouted. He stood up and walked over to where Eazy lay. "Fuckin stupid bitches." He reached down and grabbed Eazy's gun. He kicked Eazy's foot, checking for a response, but all he got were milk bubbles of blood bubbling up out of the wound in his chest. "Let's go. I'm driving."

"Yeah," Devon said. "Where we goin'?"

Rabbit scowled at him. "What are you, fuckin' retarded? We're going to get my shit back. Then we're gonna kill those bitches. Hurry up, we still got time to catch them on the road."

"Bitches," Devon said, staring down at Eazy. He wiped his face with his hands and they came away wet, which surprised him. He wiped his tears on his pants and turned away from Rabbit, sniffling.

Rabbit wasn't sure if it was a good plan or not. Right now it was the *only* plan though. They had to get away from the crime scene as fast as possible. Devon was a retard but he was right; the cops would be there soon. And they'd have a lot of questions for Rabbit and Devon. Like why Eazy was lying dead in a pool of blood and why they'd come to the motel to get the girls in the first place.

There was so much shit to do now, so many complications. He'd have to disappear for a little while after this probably, maybe take his junk and go down to Florida and visit his Aunt Carroll for a while. Let shit blow over. Maybe stay for good. *One thing at a time,* he thought as they got behind the wheel of the car.

First, catch Alice.

Chapter 31.

Alice watched the rear view mirror as she drove, checking for any sign that they were being followed. She had no doubt Rabbit and the other guy would be looking for them, but she had no idea what they were driving. Watching for them while as she was driving gave her something to focus on other than the sickening, pitiful mewling Dorothy was making. *Yeah, everything has gone to shit, but there's no reason to be such a pussy about it.*

To top it all off, Rabbit had slammed the door in Dorothy's face when he booted the door open, and she'd finally gotten a good look at it. "I'm fuggin' *roont.*" She was inspecting her face in the passenger side mirror under the sunshade, and the sight of her lumpy nose and puffy, raccoon eyes brought a fresh bout of tears.

"Will you shut up?" Alice snarled. "It isn't that bad. Stop being a fuckin' baby."

"Did you see what happened back there?" Dorothy whimpered. "It was awful."

"Whatever man!" Alice said. "I'll take you to a doctor. But later. First we gotta get out of town."

"Why!" Dorothy wailed. "I don't want to leave town! I want to stay in a motel and sleep in a real bed! And I want to get my face fixed before it stays like this forever!"

"Are you fuckin' kidding me?" Alice was shouting now. *She's making me do it, Goddamn it.* "Did you not just see me kill that asshole back there?" She grabbed Dorothy's arm but the girl pulled away. "I fucking killed someone, *okay?* Does that register at all in your head? We can't go to a motel because the cops are gonna be looking for us. We need to get out of here and lay low."

Dorothy didn't say anything. She hugged Toto and buried her face in him.

Dorothy may have been weak, as Alice had discovered, but Alice was on the frayed edge of things herself. They were both looking at long jail sentences if the cops caught up to them now. Even if they could prove she'd shot her rapist in self defense, what were the odds she'd had to shoot *two* guys in self defense? There was nothing defensive about a brick of heroin in your possession. That alone could get ten years.

You're not going to jail, the Hater muttered. *We're going to go down in a hail of bullets before that happens, right darling?*

Right.

Alice glanced over at Dorothy. *What about her?* Alice could see the girl hiding in the car during a gunfight, then being *rescued* by the cops after it was all over. She'd probably blame the entire thing on Alice, maybe walk off scot-free. Run off and get married, have a fantastic life, even have a great story to tell her rich friends one day after a few cognacs and they'd smoked a joint. *Hey guys, check this out. Remember Alice Pleasance? The Motel Killer? I knew her...*

Don't you worry a thing, pet, the Hater said. *I'll take care of that little strumpet when the time comes. And her little dog, too.*

They turned off the road and onto a larger, double lane artery that ran through town. Traffic was light, allowing Alice to weave in and out. They'd be able to follow this road out of the city and head south. Gradually they moved away from the inner city condos and strip malls for the more relaxed cookie-cutter neighbourhoods of the suburbs. The road picked up speed, and before long the girls were out of the city altogether, driving along at a steady clip through flat prairie. They were also driving away from muggy sunshine and toward large, bulbous thunderheads that split the sky between light and dark. Lightning flashed on top of the clouds, and a long way off you could see the misty gray swells of rain dropping out of the sky.

Dorothy had stopped crying, but she was still pointedly ignoring Alice. She kept her back to the girl and stared out the window instead, her face buried in her little black puppy and her fingers tracing circles on the glass.

Behind them, a silver monster was gaining ground. It pulled out behind an SUV and blew past it, then changed lanes once more as it sped toward the little yellow Volkswagen.

Alice watched it in the rear-view mirror, her stomach dropping. When it got a little closer, Alice saw the black man from the motel in the passenger seat and wiry, angry Rabbit in the driver's seat. He was leaning over the steering wheel, eyes red and twitching, and he was moving like lightning on the highway.

He's late, the Hater said, laughing. *Oh, He's late, he's late.*

The silver behemoth slid in behind them, and the moment Alice hit the gas she realized there was no way they'd ever get away from that thing. The Volkswagen just didn't have the punch that the silver wolf on their tail had with its big heavy engine. If this turned into a marathon, they might win on gas mileage, but the look on Rabbit's face told her he wasn't planning on taking all day to finish this.

"Oh my god," Dorothy said, looking back. "Is that *them?*"

Alice didn't replay. She didn't need to. They could both see Rabbit's face in that car, clear as day.

He rolled down the window and pointed his gun at them.

Dorothy shrieked and dove for the floor of the car. She was just a bit too big to sit down there, though, and she ended up on her knees, her face buried in her arms on the seat and using her dog as a pillow. Alice swallowed the urge to slap her.

There was a muted roar behind them, like fireworks going off, and the back window of the car imploded. A round hole appeared in the front windshield as the bullet continued on its merry way out of the car. A half second later the back window of the little blue car in front of them imploded as well, and the driver swerved onto the shoulder, slamming their brakes and kicking up clouds of dust in their wake. Alice blew past them, glancing over long enough to see blood on the inside of the windshield and a man screaming. His face was a frozen mask of pain.

You just don't see that in movies, Alice thought, and then she was past the car and sliding across lanes, trying to wreck the angle Rabbit was shooting at and get out of his way. She reached down and flicked on Rabbit's stereo, and then cranked it up near max so she wouldn't have to listen to Dorothy screaming. *Tool* thundered through the car, and Maynard James Keenan cheered on the end of the world.

The highway was a terrible place to be caught by Rabbit, as there were only two lanes to drive on and they both headed in the same direction. She did her best to weave around the cars in front of them and did what she could to keep Rabbit behind them. If he managed to get his car in a position to get a clean shot both Dorothy and herself would probably both be dead in short order. *He's probably beyond reasoning now*, Alice thought. *He's only thinking one thought—revenge.*

She cut off a brown station wagon and the man behind the wheel jerked his brakes and laid on the horn at the same time. It was just enough of a slowdown to knock Rabbit back a bit, and Alice kept her foot on the gas to create some space. She needed just a moment to think. She needed to get off the highway soon, because it was just a matter of time before Rabbit got off a shot that would end their little road trip forever.

She looked in the mirror again. *That moment is probably coming sooner rather than later.*

Chapter 32.

"*Jesus Christ!*" Rabbit shouted, cranking the wheel to the left and passing a brown station wagon on the shoulder. He swerved around the driver and cut back into the lane behind Alice, but she had already sped up and was now moving past a big blue pickup. The driver flashed his brakes and Rabbit could see the man flip Alice the finger. The girl was making friends all over the road.

Rabbit switched lanes. The traffic was clearing out a bit as they drove along, but there were still too many vehicles on the road for him to get a clean shot. All he needed was one, but if he used up all his ammunition before he got that shot, he'd have to run her off the road or hope for some luck.

"*Lookout!*" Devon said. He was holding onto the hand strap coming out of the ceiling of Eazy's car, and his other hand was firmly on the dashboard. His hands actually looked white.

"I got it," Rabbit said, annoyed. He avoided another car that had slowed down as Alice changed lanes again. He passed the car on his left and then came right back into the lane.

The side of the road dropped in a gradual slope for drainage, and there was knee high grass growing at the bottom of the ditch. The grass snaked up to a farmer's barbed wire fence on the far side of the ditch, and beyond that were braided rows of farmland. Rabbit wasn't crazy about the idea of going into the ditch, because there could be anything down there under the grass. Mud and water were the least of his worries. He was thinking about large chunks of wood and debris that might not just fuck up Eazy's car, but possibly kill them both.

He'd known a guy in high school who had gone into just this kind of ditch and hit a telephone pole that was lying on its side, buried in tall grass. The impact had driven him out the side window and into a barbed wire cattle fence. His back had snapped in three places. He lay in the dirt getting ant bites and having spiders crawl on him until someone finally noticed him and stopped to help. The cattle fence had collapsed under him, and his legs were flopped over backwards like a G.I. Joe doll with an elastic band hip joint twisted around backward. He never walked again. Years later Rabbit had sold Brown to the guy, and they'd gotten high together. *He never survived that accident, even though he was still alive. It didn't just break his back, it broke his soul.* Rabbit had always been wary of those fences after that, and the ditches that ran along the highway. You never knew what was lurking down there, under all that grass.

Only this time he *had* an idea, because down off the highway sitting in the grass was a white cop car, parked behind a road sign announcing an odometer test section had begun with mile one. Alice and Dorothy didn't see it; they passed that cop at full speed and their brake lights didn't flicker. Rabbit knew they were too busy looking back in their mirrors at him to notice, and he hit the brakes on his car just as the lights came on and the cop car came alive. He settled in behind it as the squad car gunned its engine and roared after the Volkswagen.

This was bad. If Alice got pinched for what happened at the motel, they'd search the car, and if they did that Rabbit had no doubt they'd find his drugs. He silently prayed for Alice to keep driving, and decided if she did he would come up behind the cop car and wipe him out. Eazy's car was big enough to push a Caprice off the road easily, and powerful enough to keep up since the cop wouldn't be passing Alice anytime soon. He'd just drive up and knock the car into the grass, and maybe there'd be nothing down there but mud and frog water. *Then again, maybe there's a hidden telephone pole lying on its side waiting to grant Johnny Law a life of pissing in beer cans.*

But then Alice's lights flashed, and Rabbit cursed. The yellow car slowed on the shoulder, and the cop car slowed behind her. Rabbit also slowed down, but then he signaled and moved over a lane. As he passed the cop Rabbit saw him speaking into a radio, an older man with a salt and pepper moustache. *Aren't they all like that?* He thought. *An old man with a salt and pepper moustache or a woman with a pony tail and a big ass.*

When he drove past Alice she was scowling at him, and he pointed to his eyes and then back at her, saying *I've got my eyes on you.* She flipped him the finger in return, and Devon made a throat slashing motion. Rabbit hit the gas and sped off, watching Dorothy appear in her seat again. Alice was focused on the cop.

"*So what we goan do now?*" Devon said. He had relaxed his grip on the safety strap, sometimes known as the *holy shit* strap, as in *HOLY SHIT HOLD ON FOR YOUR LIFE.*

"Now?" Rabbit said. "Now we wheel around at the next turn off and come back around. If we're lucky, Alice just gets a ticket. If we're not lucky, well, we might have to do some serious *gangstah shit.*"

"She's gotta die, man." Devon cracked his knuckles. It was cold in the vehicle but he was sweating profusely; his head looked like a cold beer can on a hot day. Sweat ran from his crown down behind his ears and soaked the collar of his shirt. "She killed my boy. Whatever it takes."

"If this *worksh* out, we won't even have to get out of the car." *This better fuckin work*, he thought. He didn't want to go to jail, but he definitely didn't want to be in deep with the Mexicans who had fronted him the drugs. That would be so much worse than jail. At least in jail they'd let him keep his balls. These guys were liable to cut them off and stuff them up his ass. His teeth were killing him. He'd have to blast again soon. It hurt so bad he could almost hear it, like it was screaming in both ears at the same time.

Up ahead there was a connector with a NO U-TURNS sign. Rabbit flicked on his blinker and pulled into it. He'd make his way back around, then find another connector when he passed Alice and the cop again.

Chapter 33.

The cop pulled to a stop behind them, and Alice was already gritting her teeth because Dorothy wouldn't shut up. She could see the blue and red lights reflecting in the rear-view mirror. Behind the wheel back there was a gray haired cop with a moustache, furthering her theory that *all* cops had moustaches. Or maybe they were just all the *same* cop; like clones with their genetic spooge all siphoned off some 1970s T.V. cop drama. *Simon & Simon* maybe, or that yellow haired guy from *C.H.I.P.S.*. *What was his name?* What a stupid thought. Of course she didn't know the guy's name.

It didn't matter now. What mattered now was when that cop got to the window to ask *Where's the fire?* Or *Speedometer broken?* Or *Lemme guess...you were practicving for the Indy 500?* Any of those questions would almost immediately be followed up with *Why are you girls so beat up?* Or *Why is she cryin' like that?* Sooner or later, those questions would turn to the BIG one, and they'd be up shit creek without a paddle: *What do you girls know about a dead guy in room 202 at the Emerald City Motel?*

They might even have Rabbit's car in their system now; being driven by a 'person of interest'. She was sure Rabbit hadn't called the car in stolen because he wanted his drugs back. But if there were people standing around in the Em City parking lot when the shootout happened, they would have seen everything. Rabbit's boy was too stupid to even close the door. They would have seen Alice shoot that guy. It was self defense, yeah, but the Hater said *whores don't get to play that card.*

He's right, Alice thought. Nobody would believe her.

She'd know in about two seconds if the cop was coming to arrest a murderer or ticket a speeder. His body language as he approached their vehicle would tell her everything she wanted to know about his intentions. If he came to the door with his ticket pad in hand, she might let him live. If he came with his gun drawn, there was a good chance he'd have to use it in quick fashion.

"We're fucked." Dorothy's voice salty and crackling. She choked on her sobs and snot ran from her nose.

"Hold on a sec," Alice said. "Just give me a moment." She had jammed the pistol into the gap between the seats, and now she scooped it up in her hands and slid it handle-up between her thighs. The metal was still warm, and it made her skin tickle at the thought of death being so close to her pussy. *Is that what it was like for that guy before I blew his head off?*

"Alice!" Dorothy cried, looking up at her, "*What the hell do you think you're doing?*"

"I told you to shut up," Alice said.

"No!" Dorothy said. "That's a *cop* out there, Alice! You can't just shoot a cop!"

"*WHY NOT?*" Alice shouted, then snapped her mouth shut. Behind them, the officer was getting out of his car. He seemed to be in no hurry. His gun was unlatched but undrawn on his hip, and as he slammed his car door, he rested a lazy hand across the back end of it. So maybe they weren't suspects. Not yet, anyway. *But soon enough.*

"You can't just shoot everyone who gets in your way!" Dorothy said.

Alice looked down at her then back into her mirror. "You have snot on your face," she said. Her voice was calm, like ice. *I'm cool as a cucumber. A fucking cool cucumber.*

"I don't care," Dorothy huffed, but she buried her face in her dog.

The cop reached the back of the car, and as he came up on the driver's side Alice rolled the window down all the way. Her right hand was buried in her crotch, covering any part of the gun.

"Where's the fire?" he said, looking straight down the front of Alice's shirt as he spoke. His badge said *Officer Reynolds*.

Alice laughed. She adjusted herself so he could get a better look. *Atta boy. Get a good long look. Keep your eyes on my tits and you just might live through this.*

"What's going on?" Reynolds said. "You're missing your back window and you're driving like a maniac."

He leaned down so he could get a better look into the car. He looked across the car at Dorothy and then back to Alice. "What the hell is wrong with her?"

Alice's hand moved fast, from her crotch, pulling up the gun toward his face.

"*SHE DOESN'T LIKE GUNS!*" The Hater screamed, and pulled the trigger.

The gun puffed smoke and fire up and out of the car, leaving behind a roar that echoed in their heads. Reynolds was already moving out of the way though, and he fell back on the asphalt and rolled away from the car, yelling *Jesus Christ Oh Jesus Oh Jesus.*

Alice popped the door open and got out, holding the weapon in front of her. The cop was in the process of rolling up to one knee. He had his weapon drawn but hadn't set himself to shoot yet. Alice had.

She fired again, missed, and then she and Reynolds fired at nearly the same instant. He went down on his face screaming. Alice felt like she'd been punched in the shoulder. Or maybe she'd been stabbed with a white hot fire poker, and the force of the impact threw her back against the car and then she was bleeding everywhere at once.

Reynolds was still screaming as he crawled toward his car, one hand on a bleeding stomach wound and the other pointing his gun toward Alice. He fired again but missed; the next shot he took blew out the side window of the car and sent Dorothy into fits of hysterical sobbing.

Alice shot back and caught him in the side, either near or in his ribs, and half spun him around. He blasted a shot off wild; it went into a farmer's field away from them. He popped the door open with the hand he'd been using to hold the blood in his stomach wound and left a long streak down the side of the car door. He collapsed half on his seat, reaching for the car radio. The gun was pointed out toward Alice, and as she came closer with her own gun trained on him, he fired and missed.

Alice ducked when the gun went off, a useless gesture. She knew enough about guns to know it was impossible to dodge a bullet unless you were Superman. The human body just didn't move fast enough to get out of the way of something moving as fast as a bullet.

She looked up in time to see Rabbit in that silver behemoth on the other side of the road, driving slowly and watching the action. He must have found somewhere to turn around and was on his way back. Alice took a lazy aim and fired; a small black smudge appeared in the back door on the driver's side and the window blew out. Rabbit hit the gas and the car fishtailed down the highway.

Officer Reynolds was convulsing where he lay, half in the car with his legs stretched out on the asphalt. As Alice came around the door and pointed the gun at his face.

He was gagging on vomit and blood. His gun hand convulsed in its own rhythm apart from the rest of his body; it caused the barrel of his gun to scrape against the road with a metallic *taptaptap*.

He looked up at Alice, standing over him with her gun pointed at him, but Alice didn't think he was seeing her. His eyes had taken on a sluggish, glassy look. His jaw was working but he didn't speak. Instead, he was softly stuttering F's in rapid in and out breaths.

Alice placed the barrel of her gun against Reynolds forehead and pulled the trigger. The back of his head erupted like cherry pie, if her mother had ever made a cherry pie with chunks of raw steak and knots of hair instead of cherries. The hole in his forehead pissed blood into his half open eyes and his gasping mouth, but he was already much too far gone to taste it. His head rocked back against the seat and his feet twitched for a moment like a spider's legs after it's been crushed under heel, and then Reynolds was still.

Alice reached down and grabbed his gun off the pavement. Then she reached into his belt and pulled two more clips from a little pocket on his left side. The computer in the car was flashing and whistling at her, so Alice shot it until the gun ran dry. Then she dropped the clip on the ground and reloaded the weapon.

When she turned back to the Volkswagen, she could see Dorothy's face peeking at her from behind the passenger seat. And then the world was swimming and Alice had to prop herself up on the squad car. She staggered between the two vehicles and fell hard against the back of the Volkswagen. She slid along the side until she got to Dorothy's door. Then she popped it open. She fell again but caught herself before she landed on top of Dorothy. "You have to drive," Alice said, pointing the gun at the empty driver's seat. "*Fuh-hucker shot me.*"

Dorothy was holding her hands over her breasts. She turned at the sound of Alice's voice, but when she opened her mouth to respond it was with blood, not words. She held her hands up to show Alice what had happened. There was a tight black hole in her chest, on the top of her left breast.

"Oh my god," Alice breathed. "*Ohmygawdohmygawd.*" The sky flashed rainbow lightning; blues and pinks in vertigo brilliance. The engine of the car was ticking like a high speed clock. Alice took Dorothy's hands in her own. She whispered a word: *No.*

Alice fell to her knees. She dropped her head into Dorothy's lap. Her grief was too big; she couldn't get it out. The sky darkened and lightened around them as the sun rose and set a hundred times a minute. Someone was screaming *NO! NO! NO!* It was Alice. She sucked in Dorothy's scent with every wailing sob. Snot and blood and tears mixed and dropped from her face into Dorothy's jeans. Alice couldn't breathe. She didn't want to go on. She wanted to lay here and die beside her girl. She took a gasping breath and flowers of colour bloomed in her eyes. She coughed her tears out like they were broken glass.

Please come back. Please come back.

She was still holding Officer Reynolds' pistol. She pulled the hammer back and slid the barrel in her mouth.

Good girl, the Hater said in Rabbit's voice. *Take it all. Take it to the fur.*

This was it. The end. Alice was calm. She squeezed Dorothy's fingers with her free hand. *I'll see you soon, baby, I promise. I love you.*

"*Wait.*"

The voice came from nowhere. It floated in on the wind and danced around Alice before settling over her heart. It flitted on her chest like a newborn butterfly. She looked up, the gun banging against her teeth.

Dorothy was smiling down at her. "I'm okay. Look." She pulled her hand away from her chest. There was a lot of blood, but Alice could see it was stopping already. *A flesh wound. That's all it is.*

"Yeah," Dorothy said, as thought reading her thoughts. "It must have bounced off something. It might not even be a bullet. It might be a piece of plastic from the dashboard or something."

Alice dropped the gun in Dorothy's lap. She reached up and kissed her hard on the mouth. She pressed their cheeks together tight and whispered *I love you* over and over again. Dorothy laughed, and it was the sweetest sound Alice had ever heard.

"Come on, my girl," Dorothy said. "Everything is going to be fine. There's a storm coming."

"It's already here," Alice said, not looking at the sky but at her life. She staggered to her feet and made it to the driver's side of the car where she fell behind the wheel in a heap. Her shoulder was screaming at her, and she was shaky and sweaty from pain and blood loss. She started the car and put it into gear, and then reached over and grabbed Dorothy's hand.

Dorothy smiled back and rubbed Alice's dirty hand on her cheek. She kissed it lightly.

Above them, the clouds were a black roiling mess; lightning crashed and the sky spit fat, stinging raindrops onto the road ahead of them. The air was filled with the smell of blood and rain and wet pavement. The yellow car picked up speed, but Alice didn't think they'd ever go fast enough to escape the mess they'd created.

Chapter 34.

Rabbit was nervous about coming back toward the shit storm Alice had just dumped all over the road, but he was fresh out of options by this point. It didn't matter to the people he owed money to how many cops Alice might kill before she finally went down. All they cared about was the money Rabbit owed them, and they considered it Rabbit's *personal* debt. If Alice and her girlfriend took the drugs, well, no matter to them. They wouldn't bother collecting from the girls. They'd take it out on Rabbit himself.

"*Drive slow*," Wild eyed and alert, Devon leaned as far forward in his seat that his substantial girth would allow.

That was fine with Rabbit. *He was always the bumbler of the two,* he thought. *Devon was the brains. I guess that's what happens when someone kills your best friend in front of you.*

It was starting to rain. Ahead of them on the road they could see the flashing blues and reds of the cop car on the side of the road, its door hanging open and a man lying halfway out of it. The raindrops splashed the windshield of Eazy's car and distorted the view, but it was easy to see the cop was dead. Rabbit slowed the vehicle down as they approached, and Devon rolled his window down to get a closer look.

"Fuck me," he said. "Look at his fuckin head. You can see right through *dat* hole."

Rabbit didn't want to look at it. It wasn't that he couldn't handle the sight of blood and death. God knew he had seen enough violence the past few days to last him a lifetime. No, he was fine looking through the release valve Alice had implanted in the cop's head. *It's not the blood,* he told himself. *It's what all that blood means.* She was a cop killer now, and she'd be lucky if half the police in the state didn't line up to take a shot at her. They always took that shit so personal. It made things more difficult on Rabbit and Devon. It meant they had to get to the girls, and soon, before the world exploded in red and blue lights and trigger-happy cops started raining down on them like this spring storm was about to. They were on a time limit now, of that there was no doubt.

"What's that?" Devon said, pointing to a large bloodstain on the road, just a few feet from where the cop car. "*Looks like blood.*"

"Holy fuck," Rabbit said. He stopped the car. It *was* blood on the road. A big puddle of it. There were streaks of red on the hood of the cop car as well, but none of it matched up with where the cop was laying. In fact, the streak patterns were coming *away* from the dead cop. "I think we just stumbled on some luck."

"Huh." Devon rubbed his hands together. "That cop shot her."

"Looks like it," Rabbit said. "And if she's hit bad enough, she might be dead soon."

"Then we *jes* worry about findin' her."

Rabbit smiled grimly. He hit the gas and the car roared away from the crime scene. Somewhere up ahead of them, Alice might slowly be losing her grip on life. If they were lucky, they might find the car on the side of the road and she'd be hanging on by threads. Then Rabbit had no qualms about collecting his heroin and dumping Eazy's car in the river. They'd even give it a quick rubdown to cover their asses. He watched *C.S.I.*. If there was one thing Rabbit knew, it was covering his own ass.

But first he had to play catch-up. The rain was pounding down on them, and he was so very late already. He throttled the car and sped off toward the heart of the storm, toward Alice. Toward everything. He could feel the importance of time catching up to him; threatening to pass him and leave him behind altogether. He had to move quickly if there was any chance at all. His jaw hurt, but it was a reminder of everything that was at stake and he could handle that.

The car hit a puddle and roared. For a moment there was the sensation of disconnect as the tires crashed through water.

"Easy," Devon said. "You don't have to drive so damned fast, we're gonna catch 'em."

Oh, but I do. "I'm late," Rabbit said, and hit the gas.

Chapter 35.

Alice lay back against the seat and closed her eyes, but just for a moment. She didn't dare relax too much while she was driving. All it would take was three or four seconds and she could be in the ditch.

Once the initial pain and shock of the bullet going through her had subsided, it had been replaced with a slow burning fugue that left her both dizzy and sleepy. She knew that most of it was the blood loss. There were motes flashing in her eyes; popping and crackling in her vision. It reminded her of eating fancy sushi with its little pockets of fish eggs that burst in your mouth when you chewed them. Or perhaps they were like pop rock candies, which she'd once heard was just carbon dioxide that had been freeze-dried like beef jerky. In the back of her mind she still believed they were some kind of magic, like when she was a little girl.

Beside her, Dorothy was hugging Toto and talking about the places they would go when this was over. It was a nice, listening to her talk, and it filled Alice with a gentle, sunny feeling. Like a summer picnic. As she drove, the wipers pushed amber coloured rain to the sides of the windshield. They passed houses shaped like animals with birthday parties on their lawns. All manner of creatures attended the parties, from rabbits to foxes to turtles with pink and blue bows on their reptilian heads. They passed cakes and soda fountains and presents piled high in pyramids that stretched for miles. They passed abandoned cars and garbage heaps and burnt out homes as well. They didn't concern Alice much. She welcomed the change.

It was almost as though her real life with Dorothy and the one in Wonderland were becoming interposed on each other, the way two pictures might become double exposed on the same frame into a single, wondrous image. These days, she didn't imagine that happened much anymore, with digital cameras replacing all the old film standbys.

Just another example of technology killing the magic of things, the Hater cooed, and Alice had to agree. There was nothing magic about her life with Dorothy. It was a brackish world of pain and reality. The only thing it was good for was escaping.

"*Alice,*" Dorothy said.

What do you want, Alice thought, *aside from dragging me back into this miserable freak show?*

"ALICE," Dorothy said again, and then reached over and shook her. Alice moaned, but then her eyes fluttered open. She'd been driving down the middle of the road. Somewhere behind them a horn blasted, but all she could make out were lights and a green block.

"What do you want?" Alice said.

"You were falling asleep," Dorothy said. "Where are we going?" She sniffled and wiped her face with the back of her hand. She was covered in blood. It darkened the wrinkles and pores on her face around her mouth and her nose.

"There might be a gas station ahead," Alice said. "It's been a long time since I was out this way, but there's a little roadside town or something. We can maybe get a new car there too. The cops will be looking for this one."

"What are we going to do?" Dorothy said.

"Relax," Alice said. "And don't worry your pretty head about it. I've done this a dozen times before. We'll get a car, grab some beer, and head out into the rain like a couple sunflowers." *I talk a good game. I wonder if I can make good on it.*

Alice was right, though. Twenty minutes later they were seeing signs telling them about a roadside turnoff, a place where truckers could park their trucks, get great prices on diesel and propane, and all the travelling supplies they might need. There was also a sign advertising cheap *Axe fuck sex*, but she thought she might be imagining that one because she couldn't think of anyone who'd want such a thing. The Hater thought it might be a perfect birthday gift for someone he knew, and Alice pushed him away.

The turnoff was actually a service access that they almost passed while looking for the gas station; it was a narrow paved road that allowed truckers to bring their rigs in and slow down off the highway and out of traffic. The gas station was populated with a half dozen different vehicles. Further back in a large parking area off to the side of the gas station there were three rigs parked like slumbering dinosaurs. The one in the front was decorated with a big MacDonald's hamburger and some writing Alice couldn't make out in the rain. The vents on the dashboard kicked out stale smelling air, but it was warm enough.

"This is crazy," Dorothy said. "You don't need a gas station, you need a hospital. I need a fuckin' morgue." She giggled morbidly and kept her eyes on the service road, but all her attention was on Alice.

"I'll just get some tampons," Alice said, then chuckled. "I've got heavy flow."

"This isn't funny!" Dorothy sniffed. "You have a hole in your shoulder and you're bleeding all over the place. You could die!"

"No hospitals," Alice said. "The cops will be looking for us. The first thing they do at the hospital when you come in with a gunshot wound is call the cops."

"This is so fucked!" Dorothy cried, dragging her hand through her hair.

"It's not fucked," Alice said. "Everything is fuckin' *fine*. Just find us a car and then go in and grab some stuff. Bandages and alcohol. We need to clean this hole in my shoulder."

Dorothy looked like she was ready to collapse herself. She was pasty and trembling, and her face was red and scratchy from crying. "Me? I can't. Look at me, for Christ's sake." She held out her bloody arms for inspection, pleading Alice with her eyes. She looked like she'd bathed in blood. She was red from her nose down to her knees. The wound on her chest had bled and bled, and even though it was all done bleeding Alice could see the folly of sending the girl into the store. She looked half dead.

"You should stay here," Alice agreed."You're too fucked up. If they see you like this, someone will call the cops for sure. I'll go." She held out her hand and Dorothy slapped the last of their money into Alice's palm. It was about a hundred bucks or so.

"Grab smokes too," Dorothy said. "And beer."

Alice coughed something metallic into the back of her throat, but she swallowed it before she had a chance to look and see if it was blood. She could tell that it was. She took the money and folded it into her pocket. Then she nodded and got out of the car. "Okay. I'll be right back."

"I'll be right here," Dorothy replied.

Alice pulled the hood up on her sweater to keep the rain out of her eyes and then stalked across the parking lot toward the store. The bullet hole in her shoulder was obvious if you were looking for it, but thankfully the sweater was black so the blood running down her side was invisible. It was dripping and leaving pink spatters on the ground, but that couldn't be helped now. Her gun was in the front pocket and she kept one hand curled around the handle just in case she needed it.

When she reached the door she looked back at the Volkswagen. Dorothy was lying with her head against the door, already asleep. Lightning roared across the sky with the sound of a million kettle drums, and Alice went inside.

Chapter 36.

The automatic doors guillotined apart as Alice entered the cool artificial light and air inside the store. There were a couple truckers standing around near the front counter, rough and tumble types with a week's worth of stubble on their faces and the kind of grimy, weather born faces that told the world their version of air conditioning on the open road involved a rolled down window and the occasional welt from a bee travelling by at seventy miles an hour.

Walking the aisles was a family of four collecting supplies. They had the look of people who spent most of their time working in office jobs and doing family outings with their kids on the weekends, as if that might be enough time spent with them so they didn't grow up with a deep seeded resentment toward anything paternal. The husband was an impatient man, probably used to meeting deadlines in whatever rat race career he was in, and now he was expressing his displeasure that his two sons couldn't decide on chips or chocolate bars for their snack. He was leaning toward the chips, as though they wouldn't make a mess with them.

Alice walked down the pharmacy and auto aisle, past rows of motor oil and cherry scented car refreshers, and stopped in front of identical rows of lip balm, suntan lotion, and a handful of first aid essentials. She grabbed a box of cotton bandages, pictured the blood on Dorothy's shirt *(just get me some tampons, I've got a heavy flow, ha HA!)* and grabbed another box. Then she grabbed a bottle of rubbing alcohol and some antiseptic cream.

She thought back to the night they'd cleaned up in the bathroom of that gas station after escaping from Rabbit's house. They didn't know they were sitting on his drugs then. Had things changed so quickly? That night had been full of terror, but also promise, and they'd kissed each other's blood off and she'd cleaned Dorothy up, wiping the smell of Rabbit off both of them. She looked so helpless. *It's impossible not to love her and hate her at the same time.* Dorothy's vulnerability made Alice want to protect her and keep her safe, but it also made her want to slap the girl and tell her to get a fucking grip. But she was Dorothy's lover and her protector, and she knew that Dorothy would follow her into hell if Alice asked her to.

But she hadn't asked at all, had she? She'd just grabbed Dorothy by the hand and dragged her down into a world Dorothy had only seen in Scorsese movies, where people killed each other and fucked for money and smoked heroin. Where they shot cops and got shot in return.

Now they were here again, not in a circle really but maybe a number 6, because they'd started off somewhere good and quickly dropped into a toilet bowl, and they were swirling around in circles waiting for the final splash of water so they could be sucked down into the sewage system of the world and be spit out somewhere down river as decaying matter.

Alice wondered what Dorothy thought of her now. If her entire life had been like this. What her path must have been like to end up here and now, and to be so calm and in control about the entire fucked up scene, like Alice had been there a hundred times before and it wasn't any big deal to bleed out in a stolen car while being chased by drug dealers and killing cops. Then she thought back to the motel bathroom where she'd gouged out the Hater's eye with her fingers. Maybe this *was* normal.

Maybe for Alice a fucked up situation was something so totally batshit crazy Dorothy couldn't imagine it. Babysitting the Hater was a fulltime job, and if she let it do its own thing for a while it was like sticking your tits in a bear trap; it made no sense and caused nothing but chaos and pain and asked more questions than it answered.

What if they had been right keeping me in that hospital? Alice thought. *Maybe I really needed the therapy and the drugs and the walls and doors with their wire mesh windows and shatterproof double-paned glass.* Now there might not ever be time to find out, because she was fading quicker than she wanted to admit. She hoped they could clean up her shoulder, but it was really a crap shoot either way. *This isn't the movies, kiddo. You don't shake off a bullet wound and go on with your life. You lose blood until you pass out and die.* But that wasn't the only thing that could happen. They weren't ever going to a hospital. How could they take the risk? Alice might get an infection that rotted her organs from the inside out. She could get a blood fever so high it liquefied her brain. *One day I might just not wake up when it's time for breakfast.*

Of course, there was no reason for both of them to die, was there? Dorothy was hurt bad too. *She's taking a cue from me,* Alice thought. *She's hurt worse than she'll admit to.* But she didn't have to go down with Alice. *She hasn't done anything except get hurt.* If she got really bad, Alice could dump her at a hospital. They'd arrest her, but Dorothy could tell them it was all Alice. She could plead crazy and tell them Alice had killed people and she was afraid for her life.

After all, they were a couple crazy bitches on the run, weren't they? That's what her lawyers could say. They'd broken out of a mental health facility in the hospital. It didn't take a rocket scientist to convince a jury that they had belonged there. The state had already made that decision for them.

Alice took her medical supplies past the beer cooler and grabbed a six pack on her way by.

The truckers were still milling around, bullshitting with the guy behind the counter and drinking coffee. The family of four had apparently decided on chocolate bars *and* chips, with the mother laughing off some offhanded remark about her diet. It was a setup for her husband to say something nice about her figure, but instead he rolled his eyes.

"Do you want the damn snacks or not?" he said, exasperated. "I'm tired of listening to them whine."

Oh yeah, they'll get the snacks, Alice thought. She was just kidding after all. And he was too tired to notice. *There's gonna be a day when she doesn't care enough to make those little setups for him to say nice things, and that will be about the same time she starts fucking one of her supervisors before quitting the whole scene and taking her kids out of state to live with a relative.*

"That everything?" the guy behind the counter said.

"Need smokes," Alice said. "The 'Blues."

"Need a driver's license for those," he said.

"Forget it then. I left it in the car."

"Long way from home?" he said. "You look like you're in pretty rough shape."

"About as far as you can get," Alice said. "I guess I can't get the beer either?"

"Guess not," the man said.

"Whatever." Alice had half a mind to pull out her gun and take them anyway, but decided to hell with it. Dorothy could get smokes and beer later after they'd found somewhere to hide.

The door to the store opened, a guillotine *swish* (*off with your head!*) of an automatic sliding door, and a great fat man with a short beard came running in, flustered and serious and looking like the sky was falling. "*Hey call 911!*" he shouted. "*Some girl out there is bleeding to death!*"

"What?" the counter-man said. There was a gasp from the mother in the family of four, and she grabbed her kids close to her. Her husband looked on impassively.

"Some girl out there's been shot! The man with the beard said. "She looks bad too! She needs Tampons, STAT! She's got heavy flow!"

The counter-man looked down at the supplies Alice had gathered, her gauze and rubbing alcohol and antiseptics. Alice was looking at them too. There were four boxes of tampons on the counter, and each one said "Heavy Flow" on the front. The image underneath showed a big mouthed vagina vomiting blood. Only the blood didn't stay on the box, it was spurting out onto the counter. It pooled around a lighter tray filled with football themed lighters and poured down over the candy and magazines beneath.

"Fiddle-Dee-Dee," a man behind her said, and Alice's head spun. The fat man was gone; or perhaps he had never been. The man standing in his place was tall and bone thin, wearing a rumpled black suit and battered ten gallon hat. When he smiled he split his lips. The blood was black and dribbled down his chin. It washed over his perfect white teeth, all the same size, so *vibrant*—

He was blinking rapidly. One of his eyes had a deflated soccer ball shape and was weeping blood. Alice could see his fly leg eyelashes scrabbling for purchase, making his eyes look like they were trying to swim across his face.

Realization struck like a thunderbolt. It was The Mad Hater. The man from her dream, come to life, standing before her in the doorway to the store; standing crookedly on the mat so that the door stayed open and let the wind in, and blowing leaves and garbage and cold rain; and there was no way he could possibly be standing here because he was a *figment*, for Christ's sake. This was a nightmare standing before her, not reality.

"Hello darling," the Hater said.

Alice didn't think. There was no time to think. She pulled the gun out of the pocket on her hoodie and pointed it at The Mad Hater's face. "*You're not real!*" She screamed. *It's impossible. He can't be here, he can't.*

"*Go on, Alice. Take your shot. Kill me.*"

Alice pulled the trigger.

Chapter 37.

There was an explosion, and the rack of chips beside The Hater burst, sending potato shrapnel everywhere. The other people in the store, quietly watching until this point, suddenly came to life. They were screaming and ducking and running for their lives. The Hater stepped around the chip aisle and disappeared from view. The air was filled with the smell of salt and vinegar, nacho cheese, and burnt gunpowder.

"*NOBODY FUCKING MOVE!*" Alice shouted. She swung the weapon around in a crazy arc. She waved it at the family of four, which had begun scrambling before the door even as Alice fired the gun. "*GET THE FUCK OVER HERE NOW!*"

"Easy," a trucker in a green hat said, his hands up by his head. "Just take it easy, Miss. Nobody knows your situation here. Nobody wants to get hurt."

"SHUT UP!" Alice started toward the door. The people in the store were like cattle; they moved in a half circle away from her until they were all milling about in front of the cashier. She had no idea where The Hater was, but his presence was both unnerving and terrifying. Seeing him in the flesh brought her back to the bathroom, when she'd opened her mouth and saw him in the back of her throat. This was different, though. He was out of her now, and out in the world, and she had absolutely no control over him.

She was beside the door, and it swooshed open again. The sky outside was bloated with green and black rainclouds. A brisk, wet wind blew past Alice into the store, whipping leaves and garbage and rain around her feet. She could see Dorothy across the parking lot in Rabbit's car, her head against the glass as though asleep. She wanted to run to her now, just get in the car and get away. The wound in her shoulder seemed to pulse in agreement. She looked down and saw pink spatters on her legs, and on the floor, like she'd been doused in water based paint.

"Alice," a soft voice whispered. It was behind Alice, in the store. She turned on her heel, gun raised in both hands.

Dorothy was standing in the store, so close Alice could smell the lilac and honey in her hair. She'd changed into a clean blue and white checkered dress that stopped just above her knees. She was wearing blue canvas sneakers on her feet, but Alice saw that they were spattered with blood and marbled with dark streaks. She was standing with her hands clasped in front of her, slowly rocking back and forth on her heels. When Alice looked into her face, Dorothy smiled.

"What are you—" Alice stopped. She was unable to form her thoughts into words that made sense. *How did you get here so fast?* She wanted to ask. *How did you get so clean?* "I'm glad you're here," she said instead. Dorothy chuckled.

The customers in the store seemed to be standing around and praying that if the gun went off it killed someone else. Everyone but the mother, who was clutching at her children like she was a human shield. Alice could almost hear her whispering *Please God, if that gun goes off let it hit me before it hits my kids.*

Dorothy said something and Alice looked back at her. "What?"

"He's in here," Dorothy whispered. She put a finger over her lips, begging for quiet. Then she turned her head and gestured toward the refrigerator aisle.

You can see him? "That's…no," Alice said. "That's impossible." She looked at Dorothy helplessly. "Isn't it?" It *was* impossible, because The Hater was in her head all this time and people couldn't see in your head. But if Dorothy could actually see him, that meant he'd been more than just a voice. More than just hallucinations. The fact that Dorothy could see him made him real, and the realization of that fact made Alice very scared. If the Hater was an actual being outside of her body, there was really no way to control him. But then, maybe controlling him had always been an illusion; a game The Hater had played for his own ends.

"I don't know what to do." Alice grabbed Dorothy by the arm and held her close. She was near to tears, she could feel them hitching her throat and making her voice shake. "*Help me please! I can't deal with this!*"

"ALICE!" The Hater yelled. His voice was thunderous. It bounced off the walls and reverberated around the store. He stepped out from behind the cluster of terrified hostages and approached the girls with slow, deliberate steps. He reached out with both arms and knocked the shelves on either side clean as he stalked the aisle. "It's *Time*, girly, don't you see? Time at last! Time to extract vengeance! Time to end it all! Pull the trigger! Finish it now!

He made a flourish with his hand, toward the cluster of people standing at the front of the store, now milling about like hostages in a bank heist. All eyes were on the gun in Alice's hand. They paid The Mad Hater no mind at all; it was as though he wasn't even there.

But that's not true, because Dorothy sees him, Alice thought. *That makes them all liars.* She looked at them again, over The Hater's shoulder. They didn't seem scared at all. They were just standing around like zombies, waiting for the little drama before them to unfold and come to some kind of conclusion.

But not any old ending. Alice realized. *They're here for a verdict. They came to see blood. They're here for the trial…*

She looked hard at the crowd and suddenly felt like she was seeing them for the first time. They had hair sprouting out of unusual places; tufts sticking out from under shirt collars or in odd spaces on their heads. They were all dressed in black formal wear; the men in sharp tuxedos and the women in black and white dresses. The mother carried a small umbrella over one shoulder, and as the father reached down to kiss his little one his head bulged grotesquely under his hair. When he raised his head again Alice saw why.

He was wearing a mask; they all were. The father reached up and adjusted his face, but it was too late; the illusion was ruined. He pushed the mask back into place and a large floopy rabbit ear slid out from under the string holding his face in position.

Now Alice recognized them for what they were. Rabbits and kittens and sloppy eyed puppies, all wearing masks and wearing sharp clothes. The children milling about the mother were tiny bunnies, and they scratched at their ill fitting pants and chewed on their jacket sleeves.

"They're all guilty, Alice," The Hater said. He pointed at the gun and smiled. "The guilty must be punished."

"They haven't done anything to me," Alice said slowly.

"Pish posh, Ohmygosh!" The Hater said. "Don't you remember what the Queen said?"

The Hater's words were like a video playback button for Alice, and she found herself standing in the garden courtyard once again, the Queen of Hearts and her gibbering, idiot husband presiding over court. There was blood everywhere. There were animal heads on poles, and the heads were chanting *Meat is Murder* and clapping their hands to keep time.

"Let the jury consider their verdict," The king said, for about the twentieth time that day.

"No! No!" The Queen said.

"I *do* remember, Alice said. "*Sentence First—*"

"*—VERDICT LATER!*" The Queen of Hearts screamed. The sudden boom of her voice caused the animals in the store to scramble around in a blind panic; they threw themselves into the aisles, tripping over each other and knocking the shelves clean. And at the front of the store, where the counter had once been, now sat the Red Queen upon a rusting metal throne.

She was tall and gangly, like a giant spider, all limbs and very little torso. Her head was shaved bald and bone white. She was wearing heavy red stage makeup around her eyes, and the rouge on her cheeks was in the shape of large hearts. Her mouth was a ragged gash, as though she'd jabbed a stick in the meat of her face and dragged it from one side to the other. The tear of her lips was a vaguely heart shaped and bled continuously. She wore a long crimson and amber dress that interlocked hearts and spades and diamonds and clubs. A large yellow lily pad stretched around her neck, and a heart shaped fan spread out from her shoulders behind her head like a halo. The blood drooling from her mouth was caught in the lily pad and dripped on the floor in front of her.

The room grew dim. The overhead fluorescent lights went out one at a time, in order, away from Alice and Dorothy and The Hater, until there was only one set of lights left directly above the Queen. The walls of the gas station were melting. Colour and chrome and glass bubbled and ran together and mixed with neon and concrete.

"She's here!" The Hater said. He was standing behind the girls now, and he pointed a long clawed finger toward the queen. "Now's your chance Alice! She's without her soldiers! *Quickly!*"

The Queen of Hearts drew herself up to her full height. She threw her arms out to the side in a mockery of the crucifixion. Then she looked down the aisle toward the girls and smiled; at least, it was the best this creature could to pass for a smile. A sort of half-grimace filled with blood and sharp teeth. The room thrummed with the sound of meat being run through a hand grinder, greasy and wet. As Alice watched, the animals returned to the Queen's side, bowing and taking a knee before her in an act of fealty.

"*MEAT IS MURDER!*" They chanted. They were melting, like jujubes of flesh and bone, and as they lost their shape they ran together as amorphous blobs of flesh bursting and reforming, growing insect legs and tentacles from a dozen places all at once; growing boils with thick pubic hair and blisters with dark, writhing forms beneath the ballooning skin thrashing and swimming in vital fluids.

The blisters burst forth and chanting fetuses sprang forth like raw, skinned pigs. They squawked on the ground in puddles of gore and amber fluid before heavily-tendoned umbilical cords pulled them back into the evolving mass.

Alice had never imagined a writhing, bloody scene of chaos like the one erupting before her; she found it impossible to get her head around what was happening. She was boggled by it. *I'm slipping. I can feel it. I'm losing myself to this…insanity…*

"MEAT IS MURDER!" they screamed, and from the back of the tumor grew long wooden poles with heads on them, melting heads of Dr Weller and Alice's mother, and of Rabbit and the black men whose names she'd never known. The air was filled with the smell of burning plastic and semen, and it collected like slime at the back of Alice's throat. Glitter and ticker tape fell from the ceiling. It clung to everything. Alice could feel it sticking to her face.

"Shoot her, Alice!" The Hater shouted. He danced a jig behind the girls and finished his routine by giving them each a hearty slap on the back.

Alice and Dorothy looked at him, then at each other. They both seemed to be growing and shrinking, throbbing in time, like a heartbeat: systolic and diastolic in perfect opposition. At that moment a large bubble burst on the writhing mutation that had become the Queen and her subjects, sending an angry, chanting fetus out bouncing down the aisle toward them. It slid off the liquid tiles of the floor with wet smacks, leaving bloody jelly and reams of pus in its wake. As it closed on them Alice pushed Dorothy backward and then stepped away from the incoming missile herself. It bounced between them and latched onto The Hater's outstretched arm.

"*Meat is Murder*," The fetus whispered.

"*How SweeEEEEET!*" The Hater shouted, his voice growing in resonance until it, too, cackled like thunder. Outside lightning crashed again and the world outside the store was lit in Day-Glo whites and blues. The fetus rolled over in his hands. It seemed to take on the shape of the sleepy Dormouse. Its face elongated and its ears shifted until they sat above tiny black marble eyes. Whiskers and fur erupted from his pink flesh, coarse and tangled.

"I told you I'd get you," The Dormouse said. He opened his mouth and latched on to The Hater's arm.

The Mad Hater shrieked and flailed about like he was drowning. The cord on the Dormouse tightened, and whatever was controlling him began to reel in its catch.

The Hater grabbed Alice with his free hand. For the first time, she saw real fear on his face.

"*Alice*," he whispered. "*Help me!*" The cord tightened, and The Hater was jerked off his feet. He landed on his knees in front of Alice."Help?" he said again.

She stared down at him impassively. *This is the man who has been making you crazy. But he's not scary now. He's helpless. And he's nothing compared to this.*

The Hater's arm was flensed of skin where the Dormouse had chewed into it. It burrowed long, drillbit-like claws into the meat of The Hater's arm, down through flesh and deep into bone. The umbilical cord retreated, back toward its host, and The Hater was pulled along with it. He kept his eyes on Alice as he was dragged away from her. He screamed for help and reached out to them with his free hand. Neither girl moved. The sky lit up with a continuous peal of thunder and strobe lights that alternated from red to blue to green.

The Dormouse pulled him to the base of the Queen's mass and then further still, back into the dark of the womb it had been born from. The Hater followed, screeching and crying. The mutating ball of flesh gulped him, and the pitch of The Hater's screams changed. They became higher and more panicked, until at last they were muffled by wet meat as the globular Queen finally took him, top hat and all, into herself.

"God," Alice said. She licked her lips and they were salty. She could hear Dorothy giggling hysterically beside her, but she didn't dare look. Her bowels were gurgling. She was on the verge of shitting herself with fear. Her face was hot and sticky and caked with glitter and ticker tape. It felt like *she* was wearing the mask now. *That's more true than you know,* Dr Weller whispered in her head.

The top of the creature burst open and another long pole grew out. This one contained the head of The Hater, dripping birth fluid and melting flesh like hot wax on a candle. His eyelids liquified, revealing two luminescent red eyes. The one that Alice gored was staring off toward the window, useless and blind. "Kill me!" he squealed. "*Oh please, it huuurrrrrts! It hurrrrrrtssssss!*"

It was too much for Alice. The amount of pain blubbering out from The Hater's mouth was beyond measure. *I need to make it stop or I'm going to fucking lose it right here. Right now.* Dorothy was no help. She was a stupid, useless little girl. *It's gotta be me.*

"*I don't know what to do!*" Dorothy shouted. She was chewing on her lips; her mouth was raw and red. Blood trickled from the corner of her mouth.

"Like you don't know," Alice said, and fired her gun Then she fired again and again, hitting the writhing mass of the Queen of Hearts and opening squealing, liquid holes at the point of each impact. She fired and fired until one of the bullets hit The Hater in the skull. It burst him open like a rotten melon. The screaming stopped, but it was replaced by something much worse.

The bullets actually seemed to shatter the room itself. Cracks appeared in the walls and the floor, and the sound of breaking glass roared through the room. The girls clung to each other and buried their heads in the other's hair. The wind kicked up and rain pelted them and after what seemed like forever the crashing stopped and there was silence, beautiful silence, save for a single, *high pitched whine…*

Alice looked at Dorothy. She was covered head to foot in congealing blood. But it wasn't blood, not really. The heavy, sweet smell of strawberry tarts filled Alice's nose. That's what it was. Strawberry jam. Dorothy smiled a jelly smile, and her teeth were replaced with glazed strawberry slices.

"What did you do?" Alice said. She stuck tip of the gun into the strawberry tart filling. She pushed the barrel into Dorothy's breast and was surprised to find custard underneath instead of flesh. She pulled the gun out at the barrel dripped pink custard and strawberries. *I was too late. I'm completely out of my mind now.*

"What did *you* do?" Dorothy said, looking down at the hole. "This is your thing. I'm just along for the ride."

The woman and children began shrieking in the same awful, ear-splitting tone. It was plain to see where they got their pipes from. "Nobody is who they say they are," Dorothy said. "You're not and I'm not. The Hater wasn't. That woman and her screechy family aren't."

Alice looked at Dorothy. Dorothy smiled back and rubbed her soft strawberry hands on Alice's cheek. It came away sticky and wet.

"You poor thing," Dorothy whispered.

Alice looked back down toward the counter and saw that the scene had changed. There was no Queen. There were no amorphous balls of mutating flesh, or poles with chanting heads on them. There was still blood though, lots of blood, but the scene of complete and utter chaos was gone. It had been a lunatic hallucination. Real for Alice, but fragile like a soap bubble. And that bubble had burst the moment she began firing. The scene was gone.

What replaced it was reality, and it was *oh so much worse.*

There were bodies piled in a heap around the front of the counter. Most of the customers from the store were either dead or dying. The teller was sprawled across the counter facedown in a pool of blood. There was a lazy crimson waterfall running off the countertop and down onto the bodies below. The husband was dead too, but the mother barely noticed. Instead, her attention was on a bloody mound of flesh she'd dragged into her lap. Now she sat on the floor hugging it and gasping for air.

It was one of her sons. The taller one. He was mute now. The top of his head had disappeared in a puff of red haze. The mother clawed at the discarded flesh that had once been her boy. She didn't cry, though. It looked like there was too much emotion was trying to get out of her at once and she was choking on it. She pulled him into her bosom. His empty head stared stupidly off in two different directions with waxy, dead eyes. The other, live one was sitting on the ground shrieking like he'd been set on fire, but the mother didn't bother to acknowledge him. She was muttering something softly as she hugged her dead boy and gagged on her grief. One of his eyes was now turned up toward the ceiling tiles. The other one stared just to the left of Alice, toward the entryway of the building.

I guess you were wrong, Dr Weller said in her ear. *It was just a boy, after all. There are no monster in here. Except maybe you, Alice.*

"Dorothy," she turned, but the girl was gone. Dorothy had retreated outside, into the storm, or maybe out into the car. Alice hadn't seen her go, but Dorothy's bloodied footprints were moving away, toward the door. Alice was alone again.

Ahh yes, Dr Weller said. *And where is your precious Dorothy now?*

Dorothy was outside, of course, running to the car, terrified of the scene she'd just witnessed. Perhaps she was terrified of Alice, too. *And who could blame her? Maybe I* am *a monster, and Dorothy is just an innocent; a sweet girl that has my heart and carries the remnants of my soul like a tattered old blanket.* Dorothy used it as a cape; she used it as a shield to protect herself from the big bad world.

But who was protecting Alice?

Nobody, that's who. Alice protected herself. Only sometimes the world was a confusing, horrible place, and even playing cards could be monsters. But from the dead, sleepy look on that boy's face and the way his brains were plunking on the linoleum like a dripping faucet in a bathtub, Alice could be pretty horrific herself.

Dorothy was yelling for her to come out. Something else, too, but she didn't understand it.

Alice turned and stumbled through the automatic door. She saw Dorothy sitting against a gas pump, knees pulled up to her chest. A look of fear was stitched across her face.

On the far side of the lot, Rabbit's silver car was parked sideways. The driver's side door was wide open. Alice could see Rabbit and the black guy who had survived the motel shootout crouched behind it. Rabbit raised his head and reached his gun across the hood of the car. There was a firecracker *pop!* Alice heard the drone of the bullet as it whizzed past. She had no idea how close it was, but she was pretty sure any bullet that you could hear was probably way too close. The wind and rain were hammering down on them now, and it made firing a gun with any accuracy more than a bit sketchy.

"Holy shit," Alice said. She crouched down to make a smaller target. Rabbit fired off two more rounds as she moved but his aim was terrible; the puffy black flesh swelling around his eyes probably had something to do with that.

"*He's shooting at the gas pumps!*" Dorothy cried.

"He's retarded." Alice laughed. "He always was." Crouched down beside Dorothy now she put her hand on the girl's knee for support, but Dorothy pulled away.

"Don't touch me!" Dorothy's face was tight with panic. She was the colour of a raw chicken, milky with blotches of purple just beneath the skin.

"What's your problem?" Alice asked. She poked her head around the side of the pump and was rewarded with another buzzing slug flying by her ears.

"*YOU'RE A MONSTER!*" Dorothy threw her hands over her ears as she screamed and balled her hands into fists..

"We're all monsters," Alice said. She took aim at Rabbit's car and fired. The bullet hit the passenger side door. "You're a monster too."

"You killed that little boy," Dorothy said, her voice weepy "You killed all those people!"

"You need to get to the car," Alice said. She and Rabbit traded shots. His banged off the side of the gas pump with a metallic thud. It suddenly occurred to Alice that she might not have many rounds left in her gun. She had no idea how many it held. *How many have I used? Six or seven? Now this?*

"I'm not going anywhere with you!" Dorothy cried. "You can't just kill people!" she shook her head rapidly back and forth, as though trying to scrape the last few minutes out of her brain. "You're supposed to protect us! That's your job!"

"Do you think you can start a fire with a *bullet?*" Alice asked, her voice calm. When Dorothy looked at her, she tapped her gun against the side of the gas pump. As if to highlight her point, Rabbit thunked another bullet off the side of it. It deflected away from the girls, but Dorothy flinched anyway.

"What are we going to do?" Dorothy said.

"Run for the car. And keep your head down."

"No," Dorothy said. "I can't do that."

"Fine," Alice said, standing up. "Stay here and die. I'm getting the fuck out of here right now." She swooned as she stood up, blood loss graying out her vision for just a moment, and she put her hand against the pump to steady herself. The wound in her shoulder was worse than she was letting on, by far. For a moment Dorothy faded from view. When she came back, she was wiping snot off her face with her forearm.

"Wait!" Dorothy said, reaching up and putting a hand on Alice's wrist. "Okay. I'll go."

"Go when I say," Alice said. "I'll cover you."

"Please don't let them hurt me," Dorothy said quietly. She got to her feet and crouched behind the gas pump, one hand on Alice's thigh for balance. Alice resisted the urge to knock her snot hand away.

"*Go!*" Alice hissed, pushing on Dorothy's ass at the same time. The motion caused the girl to stumble, and it took her a moment to get her balance. At the same time, Rabbit, sensing opportunity, stood up and fired.

Just like Alice knew he would.

The first shot went way wide of Dorothy as she half stumbled, half-fell into view. The second hit the ground just a few feet from where she was standing. A small puff of cloud and shattered concrete hit the ground.

Dorothy tucked her head and ran full out for the car.

Rabbit steadied his hand and took aim, ignoring Dorothy.

But Alice already had a bead on him. She pulled the trigger just a second before Rabbit did, her bullet just a bit quicker. It left the barrel of her gun and entered Rabbit's arm. The bullet cut through flesh and was already shattering the bone in his upper arm even as he was pulling the trigger on his own gun. His shot sailed wide. Rabbit went down in a heap of blood and screams.

Dorothy made it to the car and threw the door open, and then dove in head first across the passenger seat. She clamoured behind the wheel and reached for the keys...and they were gone."Fuck. *Fuck!*"

Rabbit was screaming from behind his car but Alice could barely make out what he was saying. The black guy with him was either unarmed or too busy dealing with Rabbit's arm to be a danger to the girls. Alice slipped around the side of the Volkswagen and pulled the keys out of her pocket.

"You stay out of here!" Dorothy yelled. "Get away from me!" she reached over and slammed the passenger door just as Alice reached the car, then popped the locks. "*I saw what you did!*"

"Dorothy!" Alice cried. "I have the fuckin' keys, remember?"

"*I DON'T CARE!*" Dorothy screamed. "*I HATE YOU!*"

"Well, that doesn't make you any smarter," Alice said. She put the key in the door. Dorothy tried to hold the door shut, but Alice threw it open without a second thought. Then she collapsed behind the wheel and let out a long, satisfying burp.

"I want you out!" Dorothy's chest was heaving. She was soaked to the skin; they both were.

Alice ignored her. She put the keys in the ignition and started the engine.

"No!" Dorothy said. "You—"

"*Oh would you grow up?*" Alice said, waving her gun in Dorothy's face.

"No!" Dorothy said. "Shoot me if you have to."

"Fine," Alice sighed. She pulled the trigger back on the pistol and pressed the barrel to Dorothy's forehead.

The girl cried out and pulled back, a small red hole appearing where the barrel had touched her flesh. "*That's hot!*" she cried. "*You burned me!*"

"I was about to kill you, remember?" Alice dropped the car in gear and hit the gas. The little yellow car bolted out onto the highway. "We gotta go. The cops are gonna be here any second."

"I hope they catch you," Dorothy said.

"They're gonna catch both of us," Alice said. She was looking in the rear-view mirror. The silver car Rabbit had been driving was ripping out of the parking lot and heading back down the highway away from them. Back toward the city. She didn't know if Rabbit was dead or not, but he was gone for now, and that was good enough.

The heavy rain turned to hail about ten minutes down the road, and the sky was black and green and laced with long strips of lightning. Alice had never seen anything like it.

But Dorothy had.

Chapter 38.

The girls drove in silence for a while. The windshield wipers were fighting a losing battle, but, despite not being able to see much further than the hood of the car, Alice refused to slow down. Instead she hammered on the gas, and the car began to shake.

"You should slow down," Dorothy said. She was leaning against the door of the car, as far away from Alice as she could get. Her head was against the passenger window, and the moisture in her hair caused that side of the car to fog up. "You don't want to have to kill anyone over a speeding ticket."

Alice shook her head. She was being goaded into an argument, and she knew Dorothy was doing it on purpose.

"Boy, Rabbit sure is a terrible shot," Alice said. "Couldn't hit his ass with a couch."

Dorothy gritted her teeth. Her eyes watered up on her, traitorous and salty, and she shook the tears free.

"You cryin' again?" Alice said.

"*YOU USED ME FOR BAIT!*" Dorothy shouted, hammering the dashboard with her fist. "I thought you were going to protect me!"

"I did protect you," Alice said. "I got him, didn't I?"

"Yeah, you *did*," Dorothy said. "But you weren't supposed to let him shoot at me so you could get a clean shot! Jesus Christ, what if he would have hit me?"

"Well, I guess we'd be even then," Alice said, her voice flat. "I took one already. Maybe it was just your turn."

"You're so fucked!" Dorothy said. "I can't believe that so much crazy can be rolled up inside one person!"

"You don't know me," Alice said. "Besides, you're more fucked up than I am."

"That's impossible," Dorothy said. "Nobody could be more fucked up than you. You shot a kid. You killed that black guy, and you hacked up that fucking guy in the office—"

"Woah, *woah,*" Alice said. "*I* hacked that guy up? Sorry missy, but you are not pinning that one on me, no way."

Dorothy sighed. "I saw the eyes you drew on the mirror," she said softly. "I saw the same eyes on the office glass drawn in that guys' blood. The next day you had all our money back. I *know* it was you."

Alice barked a laugh. It made her shoulder wound bleed more, and she grabbed it to staunch the flow. "Oh my God. You really have no clue, do you?"

"I saw it," Dorothy said. "I *know* it was you. No sense lying about it, you've done way worse since then."

"Sweetie, that wasn't me," Alice said. "I went over there that night and blew him to get some of our money back, and he wanted to fuck too, so we did. I got most of it back. When I got back to the room you were gone. I figured you'd gone for air or something. Maybe the junk made you sick. So I laid down and waited for you to get back. Only when you finally showed, you were naked, and you had fuckin' blood all over yourself. I was laying there pretending to sleep and I saw you clear as day. You slipped by the bed and watched me for a long time. I actually thought you were going to try something crazy, but then you went into the bathroom and had a shower. You were in there for a while. Later, you came out and crawled into bed like nothing had happened. I was scared half out of my mind. Should still be, but I didn't much care anymore. *You are a first class nutcase.*"

"It's a lie," Dorothy clenched her jaw and scowled "You're lying."

"Oh, okay," Alice said. "How long were you in the hospital before I met you?"

"Shut up."

"I bet it was a long time. Months maybe. Nobody gets kept in a loonie ward because they lied on their fuckin' psycho aptitude test. They would have found you out a long time ago. And with the state of healthcare being what it is, I seriously doubt they would just keep you in there if all you needed was some attention."

"*You're lying!*" Dorothy cried.

"*And you're a fucking murderer!*" Alice yelled. "So don't you think for one second that you are somehow better than me or you're innocent in all this. You're just as guilty. And you're just as fucked up. At least I can tell when the voices in my head are speaking. You had no fucking clue you were a *murdering schizo bitch!*" She slammed on the breaks. The car bucked and skidded on the road before coming to an uncomfortable stop in their lane. The rain became less and the hail became more, smashing off the road and the hood of the car with thunderous applause. A truck flew by them in the next lane, the driver laying on his horn and spitting up waves of rainwater as he passed. "This actually looks pretty bad. Maybe I should get off the road."

Dorothy responded by flying out of her seat onto Alice's lap.

In the first moments the gun flew from her hand onto the floor, and then the girls were a writhing, furious ball. Dorothy hit the car horn with her ass over and over again, and the car screamed its mechanical voice as though cheering them on.

Dorothy and Alice fought, rocking the car, with each girl striking heavy blows to the other but neither seeming to care much. Dorothy tangled her fingers in Alice's hair and started jerking her head around like a weighted pillow. Alice replied buy jamming her fingers into Dorothy's throat and clawing at her pale skin. At some point they rolled out from behind the wheel and landed in a heap in the passenger seat. Each girl was giving as good as she got. Dorothy fought with a ferocity that surprised them both.

Alice didn't have much fight in her though. Each movement sent spasms of pain radiating from the wound in her shoulder, and soon she was a bleeding mess. Dorothy punched her in the face repeatedly, bloodying her mouth. Finally Alice managed to get her hands up on Dorothy's head, and she pulled the girl's face down until they met in a forceful kiss.

Dorothy fought. She tried to pull her face away and separate their lips. For a moment, she almost made it.

But then she gave up the fight and they were cradling each other as they kissed and whimpering into each other's mouths and the hail outside grew bigger and hit the car with more force. It roared off the vehicle in waves, like someone was standing outside with buckets of marbles and was dumping them on the hood and roof.

Inside the car the girls kissed the blood away from their wounds and sucked on each other's tits and put their hands into the waistbands of each other's pants. Their love was panicked and beautiful, and they used their fingers on each other because there wasn't room for them to do anything else. They came together, crying out with their faces pressed together and their hands clenched, and then sat there quietly for a while breathing each other's breath. Finally, Dorothy pulled away, and Alice pulled her fingers out of her.

She settled back in behind the driver's seat and took a deep breath. She wiped the sweat from her face. The humidity of the thunderstorm had made it muggy in there, and their rapid breathing had made it worse. Alice rolled down the window. Only a crack though, because the hail was still pounding them. She flicked on her hazard lights, and then reached for Rabbit's bag of heroin. She used the last bit of foil from her cigarette pack and pulled a straw out of an old fast food cup in the back seat.

They sat there in silence for some time, listening to the rolling thunder and the hail and watching it bounce off the road and collect in the ditch along the road like piles of shoveled snow. They smoked and smoked, until Alice's shoulder stopped hurting and her head stopped pounding and their lives went from an angry infected mess to something beautiful once more.

"I need to tell you something," Dorothy said. "For months I've been feeling it. Like some kind of angry dragon inside me, that flared up sometimes. An endless fountain of rage. I used to think that it was a puddle in the bottom of my head, and that if I layered things on top of it I could keep it under control.

"So I built up layers of earth and dirt and fertile green hills and ran a gold brick road through the middle of it. It was a magic land where I went when I wanted to feel important. And when bad things happened, I went there. A land called Oz. After a while it became easy to slip it on and off, like a mask. If something started to leak through, some bad part of my life, I'd just imagine it harder. I was important in Oz. I was needed. Best of all, everyone loved me there. I became a princess, with a sceptre and a beautiful crown and everything. It was really nice.

"And the best part was all my bad feelings or hurts and scrapes just fell into the gutter beside that gold brick road. Then they got washed away down deep in the ground where they were added to the dragon. But it was okay because the dragon was asleep and far away, far deep under me."

"That's pretty crazy," Alice said.

"Yeah well, I lived like that for most of my life. It was fine. I wasn't crazy or anything. Just a dreamer. Then one day the dragon got out and I beat a girl at school with my shoe. Hurt her really bad. I smashed all her teeth in and was trying to pull her head off by her hair when the teacher finally caught up to us. Her name was Shelly. She pushed me on the slide because I was afraid to go down, and I just kind of blacked out. They told me about it later. After that, I was in and out of hospitals for a long time."

"*What?*" Alice said. "What did you just say?"

"I said I was in and out of hospitals..."

"No," Alice said. "That's wrong. How the fuck did you know about that? Did I tell you?"

"I was there." Dorothy smiled.

"No you weren't!" Alice said. "That was me! I did that!"

"I was there."

"Stop it, please?" Alice said. Her eyes welled up. "I can't take this shit right now. Not from you!"

Another car flew past them in the hail, and Alice heard the driver yelling through his open window as he flew past.

"You ever feel disconnected from the world because you just knew you were meant for more important things?" Dorothy said.

"How did you know about Shelley?" Alice said. She needed to stay focused right now. It felt…important, somehow. Like what Dorothy had just said held some deep inner meaning, brought on by the drugs and their love for each other.

Dorothy looked into Alice's eyes. Her face was cold and perfect, with no sign of the bruises or scrapes from her fight with Rabbit. She looked perfect, just as she had the day Alice first met her in the hospital. Her face was tipped in a slight frown.

"I think you know," Dorothy said."I think maybe you forgot for a little while, but maybe you know again."

"*No,*" Alice hissed. *NO!*"

"I tried to tell you," The Hater said, sitting in the back seat. We *both* did. You're not here at all, Alice. You never woke up from your drug coma. You've been lying in a hospital dreaming this entire time."

"*What?*" Alice said. She felt like she'd been hit in the head with a sack of doorknobs. "That's...That can't be true." But was it? She was suddenly looking from The Hater to Dorothy, perfect Dorothy, between a voice in her head and the girl she'd carry to the end of the world, and suddenly she was having a hard time telling which one of them was a figment of her imagination. "That's not true," she said again.

"No, it isn't true," The Hater said, laughing. "Wouldn't that be a trip though? Bet I had yah going for a minute, right?"

"FUCK YOU!" Alice screamed. She jammed the gun between the Hater's eyes and pulled the trigger. He had time for a smile and then the car was slammed with thunder and the back of his head exploded outward in a rush of tea and digestive cookies and bits of china. The car smelled like vanilla and tea leaves and Alice clamped her eyes shut. The air was thick with brimstone and smoke.

"Alice, look at me," Dorothy said.

"No." Alice clenched her eyes shut. Everything was moving in slow motion, but whether it was from the drugs or her own fucked up mind she couldn't tell.

"*Alice.*"

"I don't want to. Please don't make me do it."

"You must."

Alice opened her eyes.

Dorothy was covered in strawberry custard.

But then she really looked, and it wasn't custard at all. It was blood. A lot of blood, and Dorothy's pale skin shone under it. There was a small black hole on her tit that she'd gotten from that cop when he'd fired into the car. The blood pooled in Dorothy's lap and congealed there, a giant mess that she'd been sitting in since before the gas station. She was cold now. Her brilliant green eyes were static and staring off into space. Her head was pressed up against the window, like she was resting.

And then something in Alice broke, and she saw Dorothy crying and digging at her belly as the blood pumped out of it, and uttering a shaking, final gasp with Alice's head in her lap. A single bloody tear had run down Dorothy's face to match the torrents from Alice. She hadn't made love to Dorothy just now. she'd been fondling a corpse. Dorothy's blood was everywhere. Alice could taste it, cold and metallic in the back of her throat.

Why didn't I pull the trigger when I had the gun in my mouth? she thought.

But She knew why. It was because her mind was broken; she saw and heard and smelled things nobody else did. She hallucinated atrocities to cover the horrors of her real life, and this was no different. Seeing Dorothy there with a hole in her tit and blood pumping out of her like a spilled beer can, her mind had done what it did best. It covered the pain with another reality, something to keep on going for a little while. And Alice was such a mess that she had gone right along with it.

There was no Hater. And now there was no Dorothy. Outside, the wind screamed around the car and hail smashed into the pavement mixed with stinging rain and the roar of the storm was calling to her. Alice could feel tears coming, and she balled her hands into angry fists to stop them, but it didn't help. They came anyway, and they burned her cheeks with salt.

Chapter 39.

After a while, Alice adjusted herself in her seat and did up her pants. She felt used up. She was exhausted and fading from the blood loss. She stared over at Dorothy's body. The space between them seemed like an eternity now. The irony, of course, was that Dorothy was now *inside* her, and closer than ever. Like The Hater had been. All of it had been in her mind. Her crazy, fucked up, heroin saturated brain had gone and scrambled everything. She'd had a delusion and fallen into a fantasy world, and now it seemed no matter how much she tried she couldn't claw out of it.

But she had saved the biggest fuckup for last, hadn't she? Just like any good story. Because now Alice was slowly dying in a car on the highway, and she was all by herself. Dorothy was gone now. And she didn't know if Dorothy would ever be back.

Worse, Alice had never told her how she felt about her. She looked over at Dorothy, and then reached over and cupped the girl's cold, hands in her own warm ones. "I want you to know that I never gave a fuck about anything really before I met you." The melodrama brought a fresh round of tears to her eyes, and she whimpered through her words. "I had drugs and I had a life, but neither of them really mattered to me at all. And I know I've been a real bitch the last few days, but I will never forget you. You were the world that mattered. And I just want you back her for just a minute, so I can tell you that."

Alice put her head down and cried into her arms.

But then he felt a hand on her head.

And she looked up smiling.

"You too," Dorothy said. "I love you. So much. It hurts me to think about you." She squeezed Alice's hands and then leaned down and kissed them.

Alice beamed. "Let's drive a bit, okay?"

Dorothy rolled the window down and looked in her rear-view mirror. There was no traffic at all. Behind them, the storm reached across the sky like a green and black oil spill. Dorothy's face lit up at the sight of it. "Yeah," she said, rolling up the window. "Let's go on ahead."

Alice wasn't afraid of the storm. She looked at Dorothy and laughed. "I'm so glad you came back," she said.

Dorothy leaned over and kissed her sweetly on the side of the mouth. "I never left," she said simply.

Alice considered her words. Then she laughed. "No, I guess you never did. The Hater is gone though. For good. It really is just you and me this time."

"Forever," Dorothy said. She scooped up Alice's hand and laced their fingers together. Dorothy was cool to the touch, but she was still wet from being out in the storm. Anyone would be a little cold after getting soaked to the bone from the rain.

Alice sighed. Now that the adrenaline of the drama and sex was subsiding, she was crashing badly. She was fighting to keep the car on the road. She didn't know how much blood she'd lost, but she was sure there wasn't much more to go before she started passing out. Maybe black out for good. Then what? She remembered hearing about people losing blood experiencing a white out when they came close to death, and Alice supposed she would see that.

"It's called an NDE," Dorothy said, reading her thoughts. "A Near Death Experience. As the blood leaves your brain, you're left with noisy, distorted snow. Like you click your brain over to an unused TV channel and slowly turn the volume down until there's silence. The long black sleep of death follows."

Alice's vision was a little gray around the edges, and there was a steady pounding of water in her ears, but that also might have been the storm. The hail was steadily growing in size, and it roared off the sheet metal of the car's body. She was hunched over the wheel squinting at the black mess in front of them. "This is really bad."

"It's fine," Dorothy said. She'd rolled the window on her side partway down, in spite of the invasive rain water, explaining that the noise and fresh air grounded you when you were driving in miserable conditions. "It also helps if the windows start to steam a bit, because of the moisture," she said.

"But you are letting the moisture in," Alice said. "You have the window down. Besides, this car is trashed and half the windows are missing anyway."

"Trust me," Dorothy said, and that was new, because Dorothy was a meek and shy creature, and she never said things like *trust me* because that required a certain level of confidence. *Confidence* was something Dorothy had in short supply. What she had in very large supply, in barrels stacked on barrels and stored in large warehouses with buzzing yellow lights for protection, was indecision and shyness. Two things Alice was attracted to, but that The Hater had despised in them both.

"Do you know where I'm going?" Alice croaked.

"Absolutely," Dorothy said. Her face hinted at a smile, but Alice saw her bite down on her lip and kill it.

Alice cranked up the windshield wipers to full, but it resulted in only short lucid glimpses of the road ahead. It showed a wall of black dotted with flecks of gray and yellow. Alice was a city girl, and used to bad weather, but there was something to be said about a full on prairie thunderstorm. The power and size of the disturbance could be enough to stop a person in their tracks. It was raw, natural energy; something people tended to take for granted when all they saw was a dark spot of cloud between buildings. Rain pounded the windshield and bounced in through the holes in the windshield. The wipers scraped across them and pushed more water into the car. It dripped down the glass and onto their legs, each drop a tiny shock of electric energy.

Ahead on the road there was a large train overpass, and underneath Alice could see what looked like rows of grinning silver mouths with red eyes.

"Dammit," Dorothy said.

"What the fuck is that?" Alice said. The grinning mouths seemed to stutter in the air, and melt down into one large mouth completely covering the underpass. The smile broadened, and the little red lights turned into bulbous cat's eyes. They were bloody moons, with craters for pupils.

Jack Sprat, he ate a cat. His wife, she ate a spleen! The Hater's words, but The Hater was gone. Alice had thought them herself. "I don't want to go in there," she said. She tried to push herself up onto the seat but didn't have the strength; the effort alone was enough to cause her vision to dim. She didn't know what it was they were driving in to, but she knew it was something terrible. Something with glittering metal teeth ready to rip and feast.

"It's okay," Dorothy said. "It's just an overpass for the train."

"It has *teeth*."

"It's fine."

"It looks like a big cat with bleeding moon eyes."

"It's *fine*."

"Dorothy," Alice said. "*Please*." She let up on the gas and immediately the car powered down. They were creeping toward the cat now, barely moving.

Dorothy squeezed Alice's hand. "It's okay," she said. "I'm right here. I'm going to take care of you. You just have to trust me. There's no cat there, I promise."

Dorothy was her friend. She was more than that, a *part of her*.

Alice once asked Dorothy if she could be trusted, and Dorothy had said *yes*. Alice believed her. They were out on the road now with nothing but death behind them, and nothing but promise ahead of them. In spite of the giant striped cat on the road, red eyes glittering like blood rubies and its mouth wide open to swallow them whole, there was promise in Dorothy's voice. The meek girl was gone. She was finally in control for the both of them. And it couldn't have come at a better time, because Alice herself was barely holding on.

And the truth was that there *was no cat*. Dorothy had said as much, and when Alice blinked, the creature was gone. There was a moment where she could plainly see the eyes and teeth left behind in a vaguely predatory smile, but then they were gone too.

The answer for the disappearance was simple: *There never was a cat*. So many things the past few weeks Alice had seen or heard and simply taken at face value. It was like sleepwalking. Dorothy was showing her another way, though. Dorothy showed her that sometimes belief was enough to make the monsters disappear.

She felt like she was coming up out of deep water for the first time in a while, since before she'd shot that guy in the car and blown his brains all over her shirt. *Maybe this is what it's like to stop being crazy*, she thought. Like a funhouse ride mixed with a horror movie, only at some point your cart banged against a pair of angry coloured metal doors with ruby red eyes and long metallic teeth and you're out of the dark and into the sunlight of your real life once more.

Maybe you come to the end of the ride and your eyes are squinty from the sun and you think about how the vampires and werewolves and spooks you just survived were made out of chicken wire and Paper Mache with little Christmas lights for eyes and Styrofoam cones for teeth. And then you feel kind of stupid, because for a little while there, for maybe *just a minute*, you *actually* believed there were vampires in the world who wanted to drain your life away from you, and werewolves were creeping around outside your cart waiting for you to put your hand outside your seat so they could tear it off. Maybe for a moment you thought the ghosts you were seeing were the spirits of the dead, and were back for vengeance because you blew their head off in a gas station or in an old blue car in a deserted parking lot.

And then here was Dorothy, to make it all go away. Dorothy, standing in the sunshine waiting for you to reappear from your trip; holding your sunglasses and your purse because you didn't want to drop them in there, and who didn't come along because this was one of those things you just had to do on your own.

By yourself. And then there was Dorothy and she was smiling at you and excited to see you because she kind of missed you even though you were only gone for a few minutes, and she was glad you took a trip on your own but very glad you were back. And she would give you a hug that smelled sweet and flowery and ask you *how was it* and *were you scared* and you say *no*, but maybe you both know that was a lie because for a minute there, just a tiny moment the funhouse was real and your whole world outside the train tracks was a big fucking lie.

You still have a bit more to see. Dr Weller's voice again. Funny that he should be here, when she barely knew the man. Dorothy knew him though, and loved him, because he had tried to reach out and help her. Or help Alice. Now, who knew what was real anymore. Maybe Dr Weller was another figment of their collective imagination. Hell, *maybe Alice was the figment*, and Dorothy had made her up so she could stick around the hospital a bit more.

It didn't matter now, because she was done with all of it.

"Excuse me?" Dorothy started to pull her hand away. She was smirking at Alice, her eyes brighter and greener than ever. "You're done *with what* exactly?"

"Not you," Alice said, holding tight and then pushing her face against the back of Dorothy's hand. "I'm never going to be done with you. I love you."

"I love you too," Dorothy said. "*Sooo* much."

They could see cars lining the ditches on either side of the road, and sitting directly under the overpass with its lights flashing was a large one-ton emergency vehicle. Dorothy slowed down as they approached it. The wind seemed to be picking up speed by the second. By the time the car stopped, it was a lion's roar that rocked the Volkswagen and showered it with topsoil.

Dorothy got out of the car. Her attention was far away, past the group of people huddled under the overpass. Past a cop in a raincoat now screaming at them to get the hell off the road. Alice opened her door and fell, but dragged herself across the hood of the car and was able to grab Dorothy's arm.

"I've got you!" she screamed. Dorothy rocked her lifeless head in response.

"I know!" Dorothy said. "For ever!"

On the other side of the overpass, its base black and miles away but kicking up dirt and death around it, was the biggest tornado Alice had ever seen. It looked like the sky itself was draining into the earth in a massive, angry funnel. Lightning cracked around its edges and thunder boomed. The noise of the wind grinding across the plains seemed to grab the sound from Alice's ears and drag it toward the center of the tornado. The monstrosity picked up a house and a car at the same time, and then Alice saw the car hurtling end over end through the shattered remnants of the house as it broke down into its base components.

The cop in the underpass was motioning for them to join him. Alice couldn't hear a word he was saying. Dorothy either couldn't hear him or was ignoring him. Judging from the look of rapture on her face, staring into the heart of the tornado and oblivious to the rest of the world, Dorothy was long gone, into her *own* funhouse horror ride. Toto was clamped tight in her arms, huddled to her chest, protecting her heart the way he always did. Animals were so much more dependable than human beings were sometimes.

"*HEY!*" The cop screamed. "*HEY GET THE FUCK OVER HERE!*" He was waving his hands at them as he approached, and he pointed to the corner of the overpass where the ground rose up to meet the road above it. There were about a dozen people huddled together trying to get out of the wind. It was their safest spot to be, as the concrete of the structure would protect them from a lot of the larger debris while providing enough of a windbreak that they wouldn't be sucked up by the tornado and thrown God knows where.

When the cop got a little closer he suddenly slowed down into a partial crouch. His hand drifted down toward his holster. He lifted one arm and pointed to Alice.

Alice looked down and realized she still had the gun in her hand.

"I'm going," Dorothy said, staring straight ahead. "Oz awaits."

Alice couldn't hear her.

The cop pulled his gun and pointed it toward Alice, and now he was motioning with it for Alice to lay down on the ground. He was probably telling her to drop her weapon as well, but Alice couldn't hear him above the roar of the tornado.

Dorothy continued to ignore him; they took a couple shambling steps toward the tornado and stopped. She looked back at Alice, confused.

"*HE WANTS US TO LAY DOWN!*" Alice yelled into her face.

"*WHO?*" Dorothy shouted.

"*THAT COP!*" Alice yelled.

"*I HAVE TO GO!*"

Alice nodded. "*I KNOW!*" She pulled the gun up to eye level and pointed at the cop's head. The act caused the man to crouch into a more defensive stance, and he barked savagely like a trained attack dog.

This is the moment where everything goes to shit, Alice thought, and then shook her head and smiled. *No. We're were way past that moment.* They might have passed that moment the second she laid eyes on Dorothy in that hospital, but maybe even before. Maybe when that guy started coming in her asshole with the business end of her gun jammed in his face, shooting hot shame and saying he was sorry at the same time, like the thought of blowing his brains out was the biggest fuckin' trip he'd ever been on.

"Bark, bark, little doggy," Alice said. The tornado loomed over top of them. The cop looked at Alice and then peeked over his shoulder. The roar of the beast was beyond anything Alice had ever heard; it drove itself into her skull like hammer hooks and pried the plates in her skull loose.

The cop started backing away from the girls with his gun pointed at Alice, but his free hand was in front of him, palm out. He was looking for a truce while he backed away from the girls. Back toward the safety of the underpass, with a *please don't shoot me when I turn and run* look on his face.

Alice let him go. She turned and buried her head against Dorothy's shoulder. Her weight was lessening int he wind. The tornado was bearing down on them. It picked up cars on the far side of the underpass and tossed them like bricks to be smashed in the dirt or bounced off one another. The air was filled with sand and ozone, like standing inside a thundercloud and a sandbox at the same time, and it made a primal, grinding noise that blocked out the shrieking wind. *This is the voice of the earth*, she thought. *This is mother nature's singing voice.*

"It's going to be grand," Dorothy said.

Alice looked into Dorothy's emerald eyes and kissed the corner of her mouth where her perfect ruby lips met. That was all they had time for. For a moment, it looked as though Dorothy was being buried in sand, and all Alice could see were those emerald pools and her perfect smile. "I love—"

But Dorothy was gone again.

Epilogue.

Dr Weller stepped off the elevator and walked toward the nurse's station with his hand already up. He knew what was coming; it was the same thing that had been coming for a week now. Every day it was the same. Newshounds, agents, and cops, *oh my*. All wanting to piece everything together. Hollywood was knocking, and everyone involved with the Alice Pleasance and Dorothy Gale saga was lining up like bums at a soup kitchen, hats in hand and their mouths open. All were eager for a piece.

Except Dr Weller.

"The lady from *The Times* called again," the fat nurse behind the desk said. "You gonna call her back?"

"No," Weller said, and flashed a grim smile when the woman rolled her eyes. She'd already sold out to Hollywood. Most of the people who worked on the ward had turned their bit parts into cold hard cash. Dr Weller had heard the guy and his dad who brought Alice into the emergency room after she'd been dumped off by her pimp were going to be on *Larry King*, and had been paid handsomely for their trouble. Hollywood always got what it wanted, one way or another.

He walked the short hall to his office and stepped inside, closing the door behind him with a flourish. Then he carefully placed his coat and hat on the coat rack by the door and found his seat behind the large oak desk that had served as a divider between him and the misery of people's lives for many years. For most of those years, he'd dreamt of escaping from that seat and moving on to bigger and better things.

Now all he wanted to do was stay there and keep the world at bay.

He knew he was missing his one shot at doing something bigger with his life. Of course, knowing something, and acting on something were two totally different entities. Maybe that's what his dad had meant when he said *head shrinkin' is just a waste of time.* Weller knew what he'd *really* meant was *why spend all that time in school if you ain't goan be a real doctor?*

Maybe he should have gone to medical school and specialized in assets and faces. Then he wouldn't be sitting here right now hiding from the press and throwing away his chance to be Mr. Bigshot Man of the Hour. The fact was he had watched in horror as the details of Alice and Dorothy's last few days started coming to light. It seemed to start so small and suddenly erupt into a ball of frenzy and carnage. Like the freak thunderstorm that had spawned the tornado itself; a once in a lifetime event formed by the stars lining up just perfectly. A handful of people had died, including a nine-year-old boy in the gas station massacre. Witnesses said they saw the girls in the last moments before the tornado hit, Alice propping Dorothy up and dragging her along and Dorothy covered in blood and looking like she was already dead, for god's sake. She walked them both right into the damn thing.

And now Dr Weller was the golden child. He had exactly what everyone in Hollywood and on CNN wanted to get their hands on; a pair of fat folders highlighting Alice and Dorothy's lives up to that point, and unique perspective on what would drive Alice into a shooting rampage that ended with her killing herself while half the state troopers in the state were out looking for her.

"People are sympathetic to female serial killers," one guy had said over the phone. "Ever since Charlize Theron made us fall in love with Wournos, we've been just waiting to get our hands on another Femme Fatale. Was Alice Pleasance ever raped as a child? That would garner sympathy with female audiences. We want to show the world how male dominated society drove this poor girl into the ultimate corner. Tastefully of course. We don't want any lawsuits…"

Dr Weller had never wanted to hit someone so much in his entire life. He settled for a big *FUCK YOU* and slammed the phone down.

Of course, Hollywood would eventually get their story, no matter if Dr Weller was along for the ride or not. Eventually someone would write a script and use artistic license to fill in whatever gaps Dr Weller was so unfairly withholding from the general public. Then they could do whatever they wanted with those girls, and victim's rights groups would whine and cry about how Hollywood was glamorizing violence, and maybe someday a disturbed child would kill her classmates and tell the world Alice & Dorothy: The Movie made her do it. Then the shit would start all over again. *Is this Dr Weller? Could we borrow a moment of your time? We're just wondering what you thought of this latest shooting spree inspired by a girl who was once in your care...*

Maybe that was the truth of it then. The girls were in his care, and he'd failed them both miserably. He'd made huge miscalculations about the stability of Dorothy's mind and her resourcefulness. He'd also underestimated how much damage Alice had done to herself and her mental state, and how she could feed off Dorothy's delusions the way schizophrenics were apt to do from time to time.

He was sure Alice had killed the motel manager at the Harvest Moon Motel. The girl seemed to wear her violence as a mask, while something else bent on expunging her guilt lurked underneath. Witnesses said she'd been screaming at someone called The Mad Hater during the gas station attack; it seemed to be an odd little tick of her personality that was constantly trying to confess her sins to the world; as though her guilt had been balled up and formed like putty into a small personality that Alice desperately wanted to expel. There was no telling what she was hiding, or what she might have been trying to protect from the world, but it must have been terrible.

Her drug overdose had almost certainly caused the fractures in her personality. If she'd just stuck around a little longer, Dr Weller would have been able to fix it. As it was, she probably died still hearing voices in her head. Still talking to people who weren't really there.

Dr Weller sighed and reached for a small bottle of rye hiding in the back corner of his desk drawer. He took a quick sip and then placed the bottle in front of him on the desk. He had a lot of vacation time banked up over the past couple years. Maybe it was time to use them. Get away from it all. Maybe go up north and spend some time with his father. Or go on a road trip for a month or two. This case had ripped the heart out of him and made work bleary. It was a sure sign of burnout.

There was a knock at the door. Dr Weller looked down at the bottle on his desk but didn't bother covering it up. A moment later, the door opened and the fat nurse stuck her head in the door.

"Dr Weller," she said, "There's a man from the *L.A. Informer* on the phone. He wants to know if Alice knew the guys from the gas station shootout. They were both killed trying to break into a police impound lot last night. Security guard got 'em. Said they were after drugs."

"Tell him to drop dead," Dr Weller said. "And next time keep that fucking door closed until I tell you to open it. Alright?"

"You're such a prick," the nurse said. She pulled her head back and pulled the door closed hard enough to rattle the glass.

"You bet your sweet black ass," Dr Weller said. He drained the rye with two sharp gulps then carefully screwed the lid back on and replaced it in the desk drawer. His pens were out of order and he fixed those. Somehow, his mother would have been pleased.

He decided he would leave, after all. He could call in a leave of absence from the road, or from home, wherever he was when he made the call. The board would understand. He was a bit of a black eye on their immaculate image now. Maybe they'd tell him to take all the time he needed off, hoping he wouldn't come back. *We just think it would be best for everybody this way,* they'd say. Weller would only agree with them.

He grabbed up his coat and hat, and started to leave then doubled back to his filing cabinet. Thumbing through his case files he found one marked *Pleasance, Alice*, and another marked *Gale, Dorothy*. He couldn't trust the nurses around here not to come in sniffing around at the first sight of a payoff.

No, if Hollywood wanted a story, they'd have to come up with their own version of things. They probably would, anyway.

The End.

About the Author

Photo by Janice Schnarr

About JW Schnarr

JW Schnarr is the evil mastermind behind Northern Frights Publishing. He currently resides in Champion, Alberta Canada with his daughter and a grumpy turtle. When not writing, editing or publishing, he can be found scheming. And watching sports.

A member of the HWA, he is the Editor of *Shadows of the Emerald City*, *War of the Worlds: Frontlines*, and *Timelines: Stories Inspired by H.G. Wells' The Time Machine*. Look for his collection *Things Falling Apart* out now!

JW blogs about his life at **www.jwschnarr.blogspot.com**

Find JW on Facebook: http://facebook.com/jwschnarr

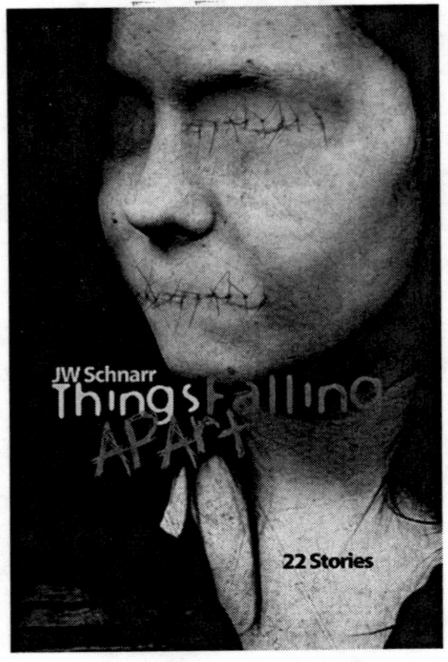

Also Available

Birth Cycles

The Oilfields of Ghawar are bleeding evil into the atmosphere as a sleeping god awakens. And while the armies of the world descend on Saudi Arabia to do battle against this cosmic horror; one man will find that while blood may be thicker than water, there are some things thicker than blood...

A *Ghosts in the Machine* digital release
$0.99
Visit **www.jwschnarr.blogspot.com** for details.

Also Available

Green Hills

Dyson's got a simple job: fly to Green Hills and make a delivery to a man named Pontius. The only problem is that Green Hills is a place unlike any other, and Pontius is not a man at all. Dyson is about to discover that if something seems like a dream come true, it's probably a nightmare in disguise...

A *Ghosts in the Machine* digital release

$0.99

Visit **www.jwschnarr.blogspot.com** for details.

CPSIA information can be obtained at www.ICGtesting.com
Printed in the USA
237257LV00001B/5/P